NEW YORK TIMES BE...

LINDSAY McKENNA

& JOAN JOHNSTON

DEADLY IDENTITY
&
HAWK'S WAY: CALLEN

HHARLEQUIN

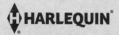

ISBN-13: 978-1-335-58010-8

Deadly Identity & Hawk's Way: Callen

Copyright © 2020 by Harlequin Books S.A.

Deadly Identity
First published in 2010. This edition published in 2020.
Copyright © 2010 by Lindsay McKenna

Hawk's Way: Callen
First published as The Headstrong Bride in 1994.
This edition published in 2020.
Copyright © 1994 by Joan Mertens Johnston

Recycling programs for this product may not exist in your area.

This edition published by arrangement with Harlequin Books S.A.

For questions and comments about the quality of this book, please contact us at CustomerService@Harlequin.com.

Harlequin Enterprises ULC
22 Adelaide St. West, 40th Floor
Toronto, Ontario M5H 4E3, Canada
www.Harlequin.com

Printed in U.S.A.

CONTENTS

Lindsay McKenna is proud to have served her country in the US Navy as an aerographer's mate third class—also known as a weather forecaster. She was a pioneer in the military romance subgenre and loves to combine heart-pounding action with soulful and poignant romance. True to her military roots, she is the originator of the long-running and reader-favorite Morgan's Mercenaries series. She does extensive hands-on research, including flying in aircraft such as a P3-B Orion sub-hunter and a B-52 bomber. She was the first romance writer to sign her books in the Pentagon bookstore. Visit her online at lindsaymckenna.com.

Books by Lindsay McKenna

Shadow Warriors

Running Fire
Taking Fire
Never Surrender
Breaking Point
Degree of Risk

Jackson Hole, Wyoming

Out Rider
Night Hawk
Wolf Haven
High Country Rebel
The Loner

Visit the Author Profile page
at Harlequin.com for more titles.

DEADLY IDENTITY

Lindsay McKenna

To the Teton County Sheriff's Department. Thank you.

And to Tara Parsons, senior editor for HQN Books, who is giving me a chance to spread my wings even more.

CHAPTER ONE

"You're a dead woman if you don't get over here."

The voice sent a chill down Susan's back and she did all she could to keep from screaming. As they stood in the kitchen, her husband of five years, Dirk Payson, cocked his fist. She had just dropped the plate with his breakfast eggs on them. The moment it shattered on the floor, Dirk leaped up from the table, rage in his face. It had been an accident, and yet, as she peered into his wild-looking blue eyes, she knew. A sickening dread washed over her while she quickly picked up the pieces of the broken plate off the floor.

"I—I'm sorry, Dirk…it won't happen again," she whispered, her hands trembling as she gathered up the pieces. One of the shards of the glass plate cut her index finger. Susan didn't feel the pain or the warm blood that flowed from the deep cut. The agony and fear clutching at her heart took most of her attention—that and not making Dirk even angrier. Breathing like an enraged bull, he stood near the table, as if frozen for a second. Was he ready to hit her again? *Oh, God, no!*

Susan's mind sought the closest escape. She was

six months pregnant and had to protect her growing baby. The last time Dirk had struck her—two months earlier—he'd broken her nose. Why did he want to hurt her like this? Why couldn't she do anything right for him? No matter what Susan did, it was wrong for Dirk. And Dirk was there to correct her with his fists.

"You bitch!" he rasped savagely, taking a step forward. "You ruined my breakfast, dammit! I was hungry!"

"I—I'm sorry, Dirk. I—I'll make you another plate of eggs. Just give me a chance?" Her voice sounded breathless and frightened. Susan placed pieces of the plate on the granite counter. With a dishcloth, she rapidly cleaned the eggs up off the floor, as well. Susan could feel adrenaline shooting through her. She needed to run! The look in Dirk's eyes was deadly this time. He wanted to do more than break her nose. Mouth dry, her hands shaking, Susan cleaned herself up under a stream of water from the faucet.

"Please…give me just a few minutes, Dirk. I'll fix some more eggs just the way you like them."

"I'm tired of you. I bet that baby isn't even mine!" That's when he lunged.

Susan screamed as his fingers wrapped around the long, blond hair that hung down her back. Wrenched backward, she felt her feet fly out from beneath her. Red-hot pain radiated from her scalp. She slammed onto the cold, hard floor. Susan threw up her hands to try and stop Dirk's other fist from striking her face.

But as she tried to twist away, he leaned over, his fist sinking hard into her protruding belly.

"No!" Susan shrieked from the impact, the pain flooding her. On instinct, she pulled out of his grip, strands of her hair still in his fist.

"Bitch! You're gonna die!"

Everything became slow motion for Susan. Somehow, she found the strength to rise, her hand across her belly where her baby lay. The pain was far too intense but she had to get away. She grabbed the handle of the black iron skillet and swung it at Dirk as he launched himself at her once again. Her entire arm vibrated from the sudden impact with his skull.

To her disbelief, he fell like a pile of rags on the floor. He had a huge gash across his brow, but at least she'd stopped him. Maybe forever. Tears splattered from her eyes. Tears of pain. She could have stood there for hours but for the sudden ripping sensation through her abdomen.

Please don't let me lose my baby! A baby she'd wanted all her twenty-three years of life. Susan had endured Dirk's beatings just to bring this beautiful, clean, innocent baby into the world.

Gasping, Susan saw everything begin to gray before her eyes. She had to escape! She had to get out of here before Dirk woke up! When he did, he'd kill her and her baby. Something raw and primal surged through her. Susan staggered forward, both hands covering her belly. Though she prayed to God that He would save her baby, Susan felt she might die.

Sobbing for breath, Susan tried as best as she could to get out of the five-million-dollar Miami estate that had been her home for all of seven months. Why hadn't she realized sooner that Dirk was a drug dealer with the Mexican cartel? That he was beyond dangerous? She'd come from a small Iowa cattle farm so what did she know? Now she was running for her life.

Warmth flowed between her legs. She knew it was blood or worse, the fluid surrounding her baby. *Save my baby...save my baby...* Susan wove unsteadily past the palm trees at the front of the house. Her world began tilting, and more fluid flowed down her legs. Sobbing, Susan ran as if drunk toward the sidewalk below. She nearly fell but she made it to the concrete walkways of the rich community. *Help!* She could never go back into the estate that reminded her of a prison. She had to escape Dirk! She had to save her baby girl that she'd named Sarah.

Cars slowed down, and drivers gawked at her. Susan wove on rubbery legs, her hands stretched outward to keep herself upright. Gasps and sobs exploded out of her mouth as the pain made her hunch over. *Help!*

Susan knew no one in Miami. Dirk had kept her inside that mausoleum, not allowing her to make friends with anyone. Her strange marriage went against her grain. At home in the small community of Greenfield, Iowa, people knew each other. They were a tight-knit community. They supported and helped one another. Susan hated Miami, hated that she'd made the stupid decision to marry Dirk Payson. At eighteen years old, when she'd fallen in love with him, she'd thought she knew everything. Against her parents' wishes, she'd run off and married him. How she regretted her choice now.

Everything had gone wrong. Susan bent over, her hands cupping her belly. Suddenly, she heard the screech of tires nearby. Looking up, Susan noticed a dark blue car stop and a man running toward her. Susan didn't know who he was, but she sank to her knees. She was too weak to stand, too weak to see if he was friend or foe. Yet, the look in his green eyes told her he was there to help her.

Then, as if someone had lowered a black curtain across her vision, Susan crumpled to the sidewalk. She knew nothing more.

Five years later...

"SUSAN, SOMETHING HAS HAPPENED," FBI agent Brenda Wilkins said, gesturing for her to sit down in a chair within an enclosed glass office.

"Oh?" Susan frowned and, automatically, her heart began to beat harder. It was snowing outside and getting to this building in six inches of snow had taken a long time. After pulling off her

black wool coat and removing her red scarf, Susan
placed them on a nearby hook.

The news had to be about Dirk. She had lost
Sarah, her baby, and nearly her own life thanks
to her ex-husband. When she'd awakened in the
hospital, Brenda Wilkins had been at her bedside.
The red-haired woman, in her forties, with thick
glasses perched on her large nose, told Susan that
the FBI needed her help. For the past five years,
Susan Donovan had no longer existed.

After testifying against Dirk, she'd entered the
federal witness protection program and become
Susan Johnson.

Brenda offered her some water from a pitcher.
Palms sweaty, Susan took the glass and murmured
her thanks.

"What's wrong? You seem upset," Susan said.
As she looked around the small, spare office, she
noticed instantly that all the blinds had been drawn
except at the front door. Brenda was meeting her
in a special FBI front that sported another name:
Garrison & Sons Life Insurance Agency.

Brenda had literally saved Susan's life. Indeed,
the FBI agent had been her gateway to a life without fear of being hunted down and killed by Dirk's
Mexican drug-cartel connections, even though he
was in prison. Oh, there was no question in Susan's mind that Dirk had sent out hit men to find
her. So far, he hadn't succeeded.

The first thing Susan had done was to dye her
hair from its original blond color to sable. And

she trimmed it to shoulder-length to add more change. Brenda gave her a new name, social security number and all the rest to complete the transfer to begin living a normal life of sorts. All these things ran through Susan's mind as she studied her handler. Brenda's red mouth was pursed. Adrenaline started to pour through Susan.

"Dirk escaped," Brenda said bluntly.

"What?" The word exploded from Susan's lips. She was on her feet with nowhere to go. The panic came back with a vengeance. "What? How could that be?"

"I know, I know. Come sit down, Susan. Please…" Brenda waved toward the chair.

Susan couldn't calm down. Dirk had sworn to kill her. He had promised to track her down and finish the job he'd started at their Miami home five years ago. Grabbing the arms of the wooden chair, Susan felt her knees weaken. She sat down before she fell down. Beads of perspiration dotted her wrinkled brow, her gaze burrowing into the FBI agent's eyes. "How could this have happened? Do they know where he is? Are they going to recapture him?" Her mind flew like a tornado around the possibilities.

"Take some slow, deep breaths, Susan. Please. You're looking pale and I don't want you to faint on me." Brenda reached over and gripped the hand that was clenched on the arm of the chair. "Come on now…breathe, breathe…"

Gulping convulsively, Susan tried. She was

gasping, her breaths shallow and rapid. Just the steadying touch of Brenda's hand helped her focus. *Oh, God, no!* The very worst nightmare that had dogged her heels all these years had finally come true. Dirk would be looking for her. Even though he didn't know where she was or what she looked like, Susan knew he'd stalk and find her. Fear of dying made her choke. She coughed violently several times, her hand pressed against her constricted throat.

"Come on," Brenda muttered, holding the glass of water toward her. "Sip this. You're hyperventilating. You've got to settle down, Susan. Not everything is lost." Brenda sat back down, her hands folded, her red nails shining against her dark green suit.

The water was cool and soothing. Susan took several gulps. Her tightened throat began to relax, but her heart pounded like a freight train in her chest. "Tell me what happened."

Frowning, Brenda picked up the report. "Dirk escaped. No one knows how. Guards suspect he was taken out in a laundry bag to the laundry truck, and he took off from there. No witnesses, though. This is all possibility, not fact. He had to have help. His cell buddies are being interrogated as I speak. And his visitors are being questioned."

"What does this mean for me?" Susan whispered. "I have a new name, a new identity. He doesn't know I'm living here in New York City."

It was a long way from Miami, Florida. Dirk hated the northeast because of the cold winters.

Lips twisting, Brenda said, "Hon, I know you've made a great life for yourself as a nanny here, and you're doing well in art school. I know you want to become a children's book illustrator someday." With a deeper frown, Brenda added in a softer voice, "But for your own safety, Susan, you're going to have to leave New York City for a while."

"But…"

Hand held up, Brenda said, "Listen to me. You're easy to find here. There's a lot of vermin, too. My boss also feels you would be safer away from the east coast. In a place where you can disappear. Don't worry, we'll do all the moving for you."

"Where?" Susan felt trapped.

"Jackson Hole, Wyoming. It's out in the middle of godforsaken nowhere. And knowing Payson's hatred of cold places, it's perfect for you. Plus, with him on the loose, you don't want him to flash a photo of you at the school and have someone recognize you. New York is a big town but it can be a small town. That's why we're moving you, hon. You need a new place and a new identity."

"That means you don't anticipate finding him soon," Susan said in a low tone. That meant her mother, who was also in the witness protection program, was affected. But so were her brothers, who lived on the family farm where she'd been born in Iowa. "You promised if he ever broke out of prison, you'd protect my family. What about my mom? My brothers at our farm? Are you doing that?"

"Already done," Brenda assured her. "We're working with local and state police. Your family has been warned in Iowa. And your mother is fine. We're not moving her. We feel she's fine where she is. They know Dirk escaped, and your brothers will be guarded 24/7 by those police agencies."

Relief poured through Susan. "Are you sure they'll be—"

"I am." Brenda sat up. "Listen, you need to move, Susan. I can see in your face that you don't want to, but you have to. We can't risk Payson finding you here."

"I don't think he will," Susan said, her voice strong. "I have my friends, Brenda. I have a publishing contact, the art department and—"

"It doesn't matter."

Susan's stomach knotted. "The last five years of my life I've found some peace, Brenda. I—I still haven't come to grips with losing my baby girl." She wanted to say the baby's name, but the word Sarah froze on her lips. To say it would make her lose all control. "I'm putting myself through art school with your help. I have a job I love and I'm good at it. I'm a nanny, but I want to tap into my other talents. I make ends meet without FBI financial assistance except for the school tuition. I shouldn't have to do this! Everything that makes me secure is here. I've just begun to feel safe."

Brenda's eyes narrowed. The woman's heavily made-up face seemed as if it would crack from tension. Already, Susan was crying inwardly. Brenda had saved her life, gotten her through the court hearings, the trial and then swept her into the witness protection program. In some ways, Brenda was like a mother to her.

"I'm sorry, Susan. I know how much you've blossomed here in New York. But I can't be persuaded to let you stay here. If Payson gets hold of you, he'll kill you. We both know that. His threat to you is part of the court testimony. Don't you want to live?"

"I want to live, not hide!" Susan cried out, her hands convulsing into fists in her lap. "I'm tired of this charade, Brenda. I want so badly to visit my mother, my brothers, but I can't. All I'm allowed is a monthly phone call with my mother. I can't ever see them! Do you know what that's like? I feel like I'm dead already!"

Brenda sat back, tapping her red nails on the glass over the desk. "I do understand," she said gently. "Isn't half a life better than no life?"

Shutting her eyes, Susan fought back tears. She'd cried hardly at all since waking up in the hospital, but the grief was still locked up within her. The shock, the stresses and pressures of the hiding, the FBI agents always in the next room protecting her, the nightmares and PTSD symptoms conspired against her. Right now, Susan felt on the edge of nothing. She could close her eyes and see her pathetic, thin figure balanced on her toes over a precipice that had no bottom.

"Susan?"

Opening her eyes, she drilled Brenda with a glare. "I'm the victim here. I was the one who was gut-punched. Dirk killed our baby."

"He damn near killed you, too. If that FBI agent who was there for surveillance hadn't pulled over after you stumbled out of that house with your nose bleeding, you'd be dead. When the agent saw you, he moved into action. He saved your life, Susan. You owe it to him and your family to keep going. I know it's hard. I know you want to see them. But right now, you *must* move. We have to put you out in the middle of nowhere. We've had a team on this for six hours trying to figure out, based upon Payson's profile, where in the U.S.A. he would *not* look for you. Wyoming tops that list."

Nodding, Susan looked down at her white fingers. Once again, her world was coming to an explosive, chaotic halt. Once more, her life was in jeopardy. Worse, this time it involved her mother and her brothers. Would Dirk go after them? He didn't know where her mother was, thank God. But he did know where her brothers lived. They had refused witness protection.

The FBI had persuaded her mother to disappear and she'd reluctantly agreed. Would Dirk kill her brothers to get even? A cold, aching chill wove down her spine. Susan had weekly nightmares of Dirk stalking her family and killing them, one by one. This mess was all her fault, and yet, her family had stood by her. They'd believed in Susan, and in her testifying to put Dirk away for good. None of them had entertained the thought of him ever breaking out of prison.

"My mother knows I'm moving again?"

Brenda nodded. "She feels it's the right thing for you to do, Susan."

Clearing her throat, she whispered, "All right. Jackson Hole, Wyoming."

"Yes." Brenda sat up, relieved. She handed Susan a file. "We've rented a small house for you. It's a cabin on a ranch. You can continue with your art career online and work long-distance with your teachers. We've changed your name, and all your records will reflect that. At least that stays solid and reliable." She managed a thin smile, hoping to cheer Susan up. "You can pick up a job there as a nanny. Your new name," she said, pulling over a file and opening it, "is Rachel Carson. We have a completely new identity for you, including a new social security number, driver's license and a deep résumé should people check it." Brenda handed her the envelope with the information.

"Then… I can't tell my friends I'm leaving, can I?" It seemed unconscionable. None of her friends knew who she really was or what had happened to her. None ever would. Yet, to leave them like this—without a word of explanation—was cruel. Susan shook her head. "This is awful. They'll think the worst of me."

"Maybe," Brenda said with sympathy. "But if they were in your shoes, they'd do what they had to do to survive, Susan."

Susan glared at the FBI agent, her wound as fresh as if it had happened yesterday. Her unborn baby, Sarah, had been dead when she'd miscarried her in the emergency room. Dead from Dirk's fist. Her baby could have lived had it not been for massive brain trauma. That was one of the few times Susan had cried. She had passed out from loss of blood and they had taken her dead daughter away.

When she regained consciousness two days later, Susan had wanted to see Sarah, but they'd said she was already in the morgue and had undergone an autopsy. She had sat in that private room, her arms aching to hold the daughter she'd carried. Something vital had fled from her spirit. She'd never got to say goodbye to her baby. Susan hadn't cared if she lived or died that day. But Brenda pulled her through.

Depression settled in on Susan as she recalled those stark, terrible days after her miscarriage. Looking at the folder, she slowly opened it with trembling hands. "I guess a sane person would be scared, wouldn't they? I mean, of Dirk being on the loose again."

Shrugging, Brenda murmured, "Hon, you're still going through the grief of losing your baby. I can see that. Grief has a funny way. Sometimes, it's fast. Sometimes, it's long and drawn-out."

"It will be forever for me, Brenda," she said, skimming the information in the file.

"Your heart was ripped out."

Just the warmth burning in Brenda's eyes made Susan rally. "It still feels ripped out. Sometimes I wonder if it will ever heal."

"When you meet the right man and get pregnant and have a second child, your healing will begin," Brenda answered softly. The silence settled between them. Finally, the FBI agent continued, "I already have a moving team over at your apartment. They're boxing everything up for you. All you have to do is take this airline ticket and go. I've got a driver waiting downstairs to take you to the airport."

Stunned, Susan realized she wouldn't even be going back to her apartment. Her cocoon was gone. Destroyed, once more. Once again by Dirk Payson. Feeling horribly vulnerable, Susan rubbed her arm. "I can't even go home...."

"Home is in Jackson Hole, hon. Look at it this way, you get to spend Christmas in a gorgeous postcard place. Don't worry, you'll make friends and things will buck up. We'll keep you apprised about Payson. If I find out anything, you'll be the first to know. I promise."

CHAPTER TWO

CADE HATED CHRISTMAS EVE. Hand tightening around the wheel of the Sheriff's Department's Chevy Tahoe, he forced himself to pay attention to the road. It was snowing, but not a blizzard. Still, at 8:00 p.m., the recently plowed roads shone with potential black ice.

He had duty until midnight, and that was fine with him. He didn't feel like going back to his home on his parents' ranch to celebrate Christmas morning with them. In fact, the heavy blanket of sadness enveloped him as it always did at this time of year. Cade knew he wasn't fit company even for the town drunk. His radio crackled with traffic from the dispatcher. There was an accident ten miles south of Jackson Hole. With this kind of weather and snow, it was messy for any driver unlucky enough to be out in it.

The highway leading back from Star Valley, about fifty miles from Jackson Hole, was dicey. Most of the deputies lived there and drove that distance to work. They couldn't afford the posh digs of the rich and famous who had taken over the sleepy ranching town of Jackson Hole. Cade considered himself lucky: his parents were from a long line of cattle ranchers come from earlier trappers. He had a home on their ranch, and it was a short drive from there to the sheriff's office.

Cade looked at his rearview mirror and didn't see any traffic. As he drove slowly up around the mountains, with the river on the other side of the roadway, Cade focused on his driving. Rounding a curve, he saw a dark SUV that had skidded into the jagged mountain cliff. Next to it, a car with its flashing lights was parked. Though visibility was poor, he noticed a woman in a black coat at the driver's side of the smashed SUV. She was trying desperately to open the vehicle's door.

After flipping on his lights, Cade quickly called in his position and requested an ambulance. As he drove closer, his heart began to pound with dread. He knew this kind of scene far too well. Worse, he recognized the dark blue Chevy SUV up ahead. It looked like Tom Hartmann's vehicle. Tom, his best friend and a deputy, had been killed six months earlier in a shoot-out with drug dealers driving through Star Valley with their cocaine.

Cade tried to bury the memory as he pulled up to the other side of the wrecked vehicle. As he passed it, he saw the familiar license plate and a new wave of pain flooded him. It was Hartmann's SUV and his widow, Lily, was the driver. Was their infant, Jenny, in there, too? Another nightmare, the one from two years ago, threatened to stagger Cade to the point where he couldn't think straight.

He was a deputy sheriff. He should know to stay calm during this kind of crisis. But he'd lost too much. Wrenching the wheel, he placed his vehicle on the upside of the wreck so no car coming around the curve would run into it.

Cade grabbed his coat and radioed in once more to the dispatcher. He gave the information about Lily Hartmann's car and asked for a fire truck. Choking on bile, Cade swung the door open, unlatched his seat belt and pulled on his heavy nylon jacket. He ran carefully on the side of the road, mud splattering across his polished black boots, and aimed for the driver's side of the car.

As Cade rounded the SUV, he saw the woman in the black wool coat and a red knit cap trying to tug open the smashed door. With his flashlight, he approached.

"I'm Deputy Garner, Ma'am. Step aside so I can see what's going on…"

Rachel willingly leaped back. She'd cut her hand on the twisted metal. It was dark. All she could see were the blazing lights of the sheriff's cruiser on the other side. The man was tall, his voice deep and calm. "I—I'm so glad you're here. I was following this SUV and it suddenly swerved and crashed into this cliff."

Cade barely heard the shaken woman's hoarse voice, but he was aware of the terror in her large eyes. The door couldn't be opened unless they used the Jaws of Life. The fire department carried two sets and they would bring them out. The window, however, was smashed in. As he flashed the light into the cab, a scream lurched into his throat, but Cade swallowed the sound.

Lily Hartmann, the wife of his best friend, lay bloody and unconscious, the air bag half empty on top of her. She hadn't worn her seat belt. Cade saw the hole in the window above the steering wheel. Lily had struck with such impact that her head had gone through the windshield. He thrust his hand through the shattered window and placed his fingers on her neck, searching for a pulse. As he shifted the light, Lily's black hair shone across her white, still face.

Oh, God, she's dead....

"There's a baby in the backseat!" the woman cried with renewed urgency. "You have to help the baby! I can't get the door open!"

Shaken, Cade combatted his personal horror over Lily's death. Nothing would bring her back. He had to act now! He jerked his hand out of the window and twisted around. As he moved swiftly to the other side of the vehicle where the other door might open, the woman followed him closely.

Cade remembered Tom and Lily, before they married, asking if he would be the godfather to their children. They'd witnessed the devastation of Cade's world, the loss of his wife, and wanted everything in place should something terrible happen to them. Cade had agreed to be their godfather. He'd never thought he'd ever have to make good on it.

"Hold the light," Cade commanded the unknown woman. After he thrust the flashlight into her hands, he gripped the handle on the door and jerked hard. It gave, and then, with more effort, Cade was able to pry the back door open just enough to get into it to see how the baby was doing. He breathed hard, his heart pounding with anguish as he wedged himself into the vehicle where Lily had put her daughter in the car seat. Tiny Jenny Hartmann with her black hair and blue eyes blinked up at him. With the light flashing into the backseat, the baby began to cry.

"Thank God," Cade whispered unsteadily. His hands shook as he disconnected the harness from around Jenny. Turning, he called out, "I'm bringing out the baby. She looks okay. I'm going to bundle her up and we'll all go to my cruiser. It's warm in there. Okay?"

"Y-yes… I'm so glad she's all right. What about the mother?"

"Dead," Cade answered, his voice flat.

"Oh, no…" she whispered, her hand across her mouth.

Cade turned and gently eased his large hands down around the well-bundled Jenny. As soon as he picked her up, she stopped crying, her eyes huge. He cradled her snugly into the crook of his right arm. Opening his jacket, he nestled the three-month-old into the folds for warmth and protection against the falling snow.

"I'm backing out," he called to the woman over

his shoulder. Immediately, she stepped away, keeping the flashlight trained so that he could ease out of the vehicle.

The woman stood mostly in shadow but he could clearly see the strain on her oval face, her full lips pursed and eyes dark with worry. "Come on," he urged her, "follow me…"

Rachel followed and kept the beam of light in front of the deputy. He walked as if he were stepping across eggs, his precious cargo in his arms. The baby was completely protected by his dark brown nylon jacket, but she no longer had a mother. It was beyond tragic. Rachel felt tears jam into her eyes and quickly swallowed them.

"Open the passenger-side door," Cade ordered her. They walked on the berm next to the cliff. Cade didn't want to take a chance of trying to climb into the driver's side with the baby. If a car came around that corner, it could clip him and kill both of them on a night like this.

Rachel pulled it open. "Now what?"

"Get in. I'm going to hand you the baby once you're inside. Then, I'll go to the other side of my cruiser and get in."

Rachel climbed into the passenger seat. She left the flashlight on the dashboard so the deputy had light and they both could see. She watched as he tenderly brought out the baby wrapped in a pink, yellow and green quilt. Opening her arms, Rachel received the infant.

"I've got her," she quavered. A baby in her arms

for the first time. Images of lying in the hospital dazed and wanting to hold her Sarah flashed through Rachel's mind. Gently, she adjusted the baby into her arms. The deputy closed the door. She watched him walk around his cruiser.

Cade climbed in and immediately radioed what had happened. The dispatcher told him help was on the way and it would take at least thirty minutes to get there due to the icy conditions on the highway. He turned up the heater and pressed on console lights. The darkness disappeared. Turning, he looked into the eyes of the woman who had been the first on scene. She held Jenny in her arms and gently rocked her. The infant had closed her eyes. Her tiny hands were visible beneath the sleeves of a crocheted pink sweater that Lily had made for the christening. Cade wanted to cry for the little girl.

Jenny was now without parents. Cade knew Tom and Lily had both been adopted only children and there was no family to take Jenny. That was why they had wanted Cade as the legal guardian for Jenny if the worst happened. The adoptive parents had agreed to Tom and Lily's request. Legal papers had been signed. Well, it had happened. Mind spinning with the implications, Cade realized he was a father…again.

"Let's see if Jenny is okay," he murmured, holding out his hands. "She was strapped in the right way, but I want to make sure nothing's broken. The ambulance is on its way, but it will take at least thirty minutes under these weather conditions to arrive on scene."

"Of course," Rachel said. She managed a nervous smile. "I'm glad you're trained because I'm not." She passed Jenny to the deputy.

Cade carefully began unwrapping the infant who now stared up at him with curious eyes. Jenny recognized his voice. She should. He'd been a daily fixture in the Hartmann home. He'd wanted to be around Jenny as well as support Lily, who had been very depressed since Tom's death. The baby, miraculously, had made Cade feel again. She helped him want to live once more, rather than just exist like a robot going through the motions. Lily seemed to have realized that and urged Cade to come over and simply hold Jenny and rock her. He'd taken over as a pseudo father and was determined to help Lily through this terrible period of loss and grief. He pulled out of his own mire of sadness and focused on the heroic woman sitting beside him. "What's your name?" he asked.

"Rachel Carson." She watched as the large hands of the deputy carefully pulled the quilt aside. "I just landed at Cheyenne airport and rented a car to drive out here."

"In the middle of this storm?" Cade gave her a glance. Obviously, she wasn't from Wyoming or would have known to stay put in Cheyenne until the front passed and the roads were cleared by the snow plows.

"I didn't know. This is my first time out west."

Nodding, Cade muttered, "Well, can you tell me what happened here?" Jenny began to coo as he gently took each small arm and tenderly tested it. She was cute in the pink crocheted sweater and trouser set. His worry over the baby receded. She seemed fine.

"I was driving up the mountain at a very slow speed," Rachel said, gesturing out into the blackness. "This SUV came out of nowhere and passed me going pretty fast. It scared the crap out of me before it disappeared. When I crept around this corner, the SUV had already smashed into the side of the cliff. I got out, ran over and tried to help."

"You did what you could," Cade said, his tone heavy. He wrapped Jenny back up in the blanket. There was so much to do. "Want to hold her again? Her name is Jenny Hartmann."

Surprised, Rachel nodded. "Sure. How could you know her name?"

"Long story," Cade grunted. He took the flashlight off the dash and said, "I have to be outside for a bit. Just remain in here. Okay?" He eased out of the cab and shut the door.

Rachel was happy to stay where it was warm and safe. Jenny felt good in her arms. Protectively, she nestled the cotton quilt around the baby's head to keep her warm. Rocking her, Rachel felt as if she were still in deep shock. Yet, there was a baby in her arms. *Alive.* Jenny smiled up at her and cooed. This was a happy baby, one who would never see her mother again. Eyes closed, Rachel fought back so many of her own suppressed emotions. Her welcome to Jackson Hole had been a horror. She hadn't wanted to come here anyway, but Brenda had left her no choice. It was one hell of a welcome. And on Christmas Eve, to boot. *How depressing.*

Rachel lifted her head and watched as the efficient deputy put out flares around the vehicle and behind his cruiser. She could see his dark shape in the rearview mirror as he walked up beyond the curve to place the bright red flares. While she doubted much traffic was out in this storm, those flares would warn whatever there was to slow down. The last thing Rachel wanted was to be hit from behind. Her arms tightened a bit around the infant who was now making noises and waving her hands. Smiling, Rachel leaned down and pressed a kiss to the baby's brow. Her fragrance breathed unexpected life back into Rachel. She loved the infant's sweet scent and inhaled it again. *The perfume of life.* The innocence of birth. Gazing down at Jenny, she couldn't help but smile. The infant's bow lips drew into a smile.

The deputy came back. He opened the door and quickly climbed in. His hair was wet and gleaming. The snowflakes were falling at a heavier rate. His nylon jacket had dark splotches all across the shoulders. He put in another radio call, then snapped off the light. Turning, he said, "I'm Deputy Cade Garner. I'm sorry I didn't introduce myself earlier."

"It's nice to meet you," Rachel said. Even in the muted light, she was drawn to his square face, strong jaw and large gray eyes. His pupils were large and black, giving him an intense and intelligent look. A few strands of his military-short black hair had fallen across his broad brow and Rachel felt it made him seem less formidable and a little more like the rest of the human race. With his khaki trousers, shirt and a gun strapped to his waist, he exuded a kind of cowboy appeal. It had to be her overactive imagination, Rachel decided.

As he took a quick side glance, Cade noticed how happy Jenny was in her arms. "Are you a skier on vacation?"

Carefully, Rachel gave him the rehearsed version of her story. Even to law enforcement she could never confide that she was in the FBI witness protection program. "I'm moving to Jackson Hole. I have a cabin rented on the Moose Head Ranch, just outside of town."

Surprised, Cade sat back. He'd definitely had this woman pegged wrong. Not that it mattered right now who she was. He felt grief-stricken over Lily dying, but now he had this new responsibility to Jenny. And then there was this woman with shoulder-length brown hair with such a tender look in her blue eyes. Rachel Carson had something soft and vulnerable in her manner. And Jenny obviously responded to that sweetness within her. She looked to be in her mid-twenties, and Cade didn't see a wedding ring on her left hand. "Moose Head Ranch?"

"Yes. Why?" She noticed how his eyes widened with surprise. There was a rugged quality about Cade Garner, no question. And Rachel sensed him to be a man of quiet authority, though her judgment of men was faulty. She could never forget that. After all, she had picked Dirk Payson. Still, Cade invited her trust even if she couldn't figure out why just yet.

"That's my parents' ranch. They have a group of cabins they rent out by the day, week or month." Cade usually didn't know about the visitors because he was busy with his own life. His father ran that part of the business while his mother ran the quilting store in town. Between these different income streams, they were able to stay afloat financially and keep their one-hundred-acre cattle ranch in the valley.

"Really? Do you live there?" Rachel asked. It was too personal a question, but the words flew out of her mouth.

"Yes," he said with a partial smile. "What do you do for a living?"

"Well," Rachel said, smiling down at Jenny, "I'm a nanny."

"A nanny?" Cade's mind raced. Either it was a coincidence or a godsend—probably both. He wouldn't have time to sit home with Jenny even though she was his legal responsibility. The captain could give him time off, but the winter was so demanding, Cade would have to locate a baby-sitter quickly for Jenny while he was on duty. Or there was this angel who'd come out of nowhere.

"I'm Jenny's legal godfather. And now, I'll be taking care of her until she's eighteen." Cade stared deeply into Rachel's widening eyes. "Since you're already at the ranch, would you consider being her nanny? Or do you already have a job lined up here in town? I know this is awkward, and possibly premature…"

Rachel felt as though Providence had just delivered this gift. "I don't have a job right now. I was going to come here and then start looking around. Yes, I'd love to take your offer. I can give you my references and contact information for the family I worked for."

Cade felt instant relief. Yes, he would check out her references. "Thank you…"

"I love children." Rachel's heart beat a little harder. Out of such a tragedy came this gift. Just having Jenny in her arms and knowing that she'd be able to take care of her in the future made staying here an incredible blessing to Rachel. "I'd be delighted to work for you, Mr. Garner."

CHAPTER THREE

RACHEL WAS SITTING in a curtained hospital cubicle with Jenny in her arms. Oddly enough, the hustle and bustle of the small Jackson Hole hospital made her feel more safe. After the ambulance had arrived and the baby had been checked over, Deputy Garner had asked her to go back with the ambulance crew to the local hospital. Clearly, he was worried about Jenny.

"Ms. Carson?" A young red-haired nurse came into the cubicle and smiled.

"Yes?"

"Jenny Hartmann has a clean bill of health. The doctor is signing the paperwork now." She frowned. "Do you know where to take the baby?"

"She's coming home with me, Dottie," Cade said as he halted next to the slender nurse. He felt his heart expand for an unknown reason as he got his first good look at Rachel Carson. She sat in the chair, her legs crossed, the baby in her arms. Jenny was asleep despite the noise in the emergency room. The two looked as if they were mother and daughter. Despite the trauma, Rachel appeared calm and almost happy with the baby in her arms. Cade nodded to her and gave her a slight smile.

"Rachel has rented one of my parents' cabins at the ranch. Legally, I'm Jenny's guardian, and Rachel has agreed to be her nanny until I can get everything straightened out."

Dottie nodded. "Sounds good to me. I'll tell Dr. Sherman to put down your mom and dad's ranch address and that you're her legal guardian. I wasn't sure if we needed to call in Child Protective Services or not."

Cade rested his hands on his hips. "No, you don't have to in this case."

Dottie frowned. "It's so sad, Cade. First Tom. Now Lily. Poor baby Jenny has no one."

Cade felt grief moving in his chest. "Now she has me." He'd just come from the crash site. Lily had been taken to the local morgue where the medical examiner would proclaim that she'd died of massive head trauma. There was so much to do. He needed to call Tom and Lily's adoptive families and friends to set up a funeral. Cade hated having to make the calls on Christmas Day. They would never have another Christmas without remembering that phone call, but he couldn't put it off. Tom was already buried at a cemetery outside of town. At least now, he and Lily would be together.

Placing her hand on Cade's damp nylon jacket, Dottie said, "I'll be right back."

Cade nodded and pulled the white curtain closed over the front of the cubicle. He felt strangely excited. Maybe it was a release from the day's tragic circumstances. Maybe it was because finally, after two awful years, someone needed him again. Bringing a chair with him, he went over to where Rachel sat with the baby.

"How are you doing?" he asked, searching her face. Cade began to realize how beautiful Rachel Carson really was. She had an oval face with softly arched eyebrows, full lips and a straight nose that looked a bit crooked at the top. Cade wondered how she'd broken it. As a deputy sheriff, he was used to studying people's faces. In some cases, it had saved his life. There was nothing threatening about Rachel. It was her large, expressive blue eyes that drew him. In them he could see both a flare of hope and utter exhaustion.

Rachel smiled a little. "Just a little stressed out but glad that Jenny is okay. That's what is really important here." Cade Garner's presence was palpable. He was tall, broad-shouldered, and in his sheriff's uniform, the black holster and all the other gear, he looked like a dangerous, modern-day warrior. Heart beating a little harder, she couldn't stop looking into his narrowed gray eyes. This man missed nothing. For a moment, a sizzle of panic grabbed her stomach. At some point, he might put her FBI cover in jeopardy. But then, Rachel sternly told herself, this man knew nothing about her nor would he ever guess that she was in the witness protection program. Her résumé and references were solid.

Reaching out, Cade barely touched Jenny's soft black hair, fuzz across her skull. "Poor little tyke. She got a raw deal, losing both her parents."

He was so dizzyingly close that Rachel inhaled sharply. There was a quiet, tightly sprung power around Cade. She saw it in his work-worn hands, his steady and earnest gaze. There was nothing meek or citified about this man. For one wild moment, she wanted to reach out and sift her fingers through his damp, short black hair. Just once, she yearned to touch a man who was both tender and strong—as Cade seemed to be. She watched as he gently curved his hand across Jenny's tiny head, his tough sheriff-deputy demeanor melting away.

Rachel witnessed a miraculous change in Cade's face as it transformed from an unreadable cop's expression to a man who clearly loved this baby. His mouth had been tense, and now, it softened and curved in a subtle smile.

"Have you ever noticed how sweet and clean a baby smells?" He lifted his head to meet her blue gaze.

"I know. I love it," Rachel whispered.

Cade felt himself getting lost in the family scene—tailor-made for future heartbreak. He had to get a grip fast and keep this semiprofessional. Sitting back, he lifted his hand away from the baby. "I had one of the firefighters drive your rental car into Jackson Hole. I'd like to drive you and Jenny to my home on my parents' ranch north of town. My captain has given me the rest of the night off because of the situation with Jenny. As her legal guardian, I've got paperwork to fill out at the courthouse the day after Christmas."

Rachel looked up in wonder. "That's right…it *is* Christmas, isn't it?"

Cade looked at his watch and said gruffly, "Just another day as far as I'm concerned."

The abruptness, the tightening around his eyes and mouth spoke volumes, but Rachel didn't know exactly how to interpret it. Maybe Cade didn't celebrate Christmas. It wasn't her business to ask. Everyone kept secrets. God knew, she had enough of her own to handle. Looking down at Jenny, she said, "Dottie said that Lily Hartmann fed her goat's milk, that she's allergic to cow's milk."

"That's right," Cade said. "Well, no problem there because my folks have some goats and Lily was getting the milk from their nannies. So, I'll just go out and milk them daily and put enough in the fridge so Jenny has a good supply. That's an easy problem to take care of."

"I've never milked a goat," Rachel admitted. She almost slipped by saying that she'd come from a farm in Iowa and had milked cows. Compressing her lips, she vowed not to allow anything of her past to leak out. Cade would have to think she was born in New York City and let it go at that. Still, something about Cade made her want to share details about her life—her real life. She was on dangerous ground with the deputy.

He straightened and smiled tiredly at her. "I

have a house at the family homestead. The cabin you've rented won't be that far from my house. How about we get you to your new home? I can take Jenny and care for her and you can get yourself a hot bath and go to bed."

Alarmed, Rachel stood as he did. "But she needs feeding every two to three hours."

Cade noted the concern in her upturned face, couldn't help looking at her fully. She was slender and about five foot seven inches tall. She had a model's body, not curvy at all. "I think I can handle taking care of Jenny. I want you to rest. Tomorrow morning, at nine, if you're up and moving around, come on over to my house. I have the day off and can help you get oriented with Jenny."

Rachel nodded. Cade pulled the curtain aside and she went with him to the nurse's desk where he signed some papers. As she kept pace with him, worry ate at her. Even though Cade seemed self-assured and capable of taking care of the baby, she felt anxious. Holding Jenny close, Rachel followed Cade out the sliding doors and into the night. It was snowing heavily now, the sounds around them muted. No one was up and about this early on Christmas morning.

Cade led Rachel to the cruiser and placed his hand on her elbow to help her climb in. For a second time, he felt as if an angel had dropped out of the night to help him with the infant. But she would just be Jenny's nanny—nothing else. With that thought, he shut the door and walked around the cruiser. Despite the shock of Lily's death and his sudden fatherhood, some of the emptiness deep inside him diminished. Why? He was too exhausted to consider answers right now.

Cade climbed into the vehicle. After going through the many radio calls, he then drove them out of the slushy parking lot and headed out toward the main area of Jackson Hole. Beneath the streetlights, Cade saw Rachel's profile go from dark to light and back. There was an incredible vulnerability to her. And her eyes haunted him. Cade could swear he saw fear in their recesses. Fear of him? More than likely, she was still in shock. Anyone witnessing such an accident would have a hell of a reaction. He'd seen so many he'd grown a bit immune over the years. In his line of work he couldn't afford to be emotionally overwrought. He had to think through his feelings and do the right thing at the right time. Yes, law-enforcement people had to have that edge.

"Where are you moving from?" Cade asked as he turned onto the empty main street.

Instantly, Rachel's gut tightened. Trying to keep her face unreadable, she stuck with her cover story. "New York City."

"This is quite a departure from city life," Cade murmured. He slowed for a stop light. The snowflakes continued to fall in lazy, twirling motions. At least this wasn't a blizzard coming through, and for that he was grateful.

"Uh, yes it is."

"What drew you here?"

Rachel cringed inwardly. Of course a deputy would ask a lot of questions. The FBI witness protection program had drilled her new life and past history into her until she could recite it in her sleep. "I felt a need to get out of the city. I wanted to explore the west. It's called to me for a long time. The family I'd worked for moved back to Italy. It seemed like fate that I make good on my dream." She managed a smile. "Besides, I love animals and I've never seen a moose. I thought this would be a good place to see them." None of that was a lie, thank goodness. For whatever reason, Rachel hated lying to Cade. He seemed so steady, reliable and honest that her conscience raged at her.

"You moved here because you hadn't seen a moose?"

Disbelief was evident in his low voice as well as shadowed in his eyes. Rachel shrugged. "I was getting tired of the big city. I yearned for those wide-open spaces. Cowboys have always intrigued me. Call it a sudden, illogical move." *Yeah, right.* Dirk Payson had broken out of prison and was hunting her. She could say nothing. And Cade would have been the ideal person to confide in. He might have gotten information on Payson through the law-enforcement sharing policies. He might have a photocopy of Dirk's face on his desk.

"Are you given to spontaneity?" he wondered, worrying that Rachel might be gone in a few months and he'd have to look for another nanny for Jenny. Cade could not stay home and take care of the infant. He had a job and crazy hours, as well. He liked Rachel and she appeared reliable and calm. Just the type of person he'd envisioned to help care for Jenny.

"Oh, not often. The only reason I did it was because my job had ended."

"Phew," he said, "I was worried that you'd up and take off in a couple of months."

"No," Rachel said. "I won't leave you or Jenny in the lurch."

"That's good to hear," Cade said, relieved. "A deputy sheriff's hours are always changing. We have three shifts in a twenty-four-hour period. I don't want to think of Jenny left alone for eight hours."

"She won't ever be left alone," Rachel promised him. Looking down at the baby girl sleeping soundly in her arms, Rachel silently vowed never to abandon her.

"I've got so many logistical problems running around in my head right now," Cade said, pointing at his brow. "Your cabin is about two hundred feet away from my home. I figure you could stay at my house the nights I have the graveyard shift."

"That would be fine. Or I could bring Jenny over to the cabin to stay with me."

"I'd like everything for the baby in one place. You're going to be busy enough without carting stuff back and forth."

"It's settled, then," she said.

Cade's mouth quirked. Her sable hair was shoulder-length and thick. It framed her face and brought out the assets of her eyes and lips. There was nothing to dislike about her. And for whatever crazy reason, he liked her—personally. "Your full name is Rachel Carson. Right?"

"Yes." Rachel didn't ask why he asked. She knew. If she were in Cade's shoes, she'd be doing a background check. He'd find her new life and information. All she had to do was remember it precisely because this was a man who missed nothing. And yet, in an odd way, Rachel felt safer with him than she ever had since Dirk had abused her. She sensed that Cade was the kind of man who would protect his woman and his child at any cost to himself. In a way, she mused, he was like the knights of old going around the countryside protecting the weak, the old and the poor.

"Where did you get your education as a nanny?" She told him.

"Is that a dream you've had? To be a nanny?"

Rachel watched as they left the Christmas-decorated town behind and climbed a long hill devoid of all traffic. "I love children. Nothing makes me happier than being around them."

Cade smiled. "Well, you're Providence dropping into my lap. I'm grateful that you'll be Jenny's nanny. So much has happened so fast."

Rachel was gazing down at Jenny and her loving smile made him ache. When she looked up and met his eyes, Cade felt at a momentary loss for words. Rachel seemed like the perfect nanny for Jenny, and this belief shook him deeply. Truth was, he found himself drawn to her as a woman. He tried to shove those feelings away.

"I'm in shock over all this, too," Rachel admitted in a soft voice. "I'm exhausted and yet, I feel like I'm still on pins and needles."

"It's the accident," Cade soothed, watching the twin headlights stab into the black night. At the top of the hill the highway would straighten and level out. The snow began to ease. "You're still in shock. I've got tomorrow off and the next day. Come on over when you feel like it."

"You seem to know a lot about Jenny."

Cade sighed. "Tom and Lily Hartmann were my best friends. Tom died six months ago, murdered by drug dealers. He was a deputy sheriff. Before he and Lily were married, they asked me to be godfather to their future children. If anything happened to them, I'd be the guardian. They had asked me because they came from adoptive families. Their adoptive parents supported their request. I said I would. I didn't realize it would really happen."

"Oh, dear," Rachel murmured. Without thinking, she reached out her hand and laid it on his broad, capable shoulder. When she realized her intimate action, she quickly withdrew her hand. "I'm so sorry. You must be in shock, too. It's awful to lose people you love." How well she knew. She'd lost her mother and brothers. It hurt not to be able to call them, to see them or to visit the farm where she'd grown up happy and secure.

"I'm okay," Cade said gruffly. "But my focus is on Jenny. After Tom died, I was over at their home nearly every day. I helped Lily take care of Jenny as much as I could because I know Tom would have wanted it that way." Cade shook his head, his hands tightening momentarily on the wheel. The wipers provided a calming effect on him as they whooshed slowly back and forth across the wet windshield. "I just never figured things would go the way they have. I couldn't believe it when I drove up in the cruiser and recognized Lily's SUV. I—this is just a crazy time in my life, I guess."

Rachel sensed the deep emotions barely under tight control within him. "At least Jenny is unhurt. And she's safe with you. She'll have a real father in her life and that's important."

Running his fingers through his hair, Cade grimaced. "Instant parent. I just never thought of myself in those parameters, Rachel." And he gave her an intense look. "I'm just glad you showed up. I'm sorry you had to see that wreck. I know it will haunt you for some time to come. Jenny's obviously happy and feels safe with you."

"That's a good sign," Rachel agreed, gently touching Jenny's soft, unlined brow.

"It is," Cade said with a genuine sigh. "My mother, Gwen, runs Quilter's Haven, a small fabric and quilting store in town. My father, Ray, runs the hundred-acre cattle ranch and I help out on days when I'm off duty. So, we're stretched thin."

"Yes, you are." Jenny stared at his hands. No wonder they looked roughened by hard, constant work. He was a cowboy when he wasn't a deputy sheriff. His work ethic made her proud of his responsible lifestyle. "Jenny has a father who will truly care for her in the long term."

Cade nodded. "Yes, but becoming a parent suddenly is jarring. My parents are going to be shocked, too. They'll be happy to help with Jenny, but they can't care for her, either."

"That's why I'm here," Rachel said, meaning it. Again, she saw the relief in Cade's shadowed eyes. His law-enforcement facade had dropped away. She was privy to the man, not the deputy. And what she saw called to her on such a deep level that it surprised her. Since the abuse by Dirk, Rachel had undergone years of therapy. She recognized the extent to which she was an abuse survivor. It had left her wary of men in general. She'd had a few men who were pals, but never a lover. Rachel wondered if she would ever be able to love a man. The scars from her marriage with Dirk Payson had been a prison sentence in so many ways.

"I'm sure glad," Cade said, smiling. "Once we get things set up, you'll need a car, won't you?"

"I will, yes. In New York I never needed one. I can drive, but it was nice not having a car payment."

"Maybe I can help you there. My dad has a small pickup truck he no longer uses."

Rachel laughed. "A pickup? I'm sure I can get used to driving it. That would be helpful because then I don't have to have a car payment on top of everything else."

"I'll make sure you get paid properly," Cade promised her. He made a right onto a road that was nothing but muddy ruts. "This is the way to the Moose Head Ranch. It's about a mile down this bumpy road, so hold on to Jenny."

The blackness was complete around them as he carefully threaded the car through the muddy ruts. The snow had stopped falling and as Rachel looked out, she realized that her life was changing remarkably and with shocking swiftness. And yet, a sweet joy thrummed through her heart as she held Jenny in her arms. It wasn't her baby, but that didn't matter. Her other jobs as a nanny had been with older children. Closing her eyes for a moment, Rachel savored the sense of utter safety she felt despite the turmoil in her life. Was it due to Cade's nearness? She thought so. How handsome he was. And then, Rachel wondered if he was married.

Opening her eyes, she glanced at his hands on the wheel. He didn't wear a wedding ring. A lot of men didn't so it meant nothing. Wetting her lips, she said, "For some reason, when I first saw you out there tonight, you looked married."

Cade's mouth thinned. "I was married," he said abruptly. Realizing he'd snapped at her, he added more softly, "I don't want to talk about it right now."

Taking his unexpectedly grim answer in stride, Rachel realized that was a closed topic between them. Yet, as she looked over at him, she saw a terrible grief in the deputy's eyes. What was that all about? She didn't dare ask at this point.

"I'm sorry," she said. Her apology seemed to deflate the tension that had suddenly ballooned between them. Cade was like Fort Knox, Rachel decided: closed up and private.

Cade's mouth thinned. "I'm the one who should apologize. I was married," he said, voice strained. "Abby and my baby girl, Susannah, were killed in an auto accident two years ago."

CHAPTER FOUR

RACHEL WAS TOO stunned to assimilate Cade's awful admission. He had lost his family! To some degree she understood his pain, like a knife in the heart. No wonder Cade looked so anguished.

His mother and father, Ray and Gwen, met them at Cade's sprawling three-thousand-square-foot single-story log home. It was nearly one in the morning. Rachel felt exhausted and yet super alert as Cade opened the car door and helped her out.

Gwen, a woman in her fifties with curly, short silver-and-black hair, led Rachel into Cade's home. Her gray eyes were sharp and filled with care. Ray went to the kitchen while Gwen took Rachel and the baby toward the back of the house.

"I don't know if Cade told you, but he lost his wife and daughter two years ago," she said. Motioning down the hall to an open door on the right, she added, "This was Susannah's nursery. Cade just hasn't had the heart to touch it yet. Little Jenny will claim it now. Come on in, I have everything ready."

Rachel saw the pale pink nursery with the crib and everything a mother would need to care for her infant daughter. The crib even had a baby quilt inside. Gwen took Jenny from her. The infant was just waking up, her eyes half-open.

"Cade said you were going to be the nanny," Gwen murmured, gently unwrapping Jenny and placing her beneath the colorful baby quilt. "There." She straightened and turned to Rachel. "I think you should stay in the guest bedroom. There's a door between it and the nursery." She motioned toward the wooden pine door.

"But I was going to stay at the cabin I'd rented."

With a brusque nod, Gwen turned out the light. A wall light shed enough of a glow into the room so that no one would trip or fall. "Yes, I know. Right now, Cade's in shock. He's lost Tom, his best friend. Now, Lily." She hustled out of the room and left the door partly open. With a gesture, she took Rachel to the next room. "He's going through a lot and he's going to need help. My husband and I don't feel he's in the right state of mind to be caring for this baby yet. We need your help for now, Rachel, if you're okay with that?"

Entering the bedroom, Rachel nodded. "Of course. I'm the least affected by all of this, so I'll focus on Jenny's care, feeding and bathing."

"Excellent," Gwen said, giving her a warm smile. She pointed to the queen-size bed. "This is a nice large room. If I were you, I'd keep the door open to Jenny's room."

"Oh," Rachel assured her, "I will. I'm so wired right now, I can't sleep, anyway."

"Hmm, aren't we all." Placing her hands on her hips Gwen looked around. "I've put towels, wash-cloth and soap on your dresser over there. The bathroom is right across the hall. Cade's master-bedroom suite is on the other side of the nursery with a master bathroom. This will be all yours."

"A hot bath sounds good," Rachel said. She loved the wedding-ring-design quilt across her bed. The curtains matched the fabric in the quilt. The entire room, even the floor, was knotty pine. A braided green-and-white area rug completed the rustic look.

"I'm sure it does. Just one more thing and we'll leave you alone. Jenny needs goat's milk."

"Cade told me."

Nodding, Gwen lifted her hand. "Let me show you where we keep the bottles out in the kitchen. And then we're going home to get some sleep after this crazy night."

Rachel liked Gwen's brusque, efficient man-ner. In some ways, she reminded her of her own mother, Daisy. Both women were short and lean. Gwen's hands were reddened and chapped. Farm and ranch work took a lot out of the owners and Rachel knew that from experience. Gwen walked quickly to the kitchen.

Cade looked up. He'd been speaking to his fa-ther, Ray, at the counter.

"I'm just showing her where Jenny's goat's milk is," Gwen explained, opening the refrigerator.

Rachel noticed the weather-lined face of Ray

Garner. He was as tall as his son, but more wiry. He wore a blue-and-white-plaid long-sleeved shirt, jeans and a pair of well-worn cowboy boots. His gray felt Stetson lay on the round table at the end of the kitchen. Gwen slid her hand around Rachel's arm and pulled her closer to the fridge.

"We milk our goats twice a day. Cade was keeping a good supply for Lily and would take the bottles to her every morning before he went to work. Lily was very health-conscious and Jenny was thriving on goat's milk." She shut the fridge and led Rachel to the cabinets near the kitchen sink. "Lily was very old-fashioned. She insisted on glass milk bottles, not the plastic ones. They're in here." She pointed up to them in the cabinet. And then in a lower tone, Gwen added, "Abby, Cade's wife, believed in glass bottles, too, and that's why we have them."

Heart aching, Rachel realized that Cade had not removed his lost family from the house. Could she have done if it had happened to her? She didn't think so. "That's fortunate," she told Gwen, taking some of the bottles and placing them on the countertop. "Did Abby put the goat's milk in the bottle and then set it in a pan of water on the stove to heat?"

Grinning, Gwen patted her shoulder. "You're very bright. Yes. Neither Abby nor Lily believed in using the microwave. They worried it might change the cellular structure of the goat's milk.

So, this might be old-fashioned, but we know it's completely safe for the baby."

Rachel nodded. "I was nanny for a little boy from India, and his mother insisted on glass bottles and no microwave, either."

"Whew, that's good. I don't have to train you up in this, then."

"No, you don't."

Patting Rachel on the back, Gwen said, "Listen, this is all you need to know tonight. And by the way, there's nothing but cotton diapers, no disposables, in the nursery. You okay with that, too?"

Rachel grinned. "No problem. My Indian family was the same way."

Gwen rubbed her hands. "You and I are going to get along just fine! Go get your bath and hit the hay. I'll pour some goat's milk in three bottles and put them in the fridge. That way, when Jenny wakes up hungry in an hour or two, you can stumble out here and get it ready for her."

"Sounds good," Rachel said. She walked over to Ray Garner. "Mr. Garner, I'll say good-night for now. It was nice meeting you." She held out her hand to him.

Ray nodded, gave her a tired smile and shook her hand. "It's nice meeting you, too, Ms. Carson. I don't know what we'd do without your coming like a rescuing angel into our lives right now."

"I'm not an angel by anyone's definition, Mr. Garner," Rachel protested. Not after the awful mistakes she'd made.

Ray Garner gave her a kind yet appraising look. Cade was also watching her, making her even more self-conscious. In the middle of so much upheaval, she hated to admit how attracted she was to him. She tried to ignore the feeling and managed a smile. "Cade, I'm going to get a bath and Gwen wants me to stay in the guest room next to Jenny's nursery. You okay with that?"

"That's fine," he said. "It's a better idea under the circumstances. I appreciate you doing this. Mom said that in about a week, she can transfer you over to your cabin. You don't have to stay here forever. Once I get legalities out of the way, I can start taking care of Jenny at night when I don't have duty."

"We'll sort this all out as we go along. Good night...."

CADE SAT ON the edge of the bed. He'd just taken a tension-releasing hot shower. As he dried his hair with the white terry-cloth towel, he listened to the quiet of the house. With Jenny and Rachel nearby, the ranch home felt different. He tried to figure out why, but couldn't.

Reeling from exhaustion, he noticed it was nearly 2:00 a.m. He'd made the call to Lily's adoptive family earlier, which had left him feeling worse. He padded into the bathroom, hung up the towel and turned off the light. Slats of moonlight filtered into the huge master bedroom through the venetian blinds.

After climbing into bed, Cade pulled up a quilt that had been made by his mother as a wedding gift to Abby and him. His hearing automatically keyed to the partly opened door to the nursery. When Abby had become pregnant, Cade had cut a door into the nursery from their bedroom. Closing his eyes once he punched the pillow into place, Cade remembered the many nights that they would take turns getting up to care for Susannah when she cried out in hunger. Sleep deprivation had been a way of life, but he'd never minded that.

It was happening all over again, and now Cade felt groggy as the night's events deluged him. What luck to find Rachel. His father had been right: she was an angel in disguise, regardless of how she saw herself. A sigh tore from his lips as he buried his head more into his pillow. It was Christmas morning. What kind of gift had just dropped into his life? Emotions churned through Cade, bringing up the past, the remnants of grief he still felt on some nights in the quiet home. Now, his house was a home once again with a beautiful young stranger and Lily's baby. What kind of strange, twisted fate was this? Cade couldn't stop the onslaught of his grief over Lily's death. Jenny would never know her mother. And suddenly, he was a father without a wife. He had legally sworn to take care of Jenny. Cade wasn't sure what these Christmas gifts meant. In minutes, he dropped into a deep, badly needed sleep.

THE PHONE WAS RINGING, and Cade jerked awake. He fumbled for the landline on the nightstand. Bright sunlight burst around the wooden venetian blinds.

"Garner here," he muttered, rubbing his eyes to wake up. Usually the sheriff's department used this phone to get hold of him when he was off duty. Tossing off the blankets, Cade swung his bare legs out of bed. His feet landed on the warm sheepskin rug next to the king-size bed.

"Cade? This is Gary."

Blinking, Cade pushed his hair off his brow. Gary Henderson was the commander of the sheriff's department, his boss. "Yes, sir?"

"Did I wake you up? It's ten o'clock. Merry Christmas, by the way."

"Late night," Cade mumbled thickly.

"Yes, that's why I'm calling. I wanted to make sure little Jenny was okay."

That was like Henderson. He was a father of two teenage daughters. His wife, Tracy, was a first-grade teacher. "Fine...the hospital doctor said Jenny was fine." Another scent filled Cade's nostrils: that of bacon frying. And then he groggily recalled Rachel was here, in his home. Was she out in the kitchen making breakfast? That brought back a sheet of warm memories to Cade.

"Good to hear. Well, listen, you're going to have court papers to file the day after Christmas because you're Jenny's legal guardian. Plus, I'm asking two other deputies to go over to Lily's home. We need to locate her will and find out what her requests were and try to fill them now that she's gone."

"Yes, sir, I know." And he filled him in with the calls to Lily's adoptive parents. "There's a lot on my plate right now."

"I'm authorizing you a week's leave with pay, Cade. Your life has suddenly taken a new road and there's a lot you have to get in order."

"Thank you, Captain. I really appreciate that."

"No problem. I guess in one way, Jenny is a Christmas gift to you. If there's anything you need, just let me know. We're here to help."

Grateful, Cade hung up the phone, and felt as if he needed another twelve hours of sleep. He didn't hear any noise from Jenny's nursery. Knowing Rachel was up, he grabbed his dark blue terry-cloth robe and pulled it on. He opened the door and walked into the nursery, but Jenny was gone. Probably out with Rachel in the kitchen. Standing there, Cade realized he had to get dressed. He couldn't just waltz out there like this. Rachel wasn't his wife. She was an employee.

He turned and went back into the master bedroom. As he pulled on a pair of jeans, blue socks and a blue T-shirt with the words *Teton County Sheriff's Department* on it, Cade couldn't ignore the bubbling happiness simmering in his heart. Abby had always made him breakfast when he'd had the day shift. She had been one hell of a cook. And now he smelled bacon frying once again. More warmth filled his chest.

As crazy as his world was right now, Cade couldn't ignore the contentment he felt. It was a completely unexpected emotion. Since Abby and Susannah's passing, he'd felt less than whole. Less than a man. Just a robotic nomad wandering the jungles of life without any real passion or focus, with no dream to work toward. As he finished combing his hair, shaving and brushing his teeth, Cade realized darkly that he'd stopped dreaming after their deaths. Now, the dreams had returned. How odd, how…wonderful.

RACHEL HEARD CADE coming into the tiled kitchen. It was easy to hear the scuff of boots on the polished pine floor that led into the sunny yellow room. Turning, she saw Cade saunter through the archway. There were dark circles beneath his eyes. How different he looked from Dirk. Cade Garner was clean, neat and shaven. All the things Dirk wasn't. The contrast was startling as well as powerful.

"Good morning," Rachel called from the stove.

Cade nodded and saw she had brought Jenny out in a portable bassinet that sat on a chair at the pine table. "Good morning. How's our girl?" He walked over to see the tyke sleeping soundly. Rachel had changed her clothes and now had her in a green flannel onesie. He tried to pay attention to the baby, but he wanted to stare at Rachel.

"She just gobbled down about four ounces of warm goat's milk," Rachel said, smiling as she put the last strips of the fried bacon onto a paper towel. "She's doing fine."

"Done her business?" Cade asked, tucking the corner of the baby quilt down a little.

"Oh, yes, that, too. She's a good girl."

Lifting his head, Cade studied Rachel. She looked fetching in a pair of cranberry slacks and a long-sleeved pink sweater, with her sable hair tied up in a ponytail behind her head. His body went tight on him. Surprised, Cade straightened and said, "Good."

"You look exhausted," Rachel said. She pointed to the table. "I figured you'd be up sooner or later. Would you like some breakfast?"

The table had been set with the white china plates and flatware. The salt and pepper shakers were nearby. "You didn't have to do all of this," Cade said. "I never expected it."

Shrugging, Rachel opened the carton of eggs next to the stove. "I'm here. I have to eat. Why not cook for two instead of one?" Besides, that was what she'd done in her former life: cooked for two. It felt good to do it again. "How do you like your eggs? And how many?"

Moving over to the stove, Cade saw she had found a red-and-white checked apron and had tied it around her waist. His mother had sewn that for Abby. "I'll take three eggs scrambled." He went to the toaster and opened up the whole-wheat loaf. "Toast?"

Rachel smiled. "Yes, two slices, please."

Cade liked the simple partnership that had naturally sprung between them. "You got it," he said. Out the kitchen window he could see the new snow across the backyard and beyond into the empty cow pastures. The sun was bright, the sky an amazing turquoise color above the rugged Tetons off to the right. Things were looking up. How could they not after what they'd witnessed yesterday?

He brought the butter out of the cabinet and placed it on the table. Going to the fridge, he turned and asked, "Do you like jam on your toast?"

"I do. What kind is in there?"

Searching, Cade leaned down and looked. "Some strawberry and a bit of apricot."

"I love apricot."

"Apricot for the lady," he murmured, pulling it off the shelf.

"I'll bet you're a strawberry-jam guy."

Grinning, Cade said, "Does it show?" He took both jars from the fridge and shut it with a nudge of his hip. When he looked up, her eyes were warm with laughter. There was an incredible ease between them, as if they had known one another forever.

"Mmm, you just remind me of a country-boy type," Rachel said, breaking the three eggs into the black iron skillet. She grabbed a fork, broke the yokes and rapidly mixed them all together.

"Ah, I see," Cade said, his mouth lifting. "What does a strawberry-jam man look like?"

She grinned. "Like you, I suppose. As an artist I see the colors, connections and symbols between things." And because of her abuse from Dirk, Rachel had become hyper-alert and missed nothing. Brenda had told her she had post-traumatic stress disorder. It came from feeling so threatened that she feared for her life. And although several years had gone by without such a threat, the hyper-alertness never left. It was always there, like a frightened animal on the verge of running away in order to survive a coming attack.

"So, cowboys and deputies are strawberry-jam men?" He ambled over and poured himself some coffee. Rachel already had a cup of her own next to the stove. He was interested in how she perceived him. Still, Cade reminded himself that he was going to do a background check on her. Over the years he'd learned never to judge a book by its cover. As he leaned against the counter and watched her scramble the eggs, he hoped the report would come out clean. If it did, then he could trust his eyes…and his heart.

"I guess so," Rachel said with a shy smile. The way Cade stared at her made her feel incredibly feminine, which was new to her. There was no question Cade Garner was a fine-looking man. Handsome in a rugged, outdoors sort of way, with straight brows above his intelligent gray eyes. The way he slouched comfortably against the counter—that lazy kind of masculinity beckoned strongly to her. Would she be able to keep these new feelings at bay while working for him?

Cade noticed she wouldn't often meet his eyes. She was shy. Maybe she was an introvert by nature. He supposed that could account for her demeanor. "Are you okay being here in this house with me?" he asked her.

Rachel's hand poised over the skillet for a moment. Startled, she asked, "Why…yes. Is anything wrong?" She scooped the scrambled eggs onto the plate he'd brought from the table.

"No, no, everything's fine. I realize we're strangers and a lot is being asked of you out of the blue. A woman might feel uncomfortable with a man she doesn't know, more so sleeping in the same house with him."

"Thanks for your sensitivity," she said. Breaking two more eggs, Rachel quickly scrambled them for herself. "I always had my own apartment in New York City but sometimes I'd stay overnight at my employer's home when they were out of town. I'm okay with the arrangement." Cade couldn't know that she'd awakened at 7:00 a.m. feeling joyous and safe. Two emotions she hadn't felt in a long, long time. And Rachel knew it was due to that protection that emanated from Cade like a powerful beacon. That and the baby. For Rachel, Christmas had given her the one thing she yearned for the most: a baby to care for. It didn't matter that Jenny wasn't her biological child. Just getting to take care of a baby fulfilled her in a way she would never be able to put into words. Maybe, too, it was because of her large, tight farm family in Iowa.

"Thanks," Cade said. He put the toast on his plate and loaded two more slices into the toaster. "So, if I'm a strawberry-jam man, then that makes you an apricot-jam woman. Right?"

Laughing softly, Rachel brought her scrambled eggs over to the table. Cade positioned himself next to Jenny's bassinet and Rachel sat down opposite him. "I don't know. I hadn't really thought of myself in that way."

Buttering his toast, Cade studied her. Rachel's cheeks were flushed, almost as if she were unaccustomed to this kind of attention. Either that or she was hiding something. He realized upon closer inspection that sable was not her real hair color. She was more a blonde. "I hadn't, either," he chuckled.

The toaster popped. Rachel stood and retrieved the browned slices. When she sat back down, her expression was more serious. "Today is Christmas."

"I know. Merry Christmas. Bet you didn't think it would be like this, did you?"

She buttered her toast. "I feel like I'm in some kind of dream." She looked out the window. "And your ranch is like a beautiful picture-postcard to me. This area of the country is truly breathtaking. If you take out yesterday, it's a merry Christmas for me."

As he salted and peppered the steaming pile of

scrambled eggs on his plate, Cade felt a wonderful familiarity settling over him. Rachel was bright, quick and easy to talk with. Suddenly, breakfast was something special once more. And with baby Jenny sleeping between them, Cade swore he felt giddy. He hadn't felt this way since his family's death. "Well," he said, "at least you didn't wake up this morning thinking you were in a nightmare."

Rachel forced a smile. Cade would never know about her nightmare. Slathering a thin layer of apricot jam across her toast, she murmured, "Oh, no, this is a dream. A wonderful one."

One that Rachel wanted to last forever. But could it, with Dirk Payson out to kill her?

CHAPTER FIVE

DIRK PAYSON SMILED a little. He sat in a motel in Des Moines, Iowa, thumbing through a roll of hundred-dollar bills. He picked up his cigarette, took a deep drag and let the smoke drift out of his thin lips. Everything was going along fine. The Mexican drug cartel had welcomed him back like a long-lost brother. Of course, Dirk knew that that was because he'd been one of their best movers of cocaine into the U.S.A. and Canada.

His contact, Pedro Morales, had the Iowa territory to ply his cocaine to the hooked addicts. He gave Dirk ten thousand in cash to reestablish his life after the prison escape. The green felt fine between his fingers. He was free and he had money. Life was good. He was letting his blond beard remain on his face. Last night, he'd bought some dark brown hair coloring. Every day he'd have to add it to his scraggly beard. And he was allowing his blond hair to grow. Luckily for him, he only had to dye it a couple of times a month. Now he knew what a woman went through. Shaking his head, he stood up and put most of the bills in a money belt beneath his red long-sleeved sweat-shirt. The rest he put into a billfold.

Looking out the venetian blinds, he saw snow-flakes twirling outside. Iowa at Christmas sucked. He hated the cold and snow but he had to connect with Pedro in order to get back into the organization.

His mind turned, as it always did, toward Susan. His sources in prison had been trying to get a lead on her since she'd entered the witness protection pro-gram. And on her mother, Daisy Donovan. So far, no luck. But he knew the Iowa farm where Susan had been born was nearby. In the phone book, he'd found the three Donovan brothers, Robert, Marvin and Donald—Susan's three big brothers. She had been the baby and only girl in the family.

As he moved back to the bed, Dirk turned over possibilities. Because Susan had testified against him as his wife, the FBI had given her and her mother, Daisy, witness protection. The sons had refused it because they didn't want to leave their five-generation family homestead. *Good for them.* He grinned, the cigarette clamped between his lips. The smoke made his eyes water.

Having had plenty of time to understand the federal witness protection program, Dirk knew that neither Daisy nor Susan could ever contact their family. Did Daisy and Susan talk, though? Were they allowed to do that? Dirk had not yet been able to find that out. Now that he was free, he would turn to other field assets, a group of com-puter-hacker friends.

Dirk paced the small room carpeted with a brown rug that had seen much better days. He knew one thing: he wanted to kill Susan. She was the initial target. His mind ranged over trying to find Daisy, but she was of much less interest to him. The three sons lived on the farm with their families. Could he believe that Daisy and Susan never contacted them? He found that tough to swallow. Susan was so tight with her Iowa farm family that she squeaked. And her loyalty to her family had always made him angry.

Sitting down, he snuffed out the cigarette in a yellow glass ashtray on the nightstand beside him. He was just the opposite of Susan: a kid from a broken home with a meth mother and father who were still serving prison time in Alabama. His Southern heritage, however, came in handy from time to time, he'd discovered. With his soft, Southern drawl and good manners, Dirk could fool everyone. His mother, her face pockmarked with craters the size of those on the moon's surface, had taught him guile and manipulation. That was the way she was and Dirk had learned at an early age how to get his way.

He was the ultimate chameleon—able to bend, shift, change and become what people wanted him to be. It was all a huge manipulation dance, of course, but he'd learned from the best: his mother, Enid. Taking out the phone book, he thumbed through it some more. He wrote down the address of the farm, the full names of the Donovan brothers, and closed it.

First things first. He needed to get a PC laptop.
Pedro had given him an email address and a couple
of throwaway cell phones so that they could remain
in touch. Pedro paid hackers a lot of money to get
info, to break into banks and other repositories in
order to steal social security numbers. He'd given
Dirk a new name and the stolen number of someone who had recently died. Now, he was Steve
Larson. Liking his new moniker, Dirk chuckled.
Once more, he was a fish in the big sea of drug-
running. A chameleon fish.

What to do now? His stomach growled. Across
the street was a chain restaurant. Having money to
buy food made him feel euphoric. He went to the
closet and shrugged into his black parka, pulled a
knit cap over his head and tugged on the leather
gloves. He'd go out and enjoy his freedom. Dirk
sighed and smiled. How damn good it felt to be out
of prison! Knowing the authorities were looking
for him, Dirk stayed on the move. He didn't look
anything like his prison picture so the authorities
were going to be hard-pressed to find him. All he
had to do was stay smart, not drive the rental car
over the speed limit and get stopped by some cop.

From the dresser drawer, he pulled a .45 pistol.
Pushing it into his coat pocket where it would be
unseen, Dirk felt secure now. A gun always made
the difference. He took a wool muffler, wrapped
it around his neck and tucked the ends of it into
the front of his coat. Now, he was prepared to go
out into this below-freezing snowstorm.

Trudging through the few inches of snow that had fallen last night, Dirk made it to his Toyota Corolla. The dark blue car was nondescript and that's how Dirk wanted to be: unseen and unnoticed. He'd have preferred to get a bright red sports car, a Corvette, but that was out of the question. No, he was smart enough to know when to blend in instead of standing out.

Over a Christmas breakfast in a nearly deserted restaurant, Dirk felt the joy of his freedom as never before. Few patrons were around on Christmas morning. As he savored each bite of his ham, cheese and onion omelet, Dirk remembered the holiday with simmering anger. His parents, who were meth dealers, had always been so out of it they didn't know when a day was or wasn't a holiday. Dirk recalled the year he was nine years old when his parents had completely forgotten Christmas. When he'd gone back to school after break and all the children were excitedly sharing what they'd gotten, he'd avoided them. Worse, no tree had been put up and decorated, either. Dirk knew about these things because he'd go visit friends and see those glittering, beautiful trees in their homes. Aching to have that in his home, he'd made the mistake of asking his father, Joe, about it.

Dirk tried to avoid that memory—but it stuck with him like a festering cancer. Joe had jerked him off his feet by his T-shirt and slammed him against a wall. The power of his throw had broken the drywall where Dirk had struck it. For that question about Christmas, he'd received several fractured ribs. His mother had been shocked by her husband's anger. But then, Dirk realized later, his father was high on meth. And meth users were very emotionally unstable when high. Dirk always tried to walk on eggshells around his father during those times. Except for that one mistake when Christmas had seemed really important to everyone except his family and he'd opened his mouth. Dirk learned after that to ignore Christmas and make up lies to his friends at school about the presents he received. Each year, it became easier. The experience taught him how gullible people really were. No one ever checked out his story. This one lesson was intrinsic to his ability to manipulate others to do his bidding. And it had made him a rich man until Susan had squealed on him. *The bitch. I'll find you. And then, I'm going to kill you...an inch at a time. Nothing fast. Just real slow. I want to watch the fear come to your eyes when I walk up to you. I want to hear you beg, see your tears and watch you scream.*

IN THE LATE AFTERNOON, after clearing off the sidewalk of snow, Cade entered his home to hear singing. Halting on the mud porch, he listened to Rachel's bell-like voice. Cade simply stood and listened. When he realized she was singing one of his favorite Christmas songs, "The Angel's Song," his heart burst open with an outpouring of gratitude. Abby had had a beautiful voice and belonged to the local church choir. This brought back poignant memories to him.

After Cade removed his boots and walked into the kitchen, warmth surrounded him. Rachel's alto voice was clear and moved him. He walked quietly to the entrance to the living room and saw Rachel in the rocking chair with Jenny in her arms. She was feeding the baby and singing to her. If anyone was an angel, it was Rachel. Her profile was clean, the soft smile on her mouth made Cade realize just how lost he'd been until just now.

The baby suckled happily on the bottle, her arms waving back and forth. Rachel had a diaper thrown over her shoulder. She took the bottle away from Jenny, lifted her and placed her gently over her shoulder. Her soft, gentle pats on the baby's lower back brought up several burps.

Laughing, Rachel lifted her up. "My, what a big voice you have." She grinned at the baby who met her eyes. A smile bloomed on Jenny's bow-shaped lips. "Hungry for some more now?"

Gurgling, Jenny lifted her hands after Rachel placed her back into the crook of her left arm. The infant suckled strongly and Rachel closed her eyes, feeling as if she were in bliss. Or, maybe it was heaven. Whatever it was, she was happy. Happier than she could recall.

"So," Cade said, walking into the room, "you're a singer, too."

Cade's gray gaze burned into Rachel. He had just come in, coat in his hand and in his sock feet.

There was something vulnerable about Cade despite his remoteness and it tugged at Rachel's heart. "Oh, I'm no great singer. I just love to sing is all." She was struck by the sudden thaw in his expression. Generally, when she had seen him, he was scowling. "There's a difference, you know."

Crouching down in front of her, Cade gently brushed his index finger along the chubby curve of Jenny's flushed cheek. "I'd be happy, too, if you were singing to me. My favorite song is the one you were just singing. It's a Christmas carol we sing in church at this time of year."

Rachel sucked in a breath as Cade leaned down. His closeness made her heart beat faster. She could feel his warmth, his masculine strength, and, hungrily, she absorbed Cade's unexpected closeness. Her knees almost brushed his. As male as he was, he was so tender as he grazed Jenny's cheek and then smoothed her fuzzy black hair across her tiny skull. *He's the opposite of Dirk.* Rachel felt her stomach muscles lose their tension over that realization. How could she have been so blind as not to see Dirk for who and what he was? It was a question she'd asked herself a thousand times without a good answer. Her mother and brothers had warned her not to marry him, and she'd ignored their pleas. She'd paid the price.

Rachel sat very still as Cade crouched, smiling at the baby. Why couldn't she have fallen in love with someone like Cade, a man with strong morals and values? Whatever the answer, Rachel hadn't

pinned down her reasons for choosing Dirk—and
why she'd stayed with him. Her family had understood and supported her through it all. She cherished her monthly phone calls to her mother. Once
a year, they were allowed one wonderful week together in Puerto Rico.

"She's really happy," Cade noted, looking up
at Rachel, the baby's fingers wrapped around his
finger. Immediately, he detected pain lingering in
the recesses of her blue eyes. A profound sadness
surrounded Rachel, and he couldn't explain why
that suffering was there. Maybe a search on the
law-enforcement network at his office would give
him answers. Though, of course, he didn't want
Rachel to show up on any lists. He wanted her to
be free of any illegal past. While it made him feel
a little guilty, Cade knew he had to do it—especially for Jenny's sake.

Rousing herself, Rachel smiled nervously and
saw that Jenny was done with the bottle. She removed it from her mouth and blotted the baby's lips
with the diaper from her shoulder. "Yes, she is."

"Now, she'll go to sleep," Cade said. He stood
up and held out his hands. "Do you want me to
put her to bed?"

"Not yet," Rachel said, beginning slowly to rock
once more. "I want her fully asleep before I do
that. Less chance of her jerking awake and then
being cranky."

Nodding, Cade said, "I'm really glad you have
baby experience."

She remembered that he'd lost his family. And he hadn't divulged much, so she wasn't going to bring up the topic, either. Instead, she said softly, "Don't worry. You'll be a great father for Jenny." And he would. It irked her that she kept wondering what it would feel like to be touched by Cade. He was a man's man and so kind to her. Rachel couldn't stop imagining being with him no matter how much she tried to put it out of her mind. In one day, she'd managed to become attracted to another man.

"Maybe..." Desperately, Cade scrambled to change the direction of their conversation. It was getting too personal.

"Have you gotten your art assignment?" Cade asked, instead. Since she was taking an Internet art course, he'd invited her to use her laptop in his office.

"I just downloaded the instructions on my next one," she admitted. "I'm to draw an animal, and I've decided I'll try a moose."

"The snow is pretty much gone by May, and I can take you into some good places to see the real thing then." Cade was shocked at his offer. Where had that come from? He saw the surprise in Rachel's features, too. What was it about her that softened his hard edges and the wall of grief around him?

"I'd love that. I have a camera and can take some photos to bring back here."

Rachel was easy to converse with. Normally,

Cade would come home from work, say hello and disappear to do his chores. Something had changed, and he wanted to take the time to talk with Rachel. He was hungry for her company. "Have you always wanted to be a children's illustrator?"

"Always," Rachel said, "I got an opportunity to go to the art school in New York in the evenings. I found out all kinds of commercial art existed out there, but I loved the children's illustrations the most."

"What else did you want to be?" Cade noticed how she avoided his look and her mouth tightened briefly at the corners.

"I dreamed of being married and having a bunch of kids." It wasn't exactly a lie, but not quite the truth, either. If she hadn't married a drug dealer, she would have married someone in Iowa and continued her farming life that she loved so much.

"Not exactly what the modern-day woman wants," Cade noted.

Rachel shrugged. "I think family is the core value of everything." Cade wouldn't know about hers and it made her feel badly.

"Brothers? Sisters?"

"No, an only child. My parents died in a plane accident five years ago." All lies, but that was her ironclad cover. Rachel didn't want to lie to Cade, but what else could she do under the circumstances?

"I'm sorry about your parents," he said, meaning it. Again, she avoided his gaze and seemed unusually tense. "Tell me, are all artists introverts who hate being grilled on their backgrounds?" Cade tried to add a hint of a smile to go with his serious question. Maybe that would help her relax. He didn't want to chase Rachel off, leaving him without a nanny.

Rachel quirked her lips as she rocked Jenny. "I'm an introvert, for sure. I just don't get many men who are interested in me or what I want out of life, is all."

"That shocks me. You're young, beautiful, talented…."

Feeling heat rush to her cheeks, Rachel wanted to shrink and disappear into the rocking chair. Cade's penetrating gray eyes lost their normal hardness when he whispered those words. He meant it. His unexpected compliment touched her racing heart. "Thank you."

Cade figured that her shyness and her nanny duties hadn't given her much luck with relationships. There was no ring on her left finger, and she hadn't mentioned a boyfriend. As much as he hated to admit it, he was glad that she was single. He hadn't been interested in women since Abby had died two years ago. Maybe he was ready to start living again. Confused on several levels, he cleared his throat and tried to make his conversation lighter. "My parents have invited us over for Christmas dinner. Ham, mashed potatoes, red gravy and pumpkin pie for dessert. Sound good?"

"Are you sure you want me to come?" She saw

surprise flare in his gray eyes and then disappear. From his gruff demeanor, Rachel hadn't even been sure he wanted her underfoot, much less in the same house with his parents.

"Of course," Cade said. "You're part of our extended family now."

She stared up at him for a moment, and then quickly averted her gaze. Those three words embraced her like a warm blanket. How badly Rachel wanted to believe that. "I'd love to join you."

"Wouldn't have it any other way," Cade said. He wanted to reach out and touch Rachel's cheek. There was such a sense of peace surrounding her. It seemed to Cade that her world was anchored around the babe in her arms. "I'm going to get a shower. Dinner's at 6:00 p.m."

Cade left the room and it seemed to lose its radiance. As the baby slept soundly, her tiny hands on her chest, Rachel tried to shake herself out of her sudden dreaminess. Dirk Payson had escaped prison, and, no doubt, he was looking for her. And yet, her life had taken a sharp ninety-degree turn and here she was in Jackson Hole, Wyoming. And with a baby she already loved fiercely, not to mention the handsome rancher's son who was easy on her eyes.

Rachel rocked and stared out the picture window at the Grand Tetons in the distance. In the past twenty-four hours, since the accident, Rachel had questioned her presence here and sudden employment as Jenny's nanny. With Dirk out of prison, anyone she associated with was in potential danger. She'd been so worried about the situation, she had called her handler an hour earlier when Cade had left the house. Brenda had told her to stay exactly where she was and maintain her cover. The FBI agent reminded her she had to have a job to support herself. No matter where she worked, whether as a nanny or in an office or a manufacturing facility, everyone was potentially in danger because of her. But what else could she do?

Rachel wished she could transport herself to another planet to keep everyone safe from her bad decision made when she was eighteen years old. Brenda had tried to soothe her worries, telling her she was on edge because of Dirk's sudden escape from prison. Brenda was confident she was fine right where she was.

In her gut, Rachel wanted to run. But run to where? The FBI insisted on knowing where she was at all times. She had nowhere to go and she would never escape. God help her, she didn't want to put anyone in harm's way. Least of all this beautiful little baby in her arms.

As she lifted Jenny and pressed a chaste kiss to her smooth, unmarred brow, Rachel now understood what it was like to stand between heaven and hell.

CHAPTER SIX

CADE BREATHED A sigh of deep relief. He stood over the printer that spewed out the final criminal background check on Rachel. The sounds of people in the sheriff's office hung around him but he didn't pay any attention. His undivided attention remained on the fact that Rachel's record was spotless. There was nothing to suggest she was anything but the beautiful, talented woman who was caring for Jenny—and him. Shredding the information next to his desk, he turned and met Gary Henderson, the captain of the department.

"What are you doing here the day after Christmas?" Gary asked, cup of coffee in hand. "I gave you a week off."

"I'm just checking up on the nanny I hired to take care of Jenny," Cade told him. The older man's black brows moved upward and then he became more grave, nodding with understanding.

"It used to be when people were exactly who they said what they were. Nowadays, we can't trust anyone. Pretty sad state of affairs our country has slid into."

Cade couldn't disagree. He told the captain

about the funeral arrangements for Lily to be held the next day.

The captain took a sip of his coffee. "I'll tell Joann to spread the word through the duty roster."

Joann was their front-desk receptionist. She had been with the sheriff's department for fifteen years and knew everyone in Jackson Hole. "That's a good idea."

"You'll be there?" the captain asked.

"Yes, of course. My whole family is coming. I asked Rachel to stay home with Jenny. No sense in them coming out to stand at a frozen, cold grave site."

"Right as rain," the officer agreed. "Get out of here, Cade. Relax for the rest of your week as you get Jenny's legal affairs in order."

"Yes, sir. There's the reading of Lily's will. After that, I'll be over at her home. Her adoptive parents are going to help me sort through everything." He shrugged. "It's going to be a busy time for me. I also have to stop at the courthouse to get the adoption paperwork started." Cade pointed to a dog-eared tan briefcase sitting on the desk next to the printer. "Wish me luck."

The captain said, "Paperwork is our nightmare in this world. Hope you have every piece of paper the court demands."

Cade picked up the briefcase. "So do I. See you next Monday."

Lifting his hand, the captain nodded.

The bright morning sunlight of December

twenty-sixth felt good on Cade's shoulders. He hadn't worn his uniform since he was officially on leave, and was dressed in ranch wear of jeans, a red-and-black flannel shirt and his sheepskin coat. He headed across the parking lot to one of the courthouse subdivisions. Today, he was starting a new life as the father of a beautiful baby girl. Jenny wasn't his by blood, but Cade loved her fiercely because Tom and Lily had been like an extended family to him. He wondered if they were in heaven looking down on him and feeling this was a good thing for their baby daughter.

As he swung through the glass doors, the security guard greeted him. Cade put his coat, his pistol and briefcase on the conveyor belt and then walked through the detector. Even as an off-duty sheriff's deputy, he carried his weapon. The young man in the starched white shirt and blue trousers nodded respectfully toward him. Cade picked up his pistol. He placed the coat over his left arm and pulled the briefcase off the conveyor belt. He knew every office in this building. As he swung down the polished white-tiled hall, his heart rose. Jenny would have a father. Cade would anchor her life. He just had to make it official. He walked past several open doors, watching court business in full swing. Murmuring voices could be heard, along with Christmas music softly playing in the background.

What about Rachel? Cade slowed his walk. She and Jenny seemed to connect solidly. The fact that her record was spotless made Cade want to give a wild whoop of joy. Nearly overnight his world had gone from a mundane gray to a scintillating rainbow of colors. He'd been so lonely since Abby and his daughter had been torn from him. His heart turned with grief over the loss of Lily. That brought up more sadness because Tom had been like a brother to him. It almost looked as if this Christmas, two years later, gifted him with a new baby daughter and an interesting yet mysterious woman. Cade felt overwhelmed in some respects; life had suddenly given him a present of hope combined with happiness. As he stepped into the office that handled adoptions, Cade yearned to be home. Rachel's singing haunted him. He was hungry to get to know her better.

"MOM? HOW ARE YOU?" Rachel stood in the living room after she'd put Jenny to bed after her morning feeding. She always carried several throwaway cell phones, which was the only way to protect her mother from detection. With Dirk on the loose, this was even more important.

"Hi, honey, I'm fine. Where are you?"

Rachel chuckled. "Mom, you know I can't say."

"I know," her mother sighed. "If I'd known what witness protection was all about, I swear I'd not have taken it. I miss our farm so much. I miss my boys and you. This is a special hell."

"Yes," Rachel whispered, sitting down on the couch and gazing at the shining Grand Tetons, covered with fresh snow from last night. "I'm so sorry I got everyone mixed up in this, Mom. I was so stupid to run off and marry Dirk. I don't know how I could do such a stupid and dangerous thing."

"Honey, don't go there. You were in your rebellious mode. I've forgiven you. I wish you could forgive yourself."

Mouth compressed, Rachel closed her eyes. "I know you have, Mom, but I've changed everyone's lives with my one stupid decision. I keep asking myself why I didn't see that Dirk was no good. I had three brothers and a mother who saw it. What is wrong with me?"

Daisy sighed. "Baby girl, you did the best you could at that time. I remember when I was your age. The teens and early twenties is a period where they think they know better than their parents."

Opening her eyes, Rachel whispered, "Maybe if Dad hadn't died…"

"Oh, he'd have put up a fuss on your wanting to marry Dirk, that's for sure," Daisy said. "But you can't control a young woman or man who has their mind set. What should I have done? Had your brothers build a cell and lock you up in it so you couldn't run off with Dirk?" She laughed. "Real life doesn't work that way."

"I know…but my one bad decision has torn our family apart forever. You and I can't go back to the farm—ever. And my brothers do the work now and I worry about them, Mom. With Dirk on the loose…"

"I know, sweetheart," Daisy soothed. "But listen to me, will you? My handler said law enforcement is out at the farm. They are protecting your brothers, so stop worrying."

"You don't know Dirk like I do. He's like a coyote, Mom. He'll sit, watch and wait a long time and get to know the system and then he'll strike during a weak moment."

"Rachel, stop plowing that furrow."

Laughing a little, Rachel sat up. A fierce love for her feisty mother smothered her in a warm blanket and dissolved her fear. "You're so practical. So upbeat."

"Common sense got me to where we are," Daisy archly reminded her. "So tell me, are you happy in your new place?"

Rachel knew that even when they got together once a year, she still couldn't tell her mother anything about her move. "I'm very happy, Mom. I'm a nanny again and I'm balancing that with my artwork." She could talk in vague terms but never specific ones.

"Ah, good, nanny work supplies you with what you lost," Daisy murmured. "How old is the tyke?"

"Three months. She's adorable."

"Good, good."

"What about you?" Rachel heard her mother give a snort at the other end.

"Well, let's just say that it's fine in the winter, but it will be hell to pay in the summer. Not my favorite place."

Rachel figured it was somewhere in the southern United States. In Iowa, they didn't have the weather phenomenon known as "dog days." They occurred during the months of July and August. The humidity was nearly a hundred percent and matched the high summer temperature and was miserable for everyone. "I feel for you."

Grumpily, Daisy muttered, "Yes, well I'm telling my handler this isn't going to do. I've already got a request in to move elsewhere and they're working on it. The next time you call, I hope to be out of this sinkhole."

"Are you getting to sew?" Her mother was a wonderful seamstress. She'd made clothes for her family since Rachel could remember.

"Oh, yes, I am. You know what? I traded in my trusty Singer for a state-of-the-art Bernina sewing machine. Now, that's a computer and I'm having to learn all the buttons and stuff like that. But I love it." ·

"You still have Grandma's Singer, though?" Rachel asked. That old machine had been passed down lovingly, and she couldn't think that her mother would ever part with it.

Laughing, Daisy said, "Oh, no! I wouldn't dream of parting with that! No, that will stay in the family and be passed on to you when I decide it's time to leave this earth of ours."

A momentary sadness over that thought hit Rachel. "Mom, you're only fifty years old. You have lots of years ahead. Look at our family—they've all been in their nineties when they pass on. Dad would have been, too, if not for that awful car accident."

"You're right. I'm not intending to go anywhere soon."

Rachel smiled softly. "Good, because I couldn't stand the thought of losing you, too. I miss Dad so much. I know we all do." Her father had been the framework for the hardworking family. He had been a serious, conservative person with a dry sense of humor. Her mother had been the light one in comparison. Rachel had grown up in a loving family. The ache grew in her heart. She missed them so much.

"I know you do," Daisy said, a catch in her voice. "We all do. In a way, I'm glad he isn't around to see what happened."

Pain dove into Rachel's heart. Daisy was right, of course, but it once more reminded her that her one bad decision had scattered her family and torn the fabric of their existence apart. "I wish there was some way I could repair what I've done to all of you," Rachel whispered.

"Only when that dirt bag is dead," Daisy reminded her grimly. "And now, he's out running around free. Are you safe?" her mother asked.

"I have extra police protection. How about you?"

"Even a bloodhound couldn't pick up a trail here."

Her mother laughed heartily, and Rachel joined her. She longed for the day when they could talk for longer than a few minutes once a month. It wasn't enough, but it was better than nothing.

"We'll have to be extra watchful now that he's on the loose," she told her mother.

"My handler said they've got a team searching for him."

"I'm glad, because I'm scared he'll go to the farm…" She couldn't finish her sentence. Rachel worried that Dirk would kill her brothers. Or try to. She felt completely safe in the witness protection program, but the rest of her family were at risk.

"I know, I worry, too. Your brothers have been informed, Rachel. They aren't going into this blind. They're smart and they're alert. And they're carrying weapons on them at all times. So, don't lose sleep on this, okay? My handler thinks Dirk will go south into Mexico and back into the cartel down there. He knows he's a hunted man up here in the States."

"Mom, our ten minutes are up."

"I know," Daisy fumed. "One day, this will all be over. I'll go back to my home and farm. You can come home and be with us. We can be a family again, Rachel. That is idealism, but it's also hope for me. That's what I cling to and believe. It helps me get through this."

"I know, Mom. I dream the same dream as you…."

"I love you, Rachel. You're in my nightly prayers. I'll look forward to talking to you next month."

CHAPTER SEVEN

"IT'S NEW YEAR'S EVE," Cade said, hoping his gruff voice hid some of his nervousness. He held out a bottle of champagne to Rachel, who stood at the kitchen sink cutting up vegetables for the stockpot. She was making beef stew for dinner later that day. He'd just come in from a grocery run to town for her. Getting champagne had been an impulse, possibly a foolish one.

Turning, Rachel's heart melted as she noticed him holding the green bottle. Most of the time, Cade was walled up and unapproachable. Sometimes, like now, he suddenly thawed. Rachel had given up on figuring him out. "That's so thoughtful of you. Thanks." She dried her hands and took it from him. Their fingers accidentally touched. Instantly, Rachel felt the warmth that moved into her hand and up her arm. There was uncertainty in Cade's gray eyes which belied an innate self-assurance in his stance. He wore a black cowboy hat, a sheepskin jacket and boots. He looked right at home with his surroundings except for this sudden shyness.

"Beef stew, corn bread and a little bubbly for

later," she said brightly, putting the bottle into the fridge. That would be their New Year's Eve dinner.

Cade removed his coat and hat and hung them on the wooden pegs where the kitchen wall intersected the hallway. "I didn't know if you drank alcohol or not," he muttered in apology. Cade felt his chest expand with a quiet joy. He couldn't put into words how nice it was to see Rachel in his kitchen cooking. The odor of freshly perked coffee scented the air. He ambled over to the coffeemaker on the corner of the tile counter.

Quickly cutting up several peeled carrots, Rachel said, "I love wine and champagne. In moderation, of course."

Cade poured himself a cup of coffee. "Want a cup?"

"No, thanks. I've had three already. One more and I'll be on the ceiling," she said, tossing the carrots into the pot. Rachel was having quite a time figuring him out, but Cade seemed to be in a good mood. She wanted to make him happy because he'd suffered so much loss in his life. He rarely smiled, but then she didn't smile often, either. They had that in common.

Cade leaned against the counter, absorbing Rachel's nearness. Since he'd lost Abby, his social skills had taken a dive. He didn't know how to act, especially around someone so lovely. He cleared his throat. "I could cut up the potatoes I just brought home."

Glancing over at him, she managed a soft smile.

"Sure." She handed him a cutting board, knife and the potatoes. For such a private man he was making an effort. But then Rachel could also see a flicker of happiness in those gray eyes. She didn't dare presume she had any positive influence. How could she? The man was just showing his appreciation. Well, eventually she would need to leave. As the shock of seeing Lily dead at the accident on early Christmas morning had worn off, Rachel had begun to rethink being here. All morning long, she had waffled on this terrible dilemma. Should she leave? Just get up and walk away one day? Leave a note saying, "It didn't work out"? Or give a real explanation and blow her cover? Rachel only wished her handler could make the decision for her and tell her to move on. But she hadn't.

Cade noticed Rachel's long hands trembling as she picked up a carrot. The way her lips pursed bothered him. His intuition was strong and had saved his life a number of times. "Didn't you get any sleep last night?" They had agreed upon a routine where they took shifts caring for Jenny during the night.

"Oh, no, not really." Rachel shrugged as she focused on peeling the carrot. "Sometimes I have a restless night." Rachel saw his brows drawn downward and his eyes conveyed his suspicion. Rachel hated lying to Cade and to his wonderfully warm family. Her conscience ate at her. The hardworking and caring Garners didn't deserve her lies. "It takes a while to get used to the sleep schedule. My biological clock has to adjust," she joked, hoping this would ease the expression on his face. It didn't.

"I see," Cade murmured, taking a sip of his coffee. "It is tough."

"Being able to do it once every six hours is nice," Rachel quickly added, cutting up the carrots and dropping them into the pot. "But you're going back to work shortly and I'll be the one waking up every three hours."

"I know." Something bothered Cade about her reactions. The expression in her beautiful blue eyes spoke of fear. Why fear? This was one time that Cade wished he could be a mind reader. He finished cutting up the potatoes and put them in the pot. "Listen, we need to talk about house arrangements. I realize I've put you in a spot by asking you to stay here in my home. Would you be more comfortable in your cabin? I know I'm a stranger and a man, and a lot of women wouldn't be relaxed with that arrangement."

Rachel's hands stilled for a moment as she thought through his offer. Looking out the window, her gaze went to the morning frost glinting on several bare-branched trees, sparkling like diamonds beneath the sunlight. Of course, she wanted to be close to Cade and be a part of this beautiful home. "Why, no. I'm okay with it if you are." She searched his face. She didn't know Cade well enough to interpret his expression. Maybe he was concerned for her welfare and that was all.

"Are you sure?" Cade asked. "Because I don't

want you to think you have to be in the same house with me, Rachel. You're an employee, and, as such, you need to have your own autonomy. I want you happy and feeling that you can relax around here. Taking care of an infant is demanding, with a lot of sleep deprivation in the first year."

If only Rachel could honestly tell him just how euphoric she was to be here. "Cade, I'm really okay with this."

Mouth quirking, Cade sipped his coffee. Something didn't feel right, but he couldn't put his finger on it. She seemed sincere. The darkness that he normally saw in the recesses of her eyes was gone. In its place was happiness. "Okay, but if it ever becomes a problem for you, the cabin is available and we'll just work things out differently caring for Jenny."

"You have a deal," Rachel said. She finished with the veggies, carried the stockpot to the gas burner and turned it on. Putting on the lid, she turned and said, "Beef stew at 6:00 p.m. tonight?"

"Yes, 6:00 p.m.," Cade said. He gazed down the other hall off the kitchen that led to the bedrooms. "Jenny sleeping?"

"Yes. Thank goodness she's one of the 'good' babies. You feed her and she drops off to sleep for three solid hours."

Cade raised his brows. "I have friends who have had cranky babies and it's miserable on them."

"Right," Rachel said, feeling his eyes upon her as she washed her hands at the sink. If only Cade

wasn't so masculine and handsome. She kept trying to stop her body from responding to his looks,
the easy way he smiled or the tenor of his voice.
She was secretly glad that he was single and available. But what good would that do her? Rachel
couldn't have a relationship. The idea of marrying or living with a man she had to lie to didn't
sit well with her.

In New York City, she had had male friends,
but never a lover. Dirk had scared her off getting
too close to a man. Her judgment was faulty if she
couldn't spot an abusive man. But then, she had
a gut sense that Cade was a good man—not like
Dirk. She still fought the need to be touched by
him. And Rachel wasn't about to reveal her torrid
dreams of kissing him. Most of the time he was a
gruff curmudgeon who spoke in one-or two-word
sentences. And sometimes, he came out of that
prison and she found herself wanting to know so
much more about him.

Cade set the emptied coffee cup in a drainer in
the second sink. "Feel like a little fresh air? I'd like
to take you over to the barn and introduce you to
the goats that give Jenny her daily milk."

Heart lifting, Rachel managed a nervous smile.
"I'd love to do that."

"I don't want you cooped up in here," Cade muttered. "You need to get out more."

Rachel shook her head. "Don't worry about me.
I'm fine. And I've got to tell you, Wyoming win-

ters are fierce compared to New York City's idea of winter."

Cade walked over to the wall of pegs and lifted off his sheepskin coat. "It's a hard winter," he agreed. "We don't even get a ninety-day growing season at this altitude. My mother still puts in a garden and we get what we can from it."

"So, you get four months of sunshine and the rest is winter coming or going?" Rachel asked, walking over and picking up her black wool coat.

Cade settled the cowboy hat on his head. "Yes, ma'am, that's about it. But when spring comes in early June, the Grand Tetons are like heaven. There's no place like this anywhere on earth." Cade watched as she shrugged into her coat and buttoned it up. Just the graceful way Rachel slid on her black leather gloves made him want to grab her by the shoulders and draw her against him. Cade reined in his desires as he walked to the back door. "Come on, let's get you used to our hard winter and knowing you can still move around despite it...."

THE SNOW CRUNCHED beneath their feet. Rachel followed Cade along a well-worn snow path to the huge wooden barn with the steep, green tin roof. Corrals were all around the building and in some of them she noticed shaggy-coated horses; and in others, Herefords raised as organic beef. The sky was such an intense blue at this time of day that Rachel had to squint. The sun made every color leap with radiance and brightness. Even the gray-limbed, naked trees that surrounded the main ranch home sparkled with frost. Her breath came out in white clouds. She wobbled here and there because the path from the ranch house to the barn had grown slick overnight.

They had almost reached the barn when Rachel slipped. She let out a gasp, her arms flying outward. Landing with a thud on her butt, she felt the jar throughout her body.

In one smooth movement, Cade had turned. She was trying to push herself up on her elbows, snow scattering over her from the fall.

"Rachel? Are you all right?" Cade knelt down and slid his arms around her shoulders and brought her into a sitting position. His face was inches from hers. He could smell the fragrance of her skin. Her lips were so close, begging to be touched and explored. Inwardly, Cade groaned.

"Oh, I'm fine," she laughed, embarrassed. "Look at me!" She tried to ignore his nearness, but it was impossible. Rachel made the mistake of looking up at Cade. His eyes were dark with fear. His gloved hands pressed against her shoulders. What would it be like to kiss this man? Gaze moving to his mouth, Rachel felt a burst of heat that grew into an ache between her thighs. The reaction was so strong, it shocked her.

Cade knelt down on one knee and released her shoulders. He didn't want to, but he had to. Rachel was too close, too...well, too desirable to him.

Snow glinted in her sable hair like tiny diamonds. He removed one glove and began to pick some of it out. Her hair was strong and sleek between his fingers. Though he wanted more, Cade settled for this simple act of intimacy.

"You're looking more like a snowman," he chuckled, meeting her smile. "There, I think your hair is free of most of those little snowballs." Just the simple act of touching Rachel's hair sent a frisson of joy through Cade. For the first time in two years, the walls started to melt around his wounded heart.

"Thanks," she said breathlessly, shaken by his attention. Her scalp tingled wildly. What would it be like to have Cade's strong fingers move through the strands of her hair? His touch was light and yet, Rachel knew without a doubt, that he would be a tender lover. She didn't know how she knew this, for she'd slept with only one man, one she wanted to forget.

"Ready to get up?" he asked, standing and holding out his hands to her.

Rachel laughed. "I feel like a fool, Cade." She put her gloved hands into his, and he pulled her up easily. For a moment, their hands stayed entwined. And then, reluctantly, Rachel pulled hers from Cade's grip.

Cade stood over her, unsure of what to do or say next. He was like a bumbling teenager who had a crush on a girl. Rachel's hair gleamed beneath the sunshine, a beautiful frame for her reddened cheeks and smiling lips. Lips he desperately wanted to capture and taste. "Don't feel bad. I can't tell you how many times Dad and I have slipped on our rears, too. It's just part of living out in the wilds during a Wyoming winter."

Rachel brushed her coat free of the snow. "Makes me feel like part of the family," she joked. Cade made her nervous, but it was only because he was her employee, right? It wasn't as if they could be anything more.

"Well," he said, putting his hand beneath her elbow as she straightened, "you are part of the family now." His fingers cupped her elbow and he felt Rachel's womanly strength. She was lean and fit, and Cade could sense her quiet courage. He wanted to put an arm around her shoulders, but that would be taboo.

Glad for his unexpected support, Rachel walked with him into the barn. Inside, the wonderful, sweet smell of dried timothy and alfalfa hay scented the air. There were several windows, and light poured through the two-story barn. She stood beside him and simply absorbed it all. This was like home in Iowa. How badly Rachel wanted to confide in Cade.

With great reluctance, Cade allowed his gloved hand to fall away from her elbow. Still, it was enough to stand so close to Rachel. She put her hands in her coat pockets and looked around. "Here in the lower area are the stalls for horses, the goats and some of Dad's milk cows." He walked forward down a clean concrete aisle between the wooden box stalls.

Rachel heard bleats. "Are those the goats?"

"Yep," Cade said, feeling the urge to take those few steps forward and pull Rachel into his arms. Kiss her. Stunned by the realization, Cade deliberately took a step away from her. What was going on with him? He'd never felt this nervous before. He scowled and became abrupt once more. "I don't like the pesky creatures. Dad had a Belgian plow horse he was going to show at the country fair one year, but a goat ate off the horse's mane, so it couldn't be shown. Goats will eat anything."

Rachel nodded. "Oh, they'll decimate a garden in a heartbeat, too." And then, she snapped her mouth shut. The Iowa farm was a part of her past. She glanced over at Cade who was sliding the bolt to the roomy box stall free. Panic flooded her. It was too easy to talk to Cade, too easy to trust him. Her normal habits seemed to dissolve beneath his powerful masculinity. She gulped. Of course he'd noticed her slip. *Oh, God...*

"Then, you know about goats?" Cade had thought she was a city girl. He saw the discomfort in her eyes for just a second.

"Oh," she stammered, walking forward, "it was just something I heard. I had an artist friend who grew up on a farm in the Midwest and he told me about the Angora goats his family raised for the wool." Would Cade buy that lie? Actually, it wasn't totally a lie. Her family had a herd of one hundred

Angora goats. One of her brothers sheared them twice a year and the wool, which was always in high demand, sold for a lot of money.

Cade stepped aside to let Rachel look at the four nannies straining their necks over the wire fence within the box stall. "Your friend is right. You let a goat loose on your property and everything is fair game. My dad lets these four nannies out after milking." He glanced at his watch. "Which is about 10:00 a.m. He then releases them into a specially built paddock so they can't get down on their knees and escape under the rungs."

Looking at the goats, Rachel felt her terror melt just a little. She walked in and petted the adorable animals who seemed eager for contact. "Oh, they're so pretty!"

Cade couldn't tear his gaze away as he watched Rachel pat them on the head, scratch their ears and run her gloved hand down their slender necks. His discomfort escalated since he wanted that kind of attention from her. He felt conflicted by what his heart and body wanted versus the right thing to do. Rachel had a special touch, a special aura around her that he, Jenny and the animals automatically responded to. He was transfixed as her hair fell over her shoulders. When one of the nannies tried to get up on her hind legs and grab a strand, she pulled back out of the way.

"They sure are hungry, aren't they?" Rachel said, gently pushing the nanny back down so she was on all four feet once more.

"They like your hair," Cade said, jealous of the goats. He'd touched those strands, threaded his gloved hands through it moments before. He wanted to do it again. His hands itched, and Cade purposely curled them into fists at his side.

Rachel pushed the strands across her shoulders, turned and looked at him. "No kidding!" Again, she saw a frown on Cade's face. Automatically, her heart shrank in worry. Had her stupid comment set off his warning signals? It was hard to think straight, when his male mouth sent a tremor of longing through her. Even now, her scalp continued to tingle from the snow he'd brushed from her hair. It had been an intimate, unexpected touch. In that moment, Rachel ached to discover him, not as a protective law-enforcement officer or employer, but as a man.

"Come on, let me show you around," he muttered. "It's time we got you out of the house and into fresh Wyoming air." Cade was anxious over the power of his impulses. He couldn't touch her again. For a moment, he'd seen what he thought was yearning in her eyes as she glanced over at him. Yearning for what?

Once more, Cade placed his hand beneath her elbow as he walked her out of the barn and into the surrounding area of the corrals. Rachel didn't want to pull away from him. It was as if being near Cade erased all her fears, anxieties and worries about Dirk finding her. And for a moment, Rachel convinced herself that everything was all right, that

Cade was interested in her. It was an idealistic thought beneath a daydream. Rachel knew it was only that: a dream. But Cade's strong, supportive hand on her arm was not. It was real. He was real.

The Grand Tetons rose like sharp, jagged peaks out of the snow-covered plain. Rachel loved looking at them. The snow gleamed on their blue granite slopes, the pine trees below ten thousand feet were a green-and-white mantle about their bases. As they walked to the corral where the four Belgian plow horses stood happily munching on hay, Rachel asked, "Do you ever get tired of looking at the Tetons? As an artist, I find myself wanting to paint them every time I look at them." How badly Rachel wanted to lean against Cade, but it was wrong. He was her employer.

Keeping her close as they crunched through the little-used path around the Belgian's pen, Cade said, "I never get tired of it." Monitoring his support of her elbow, Cade felt himself wanting Rachel on purely a physical basis. For so long, he hadn't felt the need for intimacy. Abby's death had snuffed out his life in all respects. The loss of his daughter had traumatized him into numbness. Now, his body was awakening because of Rachel. Or had he transited through the worst of his grief over the loss of his family? Cade was unsure, and tension sizzled through him.

Her elbow tingled with heat. Rachel swallowed nervously. She cast about for anything to talk about. "Do you hike in them?" Their breath looked like miniature clouds around them. The temperature was ten degrees and, luckily, no wind was blowing to make it even colder.

"Yes, quite a bit. My dad is a hunter. I'm not, but he is. I go with him during elk- and moose-hunting season. But when my schedule allows me, I like to hike with my camera." Cade decided to simply absorb and appreciate Rachel. He couldn't do anything else, not under the circumstances.

"Ah," Rachel said, stopping at the metal rail behind which the horses stood, "you shoot with a camera, not a rifle. That's good."

Releasing her elbow as if he'd been burned, Cade moved to the pipe railing and leaned against it. He kept plenty of space between them. "Maybe being in law enforcement and carrying a weapon you know can kill someone has taken the edge off my desire to hunt. When I was a kid, I did hunt. But after I had to shoot and kill someone about four years ago, hunting didn't seem as important to me."

Rachel heard the pain in Cade's tone. He leaned his elbows across the pipe rail and watched the horses eat their hay. She walked up to him. "I couldn't do what you do. I—well, taking a life… any life…it just isn't something I could do." His profile was clean and strong. Yet, the corner of his mouth flexed inward. Rachel sensed pain and sadness over taking that life. Reaching out, she placed her gloved hand on his shoulder. "I'm really sorry that had to happen to you, Cade. I can't imagine what I'd do if I'd been in your shoes." She shivered.

Quirking his mouth, Cade felt the butterfly touch of her hand, tentative on his shoulder. He twisted a look toward her. "I didn't want to do it." And then, the words came tumbling out of his mouth. "He was a local drug dealer in cocaine and knew that the feds had figured it all out. We were working with them and going to pick him up and charge him. I couldn't believe it when he came out of his house firing that automatic weapon at all of us." Stunned that he'd talk about something so personal, Cade was angry with himself. Was it her hand on his shoulder? Is that what had caused this avalanche of personal information to come out?

Her fingers tightened on his shoulder. How badly Rachel wanted to step closer, slide her arms around Cade and just hold him. Because right now, that's exactly what he needed, a little protection from the storm of life and what it had handed him. "How do you know you killed him?"

"I was the one who had walked up to the house," he muttered, remembering that day too well. Helpless, Cade added, "I don't know how he missed me, but later the coroner said he was pumped full of cocaine, he couldn't hit the broadside of a barn the shape he was in."

Cade hungrily absorbed Rachel's touch. Two years without a woman's touch or voice had left him feeling raw and needy. Cade had had plenty of chances to start up a relationship, but no woman had interested him—until now. What was it about Rachel? Her gentleness? That wonderful vulnerability that she couldn't hide from anyone? Her obvious love and affection for Jenny? Cade didn't know. He swallowed hard.

"I'm so sorry it happened, Cade. You didn't deserve that."

Her soft, trembling voice cut through his sadness. In that moment, Cade saw and felt something else around Rachel as they stood together at the corral. His gut and heart told him something terribly tragic had happened to her. And then, that look in her expression and eyes disappeared. Her hand left his shoulder. "Bad things happen all the time to good people," he offered gruffly as he searched her soft blue eyes. "In my job, we see that all the time. Even people who are bad, like this dude was, I didn't want to shoot him. But I had to or he'd have taken me down. I had no choice."

Rachel nodded. "I understand, Cade." More than he would ever know. Giving him a sad smile, she offered, "When bad things like that happen, it makes us appreciate the goodness that life can bring us."

Without meaning to, Cade reached out and grazed her hair with his glove. "Yes," was all he managed to choke out. For whatever reason, Cade sensed that Rachel did understand on such a deep, visceral level that it shook him to his core. What was happening to him? To them?

CHAPTER EIGHT

"It's already February fourteenth and law enforcement hasn't found Dirk yet," Rachel's mother Daisy said, her voice despondent.

Sighing, Rachel looked out the large plate-glass window that framed the Grand Tetons. "I know. I can't believe it. No one has a clue where he is."

"Are you feeling anxious?" Daisy asked her daughter.

"Of course. What's worse is I'm with a wonderful family. A family I worry about. What if Dirk finds me? What will he do to them? Half the time I'm thinking of just disappearing one day. But I can't, because of the baby I'm taking care of. I go through minutes of sheer terror followed by calm logic."

"I'm getting jumpier by the day myself," Daisy murmured. "My handler said that Payson could target the farm and your brothers, me or you."

"Knowing Dirk, he has some dark, devious plan for all of us," Rachel said, terror eating away at her. It was a warm February day for freezing Wyoming. Gwen had come earlier and told her it was their annual February thaw. Warmer weather would arrive for about a week. Snow and icicles would start to melt. The sun was bright at 1:00 p.m. and the sky a brilliant blue, unlike most days when it was cloudy and gray.

"What does your handler advise? Should you leave? Be on the move more?" Daisy asked.

"She said to stay put. I'm new to this area and few people know me. As a matter of fact, the last couple of months I think I've been in town only two times. I'm trying to keep a really low profile here until they can capture him."

"Hmm, good idea. I don't have that luxury. I have to go out and do all my running around for myself. The police do drop by and I do have increased security here. It's good, you have people who can do your errands for you and you can stay in a house. That makes me feel more at ease."

"Don't worry about me, Mom."

"Are you starting your illustrations with your school online yet?"

"Yes, I am. Not only that but I'm rediscovering how much I love being in the country again. About a week ago I was out at the barn and I saw my first moose! It was enormous and looking longingly at the hay inside the corral."

"Wonderful! I've never seen one, but then Iowa doesn't have them," Daisy laughed.

Rachel warmed with love for her mother. "I remember." In her eyes, Daisy Donovan was the epitome of farm values and strength. No matter what had happened in the lives of her brothers and herself, Daisy had been their eye of the hurricane. She was always practical, sensible and had a quiet voice that commanded attention and immediate respect. Her mother had abilities Rachel wished she had.

"I wish so much that they'd let us talk more than once a month for ten minutes, Mom. I really miss you. Especially now."

"I'm sorry," Daisy murmured. "I wish I was there to hold you, to tell you it would be all right."

But it wasn't all right. Rachel loved her mother fiercely for her desire to try and make her feel better than she did. "I know. I wish you were, too. Why couldn't we have entered the witness protection program together? That way, we wouldn't have to suffer this awful separation."

Daisy chuckled. "Oh, I agree completely! But listen, buck up. I refuse to let that monster ruin the rest of my life. And you should try to get on with yours. He's going to get caught. I know he will. You hold on to that, Rachel."

"I'm trying to, Mom." She looked around the living room. Soft instrumental music floated from the kitchen where she had a small radio on the counter. Rachel liked unobtrusive music when she was cooking, taking care of Jenny, sketching and writing.

She heard the crunching of tires on snow near the house. "Mom, someone is here. I have to go. I'm sorry…"

"Oh, don't be, honey, I understand. I love you

and you're always in my prayers and heart. Keep your head high and keep your hope alive. Love you. Bye…"

Putting the throwaway cell phone in her pocket, Rachel got up with a frown gathering on her brow. She couldn't see who had driven in, but the icy crunch of snow beneath the tires couldn't be ignored. Maybe the propane truck had arrived. The driver came once a month to fill the tanks at the various houses. Walking out of the living room, Rachel went into the kitchen.

"Cade!" she said, surprise in her tone.

Feeling nervous, Cade closed the door behind him. "I was trying to surprise you and you caught me red-handed. I'd thought you would be at the barn or over at my parents' home."

Shock bolted through Rachel, but not from fear this time. Cade looked handsome in his sheriff's uniform of tan slacks and dark green shirt. He wore his pistol and his Kevlar vest beneath his shirt. What got her attention were the dozen red roses he held in his hand along with a box of candy beneath his arm. He appeared unsure.

"Oh, Cade, you shouldn't have." Rachel came forward. The past couple of weeks he had been standoffish and she'd seen very little of him.

"It's…uh…just a small gift for Valentine's Day," Cade managed. Somewhere in the past two years he'd lost his social skills. He'd hemmed and hawed over whether to get Rachel a gift at all. Was it proper for an employer to give chocolate on Valentine's day? Cade didn't know. His heart, however, had insisted. "I figured you could use a boost. Come February, most people are pretty sick and tired of the cold and snow." He awkwardly thrust the bouquet of red roses toward her outstretched hand. Their fingers met unexpectedly and he absorbed her warm contact for those brief seconds. The look on Rachel's face was one of utter surprise mixed with tenderness. She took the roses, buried her nose in them and inhaled deeply.

"This is so nice." Rachel smiled as she lifted her face from the roses. She saw him put his hands on his hips, frown and take a step back. For the past few weeks, Cade had become a shadow in her life. Then, suddenly, he showed up at lunchtime with flowers and chocolate! She would never understand Cade's personality.

"Well," he said, a bit embarrassed, "there's more." He pulled out the candy from under his arm. "A little chocolate always makes a person smile. Happy Valentine's Day…" Cade watched her eyes grow misty for just a second. Then, the tears disappeared. Shuffling his feet, he stared down at his boots.

Rachel held the heart-shaped red velvet box of candy. "You know my Achilles' heel—chocolate."

Taking off his coat and hanging it up, Cade decided it would be rude just to turn around and leave. It was lunchtime and he was hungry. Still, he continued to feel jittery over his gifts. "Every time I go to the store for you, there's always 'chocolate bar' written on the list. I think I got the message." He managed a smile he didn't feel. Cade felt trapped—by himself. And by his own thumping heart that took off in beat when Rachel looked at him.

Heat swept up her neck and into her face. Rachel couldn't handle the tender fire burning in his gray eyes. In uniform, he looked dangerous—in a good kind of way. Just seeing Cade at midday like this, unexpectedly, made Rachel's heart race. "Well, you certainly surprised me." And then she gave him a helpless look. "I didn't get anything for you, Cade. Now I feel bad about it."

Cade shook his head and walked to the counter. Bending down, he retrieved a glass vase from one of the cupboards. "Don't worry about it. I wasn't sure I could pull this off today, anyway," he groused, closing up. "We've had so many calls this morning, I didn't think I would get an hour off, but at the last minute, it happened."

Turning, Cade didn't know what to do next. The thought struck him that the roses would need to be put in water. He took the vase, filled it with water and set it on the counter. Rachel came over and began to cut the stem of each rose. He leaned against the counter and watched her put the roses into the vase. The redness staining Rachel's cheeks only enhanced her beauty. Her hands were graceful and spoke eloquently of her vulnerability and artistic talent. There wasn't anything to dislike about Rachel, he had discovered in the past two months. His house was now a home. She lived with him and Jenny. And the baby had bonded completely to Rachel, like mother and daughter. Happiness thrummed through Cade. It was a feeling he'd thought he'd never experience again. Ever. And he wanted to kiss her. Right now. Here.

Stunned by his need, Cade needed to divert himself. He asked, "How's the little one?"

"Oh, she's fine." Rachel looked up at the clock above the sink. "In about forty-five minutes she'll be awake and fussing for her goat's milk." Cade's nearness intoxicated her. Rachel tried to still her beating heart. He was so near. So masculine. Even though he was gruff once more, Rachel now realized that beneath that hardened, rough exterior was a man with a heart of gold. He appeared restless, his gaze moving around the room. He shifted his stance, as if wanting to run away once more. Rachel gave up on trying to figure him out.

"Right on schedule," Cade said, furtively looking around. "I've got about fifteen minutes before I have to go back on duty. Think I'll make myself a grilled cheese sandwich. Have you eaten yet?" He needed to move away from her. Rachel was too close. Too available. Getting his hands busy on something else other than touching her was what he needed right now.

"No…not yet," Rachel said, putting the roses and vase on the kitchen table. "If you're making yourself one, I'll have one, too." She was pleased with his offer. This was a new side to Cade: the man in the kitchen. Another surprise: he knew how to cook.

Nodding, Cade got busy at the stove and refrigerator. "Two grilled cheese sandwiches coming up." Whether he wanted to admit it or not, Cade liked this kind of teamwork between himself and Rachel. They had established a rhythm, and it worked well. In some ways, it was as if they were really married. And every time he went there emotionally, Cade reminded himself he was available. He'd thought often of entering a more intimate relationship with her. What stopped him cold was the fact she was his employee. And he wanted Jenny to have someone like Rachel around for a long time. Also, Rachel had never given him any type of signal that she wanted such a relationship with him. He had to keep his yearnings to himself. It was the only way.

"So," Rachel said, putting the chocolates on the table, "how's it going today?" She realized Cade was nervous and tried to put him at ease.

"Insane," Cade said, putting the sandwiches in the black skillet. "Spring thaw brings out a kind of craziness in the local population. Since it hasn't snowed the last week, people can get around a lot easier. The older folks get into trouble because if they drive early, black ice is still on the road. We've had a number of fender benders all morning." Cade felt somewhat better with his hands busy.

"Anyone hurt?" Rachel asked, going to the cupboard and taking down plates for the sandwiches that Cade grilled over the stove. Even his shoulders seemed tense to her, the fabric pulled across his back showing off his physique. Cade worked out every day in the house's small gym. Rachel wondered what he looked like without clothes, and the thought brought stinging heat to her cheeks.

"No, and that's the good part," he said, concentrating very hard on the sandwiches. "It just means a lot of paperwork for me on something very minor." Shrugging, he added, "That's how it goes, though." He glanced over his shoulder at her placing flatware on the table. "How's it going with your illustrations? Did you get some time this morning to work on them?" He was stumbling over his words, which happened when he was nervous around Rachel. In his job, he was mostly cool as a cucumber. Something about this woman addled his brain.

"Let me show you what I've done." Rachel walked out of the kitchen and went to her bedroom to collect the illustrations.

Cade used a spatula to scoop up the sandwiches and place them on plates. When Rachel returned, she put her sketches at the other end of the table. "You have been busy," he said, relieved to be focused on anything but her.

Smiling, Rachel poured them some coffee and sat down. "Yes, I have. After Jenny eats, she goes to sleep. I get about an hour and a half to work on my sketching."

Cade sat down at the head of the table and settled the paper napkin across his lap. "I'd like to look at them after I eat and clean my paws," he said. Close, he was so close to Rachel. What to do with his hands? Cade grabbed the knife and cut his sandwich in two.

Rachel felt euphoria. This was the first time Cade had been home at lunch. And he seemed far more chatty than normal. Was it because of Valentine's Day? Was he trying to make her feel valued? Rachel tried to quell her nervousness as she sat down. "They're just sketches. When I'm in the art mode, they get coffee spilled on them, so don't worry about that."

Cade nodded and took a bite of his sandwich. It was a special hell looking across the table at Rachel. Her movements were so graceful. Her fingers long and beautiful. Again, his heart entertained those fingers grazing his flesh.

Happiness threaded through Rachel. Sitting in the kitchen eating lunch with Cade was heaven on earth for her. His unexpected arrival flushed her with a joy she'd never experienced. As she munched on her sandwich, she gazed at the vase of roses. "That was so sweet of you to get me flowers and chocolate, Cade. Thank you." Dirk had never given her anything except pain. Since settling down with this family, Rachel began to realize just how naive she had been when she'd run off with Payson. It had taught her to think carefully through any decision. How would it affect others?

"I get off at 4:00 p.m. today," Cade told her. And

then, the words flew, unbidden, out of his mouth. "There's a Valentine's Day dance at the armory in Jackson Hole. Would you like to go? It's just locals and it's a lot of fun, maybe a good way to meet people I work with." He hoped she would say yes, but he saw shock and then hesitation in her blue eyes. He shouldn't be asking, but something had compelled him. He was at war within himself. His head told him this was a stupid thing. His heart desperately wanted some intimate time with Rachel. He was emotionally being torn apart. Even worse, he seemed to have little control over himself where she was concerned.

"But," Rachel stammered, reeling at the request, "who would take care of Jenny?"

"My mom and dad," he said abruptly. "They're staying home. Automatic babysitters." Cade hoped his anxiousness didn't translate to Rachel. "Would you like to go? It would get you out of here for a while. I worry about you being cooped up so much here at the ranch. You've barely left the place since you've moved in."

What could she say? Rachel didn't want to raise any suspicion but she also couldn't be too visible. "I'm not a very good dancer," she said.

"Me neither." Cade smiled ever so slightly. "We could go out on slow dances only and try to avoid one another's feet?" Cade told himself he was doing this for her own good. Rachel stayed holed up like a proverbial bear in hibernation mode. There had to be a good reason, and he just wanted to spend more time with her. "Listen," he murmured, reaching out and briefly touching her hand, "I don't want this to be a prison sentence to you. It's just going to be lighthearted fun, that's all. Nothing serious. No commitment. Just a little midwinter lift for the spirit. The whole town looks forward to this dance. It gets people out of their homes to catch up with one another." God help him, he'd touched her. He had to stop this. Cade clenched his jaw and forced his hands to his sides. What the hell was he doing? Why was he so out of control? Rachel had done nothing to trigger these needs in him.

Rachel knew she was trapped. Her hand tingled wildly in the wake of his touch. He was her employer and the tension between them felt far too intimate. What was he doing? What did he want from her? Rachel's mind careened from one question to another. One of the tenets of the federal witness protection program was to appear normal and blend in. By now, Cade was well aware she'd turned down every offer to go to the grocery store with him. That wasn't exactly normal behavior. Of course, Rachel wanted to go to the dance with him. But she knew from hard experience that selfishness did more than just harm her—it had harmed her entire family. "That sounds nice, Cade," she managed in a strangled tone. "How formal is it?"

Relief flooded Cade. He sat back in the chair and tried to seem nonchalant about the whole thing. "There's nothing fancy about it. Women wear dresses or slacks. It's country people being relaxed, down-home and simply enjoying one another's company."

"Sounds like fun," Rachel said, trying to mean it. *Blend in or stand out.* Well, she'd managed to hide in this town for two months. She doubted anyone would know her. But now, they would. If she didn't go, Cade could get even more suspicious. And truth be told, she could already feel how wonderful it would be to slow-dance with him, walk around on his arm, be his date.

Cade looked at his watch. "Gotta run," he said, rising from the chair. The need to run pushed him hard. What had he just done? Shell-shocked by his own behavior, Cade walked over to the peg and shrugged into his brown nylon coat.

Rachel remained at the table feeling partly excited and partly fearful. "What time is the dance?"

"Seven to ten o'clock," Cade said, settling his trooper's hat on his head. "We'll stay only as long as you want." He had to give her choices. If he had his way, they'd stay until the dance closed up.

"I'll have dinner for us at five-thirty, then." She gripped her hands in her lap beneath the table. Nerves fled through her. Wild, unreasonable dreams were coming to life. She saw him scowl again, closed up and unreadable once more. What could he really be thinking and feeling? Was he an employer being "nice" to her? Or was he about to cross that line she wasn't sure she wanted to cross? Fear mingled with excitement.

Opening the door, Cade lifted his hand, feeling as if he were both floating on a cloud of joy and walking a path straight to hell. "See you later..." He fled out into the cold air, which revived him. Why was he feeling trapped? As he got into the SUV, Cade shook his head, angry at himself. He felt bad for Rachel. Maybe that was why he did these stupid things. All he wanted to do was make her happy. He shut the door of his cruiser and slipped the key into the ignition.

As he called in to the dispatcher to let her know he was done with lunch, Cade drove slowly off the ranch. Yes, that was it, Cade felt sorry for Rachel because she was holed up in the house and never left it. He was a sucker for those who needed help. Was it really romantic attraction? His mouth went thin and he headed back toward the town. Who was he fooling? With a sigh, Cade knew it could never be. The people he loved died on him. And more than anything else, Cade could not stand losing someone he loved again. His hands gripped the steering wheel hard for a moment. Yes, he simply felt sorry for Rachel. That was all.

THE DOOR CLOSED. Rachel sat, hands in her lap, staring at the roses. Dirk had never given her flowers. After the rushed wedding in Las Vegas, Rachel hadn't seen any more. Her life had switched to fast-paced Miami, Florida. Oh, Dirk had brought her chocolates from time to time, but when he did, he wanted something for them. Rachel shivered. Everything Dirk gave her came with a price.

Rachel reached out and touched the red, velvety petal of one rose. It felt so soft and pliable. The scent already filled the kitchen like a heady perfume. What did Cade want? Rubbing her face, Rachel scolded herself for being so naive and stupid. The pain of the past overpowered this happy moment. Could a man give her such gifts and not want something for it? Her body? Her kisses? Those were the things Dirk always expected from her whether she was in the mood or not.

Rachel tried to calm herself. The look in Cade's eyes was like that of a little boy shyly giving the girl he likes a gift. She could see the light in his expression, the need to please her, to make her happy. But that look had been there for a second and was quickly swallowed up by that implacable gaze that was always there.

The most important thing was that she remain brutally honest with what she saw in others as well as in herself. This helped her form better judgments about people. But Cade confused her. She sat staring at the roses. She liked the gifts. She loved being surprised. And most of all, Cade had been thoughtful toward her. It could be innocent.

Getting up, Rachel cleared the table and put the dirty plates in the dishwasher. The fact was that she longed for intimate contact with Cade. Each time he touched her, her entire body blossomed like a ripe peach. No question, she was coming alive once more. The long tunnel of suffering, grief and depression was finally dissolving. Was it because of Cade? His family? Or maybe it was just time.

Rachel wiped the crumbs off the table and rinsed the cloth beneath the tap. The wintery, sunny scene outside the window cheered her up. The place looked like a picture-postcard and Rachel wanted to do a watercolor of it someday. When she wasn't doing her illustrations and writing, she was building a portfolio of watercolor landscapes that she hoped would be seen in a gallery.

Cade…what to do about him? Hands resting on the sink, Rachel stared out the window, lost in the turmoil of that dangerous question. What to do about herself? She ached to be in his arms. Dreamed about making love with him. Wondering if he'd be a gentle lover. She had only Dirk to compare him to.

What did she want? She wanted Cade! She wanted this life. Rachel didn't want to admit how happy she was right now. Happier than she could remember in years. She was on a ranch, not a farm, but to her, it was the same thing. Nature surrounded them, the animals and the hardworking people who made it thrive fed her thirsty soul. Yet, they were things out of her reach forever. A gutting sadness cut through her. It wasn't fair that she be denied happiness, a way of life, because of Dirk. The whole notion made her angry, which felt far better than being scared.

With a damp cloth, Rachel cleaned the tile counter. Her mind and heart were centered on Cade. He was just coming out of his own long tunnel of grief over the loss of his wife and child. Rachel felt that something had put her in front of him and Jenny for a reason. So many synchronistic things had happened that it left her marveling at it all.

Was she allowed to be happy? The FBI had told her that if she ever fell in love and married, her husband could never know of her past. None of it. Ever. Rachel found that harder to accept than anything else. Her life was one big, continuing lie. Squeezing her eyes shut, Rachel pressed her palms into them for a moment.

Dropping her hands away from her eyes, Rachel stared at the roses. That was why she'd avoided relationships in the past. She didn't lie well. She knew she'd trip up. She'd nearly done that with Cade out in the barn over the discussion about the goats. No way could she stop her real life, her past, from bleeding into the present. That was why she had avoided serious and personal relationships with men in the past.

Now, it was different, for whatever reason. Cade symbolized the man she'd dreamed of—someone who was honest, hardworking and ruggedly handsome. Cade was also kind, thoughtful and sensitive. All those qualities Rachel had craved in her dream partner. Cade loved children. There was nothing to dislike about this man who had made his house her home. And he was honorable. Rachel couldn't name a time when he'd gone out of his way to touch her flirtatiously or sidled up to her. No, he'd treated her like a valued and respected friend, not a lover. If he had come on to her, she'd have left long ago.

Maybe that was the difference with Cade. They were becoming friends. Rachel had had male acquaintances, but had never found a true friend among them. In fact, she hadn't wanted to get too close because of her fear of divulging her past. Some of her emotional turmoil subsided. Cade was a friend. She could have a friend. And she could continue to allow herself to appreciate and like him as a friend.

Somehow, realizing this made her attending a dance more palatable and less threatening to her heart. Rachel could never fall in love. She wasn't going to lie to that person who held her heart. She could allow Cade into her life as a friend.

Rachel's ears picked up on Jenny's fussing as she awoke. Turning, she put away her angst and walked down the hall to get the baby. Humming a tune, Rachel felt some of the weight lift from her shoulders. Tonight wouldn't be torture. No, it was two friends going to a dance to enjoy the night. That was all.

CHAPTER NINE

CADE TRIED TO not stare at Rachel. She had brushed her hair up into a youthful style with several combs. It showed off her slender neck. He drove his dark blue pickup along the wet highway, the black asphalt gleaming with recent snow that had melted. Even in her black wool coat and red muffler, he thought she looked beautiful. As headlights passed them, Rachel's clean profile and her soft, full lips were illuminated. His body tightened. Groaning inwardly, Cade felt as if he were a prisoner between heaven and hell. He knew what hell was; he'd lived in it for two years. With Rachel coming into his life, Cade was in heaven. He was constantly battling himself not to touch her. Savagely, he reminded himself he was doing this as a compassionate gesture. Nothing else.

Cade stared straight ahead and tried to stay focused. His thoughts strayed to how happy Rachel looked. Happy to get out of the house? To be with him? His gut tightened with anxiety. Rachel was so good with Jenny and the baby was thriving happily beneath her care and love. It stopped Cade from rocking the boat. He frowned. Besides, in the months Rachel had been under his roof, she'd never given him a signal that she was interested in him.

Was that why he'd brought her the roses and candy? Cade tried once again to concentrate on his driving. As they breasted the hill, the colorful lights of Jackson Hole glimmered down below.

"The town looks like a Christmas tree," Rachel confided. Indeed, the town was in a "hole." She had found out from Gwen that her ancestors had been a mix of Native American and French fur trappers who had come in here. At that time a valley was referred to as a "hole" and the name had stuck. Although, Gwen told her, the mayor wanted the town to be known simply as Jackson and not Jackson Hole. Rachel didn't know why. The romantic story of how the Wyoming town came into being was pure Western nostalgia and should remain as is, she thought.

"Yes," Cade said, "it does."

Out the side window Rachel saw that the darkness was complete. On her right, she knew a huge mountain stood, invisible at night. To the left of them was a wide, flat expanse, the Elk Refuge where thousands of animals remained. They came out of the mountains to the lower altitude in order to survive. In the spring, they would all leave and go back to the mountains. Closer to Jackson Hole were wetlands and a river, perfect habitat for the elk herds.

"Why aren't you getting out more?" Cade asked abruptly. "My mother is worried that you're holing up too much in the house. She thinks you need to get out more often."

Rachel went into her defensive mode of lies. "I guess I'm a natural homebody," she offered, trying to make light of his concern. Opening her hands, she added, "I'm used to working at my employer's home."

"Mom said you've only driven your car into town twice."

"Your mother is like a tornado on the run," Rachel said with a chuckle. "I'm sure she doesn't stay more than five minutes in any given spot."

"That's true," Cade agreed wryly, glancing over at her. The smile on Rachel's shadowed features was anxious, her eyes darkened so he couldn't accurately read them. "She's a hard worker 24/7," he agreed. Again, tension sprang to the cab of the truck.

"I don't know how she does it all," Rachel admitted. "She runs a quilting shop and then comes home and works on the accounting for her store and the ranch. Your dad is always busy, but then, on a farm or ranch something always needs to be done." Rachel allowed herself to linger over Cade's handsome profile as he drove. "And it's a good thing that you're pitching in and helping him when you don't have duty as a sheriff's deputy. It looks like he needs a full-time wrangler."

Cade nodded. "He does, but he doesn't have the money to pay a hired hand. That's why I pitch in." And then he muttered, "I guess the whole family is manic."

Laughing, Rachel remembered growing up on their Iowa farm. "Oh, no. Farm and ranch life is demanding, that's all." She wanted to ignore how good he looked in his crisp white cowboy shirt, dark slacks and coat. Tonight, Cade was a cowboy, not a sheriff's deputy. His black hat sat on a rack behind them. Rachel felt that deep down, Cade was a rancher, not a law-enforcement officer. However, this area had little to offer in the way of affordable middle-class housing. A deputy didn't make enough to live in the town he protected. Cade was able to live here because of his family's ranch. Rich corporate retirees, oil moguls, mine owners and Hollywood types made this town the Palm Springs of the Rockies. As a consequence, for middle-class people it was nearly impossible to afford the price of an apartment rental, much less a home.

The silence hung in the truck as they moved slowly down the recently salted highway to the sparkling lights of Jackson Hole. Cade glanced over at her. He swallowed hard and rasped, "Are you happy being with us, Rachel?"

Taken off guard by the quiet question, she stared at Cade for a moment. Rachel had learned a long time ago to stop and think of the right answer before she engaged her mouth. She used to blurt out answers, but now that could prove deadly. "Of course I am. I love taking care of Jenny."

Nodding, Cade felt his heart racing a little more than usual. He kept his hands on the steering wheel. At this time of night, the temperature was falling and despite the best efforts of the salt trucks, the water that had melted during the day would turn into deadly black ice. He had no desire to go skidding off the two-lane highway. "You seem happy. I'm glad you set up that other room as your office."

"It's all working out, Cade." Far better than Rachel could ever have dreamed. "What about you? Are you still okay with me living under the same roof with you?"

Cade saw the seriousness of her expression as headlights flashed into the cab. He cleared his throat. "I want you to be comfortable, Rachel. I worry that you aren't relaxed or that you need more privacy. I worry about being underfoot, sometimes."

Rachel was touched by his concern. "I'm happy, Cade." That wasn't a lie, and her tension dissolved. "In fact, I can't remember ever being this happy." She gestured at the darkness that surrounded them from the cab. "The Grand Tetons are the most beautiful mountains I've ever seen. I love small towns and being close to nature."

Frowning, he said, "Then why did you live in New York City?"

Instantly, anxiety gripped Rachel. "For work and school." She hoped he would buy her explanation.

"I see," he murmured. "And now you want to be closer to nature?"

"Yes," Rachel lied, feeling badly. Cade was such a stand-up guy that he and his family did not deserve this kind of treatment. "I really love being here, Cade. Your family is wonderful. I have everything I've ever dreamed of." Except for a meaningful, long-term relationship. And a family of her own. A mother who could go back to her own farm and live out her life. And being able to see her brothers…

"That's good to hear," Cade said, making a turn toward the armory. The Christmas lights were still up in the town. It cheered the locals who wanted them left until March. With the winter ski season in full swing, the lights gave an ongoing holiday air to the famous fur-trapper town.

The armory parking lot had been plowed clean of snow, the white stuff was piled up in three- and four-foot walls around the edge of the rectangular area. Rachel saw that the armory, which doubled as a VFW center, was lit up with pink, red and white lanterns to indicate Valentine's Day. Crowds of people chatted excitedly and walked toward the main doors. Her heart lifted. *Tonight I'm going to forget who I am, what happened and the twists and turns of my life. I'm going to enjoy being with Cade.* And how she wanted to be held in his arms! What would that be like? Anything to rival her nightly dreams? Anticipation soared within her as she climbed out of the truck. Throughout the years, she'd never really been in the arms of a man. Maybe that's why she looked forward to this night with Cade. A human being wasn't made to live alone.

Wrapping his arm through hers, Cade said, "This parking lot gets icy. Let me escort you to the door." He settled the cowboy hat on his head and managed a thin smile down at her. Secretly, he was thrilled to have her arm hooked through his.

Rachel said, "It wouldn't look very good if I slipped and fell on my behind, would it?"

Enjoying her closeness, their bodies touching here and there as they walked between the many cars, Cade answered, "You look pretty in that outfit. It would be a shame to get it wet and dirty."

Rachel had chosen to wear her cranberry wool slacks and a pink angora sweater with a mock turtleneck. A long time ago, she'd bought a hand-dyed rainbow-colored silk scarf, and she'd draped it around her neck so that it brought more color to the ensemble. "Not exactly the grand entrance I'd like to make," she agreed, meeting his eyes. Her heart opened and Rachel thought she saw need burning in Cade's eyes. Need of her. She wasn't so naive as not to know when a man was interested in her. Could she read Cade accurately? Or was it her silly, lonely heart wanting some attention no matter who it was? Trying to tamp down her excitement and yearning, Rachel struggled to remain immune to him, but it was nearly impossible.

The people entering the armory were in a festive mood. They gave their coats to the coatroom attendant and moved with the jovial crowd toward the dance floor. Rachel met more people in that five minutes than she had in all the time she'd lived in New York City. Knowing that this put her at risk but needing the human connection, she shook a lot of hands and shared social pleasantries. Cade knew everyone. And everyone, it seemed, admired and respected him in return. There were plenty of jokes, back-slapping and handshakes.

Finally, out on the shining oak floor, which was crowded with people of all ages, Cade led her as a slow song began. The local band struck up a 1940s-era song. Swept into his arms, Rachel allowed herself to be pulled close. Cade still kept a bit of distance between them and guided her expertly around the dance floor. She absorbed the warm strength of his hand enclosing hers and the way his other hand fitted into the small of her back. Her spine tingled wildly under his touch. Rachel fantasized how it might feel to have Cade slip his hand beneath her soft sweater. Her breasts tightened. Her nipples puckered. Alarmed, Rachel hoped the fuzziness of the sweater hid her feminine reaction to him.

"You're a good dancer," Cade whispered, his lips near her ear. He wanted to say, *You feel so damn good to me. You're all woman. I want to kiss you, make love with you.* Choking all of those words back down, Cade lifted his head to search her face. Rachel didn't wear any makeup except for some pink lipstick. Her cheeks were flushed, which only emphasized her warm blue eyes and their huge black pupils. She never wore mascara or eye color—didn't have to. She had thick sable lashes that framed her eyes like those in an old master's painting. Cade felt himself spiral helplessly into them. There was such happiness within them. Was it because she was in his arms?

"Thanks," she said, her voice husky with sudden emotion. Cade's face was shadowed by the light above, the semidarkness intimate. There might have been forty other couples on the dance floor but she felt as if they were all alone in that moment. His gray eyes were large and intent-looking—upon her. Without thinking, she dropped her gaze to his very male, strong mouth. His lips were so close to hers. What would it be like to just take a tiny step forward, press her body against his and place her mouth on his? The need nearly drove Rachel forward.

And then the dance ended. People clapped enthusiastically for the local band that consisted of a saxophonist, a drummer, a singer, and trumpet-and piano-players. The men were dressed like 1920s gangsters, their felt fedoras reminding Rachel of the bootleggers of that era. The singer was dressed in a bright red sequined dress straight out of the 1940s. Her blond hair was long and wavy around her shoulders.

Rachel reluctantly parted from Cade's arms but she didn't want to. Cade kept his hand in the small of her back and led her over to the beverage table.

Standing near the wall, crystal cup in hand, Rachel appreciated the decorations. In the center of the room a flashing silver ball slowly rotated. Each facet sparkled and cast light around the spacious area. Red, pink and white crepe paper was strung from a central point on the ceiling and fanned out like octopus arms across the expanse. Someone had tied small, medium and large red cardboard hearts here and there along the colorful streamers.

It was a perfect Valentine's Day dance. The people who attended were of all ages and walks of life. As Cade had said, during the harsh winter in Wyoming, there wasn't much for people to do. And with the winter so long, everyone, young and old, looked for any excuse to get out of their homes and mingle with one another. Rachel could see that this was the perfect place for people to catch up with one another's lives and listen to town gossip.

Without thinking, Rachel scanned the assemblage. It was a habit she'd developed after going into the program. Focusing on the men in the noisy crowd, Rachel wanted to make sure she didn't see Dirk among them. The FBI had taught her always to be alert. Always to be aware of her surroundings. She didn't want to do it tonight, though, because happiness bubbled through her. Just one night! For one night Rachel desperately wanted to forget her past. Wanted just to focus on the present. *Now.* With Cade.

Another slow dance started.

"Shall we?" Cade invited, setting his emptied glass on the table.

Rachel threw caution away and set down her glass. Tonight, she would drown in the arms of Cade Garner. Everything else in her miserable life would be forgotten. "Yes, come on." Rachel gave him a playful smile and pulled him out onto the dance floor. The couples rapidly filled up the dance floor as the woman launched into a torch song.

Cade grinned at Rachel's sudden and unexpected spontaneity. He liked it, especially the glint in her eyes. Was she letting go and just being herself? Whisking her into his arms, Cade was pleasantly surprised once more as she lightly pressed her body to his. His hand settled on her back and he kept her close. Rachel didn't resist. When she rested her head on his shoulder, joy exploded through him.

The scent of Cade was all male. Rachel inhaled the woodsy soap he'd used when he'd showered. The black wool of his coat was mildly scratchy against her cheek, but she didn't care. The need to be held in the arms of a man who radiated with such powerful masculinity and protection gave Rachel the permission she needed simply to be a woman. They moved slowly, the song surrounding them and, again, it was as if they were the only two people out on the large dance floor.

"You smell good," Cade murmured, his lips against her silky hair. "Part winter night, part snow and part sweetness only a woman can be."

His words filtered down through her. His voice was low and gruff, the vibration a delicious sensation that moved to her breasts and then to her lower body. Rachel could feel Cade's masculinity, the tautness of his body, the unspoken strength hidden and just waiting to be unleashed. Most of all, she could feel that he wanted her. She wanted him.

As she lifted her face, his lips were scant inches from hers. Rachel met his hooded, darkened eyes that burned with need, and a soft sigh whispered from between her lips. Without thinking for once, Rachel leaned upward, her mouth sliding against the line of his. She initiated the contact out of some wild, deep part of herself. Instantly, Cade's mouth took hers, sweeping her into a world of heat and melting desire. As his lips slid across hers, rocking them open and claiming her swiftly, Rachel surrendered to the power of him as a man wanting her. All of her.

The music faded. The sense of being on a crowded dance floor slipped away from Rachel. She allowed her fingers to tangle in Cade's short, dark hair. As his hand pressed her hard against his front, Rachel felt her well-ordered world disintegrating. His mouth was searching, tender and coaxing. A ravenous hunger burned between her legs, so sharp and needy, that she surged against his mouth, tasting him, glorying in his maleness and absorbing it like the greedy sex-starved woman that she was.

In the back of her spinning mind, Rachel wanted to forget everything. All she wanted right now was Cade. Naked. In her bed. She wanted to feel him thrust inside her, take her as they melted hotly into one another. Her need as a woman overwhelmed her sensible mind. Cade moved her slowly around in a circle, his left hand caressing the length of her spine. It was as if he were making love to her right now. His mouth was commanding and yet teasing. His kiss was unlike any other she'd ever experienced. Cade wanted her to celebrate the joy of their coming together with each gliding, nipping touch of his lips upon hers.

The music ended. Somewhere in her dizzied senses, Rachel heard it stop, but it didn't register. Cade tore his mouth from hers. They stood facing one another, his hands on her shoulders. Her whole body vibrated beneath his touch. His intense gaze made her tremble. Rachel could only stare up at Cade, at a loss for words.

"I'm sorry," he managed in a strangled whisper. "I shouldn't have kissed you." Oh, God, what had he just done? Cade could barely think. "I didn't mean for this to happen."

Her world exploded in front of her. Rachel saw the raw anguish in Cade's narrowed eyes. His hands gripped her shoulders, his fingers digging into her flesh.

Rachel seemed excruciatingly vulnerable and shocked to Cade. He tasted her on his lips. He had felt her soft breasts pressed insistently against his chest. The ache in his lower body was painful. Without a word, he pulled her off the dance floor and sat down with her. His hand felt burnt as he released his hold on her arm. He didn't want to let her go. Not now. Not after that life-affirming kiss.

Avoiding his gaze, Rachel touched her lips. "I—

I'm sorry. I don't know what happened." Her heart was pounding but his words had hurt her. The pity in his eyes didn't help, either. Was she that pathetic that he regretted kissing her?

Cade could see Rachel was struggling with her confusion. As for him, his emotions were in utter tatters. He could barely think. All he really wanted to do was drag Rachel out of the armory, back to his home and carry her to his bed. And love her until he lost himself. Two years without intimacy had left him wildly needy. Oh, he'd had other women ply their looks, their suggestions to him, but none of them had ever captured his heart as Rachel had. And yet, he told himself, he'd only been trying to be nice, to get her out of the house. How could he have kissed her?

Rachel wanted his strong, callused fingers to move up her arm and… Trying desperately to wrestle with the shock of his words, she did her best to stay with reality. She felt helpless against the bright, joyous emotions and the clamor of her own body that wanted Cade without reserve. "I—I didn't mean… I'm sorry…it just happened…."

"I'm sorry, too," he admitted. "I never expected this to happen." And Cade hadn't. She had given him no signal that she was interested in him until tonight. His mouth tingled hotly in memory of her searching, hungry lips meeting and mating with his. She had been bold and he'd loved that about her. Although Rachel seemed meek and mild, Cade realized a cougar lay beneath that veneer.

"I wasn't thinking," Rachel said, giving him a wan smile. "So much of my life, I've made risky judgments. This is another of them. I didn't realize…"

Shaking his head, Cade studied her as another song began and couples began to drift back to the dance floor. "Life is a risk, Rachel." Cade turned so that their knees brushed against one another. "This changes everything. You know that, don't you?"

"Yes…yes, it does." Would he fire her? Would she be leaving tomorrow morning? Just the thought made Rachel wince. She had come to love this new life. And to love Cade.

"I'm reeling from it. I guess I felt sorry for you. For being stuck in the house." There, he'd come clean. Fear jagged through Cade as he saw Rachel's brows dip. Her mouth pursed and she looked away for a moment. Finally, her eyes met his.

Rachel dragged in a deep breath. "I took the job as nanny to care for Jenny. I wasn't looking for a relationship of any kind. Please believe me." Her heart wrenched in her chest—that he could feel sorry for her. She could barely breathe.

"I believe you," he rasped. "That's why I said this kiss changes everything and we've got to talk about it."

Rachel was struck by Cade's sense of responsibility. He was the opposite of her ex-husband in every possible way. "Yes, we need to talk." Shutting her eyes for a moment, Rachel tried to think through her hurt.

Cade gave her a helpless look and shrugged. "I wasn't looking for a relationship. I really wasn't."

Nodding, Rachel could see the turmoil in his eyes, as well as his desire for her. "I believe you."

"Good, because it's the truth."

"I don't know where this is going," Rachel admitted. She was trying to prepare herself for the fact that she might need to leave—he may send her away.

"I don't, either," Cade agreed. Sitting up, he said more strongly, "Look, if you want to move out, I'll understand. I don't want you to feel like you have to stay in my home any longer. The cabin is ready for you and—"

She stared at him in shock. "You aren't going to fire me?"

Brows rising, Cade blurted, "Why, no..." And then he realized she'd thought she would be fired for kissing her employer. What a mess! "Jenny needs you," he emphasized. He cursed himself for his weakness. He could lose the one person who had brought stability to Jenny's life.

"I don't want to quit my job, Cade. If you need me to move out, I will. I love Jenny. I—I don't want to be separated from her."

Sitting there, Cade digested her words and felt sudden relief. For a moment, he'd thought Rachel was gone. Forever. "Jenny needs you," he said, choked up with worry for his adopted daughter.

"She wouldn't do well if you were gone. She's bonded with you, Rachel."

"Yes."

He tried to still the heart that pounded hard in his chest. "I'm not forcing myself on you nor do I expect more of the same when we go back to our home tonight. What happened here tonight was an accident. That's all."

Both relief and pain engulfed her. The hunger in her wanted Cade at home. Tonight. In his bed. Yet, Rachel realized that she'd just unwittingly taken a step in a direction she'd sworn she would never take. The shadow of Dirk Payson had finally dissolved and in its place she had just discovered how much she liked Cade. Even worse, she wanted to pursue a long-term relationship with him.

But at what cost? Dirk was on the loose. Her conscience ate at her. Staring into Cade's shadowed, intense face, Rachel began to realize that she had to make some very hard, gutting decisions, even if the FBI thought she was safe where she was right now. Her feelings for Jenny were pure love. Her feelings for Cade were…she didn't want to go there. Instead, Rachel knew her time at the ranch was coming to an end. And the last thing she wanted to do was hurt Cade and Jenny.

CHAPTER TEN

"SURPRISE, RACHEL! A spring equinox cake for you and Cade!" Gwen Garner called as she entered the back door to Cade's home.

Looking up from the counter, Rachel smiled at the unexpected visitor. Gwen was dressed in a long quilted skirt with colorful patches, a bright yellow long-sleeved blouse and dark blue quilted vest. In her hands was a white-frosted cake decorated with pink springtime roses.

"What a pleasant surprise, Gwen. Hey, that cake looks good," Rachel called, drying her hands on a towel. She came forward and Gwen handed her the cake. "Cade will like this tonight. I was just standing here at the sink wondering what to bake for the week." She grinned. "You solved my dilemma. This is a great way to celebrate March twenty-first, the first day of spring."

Gwen shut the door. "Around here, because of the long winters when everyone goes stir-crazy, we try to find any excuse to celebrate the littlest of things. And spring has sprung!"

Placing the cake on the counter, Rachel laughed.

"Do you have time for a cup of coffee, Gwen or are you racing off to open your store?"

Waving her hand, Gwen pushed her short silver-and-black hair off her brow. "I have time for a cup, thank you. I have Stephanie opening the store for me this morning. You really ought to come down, Rachel. I'm starting a beginning quilting class this afternoon. It's once a week. You need to get out of this house. You spend too much time in it." Gwen pulled out a chair and sat down.

Rachel poured both of them coffee and set the mugs on the table. "I've been thinking about getting out more," Rachel confided. She placed the creamer and sugar bowl on the table. Handing Gwen a spoon, she sat down opposite the woman.

"Good," Gwen grumped. "About time! Cade is worried about you," she said, stirring the cream and sugar into her coffee.

Rachel lifted the mug to her lips and took a sip. "Oh?"

"He feels you're housebound. I know you have Jenny to take care of, but you need to get out more." She gave Rachel a pleading look. "Why don't you come out once a week and take my beginning quilting class?"

"But I don't have a sewing machine," Rachel lamented. "I love to sew. I got away from doing it after I left home." That wasn't entirely a lie. Before Dirk had swept her off her feet and she'd fallen for his manipulations, Rachel had been a first-class seamstress like her mother Daisy.

"Ah!" Gwen triumphed, giving her a wide grin. "I bet you didn't know this, but Cade's wife, Abby, had a sewing machine. Why not come and take my class this afternoon? We have Bernina sewing machines for those who don't have one. You can spend about three hours with us in our classroom. And when Cade gets off duty tonight, you can talk to him about the sewing machine. He keeps it in a hall closet. Ask him if he minds if you use the Bernina. I don't think he'll object at all."

Rachel admitted to herself she had a little cabin fever. When she wasn't taking care of Jenny or working on her art assignments, she helped Cade's dad, Ray. Often, she was cleaning out box stalls and taking wheelbarrows to one of the five huge compost bins. She had also taken over the milking of the nannies twice a day. Ray thought he had taught her the art of milking, but in reality, Rachel had already known how. With all the snow, there wasn't much else she could do to help out. Still, it was a way to get outdoors and get some fresh air and exercise.

"Well? I can see you're seriously thinking about it." Gwen raised her thick eyebrows. "You'll love quilting. Just look at it this way—since you're an artist you can paint with fabric instead of tubes of paint."

"I like the idea that quilting is like painting on fabric. What a beautiful way to see your work," Rachel said. After all, she had bought a car, a Toyota Corolla, and could drive to and from the quilting store. Wanting to be more independent and not so reliant on the Garner family, Rachel had made the purchase. Dirk Payson wouldn't be showing up in a quilting shop to find her so Rachel felt fairly safe in taking the class. She was hungry for the company of women because they gave her such strength and support whether they knew it or not. Her mother had never quilted, but her grandmother had. At the farm in Iowa, many of her grandmother's quilts were still used. Maybe it was time for Rachel to restart that tradition in her family. It was a warm, loving tie from her past.

"Okay, Gwen, I'm signing up!"

Clapping her hands, Gwen whooped. "Atta girl, Rachel! I knew you had it in you! Cade is going to be happy about this. He's got enough to worry about as a deputy. He doesn't need to be chawing on what you are or are not doing."

Heart twinging, Rachel sipped her coffee. "You're right, Gwen. He has enough on his plate."

"Well," she said primly, "I think he'll be overjoyed to hear you're going to learn how to quilt."

"What about Jenny? Who will take care of her when I'm at your class?"

"I'll talk to Ray. He's an old hand at taking care of babies of all kinds, four-footed or two-legged." She chuckled.

Over the months, Rachel had come to love Ray Garner. He was a tall, lean drink of water with a real quiet nature. But he was kind and thoughtful. And he did have a way with babies, whether they were newly born calves, foals or kittens. "Wonderful. So, he knows how to change a diaper?"

"Oh, yes," Gwen chuckled. "I wouldn't marry a man who can't do the same work I do and vice versa. In my younger years, I was out there branding and lassoing cattle for him and his crews. Now, we're a team. I admit that we're older now and I still love to ride with him on horseback to inspect our herds, but I'm not doing any more of the ranch work."

Rachel could see where Cade got his sense of helping her around the house. He cooked, ran the vacuum, did the washing, folded clothes and washed windows. "I'm glad you trained your son to do all those things."

"Listen, today's world is a lot different from when Ray and I grew up. It takes two people working hard to make a living and when they get home, the team has to do the housework together. It's not right to dump it all on the wife. She's already worked eight hours, too."

"No argument there," Rachel said.

Gwen rose and took her cup over to the sink and rinsed it out. "I gotta run. We're having a spring fabric sale, fifty-percent off today. You'll be able to choose some nice quilt fabric for a lot less." She hurried to the door and turned and smiled. "I'll tell Ray he's babysitting Jenny from one to four this afternoon."

"Great," Rachel said. "Thanks so much, Gwen."

"See you this afternoon. Bye!" She was out the door and gone.

Quiet surrounded Rachel once more. Jenny had another hour to sleep before she awakened. Cade had brought out a small playpen and it was set up in the living room. Jenny was at a point where she was crawling around a bit and rolling from side to side. Having the portable playpen was perfect. Outside the kitchen window the icicles dripped. It was cloudy but nearly forty degrees, a warm day for Wyoming.

Rachel mulled over the many advantages to quilting. It was a safe activity for her. And Gwen was right—she was starting to climb the walls here. She wanted to be outside, put in a garden and get her hands into the soil. In New York City, none of that had been possible. But here, it was. Gwen was excited about her helping put in the garden come early June. But even before then, she had to get out of the house more often and yet keep a low profile.

How she wished she could call her mother. Rachel hated the once-a-month rule the FBI had imposed upon them. Daisy would be delighted about her taking up quilting.

As she glanced around the quiet kitchen, checking for tasks yet to be done, Rachel continued to sip her coffee. As always, the torrid, searching kiss she'd shared with Cade came back to tease her. He'd been true to his word—since then, he had not made a move. In fact, Cade was gone more than he was home. When she asked about it, he shrugged and said that some of his deputy buddies needed time off for personal reasons. He was picking up their shifts so they could have that day off.

Or was he taking on the extra duty to stay away from her? Rachel didn't know for sure. They'd never spoken again of the Valentine's Day dance or the kiss that had rocked her world. Sighing, Rachel frowned. Hands around the warm mug, she stared unseeingly down at it. Her mind and, if she was honest, her heart were all centered on Cade. Since the kiss, Rachel had tried to find fault with Cade. Oh, he left his laundry on the floor of his bathroom, and he wasn't perfect. Compared to Dirk, he was a true prince. The more Rachel lived under Cade's roof, the more she realized how bizarre the lifestyle she'd lived with Payson was.

Was Cade avoiding her? Was she avoiding him? Rachel couldn't ask him and she couldn't act upon her desire. Better just to leave things as they were. They needed to reestablish a professional relationship. Brenda, her FBI handler, had told her at the beginning of March that they had a lead on Dirk, that he'd been positively identified in Florida. That gave Rachel some relief from the burden of worrying that he would come here and hurt Cade's family. Brenda had felt Dirk would go back to his old haunt and love—Florida. And, she'd been right.

When Rachel told Brenda of her fears for the Garner family if she remained here, the FBI handler had told her to stay put. She had excellent cover. Dirk Payson was a warm-state person and Wyoming was well-known for its winter—from October through June. No, the handler felt Rachel was safe.

No matter what Rachel did, she still felt fear eating around the edges of her happiness. There was natural contentment on the Garner ranch. Ray and Gwen were wonderful to her. Jenny was making great progress and Cade fed, diapered and played with her every chance he got. In some ways, the baby was helping to heal not only her loss, but Cade's, as well.

Feeling a bit more reassured, Rachel got up and walked over to the sink. Tonight, she would make spaghetti with French bread slathered with garlic and butter. It was one of Cade's favorite meals. Her heart warmed. Rachel wanted to make him happy. Cade had given her so much. Still, she could never forget that he'd felt sorry for her. The dance invitation was purely out of sympathy, that was all.

As she picked up the clean glass baby bottles from the steamer, peace blanketed Rachel. She gathered the baby's items for Ray. The idea of making a quilt suddenly seemed like an exciting venture to Rachel. She was looking forward to driving into Jackson Hole and finding out more about Gwen's quilting store. It was a safe place to be.

"Now, THIS IS your palette," Gwen told her briskly as she guided Rachel through four thousand bolts of colorful fabric. She grinned over at Rachel, who carried a paper and pen. "Take all the notes you want. I believe in bright, colorful fabrics, Rachel. You need to know that our quilting shop carries the highest grades of cloth."

Stopping at the red section, Rachel marveled at the various shades of red, fuschia and magenta. "Grades of cloth? What do you mean?" She almost added that her mother had bought all her cloth from a local store in Iowa, not a quilting store.

Gwen patted one of the bolts of cloth. "When a cloth company makes the first run on a new fabric pattern, they're trying to adjust the weave. What most people don't realize is that the first runs are the lowest grade of fabric precisely because the tension of their machine isn't quite as calibrated as they want it. They do this through a series of trial runs. Your first-run fabric goes to discount stores. This fabric has too loose a weave and if you make a quilt out of it, you'll run into a lot of trouble trying to get it to remain stable."

"Stable?" Rachel loved learning new information and this was fascinating.

"Yes," Gwen said, pulling out a bolt of red batik-patterned cloth with light pink splotches. "Come here." She led her to one of the cutting tables. Gwen opened up the bolt and spread it out before Rachel. Then, she brought over two samples of other cloth labeled First Run and Second Run. She laid them out before Rachel. "I want you to feel each one of these fabrics. You tell me which one feels the best to you."

Fingering each one, Rachel pointed to the batik material. "This one."

Pleased, Gwen said, "Exactly. First run has a loose weave." She lifted a length of cloth up for Rachel to look at. "You can see it here particularly along the edges of the fabric."

Rachel squinted upward. "Yes, I see that."

"Okay," Gwen said, laying the cloth aside and going to the second-run material, "look at this. Check the edges because that's where you can see the weaving. This one isn't as loose. It's a little tighter. Right?"

"Right," Rachel said.

Gwen lifted the material from the batik bolt up for her to look at the edge. "Now, see how tight this weave is compared to the other runs?"

"Oh," Rachel said, impressed, "I do."

"You want a tight, consistent weave in your fabric," Gwen told her, folding the bolt of material back up and pinning it into place. "As you create block or rail patterns, you want the material to stay put. First and second runs are too weak and the fabric moves around a lot on you. What will happen is you'll never be able to get the exact meeting of seams along your rails or blocks or they'll slide and you'll be in a pickle." She shook her head. "It's always best to go with the finest run of fabric, which is what they call quilting grade. Yes, you pay more. Usually, nine or ten dollars a yard, but when you start working with the cloth, it won't move on you, causing you a lot of ripping out and resewing of seams. And it gets really dicey if you're stitching in the ditch. You really want a fabric that is strong and steady."

"Stitching in the ditch?" Rachel laughed. "It sounds like a rhyme for a child's book!"

Gwen giggled. "Well, who knows what you will do with all this classroom information you'll be getting week after week."

"I've already got some ideas," Rachel admitted, sharing her smile.

"Okay, so you know you use only quilting-quality cloth."

Looking at all the colors, Rachel felt amazed. The store was chock-full of women who were each buying from ten or fifteen different bolts of cloth. The quilting shop was large, airy and with plenty of room for browsing. A number of them had carts with many bolts of cloth in them. Gwen had told her that these were longtime quilters buying cloth for new quilts they'd be making. It was an exciting process.

A young woman in a U.S. Forest Service uniform came in. She removed her hat. Rachel leaned over and ask, "Who is that?"

"Oh, that's Casey Cantrell. She's our newest forest ranger to be stationed up at the Grand Tetons National Park." And then, Gwen sidled up to her and whispered, "Rumor has it she's got a colorful past...."

Inwardly, Rachel grimaced. If only Gwen knew about her own colorful past. "I imagine you see and hear a lot in here."

Gwen chuckled. "Oh, yes. If you want to know what's really going on in Jackson Hole, you come here." She pointed her index finger down toward the floor.

Another woman with red hair, clad in fur, entered. Rachel thought she looked svelte and model-like compared to the slightly frumpy Casey Cantrell.

"Uh-oh," Gwen muttered, her brows dipping. "That's Senator Carter Peyton's wife, Clarissa. She's a handful. Treats my girls like dirt on some days. When Clarissa has had a fight with her husband, she takes it out on all of us. When she's in a good mood, she's the kindest person you could know. She raises millions for charity."

Watching the woman who held her shoulders squared beneath the three-quarter-length red fox fur, Rachel nodded. "Does she quilt?"

"No, but she's got a cousin who lives in Cheyenne who does. Probably coming in to buy her some patterns or such. Clarissa is only thirty years old. Her husband has been a senator here in Wyoming for eight years. Kinda sad," Gwen murmured. "Two years ago he left his wife and two children at home and flew to a Republican fundraiser in Cheyenne. Their house caught fire and everyone died."

"Oh," Rachel gasped softly, "how *awful!*" Now

she watched Clarissa with new eyes. Feeling deep compassion for the woman, she whispered, "He must be devastated."

"It's the senator that's the troublemaker," Gwen said. "He blames lieutenant Matthew Sinclaire for letting his family burn alive. He's got a real grudge against him."

"A grudge?"

Gwen tucked some of the fabric bolts back into order and muttered, "He's threatened to kill Matt. Now, Matt's born and raised here. I watched him grow up into a fine young man. Not a mean bone in that firefighter's body. You know? The night that fire happened, it was during a blizzard. The two-mile dirt road to his home was mud. The fire-fighters' trucks sank to their axles, and they were stuck a mile from the burning home. Matt and two other firefighters slogged through foot-deep mud that last mile trying to save the family. But it was too late." Shaking her head, Gwen added more grimly, "The senator thinks it's Matt's fault, and he's out to get him."

"What do you mean?" Rachel asked, alarmed.

"One thing you'll learn about Wyoming men— some of them are meaner than a pissed-off rattle-snake. Peyton is one of 'em. We've thought for a long time that he's mixed up in drug dealing from Mexico. Can't prove it, but he acts crazy at times. He's a loaded gun ready to go off. I feel sorry for Matt. You know he's widowed? He has a little girl, Megan, who's eight now. There was a 'mysterious' fire about a month after Peyton's place burned to the ground. Matt lost his wife, Beverly. Megan managed to get out alive, but the poor child is utterly traumatized. She hasn't spoken a word since the fire."

Rolling her eyes, Rachel whispered, "That's awful. Do you think the senator set fire to the lieutenant's home to get even with him?"

Gwen wiggled her eyebrows. "You know, Rachel, you're a very smart young woman. Cade suspects that Peyton put a couple of men up to the fire. There's no proof, of course...."

Rachel turned her gaze to the red-haired Clarissa at the counter who was giving orders to Sharon, one of Gwen's assistants. Her voice sounded imperious.

"Hey, enough town gossip. Follow me," Gwen said, lifting her hand. She led Rachel over to a spinner rack containing quilting books and magazines. "We always start out our new quilters with this book." She picked one up and handed it to Rachel. "First-time quilters shouldn't be scared off with some detailed pattern that calls for nine different colors. That's a lot for a first-timer. This book, *Quilts for Baby Easy as A, B, C* by Ursula Reikes, has a very simple pattern in it."

Gwen led her back to the cutting table and opened up the colorful book. "We'll be using her Rail Fence pattern from the book." She ran her finger over the information on materials and on cutting the strips or rails. "Now, all you need is four bolts of fabric. You should try and choose four that have some fun colors that you would like to put together."

Studying the pattern, Rachel felt the excitement building in her. "This all looks like Greek to me," she said, laughing. "But I see it's going to take three fabrics for the rail pattern, right?"

"Yes," Gwen said. "There's a real art to matching up the fabrics. What I'd suggest is you go wander through the store and choose. Bring them back here and we'll look at them together."

"This is going to be fun. It's like picking paints for a picture," Rachel said.

Gwen grinned. "Exactly. Choosing fabric is one of the most exciting 'hunts' a quilter has. Off with you! Come and get me when you've chosen your colors."

Rachel felt as if she were in a rainbow store of colors. One half of the store was devoted to Hoffman batik cloth. Gwen explained that the patterns, which reminded Rachel of watercolors splashed across the fabric, had been created using a wax process and had been washed at least eight times. Drawn to this type of cloth, she ended up with a sunny yellow, a darker forest green and a rich, reddish-brown known to her as sienna. Taking her bolts to one of the cutting tables, she found Gwen just finishing up with an elderly lady with wire-rimmed glasses.

"Got them?" she called to Rachel from across the large rectangular table.

"I hope so," Rachel said, sounding unsure.

"Those are nice colors," the gray-haired woman said.

"Janet, meet Rachel. She's a first-time quilter. She's taking my class."

It was impossible to reach across the cutting area to shake Janet's hand, so Rachel nodded and smiled. "Nice to meet you, Janet."

"You're going to fall into an obsession about quilting," Janet warned her with a cackle.

"I think I already have," Rachel confided. "I got lost in all the colors. There's so many."

"Yes," Janet said, pushing her glasses up on her nose. "And that is the siren's call—all those bolts of color. Each one you see you'll begin to see it as a rail, an inner border or an outer border or a backing. Pretty soon, you'll have bolts dancing in your sleep and you'll be dreaming of how to put them together."

Excitement thrummed through Rachel. She'd enjoyed being at the quilting store. The gossip was something she hadn't been aware took place and Gwen seemed to know everyone and a little something about each person who had entered the store. As happy as she was, a bit of dread trickled through her. The store stood on the main square. A lot of people milled on the sidewalks. Could one of them be Dirk? For a moment, Rachel simply watched. It was a habit. But a good one. Would she ever be free of him?

CHAPTER ELEVEN

RACHEL COULD HARDLY wait until Cade got home that evening. She had the table set. Jenny was gnawing on a cracker in her high chair near where they would eat dinner. Dressed in a blue romper, the infant was having a lot of fun with her food and smeared it across the plastic table in front of her. Rachel sat down and gently wiped her bow-shaped mouth.

"That's just too yummy to resist, isn't it?" she murmured to the baby, smiling and gently training her hair back into place on her tiny head.

Jenny cooed and waved what was left of the cracker at Rachel.

Laughing, she heard the door open and close. Cade entered, looking especially tired, and some of her happiness dissolved.

"Hard day at work?" she guessed, greeting him.

Cade nodded and hungrily drank in the scene of Rachel sitting next to Jenny. It buoyed his sagging spirits. "Some days are worse than others," he said, shrugging out of his dark brown nylon jacket as he crossed the kitchen. "I'll get a quick shower and change for dinner."

Cade leaned down and kissed the top of Jenny's head. The infant smiled up at him and waved her half-eaten cracker around. "Nothing like a baby to change how you feel," he said. As he drowned in Rachel's blue gaze, warm with understanding, Cade straightened up. "I'll be back."

He disappeared down the hall and into the master bedroom. It had been one hell of a day. The memory of a horrific accident that had occurred just outside of Jackson Hole flashed before him as he quickly got undressed. He threw his gear on the bed. All he wanted was a hot shower to wash away the screams, the cries of pain, the panicking bystanders and the blood.

As Cade stood under the hot, pummeling streams of water, he felt the tightness ease in his shoulders. For him, water was a safe haven against the world he lived in sometimes. He scrubbed his face with the soap and inhaled its lime scent. How many times had he showered right after Abby and his baby daughter had been killed? Two or three times a day. Cade never told anyone about his abnormal habit. After a while, he didn't need them and was back to one every night before bedtime. Water was cleansing and healing.

He stood in the tile shower, the water dripping off his face after he'd rinsed away the soap. Most of all, he needed to cleanse the blood that had been on his hands earlier. After getting back to the sheriff's department, he'd scrubbed them in the men's lavatory before writing out a report on the car accident. The shower washed away the reminders of the day and made him feel as if he was truly clean once more.

Cade closed his eyes and simply allowed the streams of water to fall across his body. The steam was so thick within the glass-encased area that it was more like warm white clouds surrounding him. It all felt so good. The sense of being able to let down, to relax and let the nightmare of a day dissolve, flowed off him. *Home. I'm home. I have a baby daughter who waits for me...* In another three months, Jenny would legally be his as the adoption process crawled through its different phases in the court system. He still grieved over the loss of Lily. *I have Rachel....*

Opening his eyes, Cade wiped away the water from his face and stepped back just enough to keep the streams flowing across his chest downward. *Rachel. Oh, God, how many times today after dealing with that accident did I think of her? Of Abby and Susannah?* Cade hadn't seen an accident of this magnitude since he'd lost his family in a similar accident. And this one brought all of it back to him in spades. Cade wondered when the past would leave him alone once and for all. Turning off the faucets, he opened the shower door and stepped out into the spacious bathroom. He pulled a dark brown terry-cloth towel from the linen closet and quickly dried himself.

After dressing in well-worn jeans and a burgundy polo shirt, he retrieved his old, patched cowboy boots. Some things he couldn't part with, and this pair of boots were like old friends to his feet.

There, he was ready. Cade picked up a brush and tamed his damp hair back into place. His beard darkened his face, but he wasn't going to shave twice a day. In the mirror he noticed dark shadows beneath his eyes and the murky look to his gray gaze. He looked like hell warmed over, but it was understandable after his awful day. In his years as a deputy, he'd heard of others in the department who had seen what he saw today. To hear it was one thing. To actually see it…well, that was very different. Rubbing his hand across his hard jaw, Cade took in a deep, trembling breath. Maybe he just needed to cry. After a situation or crisis, Cade had cried alone and no one had ever known about it. Not even Abby or his parents. Sometimes he'd cry to relieve the awful pressure in his chest after an accident he'd had to handle. Frowning, he looked away from the mirror. Cade never wanted to see another decapitation as long as he lived.

Rachel heard the pleasant thunk of Cade's cowboy boots coming down the hall. She had cleaned up Jenny's mess on her table, and the little girl played with colorful rubber rings instead. Looking up, she saw Cade emerge from the hall. While he appeared a little better, she sensed something awful had happened to him today. Outwardly, he looked like the Cade she knew, but one glance into his bloodshot eyes, and Rachel knew better.

"Sit down," she invited, rising from her chair. She moved over to the counter where she had everything ready to be brought over to the table. "What do you want to drink?"

"A stiff belt of whiskey," he answered, sitting down.

Turning, Rachel blinked. "Really?"

"No...just teasing. Water is fine, thanks." Cade turned his attention to Jenny and she wrapped one of her tiny hands around his index finger. Sitting with his new baby daughter and Rachel's presence in the kitchen gave him a modicum of comfort that nothing else ever would. Not even a shower.

"Here's your salad," she said, placing two bowls with fresh greens on the table. "Pick your dressing." She pointed to the lazy Susan.

"Thanks," Cade said. "Looks great. I appreciate you doing this, Rachel. You've been such a godsend." And she had.

Coloring beneath his compliment, she teased, "Listen, if a man gives me thanks for the hard work I put into a meal, that will keep me around for a long time. It's when our work goes unappreciated that we women feel taken for granted."

Choosing a balsamic and olive oil dressing, Cade murmured, "Oh, I'll never take you for granted. Not ever."

"That's nice to know. Here's our bread to go with the salad." Rachel sat down after bringing out a plate of oven-warmed garlic French bread. She saw the frown on his brow. Something awful had definitely happened today, but Rachel knew this wasn't the time to talk about it. Let him come down from the day, relax and maybe after dinner, he would broach it with her. Maybe not.

Rachel couldn't pry. That was husband-and-wife stuff, not employee-to-employer chitchat. Still, she yearned to have a deeper connection with Cade. And that kiss the previous month had redefined their relationship in a confusing sort of way. It was always in the forefront of her mind that he felt sorry for her. He didn't feel love for her—only sympathy.

Pouring red-wine vinegar and olive oil on her salad, Rachel sought to find a way to lift his darkness. "Today your mom came over and invited me to come and learn how to quilt at her store."

"Oh?" Cade lifted his head. The salad tasted like cardboard to him. He didn't have much of an appetite. Normally, after calls like that, food wasn't high on his priority list. "You're going to learn how to quilt?"

She grinned. "Yep. And I spent all afternoon at her shop. Your dad took care of Jenny while I was gone. Gwen taught me about the different qualities of fabric and what makes quilting fabric so special."

Hearing her husky voice and seeing the happiness in Rachel's eyes lifted Cade's sadness. "My mother is more teacher than quilter, although she makes a mean quilt, too. She loves to teach others."

Rachel laughed. "I was surprised how fast the

hours went by! She taught me about choosing the right colors for the quilt I'm going to make. In a lot of ways, it's like painting with a brush on canvas. I never realized how quilters are really fabric artists."

The food began to taste better. Cade speared half of a small grape tomato. "So, did you find fabric? Did Mom give you a plan?"

"I've got the fabric and the quilt guide is in the living room. I figured if you weren't too tired later, that I'd show it all to you."

"I'd like to see it," Cade said, meaning it. "What kind of quilt is Mom guiding you to make?"

"A baby quilt." Her smile lessened a bit. "I hope you don't mind. I'd like to make one for Jenny."

Cade's normally gruff voice softened. "No, I think that's great. Thank you. She'll have it all her life. Quilts are special that way and I like the idea of your energy, your care and love going into making it for her."

Relief flowed through Rachel. "Wonderful!" Since the kiss she had tried very hard to be detached emotionally when she was around Cade. It was impossible and she struggled mightily every day. Somehow, Rachel made herself stay light and professional. No more intimacy. If Cade could do it, so could she. Yet, every time she saw the man, her body cried out for his touch, another kiss and his embrace. This would only work if both of them honored their agreement.

After Cade finished his salad, he got up and

took the bowls to the sink. He brought over the spaghetti and sauce. After setting them down, he took a seat.

"You can't have this just yet," he told Jenny, running his index finger along her smooth, chubby arm. "But soon. For now, just smell great food, dumpling."

Rachel served the spaghetti. Cade wanted a lot less than he usually took. "At six months she can have a limp piece of spaghetti to play with. I'll start working with her next week."

"That's going to be fun," Cade said. The scent of fresh basil and oregano in the sauce made his mouth water. He might have been in emotional hell but his physical body was starving for food.

Rachel chuckled. "Well, she's already on organic baby foods and she's taking well to it. I'm sure spaghetti will be a lot of fun for her."

Cade tasted the sauce. "Are you sure you're not Italian?"

"No, no Italian in my blood."

"What then? You're a really good cook."

"I'm just a genetic mutt," she parried, hoping he didn't ask for more information. Rachel was getting so tired of lying that she almost wanted to stop doing it. In reality, she was a mix of English and Dutch ancestry through her great-great grandparents who had come here and bought the family farm in Iowa so long ago.

"I see," Cade murmured, swirling his fork around in the spaghetti.

"I'm glad you like it. I stopped on the way home after my beginning quilt class and picked up the fresh herbs at the grocery store."

"I'm happy you're getting out more," Cade said, meaning it. "I was getting worried about you being cooped up in here too long."

"Your mom fixed that." Rachel laughed. "And she made us a spring cake for dessert."

"I love her cooking. You and she could win blue ribbons at the county fair."

A warmth flowed through Rachel. Jenny was cooing happily as she played with her rings. This was what a family should be like, she thought. Not the disaster she'd had with Dirk. There was such unspoken happiness swirling in the kitchen. The odor of fresh-cooked food, the sound of a happy baby and Cade at the table. She was in some kind of wonderful dream.

"I don't know about entering my food at the fair, but according to Gwen, there's a huge quilt contest. I hope to see it this fall. I think she's entering."

Brows raising, Cade said, "Good. She's one of the best quilters in the valley, but she'd never tell you that."

"Your mom is a humble sort. It was fun watching her in the store today. She has such a passion for quilting and her enthusiasm is infectious. I've never seen so many happy women in one place. There's so much laughter in that store, Cade. It amazed me. I loved it."

"Mom loved getting that store off the ground.

It took five years and a lot of savings to do it. I was ten years old when she decided that's what she wanted to do. She and dad sat down and created a business plan. Since Mom is the accountant for our ranch, she took the plan to the local bank. They wouldn't give her a loan, and she was steamed. So, for five years they pinched pennies to save enough cash up front so the bank would loan her the rest in order to start the store."

Rachel shook her head. "Anything worth wanting means plenty of hard work to manifest it."

"Right on," Cade said. To his surprise, he'd cleaned up the food on his plate. Being with Rachel and Jenny gave him a reprieve from today's horrific events. Cade was grateful. "Mom wanted the quilt store for two reasons. She's very business-minded and saw that our organic cattle operation wasn't taking off like we'd hoped. She had been a part of the quilting club here since forever. Mom knew everyone wanted a store here instead of having to drive clear to Idaho Falls, Idaho, to get their fabric and patterns."

"So, she did it because of that?" Rachel asked. "Was the beef operation not keeping their heads above water financially?"

"Right," Cade said. He pushed back his chair and stood up. He leaned over and picked up her empty plate. "Mom figured that in a five-year period after the store became a reality, it would help keep our ranch solvent. And it did." He cleaned off the plates beneath the faucet and placed them into the dishwasher. Cade was glad to be talking about everyday things. Good things.

Rachel stood up and went to the coffeemaker. "And now, from what I can see, Gwen has plenty of business."

Cade brought down two mugs from the cupboard. "Oh, Dad calls her the 'rich one' now."

Chuckling, Rachel poured the steaming coffee in the mugs. Cade was so close. Secretly, she indulged in his nearness. He couldn't know how much she savored his masculine presence. "So, your ranch is on solid financial ground now?"

Cade picked up the cups and brought them back to the table. "Yes. Mom's business has allowed Dad to improve his sales work and spread the word about our organic beef. By the time I was eighteen, we were out of the red and well into the black."

Rachel pulled the cover off Gwen's spring cake. She put two slices on nearby plates. "That's good news. It's awful trying to make ends meet. The stress is enough to kill a person after a while." Her parents' farm in Iowa had gone through lean times, too. How badly she wanted to confide that to Cade. Walking over to the table, she placed the cake in front of him. "I'm just happy for all of you. As a family you work hard all the time."

Cade nodded and watched Rachel sit down and pick up her fork. "That's it, isn't it? The middle-class path to financial stability is earned one day at a time in the trenches of work." In some ways, sitting with Rachel like this was his special hell on earth. In another, it was the most important part of his day. He always looked forward to simply sitting and talking with her. Cade privately absorbed her into his heart. Oh, he knew he couldn't go too far with her. He'd promised not to crowd or pressure her. Cade had been true to his word, but it was a struggle every minute he was around her.

"I don't know how you do it," Rachel confided to Cade, enjoying the cake. "You work a full-time job as a deputy and then you come home and trade in your uniform for your cowboy clothes and you're off to help your dad."

Cade shrugged. "By me pitching in when and where I can, it saves Dad having to hire someone. I like ranch work. I figure to put my twenty years in as a deputy and then eventually come back to run the ranch full-time after my parents decide to retire."

"A good plan of action," Rachel agreed. Jenny threw her rings on the floor. Rachel went to pick them up. After washing and drying them in the sink, Rachel went back to the table and kissed the baby.

"I think Jenny's getting tired," she murmured. Loosening the tray, she eased the baby out of the high chair. "Let me put her to bed and I'll be right back."

"Do you want me to do it?" Cade asked, ready to help.

"No, you go ahead and eat." She grinned. "I already wolfed down your mom's cake and you still have some left on your plate."

Cade watched her carry Jenny in her arms. As they disappeared down the hall, he turned and resumed eating his cake. And then, he suddenly felt nauseous. Dropping the fork, Cade shot to his feet and ran down the hall to the nearest bathroom.

Rachel heard the awful sounds of retching. Frowning, she tucked Jenny in and turned toward the door. What was going on? She'd heard a commotion in the kitchen and Cade running down the hall. Worriedly, she turned off the light and partially shut the door to the baby's room. More sounds drifted down the hall toward her. Was Cade sick?

She hurried into the bathroom and saw him standing over the sink. He was rinsing out his mouth with water. His face was pale and perspiration dotted his deeply furrowed brow. Without thinking, Rachel moved beside him, her hand moving across his tense shoulders.

"Cade? What's wrong?"

Rachel's touch was electrifying. Her closeness and the softness of her voice broke through the wall he had in place to stop the barrage of violent feelings. Lifting his head, Cade took the terrycloth towel from Rachel and wiped his face. Tears leaked into his eyes. Rachel's tender expression blurred. He opened his mouth to speak, but nothing came out. Finally, he croaked, "I'll be fine."

The snarl in his voice shocked Rachel. She took a few steps back, stung by his growl.

"Are you sure?" she demanded, her arms tight against her body.

Cade wiped his mouth roughly with a towel. "Just a bad day, Rachel."

It was more than that. Rachel knew PTSD symptoms because she had them herself. She saw the shock in Cade's murky gray eyes. She sensed deep emotional turmoil in him. Tightening her lips, she refused to be rebuffed by his brusqueness.

But when he gestured for her to leave the bathroom, she obeyed, albeit reluctantly. Her heart was in a quandary. Cade needed help and yet, he'd signaled for her to leave him alone. She went back into the kitchen, hearing his footsteps down the hall. Standing at the sink, Rachel closed her eyes and tried to reason out her next step. Her heart won out, right or wrong. Turning on her heel, she walked down the hall.

Cade was pale. His eyes were still dazed. Even more heartrending were the tears. She felt as if a hand had crushed her heart. She stood uncertainly in the doorway, and he glared up at her, his expression full of sorrow.

"I'm fine, Rachel. Just go about your duties."

She didn't believe him for a second. Stubbornly, Rachel stood her ground at the entrance. "No. Something terrible happened to you, Cade. You need help—"

"I don't need anything!" he yelled. His voice

cracked and he gave her a pleading look, wanting her to leave.

Cade was reacting like any human being. Lips compressed, Rachel moved quickly. He was like a hurt animal. The suffering in his eyes tore at her as nothing else ever had. Without a word, she sat down.

"Come here, Cade," she whispered. The moment she sat next to him and opened her arms, she saw terror mixed with need in his tear-filled gray eyes. There was a struggle in Cade. Would he reject her? Scream at her? Strike out at her as Dirk had? She had no way of knowing. Her heart gave her the courage to slide her arms around Cade and pull him toward her.

At first, he resisted. Tears blurred Rachel's vision. "Let me help you," she choked.

Suddenly, Cade could no longer stay immune to Rachel. Something old and hurting broke loose in his heart. It was both relief and anguish. As he came into her embrace, he closed his arms around her. Cade held Rachel so hard, the breath squeezed out of her. Burying his head against the crook of her neck, he clung to her as if she were the only person who could save him.

Alarm spread through Rachel as she felt a slight tremor race through him. Moving her fingers through his hair, she whispered, "It's all right, Cade. It's all right. I'm here. I'll just hold you...."

CHAPTER TWELVE

RACHEL CLOSED HER EYES. Cade gripped her as if she were a life preserver. Intuitively she felt something awful had happened at work. He held her so tightly she could barely breathe. Rachel relaxed within his grip as she heard a sob rip out of him. Reflexively, she crooned to Cade, held him and gently moved her fingers through his short, dark hair.

There was so much pain in life. Rachel had experienced her fair share. And now, Cade was in a terrible place. At least she could hold him against this world of theirs that extracted high prices for living in it. In an effort to absorb his anguish, Rachel pressed a kiss to his neck and then his hair.

The night hadn't gone the way Rachel had expected. She had envisioned a happy dinner with the three of them and then showing Cade her quilting material. She had been so excited about making Jenny her first baby quilt. All of that would have to wait. Disappointed but not disheartened, Rachel understood all too clearly how much humans needed one another in times of crisis. How many nights had she held and rocked herself after Dirk had been sentenced to prison? Scared and alone in New York City, a whole new and radically different life ahead of her, Rachel had cried many times.

At least now, she could offer Cade the comfort that she had never had. Her heart opened and warmth spread through her. Rachel began to realize that her feelings for this man were more than friendship. As she sat holding him, it dawned on Rachel that whatever was growing between them was strong and good and wonderful. Another pain gutted her, dousing the happiness of the moment. There was no way she could fall in love with Cade.

Raising his head, Cade reluctantly released Rachel. He felt as if snakes were writhing in his gut; his stomach was still churning. He wiped his tears and sat up. Just the tender expression on Rachel's face nearly drove him to kiss her senseless. Yet, in spite of his own pain, Cade realized he'd abused Rachel's kindness. He'd broken his own commandment and promise to keep her at arm's length.

"I—I'm sorry. I shouldn't have…" His voice cracked.

"No, it was all right, Cade," she whispered, touching his slumped shoulder. "Something terrible happened today. I can see that."

Grimacing, Cade got up. If he didn't, he was going to do the unthinkable: take Rachel to his bed and make frantic love with her. Cade recognized his need and placed a steel grip on himself. "I'm sorry. We need to talk, but I can't right now. I'm going to get another shower and get some sleep. I'm exhausted."

Watching him hurry out of the living room, Rachel wanted to call after him. And then what? Undress and move into the shower with him? What would that accomplish? She was at a point where she couldn't lie to Cade any more. He didn't deserve that. Nor did his family. Hands clasped in her lap, Rachel could still feel the weight of his embrace. The sense that she had been an anchor to him was very real. But then, looking at her parents' marriage, Rachel had often seen her mother and father be that for one another during a crisis. Real love was about caring, supporting and protecting the other when hurt.

Looking up, the living room quiet now, Rachel understood as never before what real love was. It wasn't the love she'd felt at eighteen when she married Dirk Payson. Shaking her head, she muttered, "How stupid were you?" and got to her feet. She walked into the kitchen and cleared the table, put the dishes in the dishwasher and put the food in the refrigerator. Having things like this to do soothed her ruffled emotional state.

Would Cade talk about his experience tomorrow morning? Rachel didn't know. Since their kiss, they had kept their conversations light and not very intimate.

Looking out the window, she saw snowflakes dancing and twisting out of the darkened sky. The light from the kitchen illuminated them for just a moment. More snow. She was beginning to understand how a long winter could drive a person to distraction. Just thinking about the quilt made Rachel's spirits lift. Gwen had been right: having a hobby made the dark days of winter speed by. Rachel knew that Jenny would awaken in an hour or two and need to be fed. She busied herself at the kitchen counter getting everything ready to heat the goat's milk in the glass bottle.

CADE FELT LIKE hell warmed over the next morning. After a hot shower and a shave, he was back in his uniform and in the kitchen making himself breakfast at 5:30 a.m. The house was quiet. It was peaceful compared to how he felt inside himself. All night, he'd tossed and turned. If it wasn't the accident, it was holding Rachel and weeping in her arms. What did she think? He hadn't communicated at all with her. He'd used her without explanation. Frowning, Cade put scrambled eggs onto a plate. The toast popped up. Setting the skillet aside, he buttered the toast and took the thick slice of ham and put it on the plate.

It was still dark outside. Cade could tell by the buildup of snow on the ledge of the kitchen window that another four or five inches had fallen overnight. Sitting down at the table, he salted and peppered his eggs. Not feeling like eating, but knowing he must, his heart centered on Rachel.

"Cade?"

Snapping his head up, Cade saw Rachel standing tentatively at the entrance to the kitchen. She was dressed in a pale pink chenille robe that brushed her bare feet. Her sable hair was tousled around her sleepy face. Never had she looked more beautiful to Cade. There was such raw naturalness to Rachel that Cade swore she'd been born in the country and wasn't a city girl at all. It was a gut sense, that was all.

"Did I wake you?" he asked, his voice roughened.

Smiling sleepily, Rachel said, "No. I just woke up."

"Jenny?"

"Oh, she's still snoozing. She'll need to be fed around seven." Rubbing her eyes, she asked, "Are you okay, Cade?"

He stood up and pulled out a chair opposite his. "Come and sit down. Do you want coffee?" Somehow, he wanted to make up for snarling at her yesterday evening.

The sense of teamwork was there, as always. Rachel nodded. "I can get it. I know you need to leave for work in a little bit."

"No, let me." He headed for the coffeemaker.

"It's nice to be waited on," Rachel teased as she sat down. How handsome he looked in his uniform. She saw the holster with the gun and leather cartridge cases on the counter. He wore his Kevlar vest beneath his long-sleeved tan shirt.

Pouring the coffee, Cade tried to gather his thoughts. He brought the mug over and placed it in front of her. "I owe you an explanation for my behavior last night. I'm sorry, first of all, for yelling at you. That's unforgivable."

"It's okay," Rachel said, wrapping her hands around the mug. "You don't owe me an apology, Cade." How badly she wanted to reach out and touch his hand. Rachel didn't dare.

"Yes," Cade said grimly, "I do." He sat down. Holding her drowsy gaze, he said, "A tough accident happened yesterday. I'm not going into the details because it's too shocking for anyone to hear about, much less see." He took a sip of his coffee to fortify himself. "I threw up because of what I saw at the scene, Rachel. I didn't know it was coming. Sometimes…" and his voice trailed off. Gathering his courage, Cade offered, "Sometimes, things like that happen to anyone in law enforcement or in the firefighting business. We're only human. We see a lot, but sometimes, it goes beyond the pale and our bodies react to it."

Rachel sat quietly absorbing his husky voice laden with a backlog of unspoken feelings. She recognized the stormy look in Cade's gray eyes and knew more than she could ever share with him. Rachel wanted to say, *Yes, I know. After Dirk punched me and killed the baby I carried, I threw up for days afterward. Only after a kind nurse saw my chart and came in to tell me what was going on, did I realize what it really was—emotional shock and my body reacting to the horror of the deed.* Compressing her lips, Rachel held his anguished stare. "I can't even begin to understand the things you experience out there, Cade. But I do know this—you're kind and caring and if you come upon some terrible accident, you have to be affected by it. Deputy sheriffs aren't immune to human suffering. You're in the business of protecting people, so it has to be pretty awful for you at times like this."

"Yes," Cade said, relieved that she understood, "it is. I had this happen twice before in my career and both times, it was pretty shocking stuff."

Rachel wanted to soothe the pain she saw in his eyes and heard in his graveled tone. Cade had a tough time holding eye contact with her. The corners of his mouth were tucked in, telling her just how much he wasn't saying. "In this career, you're going to have times like this," she said in a quiet voice. "It's important you feel the emotions and not try to suppress them. They'll only come back later to haunt you in the form of nightmares."

Staring at her, Cade blinked. "You're right." He saw the grave look on Rachel's face and realized she was speaking from experience. That shook him. For whatever reason, he hadn't thought that Rachel had had anything but a happy life. He had been wrong; the look in her eyes was clear—hard-edged anguish was evident in them. He opened his mouth to ask, but then snapped it shut. He didn't want to go there just now. With his own can of worms to deal with, there was no sense in stirring up more. If Rachel had wanted to share more, she would have. He silently cursed his need for her, knowing it was impossible. Cade felt torn apart. It was becoming an agony to resist her and the love she offered.

Rachel added gently, "I've found the best way to counter those times is to do something positive. I found drawing lifts me above it. That doesn't mean I don't feel what I feel, it just means I let it work its way through me. Life isn't pretty, but we can do things to make it look more hopeful, Cade. Brighter."

Cade blinked. "You're right about that. The last couple of times I had this happen, I made sure I did positive things in the weeks afterward to sort of balance it. And it does help." The words, the tone coming from Rachel shook him. He was seeing another facet of her unknown until this moment. And then, Cade saw her frown and quickly cover up that part of herself she was sharing with him. In its place was a mask. Or, maybe a cover or lid over her own personal past.

Squirming internally, Rachel saw the sharpened look in Cade's gray eyes. She shouldn't have said what she had. That was from her real life, not from her cover story. Yet, she was helpless not to reach out and buoy him through this tragic time. Nervously, she rose. "Listen, I have to get a bath and get ready for the day."

Cade opened his mouth to speak, realizing Rachel was afraid. Her hands shook briefly as she picked up the coffee mug and walked to the sink.

Why? What was in her past to give her such intimate knowledge of trauma? The understanding in her tone was as real as it got. She had been speaking from experience. Scraping back his chair, Cade intercepted her as she walked toward the hall to the bedrooms.

"Wait," he pleaded, his hand wrapping around her upper arm and stopping her. Rachel turned, her eyes huge. He read anxiety and fear in them. "We need to talk, Rachel. How about after I get off work?"

His hand was strong without hurting. More like steadying. And oh, how Rachel wanted to take those steps forward into his arms and embrace Cade. And he could hold her. She wasn't sure who was more in need of being held—Cade or herself. "Sure," she answered.

After releasing her arm, Cade stood, hands at his sides, and repeated, "We need to talk."

Nodding, Rachel wrapped her arms across herself. "We will, Cade. Just be careful at work today. Okay?"

He wanted to lean down and kiss her, but stopped himself. Being around Rachel was like being married all over again. Only he'd made a promise to keep his hands off her. "Yes, I will," he said, his voice gruff. Turning, he went back to the table to finish off his breakfast. His arms ached to hold Rachel. His heart cried with need of her. *Dammit.*

March, Greenfield, Iowa

"WELL," DIRK SAID to Chip Malloy, "anything yet?"

Malloy took a drag off his cigarette. "Nothing yet."

Scowling, Dirk growled, "Hey, I'm paying you damned good money to find something on the phone lines to my ex's brothers. She's *got* to call them. She's too damned family-oriented." He stared out the window. It was snowing again. He hated snow. He'd hired Chip Malloy, who leased an apartment in the small town of Greenfield, Iowa. The man glared at him.

"Listen, this is dog work and you know it. I'm a damn good hacker but what you're asking for is someone to screen every friggin' call that comes in to those three guys at that farm. I've been on this for two weeks and there's no contact so far from either your ex or the mother, Daisy Donovan. You just have to be patient."

Snorting, Dirk paced the small apartment. "You'd think even if they are in the FBI witness protection program that they'd call their family from time to time."

"Maybe they will." Malloy pointed to his desktop computer and the other gadgets hooked up to it. "Every call is recorded here on my external hard drive. And it records the phone numbers of incoming and outgoing calls. I'm sure one of these days they'll call. It's just a waiting game."

Pulling out a smoke, Dirk pushed the cigarette

between his lips. "They're a damned tight family. Susan called her mother and brothers every week without fail when we were married. It was as if there was an invisible cord tied between them." Dirk shook his head and lit the cigarette. A cloud of smoke enveloped him.

"I don't know that much about the witness protection program," Malloy said, leaning back in his chair, hands behind his head. "Maybe they don't allow them to call home."

Snorting, Dirk paced some more as he smoked. "The bitch is too tied to her brothers not to call. And I want her bad, Malloy. Real bad."

Waving his hand in a distracted motion, Malloy nodded. "I get it, dude. But we have to be patient."

"I'm paying for this apartment," Dirk reminded him. "That's a lot of money. And I'm paying you for your time."

Shrugging, Malloy said, "Hey, dude, I got this under control. I've logged every incoming and outgoing call." He flipped his hand toward the logbook beside the computer. "Check it out. It's all there. I'm not idly wasting your money. And I can't help it if there is no connection so far."

Running his hand through his hair, Dirk growled, "Fine. Fine, I get it. But I'm headin' back to Florida. This snow and cold sucks. I got business ties down there that I'm getting up and runnin'. I can't afford to fly up here and look over your shoulder every couple of weeks."

Malloy grinned. "Hey, I like the company. I have nothing else to do but wait, watch and listen."

Turning, Dirk came back over to his desk. "The phone company can't track you. Right?"

"Right. They don't have a clue I'm listening in. I'm very good at what I do. I'm pure stealth, Payson. You're gettin' your money's worth."

Snorting, Dirk turned, sucked on his cigarette and muttered a curse. "Do you think in a month's time you'll hear from them?"

"Dunno."

"What *do* you know?"

Malloy scratched his itchy jaw. He hadn't shaved in three days. "I know my business. You hired me to wiretap and that's what I'm doing. I can't *make* something happen. That's why private investigators get paid so much money—to sit and wait. Patience is the name of the game, Payson."

Dirk stared at the twenty-three-year-old computer genius. In his world of drugs, Malloy was well-known to deliver the goods. He didn't come cheap, but he was the best. "What about trying to hack into the FBI witness protection base?"

"I can try. Never did that before, but it probably can be done."

"Has anyone else done it?"

"Not that I know of," Malloy said, dragging in a deep breath of smoke from his cigarette. He flipped the ashes into a yellow ceramic ashtray beside the computer. "The feds are gonna have layer upon layer of firewalls and security to ensure their source info doesn't get snatched."

"So what? Can you try?"

"Well," Malloy said, sitting up in his chair and dropping the cigarette into the ashtray, "that's gonna cost you more green."

"Figured that," Dirk muttered. "But at least you aren't just sitting on your ass here waiting for a call."

"True," the computer wizard said, smiling. "But I'll need another computer and that comes out of your green, not mine."

"Why can't you use the same one?" Dirk demanded, angry.

"Different tasks. Each one demands a lot of RAM and memory. No, you gotta cough up the bucks for me to go get what I need."

Pulling out his billfold, Dirk stubbed out his cigarette in the yellow ashtray. "Okay," he growled, irritated, "this ought to start the ball rollin'." He handed him a wad of one-hundred-dollar bills.

Taking them, Malloy counted through it all. "I need more than that."

Dirk never used credit cards. He always carried plenty of cash on him. Going to his jacket, which held special compartments inside, he unzipped a couple of pockets and hauled out more money. "Here. Will this meet your needs?"

Pleased, Malloy smiled. "Yep, I think that says it all. Thanks, dude. I'll get to work on it in the next few days."

"Can you break into it?"

Shrugging, Malloy said, "Won't know until I try. The feds have a lot of hackers of my quality on their payroll. They know how to stop people like me." Holding up his hand, he added, "But don't look so worried. I'll do my best."

"Can they follow you, though? Track you to here?" Dirk jammed his index finger down at the wooden floor.

"Oh, they could, but I'll give them such a rabbit chase they'll never find me. Not to worry, okay, dude?"

Dirk wasn't so sure. He donned his jacket and went back out into the freezing March weather. He'd hated coming back to Iowa in order to set up another cocaine ring. Dirk was a city boy and loved the excitement of the nonstop nightlife. Out here, the only excitement was watching cattle screwing one another in the springtime and that was it.

Sloshing through the snow and slush to get to his gray rental car, Dirk remained vigilant. Yes, he now had a beard, dyed his hair and wore glasses to disguise himself. Coming here wasn't bright, but he had to have face time with Malloy. Sliding into the seat, he closed the door and switched on the ignition. He turned up the heater to high, sat and looked around at the small apartment complex. The cops were looking for him, he was sure. Dirk had seen himself on the FBI's Ten Most Wanted list. Grinning, he pulled out a cigarette and lit it.

One way or another, he was going to get Susan. He wondered what name she lived under now. Where had the FBI hidden her? Dirk tried to think like the feds might think. If she was a farm girl would they put her somewhere similar? Or just the opposite to throw him off her trail? And what about Mrs. Donovan? Had the feds put them together? Were they living somewhere in the same house or apartment? That would be choice: if Malloy could find them together that would be even sweeter revenge.

Smoking, he looked through the beaded water across the windshield. The clouds were low and gray. The landscape white, with black, naked trees here and there. Dirk thought about going out to the Donovan farm and shooting the brothers, one by one. If he did that, it would bring the feds here and the manhunt for him would intensify a hundredfold. No, he had to wait. He had to let Malloy do his job. But damn, he wasn't patient. Not at all. Being on the run didn't bother him. Dirk was a master chameleon. He looked nothing like his prison picture. And the photo of him on the Internet and in the post office was a lean, shaved blond.

Rubbing his dark brown dyed beard, which he kept neatly trimmed, Dirk grinned. He turned on the windshield wipers for a moment and cleared the glass. Time to drive to the airport. With his false identification and looking like a worldly professor who taught at a university, he knew he could get past the Transportation Security Administration and anyone else looking for him. Since breaking out of prison, Dirk had flown a lot in order to reestablish his old drug ties and get them back together. He'd created a new network of cocaine drug dealers selling for him once again. The cash was rolling in and mounting higher and higher every week. His Mexican cartel boss in Juarez was more than pleased. Yes, everything was working out according to his plans.

With a savage grin, Dirk stubbed out the cigarette and then sent the butt out the crack of the driver's-side window. Quickly pressing a button to shut it up, Dirk felt the temperature rise immediately within the car. "Life is good, dude. Just be patient. She'll call home. I know she will." Dirk put the car in gear and left the apartment complex.

CHAPTER THIRTEEN

RACHEL TRIED TO quell the nervousness that had dogged her all day. Cade would be home for dinner any minute now. Outside the kitchen window, night had already fallen. What would he say? What should she do? How much should she say? Hating the lies, hating the predicament she'd gotten herself into, Rachel felt misery. She worked at the sink cutting up carrots and then stalks of celery for their nightly salad.

Gwen had come over earlier and when Rachel told her about Cade's reaction last night, she became grim. Gwen told her that sometimes being in law enforcement was torturous. Rachel quietly agreed. Gwen had patted her shoulder and told her that over time, Cade would work through his emotions concerning the accident. He always had before.

Cupping her hands, Rachel scooped up the chopped veggies and dropped them into the bowl. When the back door opened, her heart seized momentarily. Looking to her left, she saw Cade enter the room. His face was drawn, his eyes, usually glinting with life, were a dull gray. Rachel put on her unreadable mask for the sake of keeping things stable between them.

"Your daughter doesn't like carrots," she told him with a slight smile as she placed the salad bowl on the table. "Does she take after Tom or Lily?" Rachel hoped this small bit of conversation would ease the tension that suddenly inhabited the kitchen with his appearance.

Cade perked up a bit as he shrugged out of his jacket and hung it on the wall peg. Rachel looked incredibly beautiful in her jeans and a white blouse with a pink angora shell over it. "I think that's her father she's imitating. Tom never liked carrots, either." Cade shook his head and tried to smile, but failed. "That's pretty amazing."

"Yes," Rachel said drily, "it was pretty dramatic when she spat them out all over me."

Chuckling, Cade walked over to Jenny who was happily playing with a cracker in the high chair next to the table. Leaning down, he placed a soft kiss on the baby's head. "Now, Jenny, would you do that to this wonderful lady in your life? Spit carrots out at her?"

Jenny laughed and excitedly waved her arms as she saw Cade.

Warmth eased some of Rachel's tension as she watched Jenny respond to Cade's teasing. An unexpected ache settled in her chest. When she saw Cade and Jenny together, she wondered obliquely what the lives of her and Sarah might have been like had the child survived. Bad, judging from her experience with Payson. Seeing a positive relationship between a father and daughter lifted Rachel's spirits.

"Well," she teased lightly, walking to the oven and pulling on mitts, "Jenny thought it was funny. I think she might end up being an abstract artist someday."

Straightening, Cade nodded. Somehow, he had to be more social with Rachel. He saw how tense she had become. And he knew she was trying her best to make him feel welcome. The heaviness that had plagued him all day miraculously disappeared. He understood why. It was a combination of Rachel and Jenny. What man wouldn't be happy to come home nightly to these two? "Oh? Was there a particular design that engaged Jenny?"

Laughing a little, Rachel removed the pot roast from the oven and set it on a rack on the counter. "You could say that. After she spat them out I had all kinds of orange speckles and splotches across my yellow blouse."

"That sounds kind of pretty."

Nodding, Rachel pulled the tinfoil off the roast. The odor of curry and other Far Eastern spices filled her nostrils as she inhaled. "Next time it happens, I hope it's you on the firing line. Then we'll see how well you take her abstract art attempts."

"Fair enough," Cade murmured with a grin. "I'm going to change for dinner."

The tension ebbed out of Rachel. Cade came home, said hello to his daughter, changed into civilian attire and then they ate dinner together as a family. To her, it was the most important part of her day. She wondered whether Cade was going to talk with her tonight; he looked exhausted. Had he had another bad day on his shift? She hoped not.

CADE TOOK A quick shower, unlike the long one of this morning. Changing into jeans, a red long-sleeved fisherman's-knit sweater, his dark brown socks and favorite patched cowboy boots, he was ready to eat. Truth be told, he still wasn't hungry and he sure as hell didn't want a replay of last night. Combing his damp hair into place, he tried to avoid the look in his eyes. They were flat-looking. Lifeless. Well, that's how he felt right now. Still, just having Rachel and Jenny out in the kitchen waiting for him gave him sustenance. They would never realize that, but they did and he was grateful.

Sauntering out to the kitchen, Cade saw that Rachel had everything on the table. Going to the fridge, he asked, "What do you want to drink?"

"Just water," Rachel answered, settling into her chair next to Jenny. She gave the baby another cracker.

Cade took a plastic water bottle from the fridge. "Makes two of us."

She watched him as he walked to the counter. He was incredibly masculine, and yet his vulnerability was written across his face. Normally, he wore a hard mask with no expression. Whatever had happened yesterday, he had been unable to hide his real feelings from her. Cade's beard was shadowy at this time of day and gave him a decidedly dangerous look. He was dangerous to her heart. And oh, how Rachel fantasized in her what-if world. What if she didn't have this awful past haunting her? What if she could honestly move forward in a sincere relationship with Cade? Free of the past? Of the always-constant danger? Of the entanglements?

"How are you feeling?" she asked quietly as he sat down on the other side of Jenny.

"Let's put it this way," Cade confided, pulling his chair up to the table after placing their glasses in front of the plates, "I haven't eaten a whole lot today. I don't want a replay of last night, either."

Feeling deeply for him, Rachel said, "Then just take a little. How long does this kind of reaction go on for you?"

Cade spooned some of the carrots and potatoes onto his plate. "Usually no more than twenty-four hours." He met and held her worried gaze. His voice lowered with feeling. "I never got to say thank-you for your help last night."

Rachel stopped herself from reaching out to touch Cade's arm. "You're welcome. I think you should eat lightly. Just watch some TV and chill out tonight. What do you think?"

Cade watched as she gave him a very small slice of beef and then ladled some rich brown gravy over it. His stomach growled. He knew he was hungry, but he was afraid to overeat tonight. "Sounds good," he murmured. "I'd like to sit and talk with you sometime after we get the kitchen cleaned up."

"Sure," Rachel said. Her heart contracted with absolute fear. What would he say? Do? Trapped, Rachel again felt anxiety riffle through her. The longer she stayed here, the more panic-stricken she felt. How could she balance Jenny's need for a good nanny with the danger of Payson looking for her? Most of the time, she wanted to leave the ranch in order to protect them. And every time she thought of doing that, she wanted to cry. This house had become home. Cade made it like that for her, whether he realized it or not. Plus, her handler continued to tell her she was in the best place on earth to be hidden from Dirk. *Stop worrying,* she chided herself. *Enjoy the moment, instead.*

AFTER PUTTING JENNY to bed, Cade kept the door ajar so that they could hear the baby if she woke up. He walked down the hall to the living room. Rachel had some of the illustrations she'd painted today sitting on the coffee table between the couch and the overstuffed chair.

"These look great," he said, meaning it as he sat down in the chair and picked one of them up.

Rachel tried to tamp down her anxiety. "Thanks."

"How are you coming along on the illustrations for the assignment?" he asked, setting them down on the coffee table.

"I'm on time to meet the class deadline."

"We still need to get you out of here and go hunt up a moose or two for you to see in person."

"Well," Rachel said, "it hasn't exactly been great driving weather. I've never seen it snow so often as it does here."

Cade sat on the edge of the chair, legs apart, with his elbows resting on his thighs. His hands were clasped in front of him. "You're right. Come early April, though, it begins to change and it's a good time to find them."

Rachel picked up the material next to her. "I wanted to show you the fabric I've chosen to make Jenny's first quilt." It was a diversion, but she needed one right now. Her heart was pounding with fear and anxiety.

Taking the cloth, Cade studied it. "I'm really glad you like quilting. And Jenny will love this, too."

Her heart picked up in beat as he handed the material back to her, their fingers briefly touching one another. "Thanks. Gwen came over this morning and we were talking about how to cut the material. She loaned me a cutting board, a ruler and a rotary tool to do it with."

Nodding, Cade drank her in. There was fear in her eyes once more. Fear of him? Fear of their relationship that just seemed to be there no matter how he tried to evade it? Not that he'd helped things last night. "You'll do fine. Mom has always said that quilters are artists with fabric. And you're an artist already so I'm sure you'll find this medium a lot of fun."

"I already do." Rachel sobered and held his dark stare. "You said we needed to talk?" She could no longer prolong the agony she felt in her gut. Better to get it over with.

Cade immediately sobered. "I broke the contract I had with you. I don't know what happened last night except to say I was in such emotional shock that I wasn't thinking straight. It's not an excuse," Cade said, his voice low. Holding her gaze, he once more saw what he thought was desire—for him. But Cade couldn't be sure and didn't want to go there. "The cabin is available to you, Rachel. I went back on my word to keep you at arm's length. You're my employee. I know it's more work to be trudging between the house and cabin, but I want you to feel relaxed and not tense when I come home. I don't want you thinking I'm going to hit on you again. That wasn't my intent last night, I swear it wasn't."

"Last night," Rachel choked, "you were hurting, Cade. What you did was human. I didn't see it as breaking our agreement at all. I was glad I could do something for you. Holding someone when they're hurting isn't wrong."

The softness of her tone flowed over him like sun warming the iciness he still felt inside from the trauma of the accident scene yesterday. Hanging his head, Cade stared at his clasped hands in front of him. "I don't know what happened," he admitted hoarsely. "I just—came apart. It's shock, that I know. People react to shock in all kinds of different ways. This is my way, I guess...."

Rachel had to stop herself from rising to walk over and wrap her arms around his hunched shoulders. There was such anguish in the lines of his face and body. She had to sit there and not respond, because if she did, her reaction might be read the wrong way. Swallowing hard, Rachel whispered, "Listen, Cade, I did not take what happened last night as a romantic trick to get me into your arms if that's what you're thinking." She opened her hands, her voice pleading. "You're human. We're all there at some point. I was happy to be here and be able to hold you. I wish, well, I wish I could have done more to help you. I can see how much this hurts you. It hurts me to watch you suffering."

Lifting his head, Cade melted beneath the warmth of her searching blue gaze. How beautiful Rachel was—inside and out. He almost told her that, but swallowed the words. She was an employee, not his lover. But, God, how much Cade wanted Rachel to be that—and more. "I'm just afraid—well, I'm afraid I'll drive you off, Rachel. And Jenny needs you so much." *I need you.* Mouth quirking, Cade went on. "I don't want you thinking I'm stalking you. Or trying to use a situation to manipulate you into my arms." *Or my bed, next to me where I'll try my damnedest to please you like you deserve....*

Her heart tore open a little more over his rasped

words. "Oh, Cade, I never thought that for a moment. Everyone needs comfort at bad times. I never saw last night as a manipulation of any kind. You needed to be held." Rachel forced a small smile, and the look of relief in Cade's eyes made her stomach unknot. He believed her. That was good. A bitter taste in the back of her mouth remained. If he only knew that she was a liar.

"Thanks," Cade whispered. "I really needed to know how you felt. I never want to put you at risk or take advantage of you. Because I'm not."

"You're not the type," she told him, sitting up and stretching her arms to relieve the tension in them. "Why don't you watch some TV? Just rest tonight?"

Cade shrugged. "What about you? I was thinking this morning about the fabric you had on the couch last night. I talked to my mother before I left for work. I had bought Abby a Bernina sewing machine from my mom's store." He shrugged. "It never got used. But it's here, in her sewing room. Would you like to use it?"

"Why…sure, if you don't mind?" Rachel searched his expression for any hesitation, but she saw nothing but happiness.

"Mind? No, not at all." Cade rose. With a gesture, he said, "Come on, I'll get it out for you. My mom had bought the special sewing table for Abby. I'll set it up so you can quilt away."

Standing, Rachel followed him. "That would be lovely, Cade. Thanks so much for the unexpected gift. Gwen had told me I could use one of the sewing machines they keep for classes at her store."

"You don't need to," he said as he walked down the hall. Opening a door on the left, he switched on the light. Cade came into this room once a month to clean it. There had been too many poignant memories of Abby quilting and sewing in here for him to remain in it for any amount of time.

Rachel had been in the room to clean it. Light and airy, it was almost as large as the master bedroom. She watched as Cade slid back a door on a closet. He brought out three sewing tables and set them up.

"Abby had these three tables placed around the room. Two were for cutting fabric and other stuff," Cade explained as he brought the tables upright on their legs. "This one is for the sewing machine. It's a bit lower and allows you to have the sewing machine at the right level so it doesn't kill your shoulders and back." He drew out a lime-green suitcase that said *Tutto* on it. "Now this," he said, hefting it up to the middle table, "is the special suitcase that is built to carry the Bernina she used. You can take it to class with you."

Fascinated, Rachel said, "This is like Christmas."

Cade felt the rest of his worry dissolve. It was positive to focus on something that would give Rachel joy. And how much he wanted her happy. He loved seeing the joy in her eyes. "Hey, after the rotten Christmas you had, this is a good thing."

After unzipping the side of the suitcase he carefully pulled out the Bernina.

"There," Cade said, placing the machine on the sewing desk. "Here's your Bernina. It's called a 'patchwork' machine and its focus is for people who want to quilt. Take a look." He stepped aside.

Rachel leaned over and gave the machine a thorough examination. "Gwen was telling me that they have special classes on how to use a Bernina. I think that I'll take those courses first before I do anything with this one."

A lightness moved through Cade as he walked to the open door. "Do what you want. I don't think you'll hurt it at all, Rachel."

Touching the white machine with her fingertips, she said, "Classes first."

"Okay," Cade said. "I'm going to read the evening newspaper."

Rachel stood there and listened as the pleasant thunk of his cowboy boots disappeared down the hall. She turned and looked around. The room was painted a sunny yellow color. Rachel wondered if the bright cotton curtains across the only window were made by Abby. No one, it seemed, dodged the awful realities that life threw at them. No one.

After their sweet moment, Rachel felt relief. Her talk with Cade had been open and without emotional drama. How different from her marriage to Dirk. Reaching out, Rachel touched the machine once again. How many times had Abby used it? What had she sewn on this machine? And if she'd made a quilt, Rachel had not seen it in the house. Or was the quilt on Cade's bed made by her? So many questions. Rachel knew she had no business asking him any of them.

And then, her cell phone rang.

Rachel froze. Her phone never rang and she ditched it each month after talking with her mother. The FBI had taught her to never use the same cell phone twice.

Shutting the door, Rachel pulled the phone out of her pocket. It was her handler, Brenda.

"Hi, Brenda. What's wrong?" Rachel said, keeping her voice low so that Cade wouldn't overhear her.

"Just wanted to give you an update. We had police in Des Moines, Iowa, think they saw Dirk Payson."

Her heart began a wild pounding in her chest. Rachel's voice dropped to a ragged whisper. "Are you sure? What would he be doing *there*?" Fear for her brothers' lives slammed through her. Rachel closed her eyes, wanting to scream.

"I said *think*. We're not sure yet. We got a photo ID on him from TSA video. Right now we're running it through our office to see if it is him or not."

"What if it is? What's he doing there, Brenda? My God…"

"Don't freak out yet," the FBI handler warned. "What I want to do is send you a copy of the photo. I want you to look at it and you tell me if you think it's Dirk. I'll send it now."

Rachel pulled the phone away and heard it make a bell-like sound that meant a jpeg had been forwarded to her. She pressed some buttons and looked on the small, narrow screen. A gasp tore from her. No matter how much Dirk had disguised himself, she would always recognize his narrow, close-set eyes anywhere.

"Yes, that's him," Rachel rasped. "Is he going to kill my brothers, Brenda?" Terror leaked into her voice and tears jammed into her eyes. Rachel pushed them back. This was no time to get hysterical.

"Thanks for the ID. I thought so myself, but my boss wanted to run the facial recognition on this to be sure."

"What does this mean? What are you going to do?"

"First things first. Payson has fraudulent identification. We've got all the info from TSA and I have a team working on it right now. He never uses credit cards because they're too easy to trace. Payson always pays in cash for the tickets, for the rental cars and anything else he needs."

"You said he was on a flight? To where?"

"Back to Miami."

Relief made her shake. "He's going back to his old stomping grounds."

"Yes, it appears so."

"And my brothers? Are they okay?" Oh, how she yearned to talk with them!

"They're fine. Like I told you before, they know

Payson is on the loose. The local law enforcement is keeping an eye on the farm. So, just start taking some deep breaths and relax, okay? I'm assuming you're getting out and filtering into the local population? You can't hide. You must live a normal life so people don't get suspicious of you. I know there's a fine balance between being out in public and hiding in your home, but you need to keep a balance between the two."

Pressing her fingers to her brow, Rachel nodded. "Yes, I take a quilt class. I go get groceries. But I still try to keep a low profile. I think I've met that balance."

"Good. Once we get official identification, Rachel, I'll call your mother and the law enforcement who keeps tabs on her. I'm sure Payson doesn't realize he's been located. I'll be working with Miami-Dade County law enforcement to find him. And I'll keep you abreast of our efforts."

"Thank you so much. I really appreciate that, Brenda. I just live in terror of him being close."

"I know you do," Brenda said gently. "But everyone is working on this. Stop worrying, okay? We've got it handled."

"Should I throw this cell away and go for the next one with the new number?" One call was all that could be made on it.

"Yes, do that. I've got all the numbers of the cells you have in your possession."

"Right, I will. Thanks, Brenda. This is really good news."

"Yes, it is. How are things going there for you? We haven't talked in a while."

"Okay," she answered. "Cade is wonderful. I love taking care of Jenny. I just wish—well, I wish so badly that I could tell Cade the truth. And I worry about Dirk being loose. Half the time I want to run away to protect this family from him. I know if he finds me, he'll go out of his way to kill anyone nearby."

"I know this is putting you on edge, but you need some place to hide. Wyoming is perfect. I don't want you to think of leaving there, Rachel. There's no need to run. I'm sorry you can't tell Cade, but that's how leaks get started. You can never tell anyone, Rachel. You know that."

Miserably, Rachel nodded. "Yes, I know."

"Okay, gotta run. I'll be in touch when we know more."

Rachel flipped the phone closed and slid it back into her pocket. She stood there with her hands pressed against her cheeks. Fighting back relief and fear at the same time, she wanted to cry. But she couldn't. Cade might catch her and then she'd have to explain why. No, whatever she did, she had to tough it out and remain the liar that she was.

CHAPTER FOURTEEN

"I WANT YOU to change my mug," Dirk told Mexican physician Dr. Jorge Morales. Dirk had sneaked across the border in another disguise—clean-shaven and dyed red hair. Word had gotten to him that the cops at the Iowa airport had identified him, but it was too late. He'd gotten off the Miami flight and was long gone before the news reached Florida law enforcement.

The Mexican doctor nodded. *"Sí, señor."*

Dirk grinned. He sat in an air-conditioned office in a high-rise in Mexico City. Dr. Morales worked for the drug cartels. His business was to change faces with a scalpel so that a person could no longer be identified as a criminal. "Make me look pretty," he told the doctor.

The physician nodded and smiled beneath his black mustache. "Of course, Señor Payson." He pulled out several books and opened them up. "Let's talk about what changes can be made and which ones you'd like. We'll work together this hour to redesign your face."

Leaning forward, Dirk felt excitement. He didn't like the eight weeks of enforced hiding in

Mexico's Yucatán Peninsula while his face got rid of the bruising and swelling, but he did enjoy the fact that U.S. law enforcement would no longer be able to identify him. He was also getting a new passport, social security number and the whole nine yards, so once he went back into U.S. territory, he'd be invisible to police.

"I just don't like the time it takes," he griped, moving to the "chins" section of the book.

"I understand, *señor*, but what you are asking, it will take a good eight weeks."

Dirk shrugged. "I guess I can't complain. I'll be at an exclusive resort, have my own apartment, maid service and meals brought to me."

"You will live the good life, *señor*, while you heal." The doctor smiled a little. "The authorities will never be able to use any facial recognition software to find you again. You will be the proverbial wolf among the sheep. And the sheep won't have a clue."

Dirk intently studied the chin illustrations and suggested changes for his shape of face, and muttered, "Well, no matter. I got a hacker dude looking to find my ex-wife. He said it would take time. Now, I can use that time to make some serious changes."

"You will be quite handsome when I'm done with you," the doctor said. "I will broaden your cheekbones with implants. Your nose, which is very aquiline, will have a slight curve. Just enough to fool the software. And your chin, instead of receding, will be strong and masculine-looking. I'm having my optometry department create special green contact lenses so that your eye color will change, as well."

Dirk nodded. He liked the sleek chrome-and-glass office, and this doc was efficient and organized. The doctor was a plastic surgeon of great renown. He worked for the drug cartels on the side, and cash came in by the wheelbarrow load for his face-changing work. Greed, Dirk felt, was the best motivator in the world.

"You ever botch a face?" he demanded, giving the doctor a steely gaze.

"Never," Morales said proudly. And then he flashed Dirk a toothy white grin. "Look at it this way, *señor*. If I was bad at what I did, I'd be dead by now. *Sí?*"

"Sí," Dirk said, a grin pulling at the corners of his mouth. "Listen, can you give me fuller lips? Chicks dig men with a full lower lip." He pointed to his. "Mine's too thin. Can you fix that, too?"

"Of course." The doctor pointed toward his ears. *"Señor,* your ears stick out quite a bit. I intend to pin them back. It will give your face a completely different look. It's a quick, easy fix but one that will make a world of difference."

"I like that," Dirk said, pleased. "My old man always called me Dumbo ears." He snickered.

"Excellent. We'll make the change," the doctor murmured, typing the notes into his laptop.

After choosing the appropriate chin and cheeks

as well as a less-pronounced brow, Dirk felt exhilarated. It was almost akin to the cocaine highs he enjoyed so much. The doctor had taken a photo of his face and then typed in the changes. What came out in the printer was astoundingly different. Dirk stared down at the photographic paper in his hands.

"This is the new you," the doctor said in a pleased tone. "I also suggest that you shave your head, which is now quite the fashion. With a thin red mustache that you can dye every few days and your green contact lenses, no one will recognize you, *señor*."

Dirk stared mutely at the photo in his hands. How far he'd come from a scrawny Dumbo-eared teen with acne all over his face to this. The man in the photo was damned handsome in comparison. Tears leaked into his eyes, but Dirk quickly shoved them back. Too emotional to speak, he quirked his mouth instead.

"Do you like it, *señor?*" the doctor asked, concern in his tone.

Clearing his throat, Dirk blurted, "Yes…yes, I like it. A lot."

Relief in his face, Dr. Morales sat in his chair. "*Bueno*, good. Well, look at it this way, Señor Payson, you will have eight weeks of rest and recuperation. And, like a butterfly coming out of a cocoon, you will emerge handsome and different."

"Yeah," Dirk laughed giddily, "from worm to butterfly. I like that, Doc."

"You keep the photo, *señor*. I'm scheduling you for surgery tomorrow morning. After that, you'll recover for a week here in my office in a nice little area reserved for special patients. After that week, you will then have your face wrapped in bandages and you'll be driven by limo to the resort where you'll stay for another seven weeks. One of my assistants, Dr. Gomez, will be there to check up on you. There is enough business of face-changing for me to have him there permanently, so you will not have to worry about not receiving appropriate medical attention. We are there for you."

As he stared down at the photo once more, Dirk's voice cracked. "Why didn't I do this a long time ago? I'll have women crawling all over me. They won't be able to keep their hands off me."

Chuckling pleasantly, the doctor sat up and placed his pad and pen on his desk. "Aaah, *señor*, you will truly be sought after by the ladies. Women like beautiful men and you will be one of them."

Dirk said, "Well, I've got to be in the U.S., but that can be put on hold for a while." He laughed.

The doctor rose to his feet. "Come, my receptionist will take you to your apartment here in the high-rise. She will give you instructions so that you are properly prepped for tomorrow morning's surgery."

Happiness threaded through Dirk. He gripped the photo as he left the office. From worm to butterfly. Hell yes, he liked that idea. As Dirk followed the older woman to the shiny brass elevators in the lobby, he smiled to himself. Once his hacker friend got a trail on Susan, he would find her and kill her. And she'd never see him coming. She wouldn't recognize him at all. Chortling to himself, Dirk stepped into the elevator. Yes, all of a sudden, life was looking up. He might have to spend March and April at a posh, exclusive high-end resort on the Yucatán Peninsula, but after that, in May, he'd be back in the U.S. And looking for her.

RACHEL STOOD OUT on the porch with the throwaway cell phone pressed to her ear. The March thaw was well on its way. The icicles steadily dripped along the porch gutters across the outside door. Spring was coming, thank goodness. She heard her FBI handler clear her throat at the other end.

"Rachel, I'm checking in with you. We had a lead on Payson but there was a snafu in communications between the Des Moines law enforcement and TSA down at the Miami airport."

Her heart sank. "Oh, no, Dirk is on the loose."

"Yes, I'm sorry. I'm so pissed I can't see straight. I'm glad we have a new President in office. He's made it a priority to get all law enforcement talking with one another on the same damn frequency. We could have arrested Payson as he got off the plane, but TSA muffed it."

Closing her eyes, Rachel felt her gut knotting. "What should I do, Brenda? Should I leave here?"

"No, don't do that. He doesn't know where you

or your mother are. You're both safe. Just remember that, okay?"

"What do you think has happened to him? Where has he gone? Is he in Miami? He loves that city."

"Well, I've got Dade County law enforcement turning over every nook and cranny to look for Payson. In fact, the FBI has gone above and beyond and sent every law-enforcement agency in the U.S. a new wanted poster on him. We're really hustling on this. Not only do we want him captured to keep you and your family safe, but we know that Payson will reestablish his ties with coke dealers in the Midwest he worked with before. We really don't want that, either."

A little relief flowed through Rachel. "I—I'm just worried, Brenda. I worry that this family I'm with will be killed by Dirk. I know his temper. He's a sociopath. He won't think anything of killing an infant, the parents of Cade or Cade himself. I just can't bear to think of that happening."

"I understand," Brenda soothed, "but look at this another way, Rachel: you have to live somewhere. You have to work to keep a cover. So, no matter where you might go, you will involve others simply because you have to have a job. You see that, don't you?"

"It's enough my brothers and mother pay for my choice," Rachel said, a sob lodging in her throat and making her voice raspy. "I—I just feel at my wits' end, Brenda. I'm so shaken by this. I love Jenny. I love Cade's parents…." She almost said, *I love Cade*. The shock of that startled her for a moment. Rachel had no time to feel her way through that epiphany. Choking down the sob, Rachel pleaded, "Brenda, get him! Find him and get him behind bars. Please? I feel horrible about involving the entire Garner family. They do not deserve violence coming to their doorstep. My God, Jenny has lost both her parents. She doesn't need Dirk coming here to kill her!"

"Take it easy," Brenda said in a gentle tone. "Just breathe, Rachel. Breathe. You're getting too emotional about this and that's not like you. What's different this time? Why are you wigging out?"

Anger stirred in Rachel. "Wigging out? I don't think so, Brenda! Before, Dirk was behind bars and we were safe. Now, we're not safe. I don't think my reaction and my concern for Cade's family is unwarranted. I've created enough trouble for my own family, much less involve the Garners, don't you think?"

"You're right, you're right," Brenda said. "Look, the witness protection program isn't perfect, Rachel. We're doing the best we can. We've stepped up surveillance on Payson by involving every local police department in this nation. You have no idea the cost to do that, but you shouldn't have to be concerned about it, either. We want your ex-husband off the streets as much as you do. Please, just know that we're on top of it as much as we can be."

"His drug-lord boss is from Mexico City. Could he have skipped out of the country and gone south?" Rachel wondered.

"We're looking at surveillance tapes at all border crossings right now," Brenda said. "I think Payson has skipped the country."

"He could hide in Mexico for a long time and then come back across in a disguise."

"Yes, that's what our team thinks. We're sending out special instructions to border agents and border-crossing points from one end of the U.S. to the other about Payson and his habits."

Rachel stared out the back-porch door. The temperature was in the forties, the sun shining brightly, the sky an incredible blue. Ordinarily, she'd be jumping up and down for joy over the welcome change of weather. But not now. Grimly, she said, "Dirk is a chameleon, Brenda. He was always changing his looks even when I knew him. Dumb me, I just thought he did it because he was vain. I didn't know he was dyeing his hair and changing his hairstyle to fool people in the drug business."

"You can't have known what he was really doing, Rachel. You married the guy thinking he was on the up and up. You don't marry a man thinking he's a major player in a Mexican drug cartel."

"No, I guess not," Rachel whispered, closing her eyes. "I just keep eating myself up over this, Brenda. Why didn't I see him for who he was? My mother and brothers didn't like him at all. My mother put up such a fuss over me marrying him that I ran away with him to Las Vegas. I went along with it because I was so in love with him. I wanted to marry him! I thought my family was wrong."

"Listen, honey," Brenda said in a confidential voice. "You were raised on an Iowa farm. You led a pretty cloistered life out there in the Midwest. Drugs and stuff like that aren't as active in the Greenfield area where you grew up. You were ignorant, Rachel. That's all. You can't keep punishing yourself for what happened. Payson lied to you. Here you thought he was a big-time software salesman making big bucks for his fake company. He was very good at convincing you."

"Yes, he was. I swallowed everything like the stupid ditz I was."

"Stop that," Brenda said sternly. "You couldn't know you married a drug dealer. There was a part of him that wanted a real family, Rachel. You know the readout on him and his family. They were meth parents. As a child, Dirk was a throwaway kid. His father beat him black and blue, broke his nose and some ribs later on. I think he saw the innocence in you that he'd wanted and never had himself. I think he was trying to start all over."

"I know," Rachel murmured. "The psychology isn't lost on me. I can feel compassion for him now. I know what happened to him, but that doesn't mean I condone what he did to me and Sarah."

"I'm not trying to suggest that you should," Brenda said. "I'm just trying to get you to understand that Payson saw a way out through you. Rachel, you were young, beautiful, innocent and your family loved you. I'm sure on some sick, twisted psychological level Dirk saw a way to right all the wrongs of his terrible childhood by marrying you and surrounding himself with a healthy family. He would no longer be treated as he was when he was a young child."

Rachel understood. She'd had five years to digest the "real" Dirk that the FBI had provided to her as way of information during the trial. "Yet, his dark side took over. He tried to kill me and he killed Sarah."

"Knowing what fuels Payson helps us some, but not completely," Brenda agreed, sadness in her voice. "And you paid the ultimate price for what he wanted and didn't have the ability to move toward. He fell back into being a drug dealer just like his parents."

"Bad blood."

"Yes," Rachel agreed. She saw Cade pulling into the slushy driveway. He was on duty today and was coming home for lunch. "Brenda, I need to go. Cade just drove into the driveway."

"Okay, I'll keep you informed. Throw that cell away and go to the next one on the list."

"You bet I will," she said, flipping the cover closed. Turning, Rachel walked back into the warm kitchen. Cade had asked for a grilled cheese sandwich for lunch today. That was easy enough to fix. After stuffing the cell into the pocket of her jeans, Rachel quickly went about gathering the items. Under no circumstances did she want Cade to see her on the phone. He'd ask who she was talking to and Rachel was sick of lying to him.

Her hands shook a bit as she placed the skillet on the stove. She'd almost blurted to Brenda that she loved Cade! *Where* had that come from? Upset, Rachel brought out the butter and the block of sharp cheddar cheese from the fridge. She heard the porch door open and shut.

"Hey," Cade called, entering the kitchen. "How are things in your corner of the world?" Rachel seemed harried as she sliced the cheese at the counter. Cade always looked forward to being in the area of the ranch during his shift so he could drop by for lunch. So far, it had been a quiet day and he was grateful.

"Doing fine," Rachel said, looking up to his warm gray gaze. In that split second, Rachel realized with a terrible, sinking feeling that she was falling in love with Cade Garner. "How's the day going?" she forced herself to ask with a lightness she didn't feel.

Cade set his briefcase on the table and then got out of the warm nylon jacket and hung it on a hook. "Great. I'm here. It doesn't get any better than that."

Rachel nodded. "There's no place like home."

Grinning, Cade walked to the table. He opened the briefcase and brought out a bunch of papers and set them next to the plate and flatware Rachel had laid out earlier. "Amen to that. You look worried. Everything okay?"

Trying to stop her frowning, Rachel's heart leaped in fear. Cade was a deputy. He had honed his visual skills much more than most people. "Uh, yes, just a busy morning is all."

"Jenny?"

"Oh, no, she's fine. She's sleeping right now."

"Good," Cade said, putting the briefcase on the floor next to his chair. "Anything I can help you with?"

"No, I'm fine. Thanks. Just sit there and relax." How badly Rachel wanted just to turn around, run into his arms and cry. Crying always helped relieve her tension, but she couldn't do it. And now, knowing that she loved Cade, Rachel had to be extra careful with her body language and her choice of words with him. Under no circumstance could Cade know how she really felt.

Hearing him rustle through papers, which he routinely brought home to work on, Rachel felt a tiny bit of relief. She forced herself to think about the grilled cheese sandwich in the skillet. She got a jar of sweet pickles from the fridge, and, after putting it all on a plate, she turned and walked over to where he sat.

Cade had a wanted poster in his hand. As she drew near, Rachel gasped and nearly dropped the plate.

Cade looked up sharply at Rachel. She had stopped, her face turning pale, her eyes huge and filled with terror. "What?" he asked, dropping the papers and getting up. "Rachel? Are you all right? What's wrong?" Without thinking, he put his hands on her shoulders, the plate between them.

Gulping, Rachel stared past Cade and down at the paper on the table. It was a photo of Dirk Payson. Then, she remembered Brenda had told her that they were sending out new information to every small police department in the U.S. That meant this one. Trying to breathe, she thrust the plate toward Cade. It broke the light hold he had on her shoulders.

"Here," she rattled, "take this. I'm fine. I'll be back in a minute…" And she turned on her heel and hurried down the hall to the bathroom.

Stunned, Cade stood in the quiet kitchen with the sandwich in hand. He watched Rachel disappear into the bathroom, the door shutting louder than usual. What was wrong? Scowling, he went to the table and sat down. Once more he had to remind himself they weren't married. She was an employee, not his lover, as he so desperately wanted. If Rachel wanted to ask for help, she'd ask. Muttering under his breath, Cade pushed the papers aside and sat down. Women had ups and downs men never had. He reminded himself that women had an awful lot more hormones in place than men did, too. And who knew? Maybe her hormones were making her more out of sorts than usual. As he enjoyed the grilled cheese sandwich, Cade thought that maybe Rachel was getting cabin fever. It struck anyone who faced eight months of winter every year. And she wasn't used to being housebound for so long, so this was probably just a bad day for her.

Sooner or later, Cade knew, she'd reappear. And tonight he'd broach the topic with her when she wasn't so upset. Picking up the papers once more, he read about Dirk Payson. The FBI had called his office captain and they were making a big push to find this guy and get him back behind bars. Cade committed the man's face to memory. As a patrolling deputy, it was his job to be on the lookout for such a criminal.

CHAPTER FIFTEEN

CADE WAS CONCERNED as he drove his cruiser along the dirt roads of Teton County. After Rachel had seen the wanted poster on Dirk Payson yesterday, she'd paled like the proverbial ghost. Worse, he hadn't seen her after supper that night. She'd gone directly to her room, and his shift forced him to be up and out of the house long before she was awake in the morning.

The gray, scudding clouds signaled the end of a front coming through with a promise of much more blue sky. Slats of sunlight, like flashlight beams, flooded the valley. He was on a call to another small ranch, the Bar T, where there'd been a fight between cowboys. One of them had a busted jaw and Cade had been sent to collect the information. The winters were long and hard in Wyoming and about this time of year—late March, early April— cabin fever struck even the hardiest of residents. This was no place for the faint of heart.

The snow and mud combined, and he could hear it against the cruiser as he drove slowly but surely down the rutted road toward the ranch in the distance. His mind turned once more to Rachel.

Why had she blanched when she saw that poster? Something was going on. Grimly, Cade's mind wandered from the sublime to the ridiculous. Did Rachel know this suspect? Worse, was he a family member? Their names weren't the same and Rachel had said she'd never been married. There was nothing in her background check to tie her to Payson. So why the violent reaction?

As he slowed down and drove through the large timber entrance to the Bar T, Cade decided that tonight after dinner he would gently try to broach the subject with her. God help him, he was falling in love with her and he knew it. But did she love him? Cade didn't think so. Rachel was always careful around him, didn't give him "the look" or any other body language to suggest it. Yet, their one melting kiss haunted him. He wanted to taste her more deeply, gather Rachel into his arms and make tender love with her. Cade thought his fervent dreams of needing Rachel showed that he was emerging from the death of his family. That wasn't a bad thing, but Cade wasn't interested in just any woman. He was interested solely in Rachel.

As he pulled up to the log ranch house, a couple of black-and-white Australian heeler dogs came out barking to greet him. Most ranches had sheepdogs or heelers to help herd the cattle along with the cowboys on horseback or on ATV machines. For a moment, as Cade gathered his clipboard and made a call to dispatch to let them know he'd arrived on the scene, he was still centered on Rachel.

His mother, Gwen, had fallen in love with Rachel in so many ways. When Abby had died, he'd seen a little bit of his parents die, too. They had loved her. And now, Rachel and Jenny were bringing the rest of his family as well as himself back from that dark, shocking event. Cade had seen his family go from depression and grief to hope once again. The combination of Rachel and Jenny was like an IV given at the local hospital, a blood transfusion. As Cade opened the door to his cruiser, the cold, cutting spring wind rushed into the interior, wiping out the warmth.

No, tonight, he would have to have a talk with Rachel and get to the bottom of this. What would the answer be? Something as simple as that she was repulsed by the picture? Should he not bring his work home and spread it across the table where she had to look at it? Cade felt that was probably the case and he was willing to change his habits and use the small desk in the master bedroom to work on, instead. He didn't want to upset Rachel like that again. There was no need for it.

"I'D LIKE TO talk to you about that wanted poster I brought home yesterday at lunch," Cade said as they sat with their after-dinner coffee at the kitchen table.

Rachel frowned. "Oh…that." Instantly, adrenaline shot to her bloodstream. Her heart beat harder.

Searching her closed expression, Cade studied Rachel in the tense silence that suddenly sprang up between them. He kept his voice gentle. "I know these posters can be upsetting. These guys aren't stellar and some are pretty ugly and threatening to a normal person." Searching for the words, he held her shadowed, fearful gaze. "I've had these posters out on the table before and you never had that kind of reaction to them."

All day, Rachel had found herself in the worst turmoil of her life. She seesawed violently between telling Cade the truth and trying to build lies once more to cover her reaction at seeing the picture of Dirk on the table. The weight on her shoulders pressed down upon her to such a degree that Rachel felt as if she could barely get a breath into or out of her body. Pushing the coffee cup away, she nervously folded her hands. *Oh, God! What should I do?*

"Cade," Rachel began, a wobble in her voice, "what I'm going to share with you is…is shocking… And I'll understand if you want me to go once you hear it." Rachel saw his gray eyes widen in surprise. How ruggedly handsome Cade was in his dark green flannel cowboy shirt and jeans. His stubble was always dark by evening and it gave him a dangerous and alluring look that she had come to love. Yes, Rachel admitted, she was falling in love with Cade.

Sitting back, Cade rested his hands on his thighs. "What's going on?" He felt the tension around them. The set of her mouth told him she held some terrible secret.

Cade's face was set. Suddenly, Rachel feared telling him the truth. Her handler, Brenda, had put the fear of God into her about ever telling anyone. Sometimes, Rachel realized, rules had to be broken for the good of all. She simply couldn't go on putting this family in jeopardy.

Dragging in a deep breath of air and spreading her hands before her on the table, Rachel began. The more she told Cade, the more she saw his brows draw down. She thought as she was about to tell him the worst, about losing Sarah, that she could speak about it. Instead, her throat closed up on her.

"I—uh, give me a moment, Cade." She tried to wipe the tears from her eyes.

"What else?" he demanded in a strangled tone.

The look on his face was hard. As if he were a deputy sheriff with a suspect. It didn't matter. The truth had to come out. "After Dirk put me in the hospital and I lost… I lost my baby, Sarah…" Suddenly, Rachel sobbed. No matter how much she tried to throttle back the reaction, it just wouldn't be stopped.

Cade heard the raw grief in her off-key voice. "Oh, God, no…." Cade sat there stunned. His head swam with memories. Of Rachel loving Jenny. Of her telling him all she wanted was a family and children. Now, it all made sense. In an instant, he was on his feet and pulling her out of the chair. Cade wrapped his arms around her and felt her tremble violently. Without a word, he pressed Rachel's head to his shoulder and simply held her.

All the years of never being able to let it all go hit her hard. With Cade's strong, protective arms around her, the tears flooded out of her eyes and rolled down her cheeks. The gentle stroke of his hand barely grazing her hair just made her cry all the more. Rachel had no idea how long the sounds of loss and grief tore out from the depths of her soul. The man holding her was strong, steady and caring. The opposite of Dirk Payson.

Finally, the storm passed and Rachel pulled out of his arms enough to look up at him. What she saw pulverized her raw, bleeding heart. He had tracks of tears down his cheeks, his mouth was drawn in at the corners. He was crying for her. For her loss of Sarah. And when he lifted his hand and his fingers grazed her dampened cheeks, Rachel closed her eyes. A ragged sigh escaped her contorted lips.

"You never deserved what happened to you," Cade told her in a whisper, his own voice unsteady.

His mind whirled with problems. Payson was on the loose. He and his family were in danger. His heart pounded with fear. Fear for Rachel, for his family. What should he do?

"I've put all of you in danger," Rachel whispered. She pulled out of his arms, wiped the tears from her face and stared up at Cade. "I'm so sorry. It was wrong of me to do this to you. I—I tried to tell my FBI handler it was wrong. But she said I was fine here."

Cade's slow-burning anger took over. It wasn't aimed at Rachel so much as the FBI. "When you're in the witness protection program, everyone you deal with can be in danger."

"Yes," Rachel whispered. She felt all the fight go out of her. "I need to leave, Cade. Now."

"No!"

The word was spoken so sharply that Rachel jumped. Cade's eyes narrowed.

She pressed her hand to her heart. "Cade, I love Jenny and your family too much to put you at risk." She wanted to say, *I love you,* but couldn't. Instead, she watched as he digested the whole messy situation.

"I'm putting all of you in danger. You know that," she added.

Cade held up his hand. "Give me a moment. I need to think through this, Rachel."

She went to the sink and sniffed. Outside, the April sky was blue with bright sunshine. As beautiful as it was, she felt awful inside. Gripping the sink, the tile cool beneath her damp fingers, she said, "I've lied to you, Cade. I'm sorry. I really am. I didn't want to do it to you."

"I know," he answered irritably. Pacing the length of the kitchen, Cade tried to push his feelings aside and think coldly and logically. His heart swung from abject fear of losing Rachel to the fact she'd lied. And by lying, she'd put everyone in his family in the crosshairs of Payson's gun. Rachel wanted to leave.

"Where would you go?" he demanded abruptly.

Rachel turned around and faced him. "I'm not sure. I'd have to talk to Brenda and find out."

Cade gritted his teeth. "I hate this."

"Me, too." Rachel wished she'd never said yes to coming here in the first place. The love she had for Cade would never leave her heart. She felt herself spiraling down into a black pit. She had no one but herself to blame.

"You can't go," he said, his hands resting on his hips. "Jenny has bonded with you."

Shocked, Rachel stared at him. "Are you serious?"

"You can't leave. Jenny needs you." Cade almost blurted, *I need you.* But he didn't. He searched her features.

Closing her eyes, Rachel fought his words. Jenny! Oh, God, what a mess! She met his gaze. "Dirk is a loose cannon, Cade. I don't want what he did to me done to anyone else. Especially Jenny— or you…"

Cade wanted to tell her how he really felt, but he put a steel grip on himself. She had enough to handle right now. Never had he thought something like this could happen to him. "There's more than us involved in this, Rachel. My mother and father have to know." He saw her face crumple with guilt.

"You have no idea how many times I wanted to tell them. I owe them an apology, too. I know they'll hate me for what I've done…." She chewed on her lower lip, all the guilt from the past months like a weight on her shoulders.

"Enough," Cade snapped. "This isn't settled—at all. We need to talk with them. It's their ranch. Their lives." He breathed raggedly wondering how they were going to react. It hurt to see more tears come to Rachel's eyes. "Look," he said, "this isn't your fault. I know that. I'm in law enforcement. But my parents may not understand that you didn't deliberately lie to them. They aren't familiar with the witness protection program."

Blinking back the tears, Rachel whispered brokenly, "I'm so sorry, Cade. I've hurt all of you. I never meant to, I really didn't… I   I've fallen in love with—" and she stopped the words from tumbling out of her mouth. She watched as his eyes widened, and then grew feral.

Another wave of shock washed over Cade as he stared at her. Was Rachel going to say she'd fallen in love with him? She'd already said she loved Jenny. Who was left? Staggered by the nearly blurted admission, he swiftly took strides over to where she stood. Rachel looked pathetically vulnerable, her arms wrapped tightly around her body, the tears in her eyes. His hands fell on her shoulders. "I want to help you, Rachel. My parents aren't stupid. I know they love you. Everyone's been happy since you got here." He stared into her ravaged eyes. "We can support you until Payson's recaptured and back in prison."

His hands felt incredibly steadying. There was such quiet strength in Cade. "I...yes, I'd like that." Rachel felt his narrowed gaze burning into hers. "I—I'm so afraid for you, Jenny and your family. I know Dirk. He's a sociopath. He has no conscience, Cade! If he found me here, he'd kill anyone he found beside me."

Against his better judgment, Cade drew Rachel against him once again. He couldn't stand to see her cry like this. His jaw rested against her silky hair. "I don't know how you've carried this all by yourself since it happened. You're stronger than you realize, Rachel."

Pressing her face into his shirt, Rachel gripped him hard, as if to lose him would be to lose her grip on sanity. "I'm not strong, Cade. I feel weak. Defenseless. I know Dirk. He's a chameleon. He changes his appearance. I've seen him do it, although at the time he lied about why he was doing it, and I just swallowed his explanations."

Easing his fingers down along her tense spine, Cade wanted to absorb some of her fear and grief. "Look, his kind always manipulates others. You are the innocent in all of this, Rachel. You were only eighteen at the time he hooked you in and used you." Cade's heart was in chaos. His mind tumbled with shock. Never had he expected such tragedy from Rachel. She seemed ordinary, normal and was a loving human being. Yet, she had carried this nightmare within her. Cade's respect for her internal strength grew moment by moment as he absorbed the entire story of her rocky life.

Rachel was warmed by Cade's embrace. She loved him without question. That scared Rachel even more now: did Cade love her? How could he? She had such a shameful past. And she presented a threat right now to all he loved: Jenny and his parents. Rachel couldn't grasp how Cade would allow her to stay here under his roof and protection. She pulled away enough to see his face. There was such seriousness in it, in the way his mouth was compressed, in the anxiousness in his gray eyes. Yet, his arms, oh, God, his arms felt so good to her!

"Listen, there's more we need to talk about," she quavered, searching his eyes. "Every moment here I feel like I'm putting all of you in jeopardy, Cade. I—I just couldn't stand seeing anyone else killed by Dirk. I couldn't bear it." Her voice cracked.

Nodding, Cade whispered, "Come with me. Let's sit on the couch together. We'll look at all of this and figure it out."

As they sat down, Rachel's knee grazed his. She cleared her throat. "Cade, I'm a danger to your world. My God, you just lost Abby and your baby daughter. Now, I come in here under a layer of lies, and I have placed you, Jenny and your parents in an even more dangerous place. Don't you see that?"

"Rachel, I might see it that way if I weren't in law enforcement. First off, I think the right thing to do is get Mom and Dad over here after dinner and tell them everything. They need to make up their own mind about this. We will abide by their wishes."

"If I were them," Rachel said unsteadily, "I'd tell me to leave now."

Cade shrugged. "You're seeing only one side to this, Rachel, and I understand that." He added, "There are advantages to being here, too. If my parents approve of you staying, then they can be alert for strangers coming to our ranch. Forewarned is forearmed."

"Well," Rachel said, drawing in a ragged breath, "I don't see how they would want me to stay. I've lied to them, too."

"Rachel, you had to keep your cover," Cade offered, giving her a searching look. "I know enough about the FBI program to know they put the fear of God in you about never blowing your cover."

"I—I just couldn't keep lying to you, Cade. I like you too much. I love my life here. I love Jenny. And your parents are incredibly wonderful to me."

Nodding, Cade bit back so many personal words he wanted to share with her. Right now was not a good time. He had to concentrate on Rachel and help ease her out of this world she'd carried silently on her shoulders for so many years. "We all love you, too. It's mutual, Rachel." Cade kept the *we* light so that she didn't read it the wrong way. God knew, he wanted to tell her of the love he'd discovered for her. "I believe my parents will want you to stay."

Rachel wiped her eyes, feeling miserable. "I don't see why any of you would."

"I do." The words, the need to hold her nearly ate him alive, but he kept his hands in his lap.

"If they let me stay, what then, Cade? Are you okay with me living here and taking care of Jenny? Should I move out? Live in town? Or just disappear?"

Cade gave her a level, serious look. "No to all the above. I want you here, Rachel. You've given us so much. I can't tell you how much I look forward to coming home after a shift. You have no idea of the dark world I lived in until you walked into our lives." He placed his other hand over hers. "I don't want you to leave."

"But I'm putting you and Jenny in danger!" Her voice cracked, and Rachel felt herself getting swallowed up once more by fear for their lives.

Cade patted her hand. "Once we find out what my parents' decision is and if they want you to stay here, I'll contact Brenda, your FBI handler."

Rolling her eyes, Rachel whispered, "Oh, God, Cade! She'll hit the roof! She'll be so angry and disappointed in me. She once warned me that if I blew my cover, they would drop me out of the program and wash their hands of me."

Looking into her pale, drawn features, Cade understood the risk that Rachel had taken for him and his family. "You have the heart of a lioness, strong morals and values, Rachel. You did the right thing in telling me. I don't always agree with the FBI or their rules on things like this. There are a lot of gray areas that the FBI would rather ignore. And this situation is one of them. No, I think you did the right thing."

"But, if they drop me, I won't have their protection and help like I did before. I worry about my mother most of all. Have I jeopardized her, too? I'm so scared, Cade."

"I know you are," he said, fingers trailing down her cheek and jaw. It was so easy to touch Rachel. How badly Cade wanted to draw her into his arms, carry her to his bed and love her. He could see her need in her eyes. Cade had to remain strong and steady for her right now. Making love to Rachel was not where this needed to go. He hoped there would be a time in their future when he could court her as she deserved.

"If Mom and Dad feel endangered by you being here, then we'll move you into town. I don't have a problem with that. And I respect whatever their needs are. This is their home."

"What are you saying?"

"If they want you to leave, we'll find a house and move into it—the three of us." Cade saw the shock in her eyes. Her lips parted. "Rachel, I like what we have. I believe you're safe here. Based upon what you've told me, Payson isn't going to think of Wyoming to hunt for you. The FBI was smart in placing you here. I'll talk with my captain, and we can put out an extra alert throughout the sheriffs' organization to stay on top of strangers coming into Jackson Hole. We can circulate his poster to every business in town. And we have a good working relationship with the police of Jackson Hole. They'll be with us on this. We can cover your back. If I didn't think so, I wouldn't be offering these kinds of solutions. The last thing I want to do is put Jenny in the line of fire."

Rachel absorbed his ideas and possible plans. "I thought..." and she opened her hands, her voice trailing into a shaky whisper "...that you would tell me to leave."

Shaking his head, Cade gave her a slight, one-cornered smile. "No, Rachel. I know this isn't the time or place, but you're special to me and Jenny. That little girl dotes on you. You've got to know that."

"I do. On some days I think she was sent to comfort me for the loss of Sarah."

Cade reached out and settled his hand on her shoulder. "Jenny is helping you to heal from that terrible loss, Rachel. She's good for both of us in that way."

"You've lost so much more than I have," Rachel choked out. "And now I've saddled you all over again. I've brought a killer and drug dealer to your doorstep."

"I don't see it that way." Cade allowed his hand to trail down her arm and enclose her hand. Her fingers were damp and cold. His hand was warm.

"You've brought laughter, warmth and happiness back into this cold house. Now, I call it a home again. You have no idea how much I look forward to getting off duty to see you and the baby. It means the world to me, Rachel. It's as if by coming here, you gave me life once more. And Jenny…well, she lost her parents to tragedy and like a guardian angel, you stepped in to become her mother."

Hearing the barely concealed emotions in his husky voice, Rachel could only drown in his stormy gray eyes. Cade gulped several times as if to swallow a lump of tears struck in his throat. "Oh, Cade." She turned and slid her arms around his neck. Without thinking, Rachel fell into his waiting arms, his embrace powerful and protective. Closing her eyes, she laid her head on his chest and heard his heart beating like a solid, steady drum beneath her ear. The sound was incredibly stabilizing to her. At last, the truth was out and Cade hadn't spurned her. Or become angry at her. As his hands moved in reassuring strokes down her back, Rachel released a long breath of air. And with it went the fear and anxiety. Cade wanted her here, with him. With his adopted daughter.

"Listen," Cade told her gruffly, his lips against her hair, "our homes have been broken. We've suffered a lot. But by coming into my life, Rachel, you've given me the hope I thought I'd never feel again. You've given Jenny a mother. I want you to realize how much you mean to us."

Sliding her hand across his firm, hard chest, Rachel whispered, "I'm beginning to understand, Cade. Never in my wildest dreams did I ever think you'd react to what happened like this. You're one in a million of the men out there. I really thought you'd want me to leave."

Closing his eyes, Cade pressed a chaste kiss to Rachel's soft, fragrant hair. "Not a chance, sweet woman of mine. Not even possible. I want you to hang on to one thing—we'll get through this together, Rachel. Life is never easy. And it's often damned demanding and even cruel to people. The one thing we have in our favor is we like one another." Swallowing hard, Cade had wanted to say *love* but didn't dare. "We have each other. We can hold one another when we're scared or anxious. We can talk openly and without fear of recrimination by the other, Rachel. We have so much already. I hope you see that. And that realization should give you a rock to cling to no matter what life throws at us in the weeks and months ahead."

CHAPTER SIXTEEN

As THEY SAT at the kitchen table in Cade's house, Ray Garner gave his wife, Gwen, a measured glance. "We see the dangers here, Rachel." He looked at her, a frown across his broad forehead.

Gwen nodded. "We've talked it over, honey, and none of this is your fault." Taking a deep breath, the woman addressed Rachel. "We don't like liars, but you had no choice. We want you to stay."

Relief tunneled through Rachel. At the same time, the gnawing sense that Dirk would find her brought pain and anxiety. Cade gave them a grim look and nodded. "All right," he managed, his voice tight with emotion. "It's settled."

Rachel managed to speak. "Thank you. I'm grateful in one way, but scared for all of you in another. My ex-husband is never to be trusted. He's so dangerous." She pressed her fingertips to her wrinkled brow. "I worry for all of you."

Cade reached out, his hand over hers. "He's a killer, Rachel." He looked across the table at his father who had a very serious expression on his weathered features. "I'm going to the captain today about this. He'll know what to do next. I think he'll probably call Brenda, your handler at the FBI, and discuss the situation."

Rachel felt the steadying warmth of Cade's roughened hand over hers. "She's going to be angry with me."

Gwen shrugged. "So let her be. With Cade in law enforcement, there are other ways to keep track of Payson and his whereabouts. The FBI isn't the only one with connections and info." She gave Rachel a tight smile. "Besides, Captain Henderson, Cade's boss, has been in this business for over twenty years. He knows people inside the ATF, the FBI and DEA." Gwen reached out and patted Rachel's other hand. "No one is minimizing the danger here. We know we'll be in his gun sights, too."

"Yes," Ray grunted, "we are. We'll put an alarm on the main gate into our ranch. If anyone opens the gate, it will go off in Cade's home as well as ours." He gave her a grim look. "There's only one possible route into this area and that's down a mile-long road to our ranch. You can't drive a vehicle into our area no matter how rugged it is. The land won't allow it."

Rachel began to feel a tad better. "My heart aches over this whole situation. I appreciate the security you're putting up."

Gwen snorted. "Listen, Rachel, that man does not want to come up against anyone here at our ranch. We all carry weapons on us. And we're authorized by the law to do so. Between us and the sheriff's department working with the Jackson Hole police, you'll be a little safer. But nothing's foolproof."

"You're right, it's not foolproof," Rachel agreed quietly. "Thanks, all of you." She was still stunned they would willingly put their lives on the line—for her.

"Now," Ray said in his drawl, "you need to get out and about, Rachel. Gwen and I couldn't figure out why you holed up like you did, but knowing what we know now, it makes sense. You were hiding from Payson and the possibility of being identified by him in town."

"That comes to an end," Cade said. "You need to have the freedom to come and go. With this type of security in place, you should begin to integrate back into real life, Rachel."

"It feels like I'm stepping out of prison," she whispered, giving them a grateful look.

"And coming to the quilting classes at my store will give you a start on that," Gwen said. "The women there are just wonderful and you'll make good friends."

"Quilters stick together like a quilt sandwich." Ray glanced at his wife.

Cade grinned and joined the laughter. A *quilt sandwich* consisted of the top material that had been sewn together, the thick cotton batting below it and then a backing material. Put together, the three layers were a *sandwich*.

Rachel felt the dire threat lift the tiniest bit.

Hope. Looking into Cade's gray eyes that shimmered with an unspoken promise of love, Rachel saw her future.

THE SUN WAS shining brightly the next morning. Rachel worked in the kitchen, preparing a leg of lamb with couscous and vegetables for their dinner. Despite Cade's family's assurances, Rachel felt unsettled. Worried. Now, she had four other people in danger. Had she made the right decision?

Jenny was in her playpen crawling around and making happy sounds. Soon, her legs would grow stronger and stronger. Instead of crawling, the infant would be ready to start standing up and walking. Already, Jenny would stand at the side of the playpen, her little bowed legs upright and she'd laugh and wobble around with unsteady steps.

Cade had the night shift—6:00 p.m. to 5:00 a.m. for the next week. The shifts were frequently changed so that no deputies ended up with sleep deprivation from working nights. She heard his cowboy-boot footfalls in the hall and looked up from the sink. Her stomach knotted.

Emerging from the hall, Cade shrugged into his thick sheepskin coat. He noticed the tension in Rachel's face. He hadn't slept well last night at all, his mind running wild with "what if's."

"I'm going out to help my dad put the alarms in place," he told her. Rachel still looked beautiful despite the tension, her hair soft and curved around her shoulders as she stood at the sink peeling potatoes. Coming over, Cade leaned against the counter.

"That's good." Rachel's heart took off as Cade stood a few feet away watching her. There was something so primal and exciting about him that she fumbled the potato in her hands. "It's a beautiful day. Blue sky and sunshine and almost above freezing." That was how she felt inside: icy cold with dread and fear.

Glancing out the window, Cade nodded. "It's a warm day for March." He forced a smile he didn't feel. Changing topics, he said, "I wondered why you dyed your hair sable instead of letting it grow out to its natural blond color. Now I realize why you did it."

"Brenda told me to change my appearance as much as possible."

Cade watched her peel a potato. "Will you let it grow out naturally now?" he wondered. It was important that Rachel felt safe enough to really be herself. Cade found a lot of uncharted territory now that Rachel had removed the heavy FBI mask. Who was she? Was this all an act?

"I think I will," she said. "I hated dyeing my hair." She shivered. "I'll never do it again, Cade." Rachel glanced up at him and drowned in his intent gaze. There was darkness in his eyes. He was worried, too. She could see and sense it. Despite everything, an energy built between them, the hunger, the yearning strung between them like a taut rope. It was all there to read in his eyes, along with his worry. Swallowing convulsively, Rachel tore her gaze from his. The truth was, she wanted Cade as badly as he wanted her, her whole life was crazy. Fear and love. How did they get together? Much less survive one another? She had no answers.

Cade's instinct was to move those few feet to where Rachel stood. More than anything, he craved one kiss from her. He needed to hold her. Carry her off to his bedroom and never let her go. For now, Cade checked those desires and dreams. It was way too soon and there were still hurdles in their way. Cade had no idea what the FBI would do, and knew Rachel was most worried about her mother. Would the FBI refuse to keep her cover because Rachel had broken her vow? Until he could get answers, they both had to play the waiting game.

It was getting tough not to reach out and touch this beautiful woman. Rachel was like a bright, colorful butterfly who had flitted unexpectedly into his life. Despite her deception, Rachel had given Cade hope of living once more. Jenny had blossomed beneath her loving care. What didn't flourish beneath Rachel's caring touch?

"I'm off," Cade said, pushing away from the counter. He headed across the room, picking up his black felt cowboy hat and settling it on his head. His last, most precious act was to go to the playpen, hoist Jenny up and give her a smooch on her bright red cheek. The baby gurgled, laughed and touched his nose with her tiny hand. "Okay, pumpkin," he told Jenny, "I'm off to keep Rachel safe and sound here with us." He gently placed Jenny back into her playpen.

Rachel twisted around and watched the two of them. There was such incredible love between Cade and Jenny. How she ached to be a part of this family. *Time*, she reminded herself. *Time and patience. A step at a time.*

As Cade left and the door shut, Rachel sighed. She quickly peeled three more Idaho potatoes and put them in a bowl of water. After washing and drying her hands, Rachel turned and gazed fondly around the warm kitchen. The radio was on and played the elevator music she loved so much. Jenny sat with a plop when her little legs gave out. She then rolled over on her hands and knees, grabbed the white nylon netting of the playpen's side and pulled herself up into a standing position once more. Jenny was such a happy baby. Rachel wished her whole life could be like this moment: happy. Someday, when this mess was over and Dirk was back in jail.

She went to the fridge to pull out the leg of lamb and placed it into a large rectangular glass baking dish. Her life was changing rapidly now that she'd made a decision. The heavy chains that had imprisoned her slowly began to melt away. But new ones replaced the old ones. Four people were in danger because of her choices. Dirk could strike like a rattlesnake out of nowhere. Cade looked at her oddly sometimes and that bothered Rachel. She wished she could read his mind. Was he having second thoughts about her? How did he really feel about her now? Shaking her head, Rachel muttered under her breath. Her focus had to be on her mother and what the FBI might do to her.

THE NEXT MORNING, after Rachel had had her shower, dressed and fed Jenny, she walked out into the kitchen. To her surprise, Cade sat at the table with a cup of coffee in hand. Usually, when he came in after a night shift, he'd get a shower, sleep until about 2:00 p.m., then get up to prepare for the next night shift. She halted, the baby in her arms.

"Cade?"

He looked up and gave her a tired smile. "Good morning."

Anxiously scanning his face for any sign of bad news and not seeing any, Rachel settled Jenny into her playpen. She gave the baby her favorite toy, a red dragon that Gwen had made.

"Is anything wrong?" she asked, pouring herself some coffee.

"No. Come and sit down. I purposely stayed up so we could talk." Cade tried to ignore the gentle sway of Rachel's hips.

Sitting at his elbow, she saw shadows beneath Cade's eyes. He was in civilian clothes, his hair gleaming from a recent shower. He'd even shaved. Her gaze fell to his lips and instantly, her lower body tightened with a fierce yearning. Rachel took a sip of the hot coffee. "What did you find out from Captain Henderson?"

"It's all good," Case assured her without preamble. He didn't want Rachel to worry. He'd seen the fear lurking in her gaze. "I told him everything. He called Brenda."

Her breath hitched. "And?"

"They aren't going to drop you or your mother out of the program." Cade grinned, his hands around the thick ceramic mug. "Seems that the captain has some very influential ties in the FBI hierarchy. At first, Brenda was upset, but as Henderson talked to her, they worked out a plan and a strategy. She's taking the new plan to her bosses and they're going to rubber-stamp it."

Relief shot through Rachel. She leaned back in the chair and whispered, "Thank God… I was so worried that they'd punish my mother for my decision."

"They could have," Cade told her in a serious tone, "but the fact that I'm in law enforcement changes the equation a lot. And Brenda, to her credit, saw that, accepted it and then rolled with Captain Henderson's suggestions."

Sipping her coffee, Rachel felt incredible weight lift off her shoulders. "I'm so glad, Cade. Thank you so much for doing all of this." She reached out and slid her hand into his.

Cade squeezed her fingers. They were cold and damp, from nerves, no doubt, and he couldn't blame her. Reluctantly, he released her hand. "It gets better, Rachel. How would you like your mother to come and live here with us?"

"What?" Rachel gasped.

Cade squeezed her hand. "Captain Henderson talked to Brenda about the possibility. Your mother can't go back to the family farm in Iowa—yet. Once Payson is caught, your mother will be released from the program and she can go back to the farm." He smiled as he saw Rachel's eyes fill with tears of joy. "In the meantime, because of our particular situation, Captain Henderson asked if it was possible to bring your mother here, to our ranch. You know we have these cabins that we rent out to tourists?"

"Yes." Rachel's voice quavered with sudden excitement. Her mother coming here! She would get to see her!

"We could give your mother one of the cabins." Cade held up his hand. "Now, this wouldn't happen right away, Rachel. It's going to take a couple of weeks for the FBI to make all the changes in their paperwork, get approval and all sorts of other stuff. Brenda said that someone far above her approved that your mother would come here and live here at the ranch with us until Payson is caught. Once he's caught, then the FBI will remove her from the witness protection program—as they will you— and she can go home. And you can get on with your life out of the witness protection program."

Eyes widening, Rachel stared at Cade in disbelief. "Are you serious about all this? I'd be able to visit her and my brothers any time I want?" Her voice cracked.

Gripping her hand firmly, Cade whispered in an emotional tone, "Yes, Rachel. You and your mom will eventually get your lives back. Brenda told the captain that the rest of Payson's gang in the U.S. has already been rounded up, and this changed everything. And with all of them behind bars, this paves the way for your family to be normal once more. The only fly in this ointment right now is Payson himself. Once the authorities find him, then you and your mom will be released from the FBI program."

Sitting back, she put her hands against her eyes as the tears trailed down her face. "This is too good to believe. It really is," she said tremulously.

Cade had to stop touching her. "It's real, Rachel. All of it. Your mom is coming here. That will help you and her a lot."

Rachel rubbed her tears from her eyes. "It's like a fairy tale, Cade. I would never have believed this could happen. Not in my wildest dreams." She searched his warm, inviting gray gaze. "I—I don't know what to say...."

Cade grazed her damp cheek with his fingers. "This is the beginning of a new chapter in your life." Cade withdrew his fingers because if he didn't, he would sweep Rachel into his arms and take her to his bed. He didn't want to take advantage of her shock and joy. No, he wanted her for all the right reasons. And he wanted her on her time and terms.

Wild tingles flitted across Rachel's cheek where Cade had gently stroked her flesh. How badly she craved his touch! And now, it was even more wonderful because in the future, she might openly be able to go to him. Rachel dreamed of sharing with Cade her love for him and Jenny. Maybe they could be a family. She knew this was possible because of the burning look in his hooded gaze. That look sent rivulets of heated promise from her heart to the center of her core. Rachel had never felt this kind of desire in her life. She realized that she really hadn't loved Payson at all; it had been simply what her mother had called "puppy love." *This* was real. Rachel held his intense look—the look of a man wanting his woman in all ways.

"I'm just overwhelmed," Rachel admitted with a husky laugh. Drying her cheeks, she felt shaky with joy. "I can't believe this, Cade. This is so generous of you and your family. My faith in people's goodness has been restored."

As he forced himself to keep his hands around the mug of coffee, Cade felt his heart pounding heavily in his chest. "No one deserves this more than you and your family."

"Will my brothers know about this? Will Brenda tell them?"

"Probably, in time, but not right now. Like I said, the paperwork and approval hurdles need to happen first. If I read between the lines of what

Brenda told the captain, the rest of your family will be notified once your mother has been moved out here."

"That's going to make Mom so happy," Rachel quavered, thinking about the ramifications of this sudden shift in FBI policy. "This will blow her away."

Cade held up his hand. "You can tell her about it, but don't talk about a date because it could be sooner or later."

Nodding, Rachel said, "Of course." She gave Cade a smile.

Rachel's face changed dramatically when she was happy and smiling, Cade thought, just now realizing how depressed and unhappy she'd been before. And yet, Cade hadn't seen it or sensed it. Rachel had taken the witness protection program to heart. She had changed in so many ways. What he saw now, tore the breath from him and made his heart gallop like a wild stallion racing free across the land.

Shaking her head, Rachel murmured, "I just can't believe all of this, Cade. I owe you and Captain Henderson so much."

The quiver in her husky voice tore at Cade. Reaching out, he captured her hand. "Listen," he told her gravely, "I didn't do anything. Captain Henderson did it all. One of these days, soon, we'll have him and his wife out here for dinner and you can thank him in person."

"I'd love to," Rachel said, squeezing his hand in

return. How natural it felt to have this kind of intimacy with Cade. She didn't want it to stop here. Rachel's hands literally itched to be free to explore Cade from the top of his head down to his feet. As heat raced up her neck and into her cheeks, Rachel avoided Cade's gaze and released his hand. "We always had huge dinners at home. Mom would invite our friends and neighbors to Sunday dinner. It was a busy, but a happy day. I would help her in the kitchen. We were able to catch up with our friends and neighbors. Every week, another farm family would host the Sunday dinner. That way, no one family had to feed an army by themselves." Rachel smiled fondly in remembrance of those happier times.

"Well," Cade said, "I see no reason why we can't start that same kind of Sunday gathering. People get cabin fever here in the winter and that would be a great time to initiate it. People would have something to look forward to."

Rachel couldn't find words to express her gratitude. "I feel as if this is all a dream," Rachel whispered unsteadily as she gazed warmly around the kitchen. "I can't think of a time when I was happier than I am here." She gave Jenny a loving look as she sat in her playpen with her red dragon. Glancing over at Cade, Rachel swallowed hard and added, "And to be here with you. I was so green and stupid to run off with Payson. I realize that now. And more than anything, you're a man I never believed could exist. You're my hero,

Cade. You make me want to look at having a relationship once more. Before meeting you, I wanted nothing to do with men."

Cade kept a steel grip on his thoughts. He had to be careful. Rachel was coming out of a long nightmare journey and years of hiding. The woman who glowed with newfound hope in the chair next to him reminded him of an angel who had come to earth. *My angel*. And he'd never forget when she'd sung "The Angel's Song," one of his favorite Christmas hymns.

Cade began in a subdued tone, "Give yourself the time you need to be yourself once again. You've had a lot of years of hiding, Rachel. You've grown and matured but now you need space to explore yourself in a safe, protected environment. Our relationship will define itself over time."

She closed her eyes, her hands clasped to her lips. "I've had so many dreams of me and my family being together once more." Tears momentarily blurred Cade's strong, rugged face. Rachel added in a strained voice, "My heart feels like it's going to explode with happiness. I have so much to look forward to if Dirk is caught before he can do us harm."

CHAPTER SEVENTEEN

RACHEL WATCHED THE SNOW falling and twirling past the window. It had snowed last night and this morning. The white stuff was everywhere. But even the endless winter couldn't dampen her spirits.

"Mom?" Rachel could barely keep the joy out of her voice as she stood at the kitchen sink, phone in hand. It was April first, the day she could talk with her mother for ten minutes. How she wanted all of this to end!

"Hi, honey. I'm packed and ready to come out your way starting tomorrow morning!"

"Isn't it wonderful? Brenda must have called you."

"I talked to her yesterday, and she said I'll be picked up at 8:00 a.m. for my flight out to Cheyenne."

Rachel closed her eyes with a deep sense of relief. "I just can't believe all the good things that are happening, Mom. Finally, there's a break. We get a break!"

"From what Brenda said, it's all thanks to the man whose baby you're caring for."

"Yes… Cade." Rachel gulped and opened her eyes. "He's wonderful, Mom. I—I think I'm falling in love with him even though we haven't discussed anything like that."

"He's a good man, Rachel," Daisy said in a more serious tone. "And I'm sure things have been so chaotic you haven't had time to talk to one another."

"I've made so many mistakes in the past. I'm afraid I'll make more."

"Young people make plenty of mistakes. I made mine. I ran away from home for a week until the police found me in Des Moines, Iowa, and brought me home." Daisy chuckled over those memories.

Eyes widening, Rachel said, "You never told us about that!"

"Why would I?" She gave a hearty laugh. "Then you'd get the big idea to run off, too."

"Well, it's nice to know that you weren't perfect."

"No one is," Daisy told her. "The key is in forgiving yourself and getting your children through that chaotic period. We all go through tough times, Rachel. And some of us make more serious mistakes than others. I believe firmly that as you mature, you find your way into a better life. And look at you! Brenda said you were in Jackson Hole, Wyoming. I've never been there, but I'm sure looking forward to being on a ranch near you."

Laughing, Rachel felt another layer of dread and heaviness melting off her shoulders. "Ranches and farms are similar, Mom. You'll love it here. The whole family is wonderful. Cade's mother is teaching me the basics of quilting and I'm actually completing a little baby quilt for Jenny."

"Wonderful!" Daisy said. "You know, your grandmother was a quilting queen."

"I know," Rachel sighed, sitting down at the kitchen table. "I'm so glad we have all her quilts. I remember the wedding-ring pattern she made for my birthday when I turned twelve. Grams said I was a young lady now and I needed a young woman's quilt."

"I remember," Daisy said, a faraway sound in her voice as she recalled those happy days. "Your grams and I sat down when you were in school and went through all your scrapbooks. Grams saw how much you loved flowers and landscapes. She wanted to make a quilt for you that reflected what you loved. I can't tell you how many times she traveled around Iowa to the quilting stores looking for just the right fabrics for it."

"That quilt has always been my favorite," Rachel whispered, a catch in her tone. "There are so many flowers in each circle."

"She worked a year on that one for you, but it was worth it," Daisy murmured. "Quilting is in your DNA. I'm hoping when Payson gets caught that we can all be together as a family again. That we can get on with our lives…."

Suddenly, a "pop" sound came through the phone she held.

"Mom?"

Nothing. She heard the cell phone drop to the floor. Her heart raced with fear. Was that a gun? Standing, Rachel gripped the phone so hard her hand hurt. "Mom? Mom?" Her voice cracked. Dread jagged through her. "Mom?" she screamed.

The connection went dead.

Shocked, Rachel stared at the phone. Her world tilted crazily. Stunned, she was momentarily paralyzed. What had happened to her mother? With a cry, Rachel shakily punched in the numbers to Brenda, her handler.

"Brenda?" Rachel asked, her voice wobbly.

"Yes. What's wrong, Rachel? You sound upset."

The words tore out of her mouth as Rachel told her what had happened. There was sudden silence.

"You're sure?" Brenda demanded.

"Yes! Yes, I'm sure! My mother, Brenda. My God, something's wrong. I just feel it in my gut."

"I'll get local law enforcement over to her apartment pronto. You hang up. I'll call you on your cell as soon as I know what's going down."

The phone receiver clicked off. Rachel's world had gone from bright and hopeful to the worst nightmare she could imagine. Tears jammed her eyes. Her mother… She didn't want to believe that Dirk could have found her. Hand pressed to her lips, Rachel sobbed once. She had to get hold of herself! How had Dirk, or whoever it was, found her mother? And how much of the conversation on the phone had he overheard?

Cade! She had to get to Cade right away. This changed everything. Rachel sat down, suddenly traumatized by the weight she'd carried for so many years alone. This meant only one thing: that Dirk had somehow found her mother and he would now find her. Rachel tried to slow down her thoughts and think clearly.

Her cell phone rang. Rachel jerked her hand off it, as if burned. Brenda.

"H-hello," Rachel stumbled.

"I've got the police going over to Daisy's apartment, Rachel. Are you absolutely sure you heard a gun being fired?"

"It was a popping sound. The cell connection went dead. What else am I to assume?"

"I don't know. There's too many unanswered questions right now."

"I'm so scared she's been hurt...." Rachel said brokenly. A wave of grief made her shudder. Rachel had lived with the possibility that both of them could die. Now, it was coming true.

"I don't know. As soon as I hear something from the detectives, I'll let you know. Just stay calm and do not move, you hear me?"

Nodding, Rachel wiped the tears from her eyes. "Y-yes, I understand, Brenda. Just find out about my mom."

CADE HAD JUST entered the kitchen an hour later after being called by Captain Henderson. He found Rachel at the table, sobbing, her face hidden in her long, artistic fingers. Without a word, he walked swiftly over to her chair and crouched down, his hands on her shoulders.

"Rachel?"

She lifted her hands from her face. "Oh, Cade, something happened to my mom. Someone… I don't know who…shot her…" She fell into his arms, weeping.

"When I heard I came straight home. I'm sorry, Rachel…come here…" Cade held her tightly against him. She shook like a leaf in some terrible storm. He looked around the kitchen, his mind like a bear trap considering all the possibilities. Henderson had called him on the radio and he'd come directly to the ranch. The FBI had confirmed that Rachel's mother had died of one gunshot to the head. The shooter hadn't been identified. Cade hadn't been sure how much Rachel knew until now. Gently moving his hand across her hair and shaking shoulders, he could feel her pain and terror.

No one knew how Payson had found Rachel's mother in Florida. A good computer hacker could get into any type of records and information, even the FBI files. He would bet his life that was what had happened. It would be easy for Payson to find Daisy. And Rachel…

"Oh, Cade," Rachel mumbled, lifting her head from his shoulder, "Brenda called me a few minutes ago and told me my mom was dead. She's dead…."

"I know, I know," Cade whispered, sadness moving through him. He slid his fingers across her cheeks in an effort to try and dry some of her tears. "I'm so sorry, Rachel. So sorry." Looking into her eyes so filled with grief and shock, Cade realized everything had to change. His protectiveness ballooned to new heights. He loved Rachel. He wanted her at his side for the rest of his life. He wanted to keep her safe. And he wanted Jenny and his parents safe, as well. "We'll get through this together, Rachel. You aren't alone. You have friends here. Family who loves you. Somehow, we'll sort out what's happening and you are going to be safe. You hear me?"

The words barely had an impact on Rachel. She sat there, her hands on the shoulders of his jacket. His gray eyes reminded her of a predatory eagle on a hunt. As she clung to his intense look, her fingers automatically tightened on the material of his jacket. "My mom is dead...." It was all she could think. So many past happy moments with her fled before her eyes and heart.

"Listen to me," Cade said, giving Rachel a small shake to get her to focus, "tell me what happened in that phone call. What did your mother say?"

Rachel gulped back her grief and tried to focus. Just having his hands on her shoulders gave her stability. Choking out the entire phone call with her mother, she noticed Cade's every reaction. "Someone shot her, Cade. In cold blood... They never spoke to me. They just hung up the phone.

All I heard was a click and then the connection ended."

Payson would do the same to Rachel, and Cade knew it. He kept his suspicions to himself, tried to soothe by stroking her pale cheek. Under no circumstances could she know the terror he felt. He'd already lost one woman he'd loved. Cade was damned if he was going to lose Rachel now.

Captain Henderson had ordered him to remain with Rachel at the ranch until some kind of viable plan, with all the information from the FBI, could be cobbled together. "Listen, we'll take this a step at a time. Together, Rachel. I want you in my life. Always." Cade wanted to say more, but now was not the time. He wasn't even sure she heard him. Her eyes were glazed; she was traumatized, so Cade repeated himself until she seemed to grasp what he was saying.

"First things first," Cade told her gently. "Let me work with Brenda. I'll be here all the time, Rachel. I'm not leaving your side. My mother will take Jenny over to their home for the next few days."

"No," she sobbed. "Don't take Jenny, too! I—I couldn't stand losing her, too. I'll be okay, Cade. I can care for her, I promise."

Something tore within Cade's heart. Just the high pitch of Rachel's voice, the desperation in her gaze, ripped him up inwardly. "Okay, we'll keep Jenny here. I was just worried for you. Maybe you need some time alone, some space because of what happened."

Shaking her head, Rachel placed her hands on his shoulders. "Cade, I need Jenny. I lost my baby. Now I've lost my mother. Jenny helps me stay sane through all of this. If you take her…"

"She stays with us," he promised her in a thick tone.

The cell phone on the table rang.

Rachel stared at it as if it were a rattlesnake ready to strike at her.

Cade stood and picked it up.

"This is Deputy Sheriff Cade Garner."

Rachel sat there looking up at him. He seemed so calm and in charge. A sense of protection enveloped Rachel as never before. She listened as Cade talked with her handler from the FBI. When he was done, he punched off the cell and laid it back on the table.

Cade brought a chair over to where Rachel was sitting. "Brenda said the detectives have found no evidence that it was Payson."

Nodding, Rachel sat back in the chair, eyes closed. The only thing she felt was Cade's large, warm, rough hands around hers. The world she lived in had been destroyed in seconds. All that was left were her brothers, Cade and Jenny. "What will they do with my mom's body?"

"Brenda said she would be flown back to Iowa and buried from your family farm." Frowning, he added in a lower voice, "I'm sorry, but Brenda said you can't be there for the funeral. She's afraid Payson, or a hit man he's hired, might be waiting for you."

Rachel sat up and blinked away her tears. Holding on to Cade's hand was like holding on to the only reality that was left to her. "He'll still find me."

"You don't know that," Cade said in a sterner tone. Rachel looked haunted, and there was nothing he could do to change that. "Brenda is wondering how much, if anything, the gunman heard of the conversation you two were having."

"We talked about Jackson Hole," Rachel said dully, her voice a monotone. "If he heard that then…"

"We don't know if he heard anything," Cade said. He gently pushed away several strands of hair from her brow.

"I'm so afraid for all of you now, Cade." Rachel's mind honed in on those she'd come to love in the past months. She stared into Cade's stormy gray eyes. Suddenly, she realized with a jolt that she loved him. Unequivocally. Forever. There was so much good and kindness in Cade. He was the light and Payson was the darkness that had stained her life. And now, someone had taken her mother's life. Daisy Donovan did not deserve this kind of death. Rachel knew her brothers would reel from this news, and they would rightfully blame her.

Cupping her cheek with his hand, Cade rasped, "Don't you worry about that, okay? You have enough to handle right now, Rachel. I'm here. We'll protect you. Neither Payson nor his hit man is going to get to you. I promise you that."

Hearing the steel in his voice, Rachel came out of her shock. The grim set of Cade's mouth, the fierce look in his eyes convinced her to believe him. "For so long," Rachel quavered, "I've run and survived on my own, Cade. I don't want your family harmed. I—I couldn't stand it if Dirk found me. I know he'd kill your parents… Jenny…oh, my God, I don't want her hurt like my mother was!"

"Shhh," Cade whispered, framing her face now. "Don't go there, Rachel. Don't. This time, there's help around you. We'll circle the wagons and we'll protect you. My family knows how to defend themselves, so stop worrying about that. And I'll never allow Jenny or you ever to be hurt by that sonofabitch." Cade would give his life for them without a second thought. And deep in his gut, he knew Payson was behind this killing. He didn't know how, but he knew it. Cade was sure the convict was coming here. Somehow, the bastard had found out everything. The stalking had begun. Cade knew he would stand between Payson and Rachel and his baby daughter. And if necessary, he'd take the bullets for them.

CHAPTER EIGHTEEN

DIRK SMILED MIRTHLESSLY from his hiding spot on a hill overlooking the ranch. It was May third and, through his binoculars, he could see there was a party of some sort going on down below. The temperature was chilly but he braved the cold from his hiding place. For a week since arriving incognito in Jackson Hole, Dirk had been quietly skulking around like a shadow, pretending to be a tourist. He had come to track down Susan. And then he chuckled: he'd seen her slip into a quilting store one morning as he was having coffee at a café. The FBI had done a great job of placing her. She knew how much he hated cold weather and Wyoming was a freezer. *Good choice.* It had been easy to tail her home without her knowledge. When she pulled into the ranch road, he'd passed her and then found the next road and pulled off. A quick trip to a store with topographical maps and he'd located not only the ranch, but the owners, as well. And it had been easy to hike in, find a place to hide and watch.

Even now, as he sat on a small plastic tarp to keep dry, there were huge patches of unmelted

snow on the bramble-filled hillside that over-
looked the ranch. It was half a mile from the main
compound that consisted of a barn, a number of
huge corrals, many cabins and a couple of ranch
houses. But it was close enough for Dirk. He finished his cigarette and snubbed it out in the mud
next to his tarp. Good thing he'd brought a ther-
mos of coffee. This was his third day of watching
and recording ranch activities. Dirk congratulated
himself on finding Daisy Donovan, thanks to his
hacker friend. The hacker had broken into FBI records and found her name and address before he
was shut down and walled out. And even though
Dirk hadn't known where Susan was, listening to
Daisy's side of the phone conversation had given
him everything he needed.

He saw that Susan had dyed her hair brown and
Dirk smiled. He could see the blond roots and wondered if she was letting it grow back to its natural color. Well, it didn't matter. Dirk had carefully
noted the times and people coming to or leaving
the ranch complex on his clipboard. Timing would
be everything. The fact that Cade Garner was a
deputy sheriff didn't help things, but Dirk understood plenty about the movement and shifts of law
enforcement. Right now, the deputy was on day
duty, so that would leave Dirk time to enter his
home, kill Susan and leave before he ever knew
what had happened.

The celebration below looked like an old-fashioned barbecue. There were plenty of pickups and

SUVs in the huge gravel parking lot. To Dirk it looked like a party celebrating the coming warmth of spring. He couldn't blame them. Knowing that snow was on the ground eight months out of the year in Wyoming, he was sure everyone was ready to see the spring weather arrive. He'd hate living here.

A twisted grin pulled at his mouth as he saw Susan come out the front door with a baby in her arms. Whose baby was it? The deputy's? Dirk had no way to know her new name, either. He figured the witness protection program had given her a new one. Did she have a kid by the cop? He recalled slamming her to the floor and punching her in the belly. Dirk had always felt Susan had deliberately gotten pregnant to hold on to him. And he hated any woman hanging on to him for whatever reasons. She'd deserved to be beaten up and lose the brat. Dirk was never sorry for that. He was sorry that he'd been caught after she'd knocked him out cold with that skillet. And that is why he was here on this day: to settle the score once and for all.

Pleasure thrummed through him as he watched Susan with the Garners. She was starting a new family here—at least temporarily. He'd already murdered Daisy Donovan and got all the information he'd needed from that one phone conversation. It had been so easy. He'd simply crept up silently behind her, lifted his pistol and put it two inches from her head. Daisy went down like a felled ox, blood and brains spewing all over him and the wall. Dirk had simply picked up the cell phone, disconnected it and then pressed another key to retrieve the number. And then, he'd found the location: Jackson Hole, Wyoming. After that, he'd wiped the cell phone clear of prints and thrown it down next to Daisy's body. How badly he'd wanted to speak to Susan, but he didn't want her to know a thing. Dirk wanted her to worry—a lot. He felt like a cat teasing a mouse caught in a corner. Chuckling beneath his breath, Dirk felt her day was at hand....

CADE SAW THE grief etched deeply on Rachel's face as he prepared to leave for the day shift. She had eaten little of the breakfast he'd prepared for them. How beautiful she looked in the quilted vest that his mother had made for her, the dark green sweater and jeans. Already the blond color of her hair was growing in. The golden color suited her. His heart ached for her.

"Yesterday's barbecue was a lot of fun. It was good to see the other ranching families in the valley come together," he said.

Rachel nodded and pushed her plate of pancakes away. She'd eaten a few bites and felt nauseous. "It was nice to meet everyone," she murmured. Looking up, she noticed Cade's frown, his arms wrapped across his chest. He was worried about her. "I'm okay, Cade. Really." Shrugging, she added, "I'm just grieving over the loss of my mom."

Unwrapping his arms, Cade pulled his chair over next to hers. He placed an arm around her slumped shoulders. "I know. But you're not eating enough," he said, searching her large, shadowed eyes. As he touched her hair, Cade fought to keep from becoming too intimate. Every time he wanted to speak of his love for her, something catastrophic happened to prevent it. Waiting was hell. How badly he wanted to tell Rachel that he loved her, wanted her as his wife, his best friend to be at his side forever.

Rachel absorbed his warm touch, her skin tingling pleasantly. In the past month since her mother's murder, Rachel felt nearly all her life drain out of her. If not for Cade and Jenny, she wondered if she would want to live. Plus, the threat of Dirk or his hired gunman hung over her like a sword that would someday fall. Rachel knew Dirk well enough; he was a weasel. He'd find a way to get to her. Maybe that's why she felt so depressed. The life that she loved here was already destroyed. Swallowing, Rachel forced a thin smile she didn't feel.

"Go to work. I'll be fine."

"Mom said she was coming over later to help you piece a quilt together." If not for quilting, Cade knew Rachel would drift away, it seemed, from life itself. He couldn't imagine losing his parents and understood her devastating grief. The quilting was a bright spot in Rachel's life. And Gwen Garner was filling in for the loss of Daisy. Cade was forever indebted to his mother. She came over every day and the two of them would sit and work on a traditional quilt design on the kitchen table together. It was helping Rachel get through her ordeal.

"Yes, she will."

"Mom said you were doing rails? A log pattern?" Cade knew quilting because he'd been raised around it.

Reaching out, Rachel placed her fingers over his lower arm that rested on the table in front of her. "Bright, rainbow-colored rails."

"When do I get to see it?" he teased, smiling at her. Rachel's face was wan, more ghost than human, and it ate at Cade. He wanted to embrace Rachel, take her to his bed, hold her and love her. She wasn't there yet. Maybe she never would be. If she loved him, she hadn't said as much. And every time she reached out of her own accord to touch him, it lifted his heart, fed his hope and made him want to hang on.

"Maybe tonight," she said. Searching his shadowy gray eyes, Rachel knew he was worried about her. She'd lost ten pounds. Patting his arm, she said, "Get going. I'll be fine. I'll see you tonight for dinner."

Without thinking, Cade impulsively placed a warm, soft kiss on her brow. He wished he could provide sanctuary from all of her sadness.

"Okay," he whispered, "tonight." *I love you* nearly tore out of his mouth. Cade fought hard to swallow the words as he left the chair and moved away from Rachel. God, how long would he have to wait? He shrugged into his jacket and picked up his hat. Cade understood that until Payson was found, there would be no relaxation of tension in this household. There couldn't be.

A hired security guard, Randy Evans, remained on duty outside Cade's home. He routinely drove the road coming into the ranch once an hour. And when he returned, he would check to make sure Rachel and Jenny were safe. Randy left when Cade got off duty.

Rachel lived as a virtual prisoner in the house. She'd meant to leave so that she could protect the family. They'd argued heatedly over her decision. Because of her mother's death, Rachel no longer had the endurance or strength to overcome Cade and his family's decision to keep her at the ranch. There just wasn't any fight left in her, and Rachel finally bowed to their request. Besides, Cade had told her if she did leave, he would find her. And bring her home. To his home.

"Have a good shift," Rachel called as he walked out of the room. "Stay safe…." Because Rachel could not conceive of her life without Cade in it, not anymore.

Cade smiled. "Don't worry about me. You just eat and regain that lost weight. Okay?"

Rachel nodded and listened to the boot footfalls down the hall, the door opening and then closing. Automatically, she went to lock it. That was her life: locked doors and locked windows all the time now. Randy would knock at the kitchen door an hour from now. Pushing some strands off her brow, Rachel walked back to the kitchen. Jenny played in her pen, most of the time now on her tiny legs rather than crawling around. She was a good baby and Rachel went over, picked her up and held her.

"Let's practice your walking, young lady, before I do the morning dishes, okay?"

Jenny smiled and waved her hands. She now knew *Mama* and *Dada*. And she had taken her first real steps a day before Rachel's mother's murder. Since then she worked several times a day with the baby to help strengthen her legs and body. Rachel focused on her job, a labor of love, and tried to forget the danger she was in. She sat down on the rug and placed Jennie in front of her, hands on her tiny ones.

Rachel lost herself in Jenny's little steps. Her heart rose in joy as the child eagerly stepped toward her. Finally, after about ten minutes, Rachel got on her knees and gently released Jenny's hands. The infant tottered back and forth, but eventually found her balance.

"That's a good girl," Rachel called. She scooted about two feet away from her and yet close enough in case Jenny started to fall. "Come to me, Jenny...."

The little girl smiled and tottered forward, her hands extended toward Rachel. Each step was a little more solid and less wobbly than the next. As she met Rachel's outstretched hands, she bubbled.

Rachel laughed softly. "Perfect, Jenny!" There

was a sudden, muted noise. Lifting her head, her hands on Jenny's, Rachel glanced toward the hall where it had originated. It was a cloudy day and she hadn't turned on the light. What was that sound? It might be a bird hitting one of the windows. That had happened before.

Rachel turned, her back to the hallway as she maneuvered Jenny. The infant understood what she wanted and lurched from side to side as she made her way into Rachel's arms. They laughed together and Rachel picked her up. "Enough for now, young lady," she whispered, kissing Jenny's forehead. Walking into the kitchen, she put her back into the playpen.

"Well, well…"

Rachel's head snapped up. She stood, gasping. There, in the doorway, was Dirk Payson, grinning at her. Instantly, her pulse raced dangerously. Her eyes widened as she realized how different he looked. And yet, it was him. Her murdering ex-husband.

Dirk's smile grew, as if he was glorying in the abject terror he saw in her eyes and face. "What's the matter, baby? You don't recognize me?" He held a gun in his hand. With a flourish, he pointed to his face with his left hand. "I spent eight weeks down in Mexico getting this eye-candy look. Pretty nice, huh?"

Rachel's world spun. Gripping the side of the playpen, she felt all her maternal instincts taking over. She walked around and placed herself between Jenny and Dirk. Randy was on his rounds and wouldn't return for at least forty minutes. Rage tunneled through her and yet, she knew her ex-husband's volatile temper. Jenny *had* to be kept safe! The gun's barrel was pointed at her chest. "How did you find me?" she rasped.

Chuckling, Dirk, pulled a pack of smokes from the inside of his dark green jacket. "Easy enough," he said, putting the cigarette between his lips. He slid the pack into his jacket and found the lighter in another pocket. With his cigarette lit, the smoke curled. "I hired a hacker to hack into FBI records. He found your mother's address. And then, your mother let the cat out of the bag, honey. All I had to do was find the number on her cell phone, look it up and see it originated from Jackson Hole, Wyoming." He saw the rage come to Rachel's eyes. It felt good to goad her. And Dirk wanted to hurt her. He felt the power flow into his hands.

"Y-you killed her. I knew you did it!" Rachel whispered, tears coming to her eyes. Quickly, she forced them back.

Payson sucked on the cigarette, blew out a cloud of smoke and smiled at her. A sense of absolute joy coursed through him. "I told you in court that day they sentenced me, that I'd kill your entire family," he sneered. "I meant it." His voice changed. "You're next on the list. What made you think you'd get away with testifying against me?"

Rachel struggled to hold on to her white-hot

anger. "You killed our baby, Dirk. You nearly killed me."

"Too bad I didn't finish the job then. If I had realized you were going to rat on me and then testify, I'd have finished you off right then and there."

The coldness in his eyes frightened her. She knew that as soon as Dirk finished his cigarette, he'd kill her. "Please," she pleaded, "leave the baby out of this."

His gaze cut to the infant. "Yours?" The sarcasm in his voice was thick.

"N-no. She's Cade's daughter by adoption."

"And you're living with a cop," he jeered. "How convenient a cover. You're pretty good. But it didn't work, did it? You knew I'd come for you." He kept looking at the baby girl in the playpen behind Susan.

"Dirk, please...do not harm her."

"Depends upon how nice you are to me." He gave her a long, hard look from the top of her head down to her feet. "I got a real itch that needs to be scratched. Maybe a toss in the hay will make me think about letting that kid live instead of die. What do you say?"

A shudder wove through Rachel. She felt as if she would vomit. "Yes. Anything you want, Dirk. Just don't harm Jenny. She's an innocent in all of this. This is between you and me...."

After dropping the cigarette on the floor, he smashed it with the toe of his boot. "Okay, then, come with me." He pointed the gun toward the

hall. "I broke open the window in the big bedroom. That's where we'll go." He looked at his
watch. "Deputy Dawg will be gone until noon.
And that security doofus won't return for at least
thirty or forty minutes. We've got plenty of time."
He snickered. "I'd like to see the look on his face
when he walks into the kitchen and you're laying
there with your throat slit."

Blanching, Rachel moved quickly. She didn't
want to give Dirk any reason to harm Jenny. Dirk
jabbed the pistol into her back, and she hurried into
Cade's master bedroom. The window was open,
the screen having been removed. The cool May
morning air made her shiver.

Desperation tunneled through her. She knew he
would rape and then kill her. That was when she
saw her chance. It was a simple plan, and she had
to act fast. Risking everything, Rachel grabbed
a bronze statue of a cowboy on Cade's dresser.
With all her might, she used both hands to swing
it at Dirk's head.

Startled, Dirk let out a cry and fired the gun just
as the bronze slammed into his head.

With a scream, Rachel started to fall backward
and saw him stagger. Oh, God! She was helpless.
She couldn't run. Blood oozed out of a cut on
Dirk's head.

"You *bitch*!" he roared.

Everything slowed down. Rachel screamed and
held out her hands as he raised the gun toward
her. His face was a hideous mask of hatred. He

straightened, his back to the open door. "You're gonna die…."

Rachel's entire life unwound before her. A shadow moved through the door. Cade! Before Rachel could move, he'd leaped upon Dirk. The gun went off. Rachel felt a numbness in her right leg. She fell to the floor.

Cade balled his fist as he wrestled with the lighter Payson beneath him. The gun had flown out of his hand as Cade slammed him into the floor. He'd seen Rachel suddenly flung backward, landing in a heap near the bathroom door. Blood stained the pants covering her right thigh. She'd been shot! Grunting, Cade put every bit of hatred for Payson into his fist. As his hand connected with the convict's face, Cade heard his nose break. Several teeth broke. Blood splattered out of Payson's mouth as he cried out.

Rachel's eyes widened. Payson's gun skidded to a halt right in front of her. Breathing hard, she scrambled to her hands and knees. Her right leg wouldn't work. Desperate, she crawled toward the pistol. Her hand shook violently, but she managed to grab the gun. With a thrust of her left leg, she fell backward away from him. Blood purled thickly along his left temple. He went limp beneath Cade's powerful punch. She watched numbly as Cade pulled a pair of cuffs from behind his belt and jerked Payson onto his belly. In swift, sure motions he cuffed the convict. Now, she was safe.

Looking down, Rachel noticed a huge red spot

of blood rapidly moving across her right thigh. The shock hit her. She'd been shot. Her survival instinct kicked in. She forced herself to try and stand, but collapsed again.

"Stay down," Cade shouted, getting up off Payson. "Don't move, Rachel! Let me call an ambulance...." He walked swiftly to her side, his radio in hand.

She looked up at Cade's face. She saw the blackness in his eyes, felt his fierce sense of protection toward her. He'd come back home for her. Why? She opened her mouth to speak, but nothing came out. How had Cade known Dirk had broken in here? Her tears blurred his image as he leaned down over her to examine the wound. And then, Rachel felt her world spin. The last thing Rachel remembered was Cade's anxious face as he pressed hard down on her wound to stop the bleeding.

CHAPTER NINETEEN

"HOW ARE YOU DOING, Rachel?" Cade asked after pushing aside the curtain to her side of the emergency room. The only time he'd left the cubicle was minutes earlier when he'd conferred with the deputies guarding Payson. The convict was receiving medical attention in a private room on the second floor. Rachel had been unconscious when he left. Now, she was awake.

Rachel looked up from her gurney. Cade was white-faced, his eyes dark with turmoil, mouth set in a thin line. She'd never seen him so upset. It warmed her to know how much he cared for her.

The doctor working on her right leg nodded to the deputy as he entered. Her mind was still foggy. Slowly, the details began to dribble back. She opened her hand and Cade came forward and gripped it.

"I'm okay," she said in a faint voice. Rachel wanted to ease his anxiety. The room still spun and she closed her eyes. When she opened them again, everything had stopped spinning.

She looked anxiously at Cade. "Jenny? Is she

all right?" Fear stabbed at her and tore away the rest of the grogginess. Her mind barely functioned.

"She's fine," Cade soothed. "Unhurt. My mom and dad have her over at their place right now. She doesn't realize what happened."

"Thank God," Rachel whispered, then glanced at the doctor. "Am I going to be all right?"

"It's just a flesh wound," the woman doctor assured her. "You're going to be fine." Jordana Lawton glanced at Cade. "Matter of fact, Deputy Garner has permission to take you home as soon as I get done cleaning out your wound and give it a few stitches. You just relax. This isn't going to take long."

A trembling sigh broke from her lips. Cade's hand rested on her shoulder. Rachel could feel his strength. "I'm okay, Cade."

Cade struggled to maintain his composure. But Rachel had almost died from the ordeal and the thought nearly undid him. Ordinarily, he could. The physician had already cut away the fabric of her slacks on her thigh to reach the still-bleeding wound. Rachel had fainted in the ambulance as he rode with her to the hospital in Jackson Hole. When he was sure that she was being taken care of, he'd called his parents to let them know she was going to survive the gunshot wound. Plus, he had to coordinate with the sheriff's office and make sure Payson was guarded.

"That's good news," he agreed, attempting to share a smile with her, but not succeeding. Since the doctor was working on her, he couldn't embrace her. Cade stood at the end of the gurney holding her cold, damp fingers. He could see that Rachel was still in shock. Why wouldn't she be?

"I don't remember getting shot," Rachel murmured, searching her memory. "I just remember my leg feeling numb and when I wanted to move, I couldn't."

The young doctor looked over at the deputy. The blond-haired nurse at his side handed her a sponge. "Nothing to be worried about," she assured Cade. "It's a flesh wound. She was lucky. I'm going to clean it up, give her a shot of lydocaine to numb the area and then sew it up and put a dressing on it. After a tetanus shot and an antibiotic prescription, I'm going to release her."

Relief flooded Cade. "Sounds good," he whispered, gazing down at Rachel. She looked so pale. What kind of trauma had she faced with Payson? "Do you remember what happened before I arrived?"

Rachel told him everything. When she finished the story, she felt fatigued. Talking about it drained her of whatever reserves she had left. "What shape is he in?" she asked Cade.

"Payson's in a private room here in the hospital and being guarded by two deputies. We're moving through the paperwork to get him transferred back to the prison he broke out of. He's got a broken nose and jaw, he lost three teeth, but he's going to live." Cade held up the hand he'd used to strike

Payson. His knuckles were bruised and swollen. He wished he'd hit him even harder.

Reaching out, Rachel gently placed her hand over his knuckles. "You saved me...."

Cade gently squeezed her hand. "I just thank God I listened to my gut, Rachel. I had a bad feeling, turned around and drove home. I saw Randy on the road making his rounds. When I got to the ranch and saw the master-bedroom window broken, I knew Payson had found you."

Hot tears filled her eyes. It was the first time since the incident that she'd felt weepy. Maybe the adrenaline was wearing off and exposing her to other emotions. "Cade, he admitted to killing my mom." Shakily, she wiped her eyes. "After he told me that, I don't know what came over me. I wanted to kill him for killing her. I can't believe I picked up that bronze and hit him with it."

Gently, Cade said, "Rachel, we're all capable of defending ourselves. And that's what you did. And anyone would be angry toward the person who killed their loved one. Don't feel guilty over how you responded." His mouth turned down. "I'm just sorry I wasn't there earlier." Hoarsely, he whispered, "I promised to protect you from Payson and I didn't...." That hurt him most of all because he loved Rachel and he hadn't been there to stand between her and that killer in time.

"Don't go there, Cade. You came at the right time," Rachel protested, her voice stronger with conviction. "I'm just glad it's over."

Nodding, Cade wished the doctor and nurse weren't present. He wanted to take Rachel into his arms and hold her so damn tightly they'd become one. Searching her exhausted features, he murmured, "As soon as the doctor is finished, I'm taking you home."

Looking into her weary eyes, he asked, "Are you all right with that? Would you rather not go back to that house?"

"Oh, Cade, it's *your* house. It's where I've lived and I love being there. I don't want to go anywhere else. I really don't."

Heartened, he nodded. "Okay, home it is."

Home. That word sounded incredibly healing to Rachel. Her world had suddenly imploded upon her. She had no idea what would happen next. The loss of her mother and now Dirk's unexpected attack had made her feel out of control. Cade looked so assured and strong that she greedily absorbed that energy. His hand felt stabilizing and warm compared to the iciness she felt present within herself. Though she was in shock, Rachel tried to give him a warm look.

"I can hardly wait, Cade. That's all I want right now—home, you and Jenny."

CADE STOOD AT THE kitchen window five days later. The May sun was shining. The snow was nearly gone, and he could see the muddy land starting to green up in preparation for the late spring. Sipping his coffee, he turned and waited for Rachel. It was only 6:00 a.m. Jenny was asleep in her room. He'd checked earlier on the baby and then on Rachel. She, too, was sleeping soundly.

A new sense of contentment blanketed him. He'd asked for two weeks vacation after the incident. As he drank his coffee, he felt a deep satisfaction that Dirk Payson was in prison. Payson would have another trial for the murder of Daisy Donovan. And Cade was sure he'd get the death penalty. The bastard deserved it. He was a bad seed and had made choices that took him down this particular path. At some point, Payson would permanently be out of Rachel's life. Until then, Cade wanted to be there for her. He loved her.

His heart ached with need of Rachel. Since he'd brought her home, she'd shifted and gone deep within herself. Cade recognized it as grief as well as shock. His family had rallied around her and little by little, Rachel was emerging from the darkness. Even better, the FBI was releasing her from the witness protection program. They had rounded up the rest of Payson's men who had worked with him. The Donovan family was no longer in jeopardy from the drug ring since it had been broken up and the FBI had captured the drug lord.

Rachel padded softly out into the kitchen in her sheepskin slippers. She saw Cade standing at the kitchen sink leaning his hips against it, cup of coffee in hand. He wore a maroon flannel long-sleeved shirt and jeans along with his well-worn cowboy boots. His hair was still damp, so she knew he'd recently taken a shower. Giving him a soft smile, she said, "Coffee's ready?"

Cade nodded, poured her a cup and handed it to her. Her hair was mussed and he ached to run his fingers through that mass of curls where the blond hair was now clearly evident. "Did you sleep well?" he asked. Rachel wore a pale-pink chenille robe and a sleepy look lingered in her eyes. The expression became her, and Cade forced himself not to stare at the soft curve of her lips. Wanting to kiss her, kiss away her anguish and suffering, he gripped the mug a little more tightly in his hand.

"I slept like a log. I had a good dream."

"Oh?" His heart began to race with need of her. So much had happened and Cade felt frustrated that he could never bring up his personal need for Rachel or speak of the love and dreams he had for both of them.

Settling her hips against the counter, Rachel sipped her coffee. "I dreamed I was home, at our farm. I was with my brothers and their families. We were happy and laughing." Looking up at Cade she said, "And you were there, too."

"One big happy family again?" Cade asked, heartened by the dream.

Nodding, Rachel took another drink of the coffee, eased away from the counter and set the mug down next to the sink. Moving in front of Cade, she placed her hand on his arm. "Cade, I can't stand not saying this to you." She pursed her lips for a moment and looked worried. Gathering her courage, Rachel sought out and held his suddenly intense gaze. "I love you. It just happened over time. I wasn't expecting ever to fall in love again, but here you were. You've been wonderful—you're patient and understanding. You're the exact opposite of Dirk in every way. So many times I've stood at this sink, looking out the window, counting my blessings that you'd somehow fallen into my life like a guardian angel." Her hand tightened briefly on his upper arm where she felt his muscles respond beneath her fingers. "I woke up this morning knowing I had to tell you that. I don't know if you love me…but with so much happening, I *had* to tell you how I really felt."

His mouth dry, Cade asked in a rasp, "And how long have you loved me, Rachel?"

She gave him a shy smile. "I think it started the night of the accident. I didn't realize it until later of course, but seeing you was like seeing life. A life filled with promise. With hope. I finally figured out about a month afterward that you were the man I had always dreamed of meeting, but hadn't. I made some terrible choices, Cade. I didn't listen to my mom's advice, and instead I ran away from home. She was right. And after all that happened, you were like life being handed back to me."

Her words were like sunlight flooding into his entire being. Cade set his mug down and brought Rachel into his arms. She was soft and willowy, her lower body pressed against his. "Thanks for being so honest," he said, moving his fingers across her brow to move a few strands of hair aside. He drowned in the wide blue eyes that shone with innocence. Somehow, he managed to tell the truth. "I love you, too, Rachel. I don't know when it happened, either. It just did. At first, because you came here to take care of Jenny, I thought I was reliving my first marriage. Later, I knew it had nothing to do with the past." He smiled gently and cupped her face, "I fell in love with you for you. And God knows how long I've been sitting on this. Every time I thought I could tell you, something happened to stop me."

His roughened hands made her flesh tingle. How good it felt to be cradled in Cade's arms. His voice vibrated with feeling. Rachel could see the love shining in his widening gray eyes. No longer was he the expressionless sheriff's deputy, but a man wanting to love his woman. Leaning up, she kissed his recently shaven cheek. And then, on tiptoes, her lips near his ear, she whispered, "I want to love you, Cade. Here. Now. I've never wanted anything more than you. And I know it's the right time and place. Will you?" She pulled away to look into his eyes.

"You never have to ask, sweet woman," Cade told her. In one movement, he picked her up off the floor and into his arms. Glorying in the way her arms settled around his shoulders, in the lovely smile in her eyes and on her lips, Cade carried her to their bedroom.

The stained-glass lamp on the bureau gave just

enough light to the room. With a sigh, Rachel felt him nudge the door closed with the toe of his boot. The room was like a warm cocoon to her. Cade deposited her on the bed. The beautiful quilt over the top had been an heirloom from his great-grandmother. It was old, well-worn, much loved, and she absorbed the love that had gone into its making.

Cade sat down next to her. He grazed her reddened cheek. "Tell me what you want." He grazed the line of her clean jaw and read the need in her slumberous eyes.

"Just love me, Cade. That's all I need or will ever want." Her voice went low, uncertain. "I'm not saying I'm skilled at this...."

"Then we'll teach one another as we go," Cade whispered, touched by her admission. Standing up, he began to undress. A sense of incredible inner power flowed through Cade as he unbuttoned his shirt, shed it and bared his massive, dark-haired chest. The look shining in Rachel's eyes made him feel more potent than ever before.

Rachel felt her heart beating faster and faster as Cade removed each article of clothing. His body was powerful, shaped from a life of ranch work. The muscles of his arms and legs were well developed. When he stood naked before Rachel, her mouth went dry with anticipation. Clearly, Cade desired her. There was no mistaking that, and she dragged her gaze upward to meet his. Without a word, she sat up. There was a sense of momentary dread as she eased off the bed to remove the chenille robe. Rachel wore nothing beneath it. Would Cade find her ugly? Not beautiful enough to want to love? Rachel swept past her fear and found the courage to allow the garment to drop and pool about her feet. She stood naked before Cade's burning inspection. Anxiously, she searched his gaze, worried that he would reject her. Payson had called her body deformed and ugly.

Cade lifted his hands and rested them on her shoulders. "You're incredibly beautiful, Rachel." His voice went hoarse with want. His eyes slid down and across her body. Her breasts were small, perfectly formed, and her hips wide and flared. She was built to have children, he realized somewhere in his fleeting thoughts. And how badly Cade yearned to have a baby with her. For now, he used protection and they could decide when the time was right for both of them.

Closing her eyes, Rachel allowed his words to vibrate through her, touch her heart and heal her wounded spirit. Did Cade know how wonderful those words sounded? She didn't think so, but she would let him know at another time. Opening her eyes, Rachel stepped forward into the circle of his arms, reached up and placed her mouth against his.

Within seconds, Cade's lips plundered hers, fueled by aching need. Easing Rachel down to the bed, Cade lay beside her, their bodies meeting and melding against one another. Rachel absorbed his male strength. It felt as if they had been made for one another—his body powerful, hard, and hers soft and receptive. This new discovery riffled through her like a hot, needy sensation and made the ache between her thighs even more intense.

As his mouth cherished hers, his breath hot and ragged against her cheek, Rachel moved her tongue across his lower lip. Cade groaned. The sound was like thunder moving through her, enticing her, calling to her. The knot of throbbing heat within her grew to such a point that Rachel moaned. She'd never felt this hungry before.

As Cade moved his hand in a slow, exploratory gesture down from her shoulder to curve around her small, firm breast, he felt her gasp. Smiling into her eyes, he used his thumb and index finger to caress the hardened nipple. Rachel pressed herself against him, a raw moan escaping her parted lips. His heart soared. Cade knew he was pleasuring her. He burned with a love that could only be quenched by their coming physically together. Yet, as he left her breast and trailed his fingers down across her rib cage to her waist and belly, Cade wanted this to be good for Rachel in every way. If that meant he would suffer in the meantime, that was all right with him. He knew enough of Rachel's past not to hurry her, rather, to allow her to feel what it was like to have a man who loved her bring her to full readiness.

Cade's fingers caressed the downy nest of hair at the apex of her thighs. Rachel gasped, her flesh tingling and tightening. She cried out his name. As Cade gently eased his fingers into the cleft to graze her sensitized flesh for the first time, Rachel emitted a moan of utter pleasure. Heat built rapidly within her core. Cade's fingers knew how to explore, caress and make the ache within her even more intense. Rachel arched herself against his fingers.

"That's it," Cade whispered darkly into her ear, "just enjoy this, Rachel. You're all woman, you're mine. All I want to do is give you pleasure...."

Absorbing his husky words, she restlessly slid her arms around his shoulders and pulled him forward. As his fingers left that dark, secret place of heat, Rachel felt his mouth settle commandingly over hers. She opened her legs and thrust her hips upward. Instantly, he met her aching core. She deepened the kiss and moved her tongue within his mouth. The moment that happened, she arched upward to meet his thrust into her.

Her world spun and deepened. Rachel felt him move seamlessly into her, as if they had always been meant for one another. He slid his hand beneath her hips, lifted her slightly, the sensations intensifying until she tore her lips from his. With each rocking thrust, Rachel went higher and higher. The throbbing tension in her core became so intense, she groaned. And, as if sensing what she needed, Cade thrust hard and deep within her. Their rhythm changed and grew frantic. Throwing her head back, Rachel cried out in relief as the gate within her exploded. The hot fluid flowed through her in wave after wave of utter gratification. She felt light, airy, only vaguely aware of Cade's breath next to her ear. His hips continued to thrust against hers, his male body strong and coaxing her to new heights.

It was like being spun in gold and white light, Rachel thought. She was weightless, plundering his mouth and feeling his hot, moist breath flowing across her face. Cade stiffened, groaned and tensed to immobility. Rachel instinctively knew to move her hips to give him the ultimate joy that he'd just given her. Together, they were molten lava flowing and fusing into one another. As she clung to Cade and his arms slid around her in a tight embrace, she needed nothing more. *Nothing.* For the first time, Rachel understood what it was for a man to fully love his woman. The tenderness Cade had shown, the patience, the slow movement and exploration of his hands and lips upon her body taught Rachel what real love was really all about. It made her life with Payson seem like a bleak sham. Rachel gloried beneath Cade's heavy body pressing her into the mattress. His mouth caressed her closed eyelids and sipped the honey from her parted lips.

All of the butterfly lightness slowly receded. Rachel lay in Cade's arms, his body like a warm blanket across her. There was a delicious sense of love mingling with protection, as well as care radiating from him to her. His fingers gently tangled through the strands of her hair. Her scalp radiated with delicious tingles beneath his ministrations.

Each movement made her feel wanted, needed and most of all, Rachel could feel herself healing from her traumatic past. Love did that, she realized as she slowly descended from that euphoric state.

Easing off her, Cade brought Rachel beside him. The room was warm but he wanted to ensure she wouldn't get chilled in the aftermath of their lovemaking. Reaching across her, he brought the quilt up and over them. Her eyes opened, with a drowsy, fulfilled look in them. He smiled down at her. "This is what I want to see every morning when I wake up with you," he told her in a low tone. Caressing her hair, he whispered, "I love you, Rachel. I want to marry you. I want you to be my partner, my best friend…my wife. And the mother of our children if that's what you want."

The words were like healing hands cupping her wildly beating heart. The throbbing within her lower body slowly receded and she found it difficult to think rather than just feel. Gazing into Cade's gray eyes, she nodded. "Finding you was finding myself. You've helped me find my way back to me, Cade. I can't put it all into words, but you've shown me how to have a healthy relationship between a man and a woman."

"How could you know before now?" he asked, tenderly pressing a kiss to her brow, cheek and then trailing a series of them to her mouth. Raising his head, scant inches between them, Cade held her blue gaze. "We all make mistakes, Rachel. No one is perfect. I knew Payson had hurt you badly. I hope to show you there is a good side to the rest of us."

"You have," Rachel murmured, feeling a delicious drowsiness stalking her. "I've never felt happier. Or more hopeful."

Gathering Rachel into his arms, Cade lay down, pressing his body against hers. "Let's take a nap," he urged, his face buried in her fragrant, silky hair. "We have a lot to talk about after we wake up. Right now, sweet woman, all I want to do is lie here with you and wake up with you in my arms…."

"WHAT DO YOU THINK of a July wedding?" Cade asked Rachel as they sat at the kitchen table two hours later. Jenny had been fed, bathed and was now crawling around the kitchen floor. Sometimes, she would stand with the help of a chair or with the support of their hands. She was happy to be exploring the legs of the chairs right now.

Slipping her hand over Cade's, Rachel said, "Let's see what your parents say. Gwen has a lot of things going on at the quilting shop. We need to try and fit into their schedules."

"You're right," Cade said. He gazed over at her flushed face and drowned in her joyous blue eyes. His body hardened all over again. They had awakened an hour ago and taken a shower together, then had tended to Jenny, who had just awakened.

"First, I'd like to go home to Iowa with you at

my side, Cade. I want you to meet my brothers and their families."

"I'd like that. I want to see where you were raised," Cade said, meaning it. It was nearly ten o'clock in the morning. Sunlight made the world outside their kitchen bright and hopeful after a very long, dark winter tide.

Jenny climbed up with the use of the chair and Rachel's help. She smiled and cooed.

"We'll be taking Jenny with us," Rachel promised, lifting the baby into her arms and settling her across her lap.

"Absolutely," Cade said, reaching out and allowing Jenny to wrap her tiny hand around his finger. He gave Rachel a warm look. "Maybe, after we've been married awhile, we might think of giving Jenny a baby brother or sister?"

Rachel heard the hope in his voice. So much had been taken from Cade. Now, it was as if all of life was going to be given back not only to him, but to her, as well. Their tragedies were behind them. She kissed Jenny's hair. "I'd like nothing better than to work on that, Cade. I've always dreamed of having two or three kids. I came from a large family and I know the happiness of it. I'd like to have that chance with you."

Her softly spoken words were incredibly sweet and healing to Cade. He placed his hand around Rachel's shoulders, their chairs close to one another. "You're a gift to me."

"No," she whispered, tears coming unexpectedly to her eyes, "you're my gift, Cade."

Leaning over, he smiled and pressed a tender kiss to her lips. "We'll be gifts to one another. Okay?"

"Forever," she said, her voice raspy with unshed tears. "I know life can be hard, and we'll have plenty of ups and downs. Together, Cade, we can manage them. I know we can."

Jenny bent over to crawl into her father's lap. Cade smiled with deep fulfillment. "Life guarantees nothing. What we can do is live each day to its fullest. I'm grateful you and Jenny are in my life. And I intend to let you both know how much I love you. You're all I'll ever want or need."

* * * * *

Joan Johnston is the *New York Times* and *USA TODAY* bestselling author of more than fifty novels with more than fifteen million copies of her books in print. She has been a director of theater, drama critic, newspaper editor, college professor and attorney on her way to becoming a full-time writer. You can find out more about Joan at joanjohnston.com or on Facebook at Joan Johnston Author.

Books by Joan Johnston

Visit the Author Profile page
at Harlequin.com for more titles.

HAWK'S WAY: CALLEN

Joan Johnston

For Priscilla Kelley.
Because the little things do matter.

PROLOGUE

"I'M SO SORRY about your father." Callen Whitelaw felt awkward offering sympathy to someone she hardly knew. At first she didn't think the grieving man was going to reply. When he did, he said one word in a ragged whisper.

"Thanks."

Callen tried to imagine Sam Longstreet crying with enough despair to make himself hoarse. She wanted to fold him in her arms and comfort him. But he was a stranger, even though he had been a neighbor all her life. She had known his father, E.J., better than she knew Sam, because E.J. had come to Hawk's Way often to spend time with her father.

"Is there anything I can do?" she asked.

"No." He hesitated a moment, then said, "Maybe there is. I have to go to Amarillo on business. Maybe you could meet me there, have dinner with me. I... I could use the company."

Callen was stunned by the invitation, which seemed to come out of the blue. Why would Sam Longstreet want to have dinner with her when he didn't even know her?

"Never mind," he said when she hesitated too long.

She caught his arm as he started to turn away. "Wait. Please. I'll be glad to meet you. Just tell me when and where."

He named a time and a restaurant, and then his attention was drawn by another rancher offering condolences.

Callen thought about the invitation during the entire drive home with her family, wondering what had compelled Sam to reach out to her. Once she was home, she asked her eldest brother, Zach, about Sam. Zach admitted to only a passing acquaintance with Sam. Her other brother, Falcon, hadn't come home for the funeral from his ranch in Dallas, but Zach said he could speak for both of them.

"Neither of us knew Sam very well," Zach said. "He was two years ahead of me in school, three years ahead of Falcon, so we didn't have any classes together."

Zach was thirty-four, so that would make Sam thirty-six, Callen figured. He had seemed every bit of that, his features chiseled by wind and weather, his striking green eyes webbed at the corners by the sun, his wide mouth bracketed by lines, his shaggy, chestnut hair streaked with blonde. It was a face aged by the hard life of a Texas rancher and by the grief that sat upon his brow.

"Sam wasn't too good with the books," Zach continued. "The football coach got tutors to help him pass his class work so he could play. He was a great running back, as I recall, but he pretty much kept to himself."

"Was he good enough to play professionally?" Callen asked.

"He hurt his knee in the state championship game. I guess he couldn't run fast enough after that to compete in college. He settled in to work on the Double L after high school, and as far as I know he never aspired to anything else. Why are you interested in Sam Longstreet, anyway?"

"He seemed so sad," Callen said.

"Stay away from him," Zach warned. "He's a saddle tramp with a rundown ranch."

"That's unfair!" Callen retorted in defense of a man she had just met. "Just because the Longstreets don't have as much money as the Whitelaws doesn't make Sam any less of a man."

"He's never going to amount to anything."

"How do you know?"

"If he was going to do anything with that ranch to improve it, he would have done it by now," Zach said.

"Not necessarily," Callen retorted. "Maybe he and his father disagreed about what ought to be done." Callen knew she had hit a sore spot with Zach, because he and their father often disagreed about ranching methods.

"You're speculating," Zach accused.

"You're just mad because you know I'm right," Callen shot back.

Her quarrel with Zach was loud enough to bring their mother, Candy, into the parlor from the kitchen.

"What's going on in here?" she asked.

"Callen's got herself into a snit over that good-for-nothing at the Double L."

"Sam Longstreet is not—"

"That's enough from both of you," Candy interrupted. "Zach, don't you have some business with your father in his office?" Once Zach was gone, she turned to Callen. "Now what's all this about Sam Longstreet?"

"I spoke to him at E.J.'s funeral," Callen said. "He seemed so alone, Mom, and so sad. I wanted to do something for him, but I didn't know what. He mentioned he was going to be in Amarillo on business and asked me to join him for dinner. I said yes."

Her mother arched a questioning brow but said nothing either to approve or disapprove of what Callen had done.

Yet Callen felt the need to explain herself. "I couldn't say no, Mom. I mean, there was something so peculiar about the way he looked at me. He didn't say much of anything, but I could hear him speaking to me with his eyes. It was so strange."

"Peculiar. Strange. Those are odd words to describe a man you've agreed to join for dinner," her mother mused.

"That's the problem, Mom," Callen said, shoving a hand through the dark bangs that hung slightly in her eyes. "I don't know exactly how to describe him. He seemed so sad. And lonely."

"I see. So you want to make him happy and less lonely?"

"Is that so awful?"

Her mother slid an arm around her waist and hugged her slightly. "Not if you keep in mind that what you're offering Sam Longstreet is friendship. Just don't let yourself tumble head over heels in love with a man who's too wounded to love you back."

CHAPTER ONE

"I'M GOING TO marry Sam Longstreet, and there's nothing you can do to stop me," Callen said to her father in a calm, brittle voice. Her brown eyes flashed with defiance. "What's wrong with Sam? He's a rancher, a close neighbor. Longstreet land has bordered Whitelaw land in northwest Texas for generations!"

Garth Whitelaw eyed his daughter, the youngest of his three grown children, with trepidation. She had been engaged twice, but never married. Both times, he had warned her she was making a mistake. Both times, she had disregarded his advice, only to break the engagements later when she learned the truth of what he had said. Now she was proposing a third prospective husband, this one as bad—maybe even worse—than the other two. Garth had learned that telling Callen no was like waving a red flag in front of a bull, but he felt so strongly that Sam was the wrong man for his daughter that he made his arguments anyway.

"Sam Longstreet will never amount to anything," he said. "He's a down-at-the-heels rogue with nothing to his name but a ramshackle ranch.

At a guess, I'd say he's only interested in your money."

"That's despicable!" Callen retorted. "How can you even suggest such a thing?"

"Because it's true," Garth replied in a steely voice. "You're an heiress, Sam's a dirt-poor rancher. He was lucky to get through high school, and he hasn't done anything since to educate himself. He's a loner, and he's lazy. The Double L is falling down around him. What can the two of you possibly have in common?"

"Sam's a wonderful man," Callen argued. "He's just had a lot of hard luck lately. His father made some bad investments that took all their savings. I'll agree Sam has been reclusive in the months since his dad died, but that sort of blow would be hard on anyone who loved his father as much as Sam loved E.J."

Garth probably missed E. J. Longstreet as much or more than Sam did. The two older men had been good friends. It was a shame what had happened to E.J., and Garth sympathized with Sam's loss. But that didn't mean he wanted Sam for a son-in-law. He couldn't imagine what his daughter found attractive about the rancher. He asked again, "What do you see in him?"

Callen hesitated a moment before she replied. "Sam needs me, Daddy. And I need him. He makes me feel...special."

Garth snorted. "I'm not saying what happens between a man and woman between the sheets isn't important. But you're going to find it mighty tough sitting across from a lazy good-for-nothing at the breakfast table for the rest of your life."

Callen's lips flattened and her eyes narrowed. "I didn't mean Sam makes me feel special in bed. I meant— Oh, what's the use! I'm not going to change your mind, and you're not going to change mine. I wasn't asking your permission to marry Sam, I just wanted to let you know we're going to be married and invite you to the wedding."

"I won't be there," Garth said flatly.

Callen's chin quivered. She gritted her teeth to steady it before replying, "That's up to you, of course." She started for the front door of the antebellum-style mansion that had been built more than a century before as the main ranch house at Hawk's Way. She paused at the front door, waiting, hoping her father would change his mind. Her heart sank as she heard his parting words.

"If you marry Sam, you won't have a job here anymore." Garth knew the threat was a mistake the moment the words were out of his mouth, but it was too late to take them back. Callen was the best cutting horse trainer he had. She wouldn't have any trouble finding another job. And he didn't want to lose all contact with his only daughter. Though it had been years since he had said the words to her, he loved her dearly.

Callen's shoulders stiffened, then squared, before she turned to face her father. "I hope you'll change your mind, Daddy. Because come Friday, I'm going to be Mrs. Sam Longstreet."

Callen headed for the stable to saddle her horse. She needed some time alone to think. The canyons and gullies of Hawk's Way had long provided a haven, a ready balm for her soul. Once in the saddle, Callen aimed her horse into the Texas sun. It felt wonderful on her face, and the wind brushed her bangs away from her forehead and lifted her shoulder-length black hair so it flew in the breeze. She relaxed her jaw, which she realized was still clenched.

She was furious with her father for opposing her marriage to Sam and equally terrified that he might be right. He had been right twice before. But Sam was different, not at all like the previous two men she had planned to marry. In the first place, Sam was a rancher. She had grown up on Hawk's Way, and there wasn't anything she didn't know about cattle or cutting horses. She and Sam had that in common, since he had grown up on the Double L. But she would have been hard-pressed to name the specific things about Sam that made her so sure they were right for each other.

When she had gone to dinner with Sam three months ago, Callen had found herself utterly charmed by him. There was something dangerous about Sam, about his moods and the way he carried himself. And yet his eyes were so very sad. And kind. That was the word she would have used to describe his behavior toward her.

She could remember Sam's first kiss as though

it had just happened. He had walked her to her car from the restaurant and stood there looking at her with eyes that spoke volumes. The closest light came from the restaurant, and they stood partly in shadow.

"You're beautiful," he said.

Callen had been told that before by more than one man, but Sam made her believe it. He cupped one cheek with his hand and brushed his callused thumb across her lips. She shivered at the touch. Her eyes had drifted closed as he slowly lowered his head.

His lips were incredibly soft as he pressed them to hers. He brushed them once, twice across her mouth before lifting his head to stare into her eyes once more.

He'd left her wanting much, much more.

It was only the first of many excursions together. They often went riding over Double L land and, if Callen were honest, she had to admit the place needed work. Fences were down, windmills screeched for want of oil, the barn needed some sideboards replaced and the house—at least from the outside—had seen much better days.

When she asked Sam about the rundown condition of the Double L, he had replied, "It takes money to make repairs. Not all of us are blessed with wealth."

Seeing how sensitive he was about the difference in their economic situations, she hadn't brought up the subject again.

Their second kiss had come a week after the

first, at a moment when they had just stepped down to rest their horses. She was caught by surprise because it was a kiss of hunger, and she hadn't seen the need in Sam's eyes until he reached for her and pulled her into his embrace. His body was large and hard, and she had felt enveloped by him—safe, secure, and very much wanted. His hands moved hesitantly over her body at first, barely touching, reverently touching, and finally claiming her. She felt breathless when he finally released her.

"Sam…please." It was a plea to finish what he had started.

Sam shook his head and, in a voice harsh with need, said, "No, Callen. It wouldn't be right."

"Why not?"

He smiled ruefully. "In the first place, I don't have any kind of protection with me."

She blushed furiously. She should have thought of that herself.

"In the second place, you deserve better. A soft bed and a lover who belongs to you, heart and soul."

She hadn't known what to reply to that.

"Come on," he said, lifting her into the saddle. "We'd better get back to the house."

They had been seeing each other almost daily for a month when she asked if she could see the inside of his house.

Again, Sam shook his head no.

"Why not?" she demanded, fists perched on hips.

"Because I wouldn't trust myself alone with you if there was a bed anywhere nearby."

Callen had been flattered but was so used to getting her own way that she didn't give up. She pressed herself close to Sam, feeling the way his body tensed and hardened. "I wouldn't mind, Sam," she purred in her most seductive voice.

"I would," Sam said as he caught her by the arms and moved her away. "You deserve the best, Callen. You deserve to be treated with respect."

Callen met Sam's gaze, her eyes wide with surprise. His words were what every woman wanted to hear, yet her brow soon furrowed in confusion. His ideas concerning courtship were so…old-fashioned. He had to know, since she had been engaged twice, that she wasn't a virgin who needed to be protected from the importunities of a forceful male. But Sam had apparently put her on a pedestal. She found it awkward to stay balanced there, knowing herself to be far less than perfect. But, oh, how good it felt to be so cherished!

Then the precious moment had come, just two days ago, when Sam proposed to her.

"I know I'm not good enough for you," Sam began.

She pressed her fingertips to his lips. How could he not be good enough when he made her feel so wonderful?

"You deserve better," he insisted. "But I'll do my best to make your life as happy as I can. Will you marry me, Callen? Will you be my wife?"

Her throat was so tight with emotion that she

hadn't been able to answer right away. At last she said, "Yes, Sam, I'll marry you. I want to be your wife."

He kissed her then, tenderly at first and then hungrily, his tongue sweeping into her mouth and claiming her. He hugged her so tightly she squeaked with pain. When he released her, they looked at each other and laughed with joy.

His eyes glittered in the sunlight, and for a moment she was frightened at their intensity. She shivered, and he pulled her close, murmuring, "Don't be frightened, Callen."

Until Sam spoke the words, she hadn't realized how scared she was. But the look in his eyes urged her to trust him. And she did. Sam would never hurt her the way she had been hurt before. He would never allow himself to be bought off by her father, as her first two lovers had done. Sam would only love her and respect her and protect her.

Was it any wonder she had fallen in love with him? Was it any wonder that, when he had proposed, she had said yes? Her father had suggested that Sam was another fortune hunter. That he was lazy and poor and just wanted to marry her for her money.

Callen didn't believe it. Sam loved her. She would stake her life on it. *Was* staking her life on it. Because, come Friday, she would be standing in front of a judge with Sam Longstreet by her side. And when the judge asked if she wanted to spend the rest of her life with Sam, she was going to say yes.

SAM LONGSTREET DIDN'T want Callen's money, but neither was he marrying her for love. He had wooed her and won her with one specific purpose in mind: to get revenge on Garth Whitelaw.

Garth was the one who had convinced Sam's father, E.J., to invest his life savings in several ventures that had turned out to be swindles. Sam had been shocked to discover that Garth had led his father so far astray, since the two men had been friends for more years than anyone could count. His best friend's betrayal had made E.J. moody and morose. He had started drinking and rarely left the house.

Sam had tried to console his father when things were at their worst, but E.J. was inconsolable. After more than a hundred years, he would be the Longstreet who finally lost the Double L to creditors. Sam had come home from working on the range one day to find his father, whom he cherished, dead of a gunshot wound to the head.

He had nearly gone mad with grief.

He had sat for hours in the same room with his father's corpse, unable to move. The long hours he spent paralyzed had given him a lot of time to think. The more he thought about it, the more convinced he became that Garth Whitelaw had planned to dupe his father, knowing full well E.J. would lose his ranch. Then, when it went into foreclosure, Garth could buy the land for a pittance of its value and add it to Hawk's Way, thus replacing the several thousand acres Garth had given to his eldest son, Zach, on his twenty-first birthday. It was Garth Whitelaw's greedy desire to possess the Double L that was the direct cause of E. J. Longstreet's death.

On the day Sam buried his father, he confronted Garth at the graveyard with his knowledge of the other man's perfidy. He waited until Garth was alone and approached him.

"This is all your fault," he snarled. "E.J. followed your advice and lost everything he worked for all his life!"

"I never—"

"Don't try to deny it," Sam said in a savage voice. "My father never invested a penny until he talked to you. Only this time you told him what would serve your purposes. This time you led him into a swindle. You knew how he felt about the Double L. You ruined him. You killed him as surely as if you'd held the gun yourself!"

Garth blanched.

Before he could retort, his daughter, Callen, reached his side. She was wearing her long black hair in a ponytail, with a fringe of bangs that made her look surprisingly young. Sam remembered her as a bothersome kid always trailing along behind her older brothers, Zach and Falcon, not that he and her brothers had had much to do with each other then or now. He noted in a detached way that Callen had grown up to be quite a beauty.

Sam watched as Callen looked up with adoring eyes at her father. Then he caught Garth's unguarded look of love for his daughter. At that moment the idea had come to Sam that here was one sure way to get vengeance on his enemy. Garth had stolen his father; somehow he would take Garth's daughter from him.

As Garth walked away, Callen looked up at him. "I'm so sorry about your father."

Sam checked the retort that he didn't need any Whitelaw pity, and said, "Thanks."

His face remained a thing of carved granite as he stared down at her. It dawned on him how easily he could have his vengeance.

Sam knew about Callen's two previous engagements. He knew her father wouldn't think he was good enough for her. All he had to do was make her fall in love with him. Father and daughter were sure to argue, and it would split them apart. Then he would offer to marry her, force her to choose between him and her father. Either way, she would lose. And, therefore, Garth would lose. His vengeance would be all the sweeter when he told Callen—if she chose him instead of her father—why he had married her.

Sam hadn't wasted any time beginning his conquest of Callen. He wasn't without charm, he simply chose not to employ it most of the time. There, at his father's graveside, he let his gaze linger on Callen's lips and then focus on her eyes. They were a warm, tobacco brown.

She flushed prettily. "Is there anything I can do to help?"

"You can meet me for dinner in Amarillo," he said.

When he turned his gaze back to Garth at the graveside, he was pleased with the frown he saw on the other man's face. He knew Garth wanted to warn him to keep his distance from Callen, but the older man kept his lips pressed tight as he whirled abruptly and walked away.

When all the other mourners were gone and Sam was finally alone in the tiny graveyard that held the mortal remains of generations of Longstreets, he stood near the cold headstone that marked his father's final resting place and made a solemn vow to avenge his death.

"I promise you, Dad, however long it takes, no matter what I have to do, Garth Whitelaw is going to suffer for what he did to you."

His courtship of Callen had been accomplished with surprising speed. He suspected she had felt sorry for him at first, and thus her barriers were all down. He had swept her off her feet with honeyed words and a few searing kisses. He hadn't bedded her, using old-fashioned morals as an excuse. His charade of respect and caring had worked even better than he had hoped. Within weeks she had fallen in love with him. When he proposed, she had accepted with tears of joy in her eyes.

The best part had been when Garth Whitelaw came to the Double L with his checkbook open, asking how much Sam wanted to call off the wedding.

"I don't want your money, Whitelaw." Sam hadn't

been able to keep from smiling. Garth was a fool to think he was going to be able to pay for his guilt with cash.

"I know you need money to keep the Double L from foreclosure. Tell me how much, and I'll loan it to you interest free," Garth offered.

"I don't want or need your help," he retorted. Truthfully, he was surprised that Garth had tried to buy him off with that particular offer. Sam figured the man must have had some other plan in mind to put the Double L in his debt. He wasn't going to fall for it.

"I want you to stay away from Callen," Garth said.

"She's a grown woman. She can make her own decisions."

"She's made her share of bad ones."

"And I'm a bad one?"

"The worst."

"Does Callen know you're here?"

Garth shifted restlessly, uneasily. "No."

A wicked grin split Sam's face as he relished Garth's discomfort. "Don't worry. I won't tell her you tried to buy me off."

Garth hadn't bothered thanking him, just stalked down the rickety stairs that led from Sam's sagging front porch, gunning the engine of his pickup as he headed down the dusty road.

So far, Callen had remained firm in the face of her family's disapproval. Sam had to admire her for that. He fought back the nagging conscience that told him it was wrong to hurt an innocent woman for the transgressions of her father. He was only doing what was necessary to avenge the wrong done to E.J. Garth Whitelaw hadn't given a thought to Sam's pain when he had ruined Sam's father. He quieted his conscience with the thought that when it was all over, Callen would still be alive. E.J. was gone forever.

The wedding was tomorrow. He wondered if Garth would find some way to stop it. He hoped the older man tried. It would surely put a wide breach between Garth and his daughter. It was a breach Sam intended to extend until father and daughter were totally alienated.

Sam swallowed the bitter bile that rose in his throat when he thought of the senselessness of his father's death. He needed the marriage to Callen to achieve his revenge against her father. It was important to guard against feeling anything for her. He had to bear in mind that Callen Whitelaw was just a tool he was using to achieve his goal of revenge. He had to forget about the softness of her skin, the sweetness of her kisses, the look of adoration and trust in her eyes.

Sam's lips pressed flat. When it came time to say his vows before the judge, he would do it. And crush the conscience that urged him to let the girl go free.

CHAPTER TWO

CALLEN CAME ALONE to the county courthouse for her wedding. Her father had held fast to his vow to be absent, and her mother had refused to side against her father. Her brother, Falcon, couldn't leave Dallas because his wife, Mara, was pregnant and near term, and her brother, Zach, had told her plainly that she was making the worst mistake of her life, and he wasn't going to be a part of it. In a privileged existence that had been marked by periods of loneliness, Callen had never felt so alone.

As she paced the hardwood floor in front of the judge's chambers dressed in an antique lace dress, wearing an ivory felt cloche and carrying a pungent bouquet of gardenias, Callen wondered whether she was playing the fool. Was her family right? Was Sam actually a fortune hunter?

Callen glanced at her watch. Sam was late. For a half second she wondered whether he might not show up at all. Before that thought could take root, she saw him come through the imposing double doors of the courthouse. As glad as she was to see him, Callen couldn't help the feeling of foreboding that wedged in her throat and made it difficult to speak.

Sam walked right up to her, reached for her hands and took them in his. "You look beautiful," he murmured.

Unfortunately there was no way Callen could honestly return the compliment. In fact, she was sorely disappointed by Sam's appearance. "You didn't dress up."

Sam flushed. "No."

No excuse, no explanation, just no. His sun-bleached hair was shaggy and needed a cut, nor had he shaved for at least a day. His boots were worn, and his jeans were frayed. He looked like he hadn't slept for a week, and if he had, he'd done it in his clothes. The sun-lined face that had become so dear to her was carved in granite. And his green eyes, the kind, tender eyes that had made her fall in love with him, looked as hard as cut glass.

Callen shivered. Sam seemed a stranger. This was a side of him she had never seen. He was the saddle tramp Zach had named him, shady and disreputable. Two spots of heat rose on her cheeks when she thought of the scathing comments her father would have made if he had seen her bridegroom looking like this. Callen was ashamed and embarrassed by Sam's appearance. The thought flashed across her mind that she ought to run like hell from Sam, from this marriage.

She couldn't look at Sam, afraid he would see what was in her thoughts. Appearances shouldn't matter, she told herself. She had known Sam was poor. She had seen him unshaven in the past, in fact, had seen him in the same Western shirt and jeans he was wearing now. But that didn't ease her worry. She had expected Sam to treat their marriage, the ceremony at least, with the same reverence she felt. After all, they were beginning a new life together. If anything, Sam's appearance evidenced contempt for the ritual of marriage. Obviously she had mistaken his feelings on the subject.

What else are you mistaken about, Callen?

Callen fought back the voices of her father and her brother, both of whom had warned her not to marry Sam. She opened her mouth to tell Sam she couldn't go through with it and shut it again. She couldn't be wrong about Sam. She refused to be wrong about Sam. There must be some good reason why he hadn't taken the time to improve his appearance, an emergency on the ranch or some other disaster.

"Was there some trouble on the ranch this morning?" she asked.

"No."

"No cattle stampede? Brush fire? Pack of howling wolves at the door?" she teased.

"No."

She pursed her lips ruefully. "You overslept?"

"No."

She couldn't think of another reason that would explain Sam's careless appearance…and he wasn't offering one. She looked up into his green eyes, which softened slightly as he stared down at her, and waited for an explanation.

"I went to visit my father's grave," he said at last.

"Oh." Her shoulders relaxed. Of course. He was still grieving. He must have stayed at the small, fenced plot too long, and then not had time to remedy his appearance. Now that she examined Sam's face more closely, she saw red-rimmed eyes, a clenched jaw. Yes, he was definitely still grieving. It must be awful to know his father hadn't lived to see his only son marry, hadn't lived to know his grandchildren.

The thought of producing grandchildren brought a rosy glow to Callen's cheeks. She had thought a lot about what it would be like to lie with Sam, to grow large with his child, to hold a baby in her arms and have Sam smile at her, as they admired their child together.

Callen reminded herself of everything she had learned about Sam over the past three months. He was kind. He was considerate. He was charming. He was even handsome in a rugged sort of way. And his eyes made her feel cherished and loved. Or at least they had. Perhaps it was the memory of his father, the grief and the sadness, that had stolen the warmth from his eyes and made him look so harsh and hard when she had first seen him today.

She loved Sam for who he was, not for the outer trappings of the man, not for his wealth—or lack of it—but for the way he made her feel. She squeezed Sam's hands, raised her eyes to meet his and offered him a tremulous smile. "Come on, Sam. The judge is waiting."

"Your family?"

She swallowed over the lump in her throat. "They're not coming."

"Then it's just us?"

Callen nodded. Sam's lips pressed flat and his eyes narrowed. For an instant she wanted to flee, to save herself from Sam, from the possibility of a failed marriage. But it would be devastating to break a *third* engagement. She wouldn't be able to look her father in the eye. It was too late to back out now.

Callen took comfort in the thought that she knew Sam better than her father did. Sam would never hurt her. And if he did, her father would never hear of it from her. She would do whatever was necessary to make the marriage a good one. As one of the Three Whitelaw Brats, and with a lifetime of outmaneuvering and outsmarting two older brothers to her credit, she had developed the ability to rescue herself from the toughest situations. She loved Sam. Somehow, this was all going to work out.

She looked up at Sam, her heart in her eyes. There was a flash of some strong emotion on his face before he kissed her with a combination of tenderness and fierceness that left her breathless. The thought came to her, powerful and overwhelming. *I want to spend my life with this man.*

"Come on," Sam grated in a husky voice. "Let's go."

SAM FELT LIKE sobbing with relief—and disgust. He had done what he could to keep Callen Whitelaw from walking into disaster, but she hadn't backed away in time to save either of them. He led her toward the judge's chambers. It was time to take the next step on his trail of vengeance.

His eyes were red-rimmed because he hadn't slept. His conscience had smote him the day before the wedding, demanding that he free Callen from the devil's bargain he was about to make with her. He had tried desperately to think of a way to take his vengeance on Garth Whitelaw directly, without involving his daughter. But he couldn't think of anything that was as likely to cause Garth the same pain he endured himself as stealing someone he loved away from him.

In endeavoring to free Callen from the morass into which he had drawn her, Sam made a stunning discovery. He wanted her. Somehow during the course of winning her admiration, he had come to admire her, as well. She had a wicked sense of humor, a smile that flashed often enough to lift even his leadened heart, skin softer than silk, and lips as sweet as anything he had ever tasted. His groin tightened at the mere thought of bedding her. He suspected his desire for her had contributed to his inability to come up with another route of vengeance.

By the same token, because he had allowed Callen to get under his skin, it was going to be difficult to hurt her, as he must if he was going to achieve his goal of hurting her father. In the early hours of the morning, wretchedly alone, with the grief of his father's death making his stomach spin and his chest ache, he had come up with the idea of presenting himself to Callen in such a state of disarray that she would be the one to back away from him. He couldn't push her away; she was going to have to leave him of her own accord.

It hadn't worked.

Callen's family had sheltered her from the harsher facts of life, and with the confidence of the innocent, she had simply looked past the facade he had erected to shove her away and embraced the man she found beyond it. He sighed inwardly, damning her for making him want her even more, damning himself for being bastard enough to go through with his plan.

They had reached the door to the judge's chamber when Callen's eldest brother showed up. Sam eyed Zach warily, aware of the animosity on the other man's face.

Callen appeared delighted by Zach's arrival. "Zach! You came!" She let go of Sam's hand and flung herself into her brother's open arms.

Sam met Zach's narrowed eyes over Callen's head and knew the other man would do whatever he could to stop the wedding. Sam welcomed the coming fight with relish. He had wanted—needed—to hit out at the injustice of his father's death. With Garth unavailable, Zach Whitelaw made a very satisfying target.

"I'm so glad you changed your mind and decided to come," Callen said with breathless excitement. "I would have gone through with the wedding even if no one from the family came, but I'm so glad to have someone to stand beside me."

"I'm not here to support you," Zach said in a hard voice.

Callen stepped back, aware suddenly of the hostility that bristled between her tall, intimidating brother and the lean, dangerous man who would soon be her husband. Her heart sank. There was no way the two of them were going to be reconciled in the few minutes she had before the wedding. If it came to a choice, Callen knew she would go with Sam. That would surely make Zach even angrier.

Callen stared up at her brother. "Why did you come, Zach?"

Zach's eyes were on Sam. "To tell the sonofabitch you're getting set to marry that if he lays one hand on you, if he hurts you in any way, he'll have to answer to me."

Callen heard Sam's hiss as he took an outraged breath, felt his body stiffen, saw his stance widen for battle. She put herself between the two men, laying one hand on Zach's chest and the other on Sam's to keep them from coming to blows. "Please," she said. "Don't fight."

When she turned to Zach, she found no sympathy in his dark eyes, only scorn and anger.

"You're a fool to be marrying beneath yourself like this," Zach raged. "Take a good look at him, Callen. He's a disgrace."

When Callen didn't immediately turn back to Sam, her brother put a strong hand on her chin and forced her face around toward her bridegroom.

Callen shook herself free as she heard Sam's growl of challenge.

"Let her go!"

"She's my sister. I'll do as I please."

"She belongs to me now," Sam retorted. "You damn well better leave her alone."

"The hell I will!"

"Stop it! Both of you!" Callen cried, shoving against two hard, heaving chests with the flat of her hands.

Zach continued his scorching castigation of her bridegroom without even taking a breath. His dark eyes burned as he held her gaze. "Think about who you're going to marry," he said ruthlessly. "Sam Longstreet barely made it through high school. He's got no dreams, no goals. Hell, all he wants is your money! He'll embarrass you in front of company because he looks like hell warmed over most of the time. Like now," he said, nodding with his chin toward Sam. "Is that the way a bridegroom ought to dress for his wedding?"

Callen looked, then lowered her eyes. She had been willing to disregard Sam's appearance, to excuse it. That was difficult with Zach standing beside her pointing out Sam's faults. She felt a flush of embarrassment, then a burning resentment toward her brother and, to a lesser extent, toward Sam for putting her in the position of having to defend something she had condemned herself.

"What Sam's wearing doesn't matter to me," she said stubbornly.

Zach grabbed her by the shoulders and turned her so she was facing him again. Her hand dropped away from Sam's chest, but she was aware of him standing behind her, of the leashed tension that sizzled and threatened violence.

Then Zach was speaking, his face so close she could see the temper smoldering in his dark eyes. "The man doesn't have any friends. You'll be all alone once you're living with him at the Double L," he warned. "Don't marry him, Callen. Put an end to this nonsense."

"I love him," Callen said in a quiet voice.

Zach pulled her into a protective embrace, almost crushing her with his strength. "God, Callen, what can I do to make you change your mind?"

"Nothing. I'm going to marry Sam, with or without your approval...or Daddy's blessing."

Zach's next words were spoken low in her ear so there was no possibility of Sam overhearing. "When you decide to leave him, when you recognize your mistake, you'll be welcome at my place."

He levered her away and into Sam's waiting arms. "Don't forget what I said, Longstreet. You harm one hair on her head, and I'll come after you." Then he stalked past Sam and out the courthouse door.

Callen stood there with Sam's arms wrapped comfortingly around her, hard-pressed to hold back the tears that threatened. The third time around she certainly hadn't planned on a lavish wedding. But she would have liked some of her

family to be there, and she would have liked her
groom to be a little better dressed.

She raised her blurred gaze to Sam's face and
saw a flash of sympathy in his green eyes that disappeared so quickly she wasn't sure it had been
there in the first place.

"Do you still want to marry me?" Sam asked
in a taunting voice. "Or has your brother talked
you out of it?"

Sam was giving her one last chance to back out,
Callen realized. She searched his eyes for any sign
of the affection he had shown her during their courtship. It seemed strangely absent. She felt frightened.
What if her family was right, and she was wrong?
She couldn't afford to make another mistake. But
neither could she face the humiliation of crawling
back home with her tail between her legs.

Stubborn pride kept Callen standing at Sam's
side. She wasn't going to let her family talk her
out of something she knew was right. Her relationship with Sam over the past three months had
revealed the source of a vague discontent she had
felt for years. She was thirty-two years old. She
had yearned for someone to love, someone to love
her. She wanted children, several of them, and
she wasn't getting any younger. And she needed
a home of her own, a place where she belonged.
Sam had promised to fulfill those needs.

Furthermore, Sam had been a neighbor for
years. If he had really been a fortune hunter,
wouldn't he have come courting a lot sooner? He

couldn't possibly have the sinister motives for marriage that her father and brother had suggested he did.

"Let's go on in." Sam put a hand to the small of her back and ushered her inside the judge's chambers. She wasn't acquainted with the judge, nor with the secretary and bailiff he offered as witnesses.

Callen heard nothing the judge said as he began the words of the ceremony. She was too caught up in remembering her family's accusations against Sam and her own reservations about what she was doing.

"For richer or poorer, in sickness and in health…"

He's a fortune hunter! He's only after your money!

Callen closed her eyes as a wave of nausea rolled over her. It was terrifying to defy her father, terrifying to ignore the warning signs that were all around her and follow her heart.

I love him.

That was the response that had silenced her father. That was the response that had silenced Zach. But was her love enough?

"Do you have a ring?" the judge asked.

Sam added a simple band of white gold to the diamond engagement ring he had given her that had belonged to his mother.

Then it was her turn. She knew how much a rancher worked with his hands. A ring that wasn't simple would be a nuisance and likely wouldn't be worn. So she had bought him a plain gold band.

She saw the flicker of surprise in his eyes and then what looked like pleasure as she slipped it on his finger.

The ceremony was over too quickly. The judge smiled at them and said, "You may kiss the bride."

Callen was ready for a quick peck on the lips. But Sam pulled her slowly toward him until their bodies were aligned and then lowered his mouth to claim hers. The kiss was thorough, and before he was done they were both breathing hard.

When she turned an eye back to the judge, his grin had broadened. He reached out to shake Sam's hand. "It's always a pleasure to see two people in love."

Callen noticed the smile on Sam's lips, but it never reached his eyes. Was it the mention of the word *love* that bothered him? Sam had never said the words to her, but he had shown her in a dozen different ways that he cherished her. Besides, she thought with a rueful smile, this was no time to be having second thoughts. The deed was done. She was Mrs. Sam Longstreet.

Sam was no longer smiling by the time they reached the steps outside the courthouse door. "Do you want to drive to the house together, or follow me in your car?"

"Do you have a preference?" She wanted him to say that he couldn't bear for her to be separated from him for a moment. She wanted to be romanced on her wedding day. Sam's response was too practical for her peace of mind.

"We'd only have to make another trip back for your car," he said. "Go ahead and follow me to the house." He turned his back on her and headed for his pickup, leaving her standing alone on the courthouse steps.

Callen noticed he hadn't called it a home.

She tried not to feel abandoned, tried to put the best possible face on the situation. But this wasn't what she had imagined. What had happened to the romantic swain who had swept her off her feet?

Callen pursed her lips thoughtfully. If she didn't stop seeing trouble everywhere, she was going to drive herself crazy. Things would work out. She only had to remember that she loved Sam. And he loved her, whether he said the words or not. She was married to Sam, for better or worse.

Unfortunately, when Sam carried her over the threshold of the Double L ranch house, she saw how bad *worse* could be.

Her father's description of Sam's place as a "ramshackle ranch" was very much on the mark, Callen realized. She had known the wood frame structure with its tin roof was old. But she wasn't prepared for what she found inside when Sam set her back on her feet after carrying her over the threshold.

"Well? What do you think?"

Callen searched for something nice to say. "It's...clean." Perhaps neat was a better word than clean. She eyed the dust that had gathered on every surface, the cobwebs in the corners. What furni-

ture the house contained—and it was decorated
Spartanly—was old and rat-bitten. There were no
antiques here that had been lovingly polished to
a high sheen like there were at Hawk's Way. Just
secondhand junk.

No wonder Sam hadn't wanted to bring her into
the house. There was nothing here that could be
admired. Until this moment, Callen hadn't realized how luxurious her lifestyle at Hawk's Way
had been, or how spoiled she had been by the com-
forts she had always taken for granted.

The condition of the furniture, of the house itself, suggested things had been going downhill at
the Double L for far longer than the three months
since E.J. had died. The place reeked of ongoing
impoverishment.

Her father's words echoed in her head. *He's only
interested in you for your money.* She shoved them
back out again.

"It needs a little work," she said with a hard-
won smile. "But I'm more than willing to supply
the elbow grease." She walked around the combination parlor and office excitedly pointing out the
improvements she would make.

"First thing is to buy you a new desk. Then, a
sofa placed just so in front of the fireplace, a couple of leather chairs—something comfortable with
an ottoman for you—a few tables, lamps, some art
for the walls, a carpet on the floor, and I guaran-
tee you won't recognize the place."

"All those things cost money," Sam said.

Her smile broadened. "I'm rich. I can afford it."

He shook his head.

Callen felt a well of joy. *He didn't want her money!* Her father was wrong. She was moving toward Sam when his next words stopped her.

"We'll need that money to make back payments on the mortgage and to pay debts I've accumulated. I doubt there'll be much left for frivolities like furniture and rugs."

"What?" Callen was staring at Sam as though she had never seen him before. "I have plenty of money—"

He cut her off with a harsh oath. "It's not enough. I have a fairly good idea of the extent of your fortune. I'm telling you, it'll be eaten up by the cost of keeping possession of the Double L."

"Then we'll sell this place and—"

"No, Callen. This is my home—your home now. We're staying come hail or high water." In response to the shocked look on her face, he said, "Surely your father mentioned I was in financial trouble." His mouth twisted cynically. "You must have known how bad things are. The condition of the outbuildings, the fences that needed mending, the rundown condition of the house. You couldn't have been blind to all of it."

"I…wasn't…exactly." Only she had worn blinders, refusing to see reality, lost in a fog of euphoria: a fool in love. In one respect—Sam's need for her money—her father had been absolutely right. But she wasn't going to cry craven and run. She loved Sam. And if he needed her money, he was welcome to it.

Callen lifted her chin. "Whatever money you need, you're welcome to spend. Use it how you think best."

Sam's eyes narrowed. He was astonished at Callen's generous offer. He had expected trouble when he told her he wanted to invest her fortune in the Double L. With the marriage still unconsummated, it was a sure way of goading her to run, to save herself from the fate he had planned for her. But her brown eyes had flared with a militant light and that stubborn chin of hers had bucked up. And she had offered him everything she had.

He refused to feel guilt or remorse, even though the pull of both made the skin stretch taut across his cheekbones. She had made a free choice to be his wife. She had stayed when she saw how rough things were going to be. Well, so be it. He had committed himself. It was time to get on with his revenge.

CHAPTER THREE

"COME HERE, CALLEN."

Callen saw the fierce desire in Sam's eyes and felt an answering desire rise within her. Now that the moment was at hand, however, she was uncertain what to do. "It's broad daylight," she said with a shy smile.

"I want to see you when I make love to you for the first time," Sam replied.

A rush of pleasure and embarrassment painted Callen's cheeks a vivid rose. "There's not much to see," she murmured. Her breasts weren't anything to shout about, and while she had a narrow waist and a decent pair of legs, she was closer to cute than pretty, closer to pretty than beautiful. It would have been easier to do this the first time in the dark.

"Callen."

The single word was a command that compelled her to obey. She took the several steps that brought her near enough for Sam to reach out and pull her close. His arms folded around her possessively.

Callen felt safe, secure, treasured. Those weren't the feelings she had expected and, as it turned out, weren't the feelings she experienced moments later when Sam's mouth came down to capture hers.

Hungry. Unbridled. Ruthless. Sam demanded total surrender, and Callen was helpless to resist. The blood raced in her veins, sending heat and shuddering sensation throughout her body. Now Callen understood why Sam had kept his desire under control in the past. She was overwhelmed by feelings she had never imagined. His effect on her was devastating.

"Sam," she gasped. She clung to him, breathless and almost dizzy. She was shivering and couldn't seem to stop.

"Callen," he breathed in her ear. It was a plea. It was a promise.

He lifted her into his arms and carried her into his bedroom. It was darker there because heavy curtains covered the windows. She clung to Sam's shoulders as he leaned over and pulled down the covers on the bed, barely toeing off her shoes before he laid her down. She noticed the bed was made with fresh white sheets that had been tucked in with almost military precision. He had known he would bring her here. He had cared what she would think—about this, at least.

The sheets were cool, or maybe it was simply that she was so warm in contrast. He stood above her, his green eyes lit with a fierce, primitive light.

"Take off your clothes," he said.

Callen was caught unawares. She had expected him to do that for her, had anticipated it, in fact. He stood above her, arms akimbo, legs widespread, with that devouring look on his face, and waited.

She sat up and turned her back to him before lifting her hair out of the way. "Can you get these few buttons for me?" It seemed like an eternity before she felt the brush of his hands against her nape. She felt the sweep of air as her back was exposed and a moment later the touch of his mouth against her skin. A shiver of delight ran down her spine.

When he was nearly finished, Sam slid onto the bed behind her. His hands slipped around to cup her breasts. She felt him exhale slowly as his hands shaped and molded the small mounds.

"You feel so good."

The sound of his voice rasped in her ear, sending another shiver through her. Her hands dropped to rest on his as she leaned her head back against his shoulder. "I've dreamed about this so often...."

"So have I," he confessed. "You feel so good, so right in my hands."

"There's not much there," she said with a wry smile.

"Enough. Plenty," he said as he turned her in his arms.

She gasped as his mouth latched onto one breast through the lace. She felt the nip of his teeth and laughed breathlessly. "Maybe I ought to finish taking this off."

He lifted his head and released her. "All right. Go ahead."

She was suddenly shy again. The unbuttoned dress slid off her shoulders, revealing the white silk camisole she wore. She rose on her knees and shoved the dress and a half-slip down, then sat and pulled them off over her bare legs. She hadn't worn nylons in deference to the June heat, so she was left in nothing but her silk tap pants and camisole.

She started to lower the straps of her camisole, but Sam reached out a hand to stop her. She followed his eyes downward and saw that her nipples had peaked beneath the silk. There was a damp spot near her right breast where his mouth had been. He lowered his head and suckled her through the cloth.

Callen groaned. She had never felt anything so exquisite. Her hands slid into Sam's hair, which was thick and silky to the touch, while her head arched backward in ecstasy.

Sam took his time removing the rest of her clothing. It was difficult for Callen to lie still under his sharp gaze once he had her bare.

"You're beautiful, Callen."

In that moment she believed she was beautiful, despite her too small breasts and her straight black hair that refused to hold a curl and the spattering of freckles across her nose.

"I want to see you," she said, reaching up for the first of the buttons on his shirt. She had three unbuttoned when his patience deserted him. Callen laughed as Sam tore off his shirt, yanked off his boots and socks and reached for his belt buckle.

He was naked moments later, and the laugh caught in her throat.

Whatever faults Sam might have had, his body wasn't one of them. Callen let her eyes roam from broad shoulders and muscled arms, down a chest that was furred with dark hair, past a washboard belly, to the curls that surrounded his arousal. His legs were long, his thighs sinewy and taut.

"You're the one who's beautiful," she managed to say.

He smiled.

Oh, what a wonderful smile it was! His white teeth flashed, and his eyes crinkled at the corners. She felt warm all over. Then came the laugh, up from his belly, past his chest and out of his mouth, a full, rich, happy sound.

She grinned. "What's so funny?"

"You thinking I'm beautiful."

"But you are," she insisted.

He snorted, a male sound of dismissal. "You're the special one, Callen." He sat on the bed beside her and let his callused fingertips stroke across her belly. "I can't believe you're mine."

Callen felt revered, cherished. She had done the right thing marrying Sam. She hadn't made a mistake. Sam couldn't touch her like this, hold her in his arms, stroke her mouth with his tongue in just that way if he didn't care for her.

He took his time loving her. His eyes constantly roamed her body, following where he touched. When he joined their bodies, making them one, he watched that, too. She had never been so aware of herself as a woman, never been so aware of the aching need to give everything she had to another human being.

Callen heard Sam's groan of agony and pleasure in the moment he thrust inside her, felt her muscles contract to hold him there. His hands lifted her buttocks as he made sweet, sweet love to her. She touched him everywhere she could reach, returning the caresses he had so freely given her. In her ultimate joy, she grasped his hair and pulled his mouth down to join hers as they cried out in exultation.

Afterward, she lay sated in his arms, breathless, her chest heaving. Their bodies were sweat-slick in the heat, and she realized suddenly that the house wasn't air-conditioned, that it was the breeze flowing from behind the curtains through the open windows that cooled their bodies. No wonder the curtains had been drawn, she thought. It kept out the hot sun. It was one more indication of the *worse* to go with the *better* in this marriage.

Right at this moment, Callen didn't have any complaints. She stretched lazily and felt Sam's hand slide down her thigh. It felt good, warm and rough against her skin. Sam was, quite simply, an incredible lover. She shouldn't have been surprised, but she was. She hadn't thought of him as the sort of man who dated a lot. So where had he learned to be so knowledgeable of a woman's needs in bed?

The answer to that question was easy, once Callen thought about it, though thinking at all was difficult with Sam's hand caressing her. A man as kind and considerate as Sam Longstreet would naturally be a good lover, because he would always be concerned about the other person's pleasure. She decided he deserved some thanks for his thoughtfulness. So she slid her hand along his naked flank, returning the caresses he bestowed upon her. She could feel the strength, the sinew and muscle that surrounded bone. She gave a little shove, and he rolled over onto his back.

"What's this?" he asked.

"I'm going to have my wicked way with you," Callen answered.

"By all means." His grin was far more wicked than anything she could have imagined doing to him. He lay still beneath her hands. Actually, not quite still. His body undulated beneath her onslaught, until he rolled her over beneath him and took up where she had left off.

They didn't leave the bed all day. It was full dark before either of them thought of anything except the delights to be found in the other's body. It was Sam's stomach that finally protested with a loud growl.

"I'm hungry," he admitted.

Callen snuggled closer. "Me, too."

"Who's going to get out of bed and fix supper?"

"I suppose I ought to," Callen said with a huge yawn.

"You're exhausted."

Callen heard the surprise and remorse in Sam's voice. She smiled to herself. "I hope you keep me this tired all the time," she teased.

She felt his body relax and heard his chuckle. "I might have gone a little crazy. I just never thought—"

He cut himself off and abruptly rose so that her hair, which was caught under his shoulder, got yanked hard enough to hurt. She cried out, then heard him swear as he stubbed his toe on the bedstead.

"Are you all right?" he called. Then, "Where the hell is the lamp?"

"I suspect it's where it's always been." Callen restrained a giggle as she reached out and snapped on a lamp beside the bed. She squinted her eyes until they adjusted to the light. When she could open them without pain, she saw that Sam was staring fixedly at her. She looked down and found there were small love bruises on her body where he had staked his claim. Her breasts were still flushed and rosy from their latest round of lovemaking. She quickly grappled for the sheet to cover herself.

"Don't. I..." He swallowed hard. "I like looking at you."

She forced herself to lie still. It was plain he wanted her again.

Fortunately—or unfortunately—his stomach chose that moment to growl again. He grabbed his jeans and stepped into them before heading for the kitchen in a hurry. "Stay where you are. I'll get us something to eat."

The first thing she did was jump out of bed and race for the standing oval mirror in the corner to see for herself how she looked. *Good Lord!* she thought. *That's what he finds attractive?*

Her hair was tangled beyond combing, her breasts were the same tiny size they'd always been, and she hadn't grown any taller. But a second look revealed the dreamy glow in her dark brown eyes, the heat beneath her skin that made her complexion pink and rosy, and the puffy softness of her lips where she had been thoroughly kissed. She looked like a woman who had spent most of the day making love with a man she adored.

She heard Sam returning, and scurried back to bed. Well, why not? If the man wanted to wait on her, who was she to complain? She was sitting up in bed when he entered the room, but she had chickened out and pulled the sheet up under her arms. There was such a thing as modesty, after all. She hadn't become a total wanton in one day. Had she? One glance at Sam's face, and she was afraid she had. She let the sheet fall and heard him gasp. He set the tray of soup and sandwiches on a dry sink across the room and came to her without another word.

The supper he had prepared sat forgotten.

When Sam woke, he felt disoriented. It took him a moment to realize the heat he felt came from another body snuggled up close. He eased himself away from Callen—from his wife—and sat up on the edge of the bed letting his eyes become accustomed to the dark. He wondered what time it was and sought out the alarm he kept next to his bed. The digital clock told him it was barely 10:00 p.m. It seemed much later.

He felt exhausted, but at the same time more rested than he had at any time since his father's death. He had reason to feel relaxed. His plan for vengeance had well and truly begun. He had taken the first steps to attach his wife's affections. Before he could take Callen away from her father, he had to be sure that if she was forced to choose, she would choose him. He had to be sure she was well and truly in love.

So he had made love to her as though she were the most precious of women. He had given her all of himself—or almost all. He hadn't given her his heart. He didn't love her. That would be a disaster and ruin his carefully laid plans. But he had created the illusion of love to the best of his ability.

It was only after that first incredibly powerful climax that he had realized the danger to himself. Yet he hadn't been able to deny himself the opportunity of making love to her again. She was all satiny softness and fiery desire. He hadn't been able to resist coming back for more. And more. He hadn't known he could want a woman like he wanted Callen. He was going to have to be careful. He had to remember at all times that his real purpose in marrying her was to cause her father pain.

Callen stretched and her foot reached out and stroked his thigh. "Come back to bed, Sam," she murmured.

He ought to get up and leave her now. He could feel the loose ropes binding him to her, even as he sought to bind her to himself. But he was the one in control. He could escape the noose whenever he chose, or use whatever means were necessary to cut himself free when the time came. He surrendered to the call and joined Callen in bed.

The next time he woke, it was dawn. Lately, because he couldn't sleep at night, he had dropped into bed exhausted at sunrise. But he had a mission this morning that had him out of bed the instant he realized what time it was. He had to make it to town, to the Stanton Hotel Café, where all the ranchers gathered early to drink coffee and listen to the stock and grain prices on the radio and compare notes before beginning the day. Garth Whitelaw would be there. And Sam had a few things to say to his new father-in-law.

The hotel had been built in the 1880s, and it still featured several of the original Victorian sofas in the lobby along with a Turkish carpet and some silvered mirrors in elaborate mahogany frames. The hotel café dated from the 1950s. It had a long service bar with stools that had red plastic seats and chrome backs. Someone had added trophy deer antlers on the walls, along with macramé wall hangings from the 1970s and a few pictures of the hotel when it had been in its prime.

Sam saw four ranchers at the far end of the bar. They sat in the same seats every morning. Garth Whitelaw was sitting on the stool closest to him, near the center of the bar. The stool next to Garth was empty, and Sam slid onto it.

He stared straight ahead, looking into the mirror behind the bar. He could see the faces of everyone reflected there. Sam noticed that he looked more than a little the worse for wear. He was wearing a hat that hid most of his hair, but it obviously needed a cut. He hadn't shaved and, to his chagrin, there was a love bruise under his right ear that Garth Whitelaw couldn't miss. Sam braced his elbows on the bar and ordered himself a cup of coffee from the waitress and proprietor of the café, Ida Mae Cooper.

The conversation at the bar had stopped. He let his eyes slide over three of the ranchers, daring any one of them to say anything. They each found something of interest to occupy themselves and avoided meeting his glance. When his green eyes met Garth's stony gray ones, he let his contempt show on his face.

"Offering some more good advice this morning?" Sam taunted. "You men might want to take what Garth Whitelaw says with a grain of salt. He tends to change the truth to fit his purpose."

There was an ominous silence as the men at the bar absorbed the insult.

Garth stiffened. He set down his cup of coffee and turned to Sam. "Are you calling me a liar?"

"If the shoe fits…"

Ida Mae sloshed some coffee into Garth's cup. "Don't want no fightin' in here, boys." Nobody could remember when Ida Mae hadn't been running the coffee shop. She had grown up on a ranch in the area, so she knew how to handle a rowdy crowd. Not that things got rowdy much these days. Only, Ida Mae could see that Sam had coming looking for trouble, and she knew for a fact that Garth was more than willing to give it to him.

"Why aren't you home with your wife?" Garth demanded.

A sneer cut across Sam's face. "I left her asleep in bed. She was plumb wore out."

"That's no way to talk about my daughter," Garth warned. "Or your wife, for that matter."

Sam was too intent on hurting Garth to care that he was acting in a manner that was totally alien to him. He would have killed any other man who spoke such a slur against his wife. But Callen wasn't just his wife, she was also Garth Whitelaw's daughter. She was part and parcel of his revenge. He was here to hurt Garth Whitelaw, not to protect his wife's name.

"I just thought you'd like to know I'll be going to the bank today to take care of my back mortgage payments," he said.

Garth's eyes narrowed.

"Can you believe it? Callen offered me her fortune," Sam said with a snide grin intended to raise the hair on Garth's neck.

"Why, you—" Garth started to rise, but was stopped by Sam's wagging finger.

"Uh-uh," Sam cautioned. "Ida Mae wouldn't like it if you messed up her place." He leaned closer and said in a voice not intended to be heard by the other men, "The Double L is lost to you, Whitelaw. Soon, your daughter will be, too."

"What the hell do you mean by that?" Garth shot back.

"Just remember what I said, Whitelaw." He rose, and Garth reached out to grab his arm. He yanked it free. "Stay away from me and my wife, do you hear?"

"I'll see my daughter—"

"She's not your daughter anymore," Sam said. "She's *my* wife. Stay away from the Double L, and leave Callen alone."

"If this is about E.J.—"

"You're damn straight it's about E.J.," Sam said, his face contorted in fury. "I want you to know what it feels like to lose someone you love and know they're gone forever."

"What the hell is wrong with you?" Garth demanded. "I had nothing to do with E.J.'s death."

"Nothing anyone can prove," Sam agreed. "But I know the truth. And so do you."

Garth shook his head in frustration and disbelief. "You're wrong, Sam."

"Just don't plan on seeing Callen again," Sam said baldly.

"I'll see my daughter when and where I choose."

"Not if I say no. I have some influence with my wife. She won't be working for you anymore, just so we have that straight."

Garth heaved a frustrated sigh. "I'm telling you again, I'm not responsible for what happened to E.J." He paused before adding sardonically, "And my daughter, as you will soon discover, is a woman with a mind of her own."

Sam already had some inkling of that, but he was determined to keep Callen so busy she wouldn't have time to miss her job—or see her father, even if she wanted to. "Just stay away from her," Sam repeated. "She's dead to you."

Sam whirled on his booted heel and stalked out of the café. When he reached the covered wooden porch outside the Stanton Hotel, he took a deep breath and let it out. He was not normally a vindictive man, and the outpouring of rage he had felt toward Garth Whitelaw had left him feeling drained. It was two hours before the bank opened, and he had just walked out of the best place in town for breakfast.

He thought of going home, and an image rose before him of Callen lying tangled in the sheets on his bed. Hell, he'd just go on home and get back in bed with her. There was plenty of time to come back into town later and pay the banker. He had accomplished what he'd set out to do. There was no reason why he couldn't go home and enjoy his wife…while she still was his wife.

CHAPTER FOUR

THE FIRST TIME Callen's mother called to invite the newlyweds to dinner, Callen accepted on the spot. She had been spending all her time fixing up the house, waiting to see if her father would relent and ask her to come back to work at Hawk's Way. So far, he hadn't budged an inch.

"Of course, we'll come, Mom," she said. "What time? We'll be there. Sam? Oh, I'm sure he'll be free. Don't worry, Mom. We're both looking forward to it." She had laughed at the cautious note in her mother's voice. Maybe her wedding hadn't been auspicious, but her marriage was everything she had dreamed it could be.

She was astonished, therefore, when Sam informed her he had made plans to take her out that evening.

"I was hoping to surprise you." He had a sort of sheepish look on his face that melted her heart.

"I wouldn't spoil your plans for the world," Callen said. After all, she didn't want to discourage any romantic notions Sam might have in the future. "I guess I'm not used to being married," she said, wrinkling her nose. "I'll have to get used to asking first before I make arrangements that include both of us."

Callen had called her mother with their regrets. The next time her mother called, about two weeks later, Callen said, "I'll have to check with Sam. Can I call you back later tonight?"

She had brought up the subject at dinner. Sam paused only hesitantly before he said, "Sunday dinner? I don't know why not. Sure, tell them we'll come."

Callen gave him a big kiss. "Thanks, Sam. It'll make my mom so happy. And I know you'll like my dad, once you get to know him."

Only, when Sunday came, Sam had an emergency he had to take care of that precluded going to Sunday dinner at Hawk's Way with Callen. Some fence was down along the south pasture, and his prize bull had wandered onto Abel Johnson's property. Abel didn't mind, but Sam hated giving away free stud service on his bull.

"I have to get him back right away," Sam said apologetically. "We'll have to have dinner with your folks another time."

Callen called and apologized to her mother. They set another tentative date for a week later. When the following Sunday came, Sam was sick with the flu. He looked awful, and Callen hadn't the heart to make him keep the dinner engagement with her parents.

When they had been married for three months, it came as a shock to Callen when she realized that she and Sam had not yet darkened the portals of Hawk's Way. In fact, she and her parents hadn't even crossed paths. It was easy to excuse the omission. She and Sam had both been incredibly busy.

Her time had been spent turning Sam's home—now her home, as well—into a charming, cheerful place by using lots of hard work and secondhand everything. She had managed to re-cover the couch with an Indian print in warm Western colors and was amazed at what a little polish had done to the furniture. She had bought paintings over the years, mostly by southwestern artists, which she had hung on the walls.

She discovered gallons of a pale yellow paint in the barn, which Sam confessed he had bought more than a year ago for the house. She took it to the hardware store and had it shaken up, and began painting the outside of the house. To her surprise, when Sam realized what she was doing, he stopped his repairs long enough to share the job with her. When they were done, she had stood arm-in-arm with Sam and admired the house.

"It looks so different!" she exclaimed. "It has a sort of rustic charm—"

"You mean, it doesn't look like a dump anymore," Sam interrupted sarcastically.

"You're putting words in my mouth," Callen protested. "I only meant that now I can see the care that went into building this place. Someone meant this house to survive for generations."

"It has. And it will," Sam said in a determined

voice. He was silent for a moment before he said, "Thanks, Callen. I needed to see it like this. Like it can be."

He had gone back to his work mending the barbed-wire fence. She had refocused her attentions on the interior of the house. She replaced the heavy curtains in the master bedroom with vertical blinds from a discount store so she could still block out the sun during the hottest part of the day but enjoy the sunlight in the early morning and late evening. And she had pulled up the worn linoleum in the kitchen and found a beautiful hardwood floor, which she had refinished.

She spoke often to her mother on the phone, but it had become almost a reflex to refuse her invitations. There never seemed to be time. Callen wasn't sure how much of her reluctance to accept her mother's invitations lately was a result of being busy and how much was the result of her growing awareness that Sam didn't want to have dinner with her parents.

She wasn't sure exactly when she had realized there was a problem, but the signs were blatantly evident when she finally did. Sam reacted oddly to the mere mention of her father's name. Quite simply, his lips went flat and his eyes narrowed and a muscled jerked in his jaw. She could have gone alone to have dinner with her parents, but she didn't want them to think she and Sam weren't getting along. Because they were.

In fact, Callen had never been so happy. Sam

was a dedicated and inventive lover, and he seemed to appreciate her efforts in the house. He was easy to talk to, and even though he seemed exhausted at the end of each day, he was never too tired to spend time with her. It was an ideal marriage. Except that Sam didn't seem to want anything to do with her family.

And there was something else. She couldn't quite put her finger on what it was, except she had noticed a certain reticence in Sam whenever she tried to make plans for the future, plans that included children. He said he had enough to worry about just solving day-to-day problems. He couldn't think about a family right now. And he was right. Still, it would have been nice to dream with him.

As much as it pained her to admit it, maybe Zach had been right about Sam lacking dreams and goals. For some reason Sam didn't want to think about the future. She didn't doubt that he loved her, even though he had never said the words. But she had become more and more certain over the past three months that he was hiding something from her. She was afraid to ask him about it, afraid to burst the bubble of happiness that surrounded her marriage.

Finally, she couldn't help herself. One night after supper, she blurted, "What's wrong, Sam? Why don't you want to have dinner with my family?"

He hesitated so long that she thought he wasn't

going to answer her. When he did respond, he said merely, "You know how busy the past few months have been for both of us."

But she wasn't satisfied with that answer. "Did my father say something to you… I mean, before the wedding?" Callen held her breath. She couldn't believe her father would have had the nerve to approach Sam and offer him money to call off the wedding, as he had done with her two previous fiancés. But she could think of no other reason for Sam to dislike her father so vehemently. If anything, Callen would have expected Sam to despise Zach. After all, Zach was the one who had confronted Sam at their wedding. But Sam's anger didn't seem to be aimed in that direction.

The longer Sam hesitated, the more frightened she became that her father had offered him money. Suddenly she didn't want to know. "Forget I asked," she said, rising abruptly and heading for the kitchen sink with a stack of dishes.

Sam followed her and wrapped his arms around her from behind. He nuzzled her nape as he said, "What brought all this on?"

She sighed. "You keep avoiding any contact with my parents. I wondered why."

"It's very simple, Callen," he said in a quiet voice. "I want you all to myself."

She was afraid to believe him because it sounded so romantic and made her fears seem ridiculous. "That's all?" she asked. "Nothing else? What about my father? Do you—"

"Let's not talk about your father. Right now, I just want to make love to my wife."

He swept her into his arms, making her laugh at his impulsiveness. A moment later his mouth caught hers in a searing kiss, and then it was too late for thinking. She decided to let the future take care of itself. She was too busy loving Sam to worry about it.

Later, lying in bed beside his sleeping wife, Sam wondered how much longer he could manage to keep Callen separated from her father. It had been an exhausting exercise to keep an eye on Garth's movements and make sure Callen was away from the house whenever he visited. He had come twice to the Double L. Both times Sam had taken pleasure in sending him away without seeing his daughter.

"Where's Callen?" Garth had demanded the second time.

"In town shopping."

"I don't believe you."

Sam had made an open gesture with his hand, inviting Garth inside. To his surprise, the older man hadn't taken him at his word, shoved open the kitchen door and stalked inside.

"Callen? Are you here?" His call remained unanswered.

Sam could see Garth was surprised by the look of the place. Garth had visited E.J. often enough to know how they had lived. So he had to be aware of all the changes Callen had made. Even though Sam wasn't personally responsible, he felt proud of what Callen had accomplished. He had been amazed himself at the changes his wife had wrought. Quite simply, she had made his house a home.

It wasn't just the southwestern landscapes on the wall, or the lack of dust and cobwebs, or the shine on the furniture. It was the way she had re-arranged the furniture so they could sit in front of the fire together. The way she made him com-fortable in a chair before dropping to the floor in front of him and crossing her arms on his knees and resting her chin there while she talked anima-tedly about her day. The way fresh flowers found their way inside, along with sunlight and the eve-ning zephyrs.

He wondered what Garth thought of all the changes. But he didn't ask. Instead, he said, "I told you she wasn't here."

"You can't keep her away from me indefinitely," Garth replied. "If this continues much longer, I'll just tell her what you're doing."

"Then I'd have to tell her why I don't want to see you. How you tried to bribe me out of marry-ing her." Sam relished the pinched look on Garth's face. He had the man where he wanted him. "Go away, old man. Your daughter is lost to you. Just like my father is lost to me. I hope you suffer, the way I've suffered."

Garth's face had whitened, the grooves around his mouth had deepened. But he hadn't argued, hadn't tried to defend himself again. He had simply left.

When Sam had found himself confronted by Callen this evening, he had considered telling her about the offer of money her father had made to him. That surely would have worked to alienate the two of them. But he had decided it wasn't necessary to hurt her that way. She would be hurt enough when she learned the real reason why he had married her.

Sam slipped an arm around Callen's waist and spooned her into his groin. He felt contented. Almost happy. Except that he knew all this was temporary. So there was a bittersweet quality to his life that made his chest ache and his throat swell. He wondered how long all the changes Callen had wrought in his life would last.

His personal life had undergone as many changes as his house over the three months of his marriage. Faced by Callen's boundless energy, Sam had found himself roused from a lethargy he hadn't realized had hold of him. At least he was sleeping at night, which made it easier to face a dawn that came too early, in his opinion. Sam hadn't even realized how lonely his life had been, until Callen filled his evenings with talk of her plans for the future.

He has no dreams, no goals.

Zach's words had come back to haunt Sam often in the first months of his marriage, and he had been forced to acknowledge the truth of them.

There had been a time, long ago, when he had dreamed big dreams. He had imagined himself escaping the loneliness of his life at the Double L by playing football for a pro team, traveling and meeting fancy women and living the high life. He had been fast on his feet and determined to succeed.

But that dream had been blown away with the cartilage in his right knee. He hadn't been a good student and going to college for the sake of an education—rather than to play football—hadn't appealed to him. After high school he had returned to what he knew—ranching.

He was a good rancher; he understood his business. But with a whirlwind like Callen around, Sam realized just how slow-paced his life with E.J. had become. It wasn't a matter of being lazy, exactly. He'd simply had no reason to work harder. He and E.J. had always had enough for their needs, and their needs had been simple.

All that had suddenly changed with E.J.'s death. Callen was a big part of Sam's reawakening. He couldn't imagine himself lingering in bed after she was up and working. But even if he hadn't married Callen, his life had been changed forever by E.J.'s suicide. He had been jolted out of his lethargy by the knowledge of how near he had come to losing the Double L. The last-minute rescue provided by Callen's fortune had made him realize he didn't want to live so close to the edge. If that meant working harder, then he would work harder.

Sam smiled wryly. The fact of the matter was,

it had been necessary to work harder simply to get back to where he and E.J. had been before E.J. lost his shirt to the various swindles he had invested in. Thanks to Garth Whitelaw. Although Sam still had possession of the Double L, it was a long way from being a successful enterprise. He had begun to think and plan what he could do to make the ranch more economically sound.

He had shared his ideas with Callen at first simply because she seemed to expect him to converse with her in the evenings when they sat in front of the fireplace. He wasn't really good at making small talk, so he had hesitantly revealed his idea to start training cutting horses. He was damn near as good with horses as Callen, and it gave the ranch another source of income besides beef cattle.

"That's a wonderful idea!" Callen had enthused. Her eyes had twinkled with mischief when she said, "I'll just recommend *you* to my friends who want their horses trained, instead of Daddy."

"I don't want—"

Callen had bounced up from the floor and settled herself in his lap with her arms around his neck. "I can help, can't I, Sam? I won the junior cutting horse championship when I was sixteen, just like my mom. And I've been helping Daddy work with cutting horses since I was knee-high to a grasshopper."

"I'd planned to do the work myself."

"Of course you did," she said in a soothing

voice. "Only now that you've got me, why should you have to do it all alone?"

Her words had tumbled into the deep well of loneliness he lived with and filled it up a little. He reminded himself not to get too dependent on Callen, since there was at least a chance that when the showdown came, when he forced her to choose between her husband and her father, she would choose Garth. But it had felt good to pull her close, to feel the pillow of her breasts against his chest, to feel her fingers twine around the hair at his nape, to feel her lips nuzzle his throat. His hands had tightened reflexively around her.

His conscience often warned him that he was doing the devil's work, that he would regret his efforts to take revenge against Garth Whitelaw in the way he had chosen. He fought his scruples by visiting his father's grave almost daily. Each grim sojourn stoked his righteous anger and multiplied his enmity. Those malevolent feelings festered inside him, and he had to work hard to keep the darker side of himself hidden from his wife.

He had seen in Callen's eyes that she knew something was still bothering him, even though she had recently allowed herself to be assuaged with the excuse that he just wanted them to have some time alone. Sometimes he wondered what he would say to her if she probed the situation further. But she had seemed content to let the matter rest.

Until today.

IT HAD BEEN a bad day all around. Sam had discovered two of his steers dead from eating crazyweed. A flash flood had taken out a whole section of fence. The valves on his pickup had finally ground to a halt and needed to be replaced. Then, when he got home, he had found the kitchen torn apart and no supper ready because Callen was repapering the wall.

"What the hell do you think you're doing?" he demanded.

"It's only remnants I found on sale at the hardware store," she said, apparently assuming the source of his anger was concern about the cost of what she was doing. "Isn't it pretty?"

For the first time, he looked at the paper. It had small, multicolored flowers on a white background. No man would be caught dead putting something like that on his kitchen wall. For the space of a heartbeat he wondered how he would be able to bear looking at it if she left him. The thought made him angry. Why the hell should he care if she left him? He didn't love her. Had never loved her. Would never love her.

"It's fine," he said flatly. And then felt like a worm because her face fell.

"You don't like it."

"I didn't say that. Hell, Callen, it's great paper. I just had a horrible day. And I'm hungry."

"Of course you are," she said, immediately stopping what she was doing to come and give him a hug.

He couldn't help himself. He hugged her back.

Well, hell! What was he supposed to do? He had to make sure the woman kept on loving him, didn't he?

"I'll cook," he offered. "You're busy."

She wrinkled her nose and laughed at him. "I've tasted your cooking. Give me a minute and I'll have something ready for us. You've got time to finish writing out those bills that need attention." She turned him toward the kitchen door and gave him a little shove toward his study.

He stomped off to his office—which now contained an antique rolltop desk—to work on his books, something he hated because he could never get the numbers to come out right. It was a job E.J. had always done. Which only reminded him of how much he missed his father. Now he was forced to confront the computer in the study and all those numbers. He hated numbers.

It wasn't long before he could smell something good cooking in the kitchen. Shortly after that, Callen called him in to supper. He gratefully turned off the computer and headed for the kitchen. When he got there, he stood in the doorway and stared at the table.

The wallpaper mess had miraculously disappeared. There were flowers on the table, and she had lit candles. He didn't know where she had found the china, and he was afraid to ask. The table had a cloth and cloth napkins. He couldn't remember the last time he and E.J. had put a cloth on the table, and they hadn't used candles except when the electricity went out in a storm. He had complained once that all that special stuff wasn't necessary, but Callen had told him it was no trouble at all.

He sat down with a grunt of expectation, his nose lifting for the scent of whatever it was she had on the stove.

"I just broiled some steak, threw a couple of sweet potatoes into the microwave and steamed a little broccoli on the stove."

He wrinkled his nose. "Sweet potatoes?"

"Don't you like them?"

"At Thanksgiving. With lots of brown sugar and marshmallows."

"Try one. If you don't like it, I won't make it again."

He realized suddenly she had taken the meat of the sweet potato out of the shell, mixed something into it and stuffed it back in again. "What's in here?" he asked warily.

"Cheese and bacon."

Sam grunted doubtfully, but he took a bite and found it delicious. He didn't tell her he liked it; he simply ate it all without further complaint. He had to admit that Callen was a good cook. The steak was rare, the way he liked it, and the broccoli was crisp, but not raw.

He looked up when he had finished to find her watching him expectantly. "Good" was all he said.

From the smile on her face a person would have thought he had told her she was the greatest cook in Texas. He felt guilty for his faint praise and added, "Really good."

"Are you feeling better now that you've filled your stomach?"

He thought about it a minute and chuckled. "I guess I am."

"Remind me to keep you well fed in the future," she said with a grin.

There it was again. *The future.* His irritation rose at the reminder of what he was doing with her…to her…and the words were out before he could stop them. "I'm not a child, Callen. Don't treat me like one."

He saw from the stunned look on her face that she hadn't expected him to lash out at her. The hurt look that followed a moment later made him feel guilty, because he knew she didn't deserve his criticism.

"What's wrong, Sam?" she said in a voice that was threatening because it was so serious. "I want to know. I can't live like this, knowing that something's eating you inside. What is it? Please, tell me."

At first he was terrified that Garth might have told her the truth. That she was going to create a showdown here and now. He realized in a horrified instant that he would do anything to keep her with him.

Even forego your vengeance?

He avoided answering the question, reasoning that she couldn't know the truth. Otherwise she would have confronted him with it. He met her gaze, which was dark and somber.

"Sam, please. Tell me what's wrong."

He rose so abruptly the ladder-back chair fell with a crash. "There's nothing wrong with me. I'm just not used to having someone around all the time asking me dumb questions!"

She jerked as though he had slapped her. And he had, figuratively. But the Callen he knew was full of guts and gumption, and she didn't disappoint him. She jumped to her feet and snapped right back, "I'm not *someone,* I'm your *wife.* And I only want to help!"

"I don't need your help," Sam said in a harsh voice, admiring her even as he pushed her away. "I have to handle this by myself."

"Is it your father? Are you still grieving?"

"I don't want to talk about this!" Sam said, heading for the privacy of his office. Damn, if the woman didn't get to the kitchen door before him and bar the way!

"You're not leaving this room until you tell me what's wrong," Callen insisted.

"Get out of my way, Callen."

"No."

He stood there a minute, trying to decide what was best. The solution to his problem was simple when it finally came to him. He turned on his heel and headed for the kitchen door that led outside. He slammed it on his way out.

It occurred to him much later that he was going

to have to face Callen eventually, or end up sleeping in the barn. When it came down to it, he decided sleeping in the barn wasn't such a bad idea after all. Maybe a night spent on her own would convince Callen that his business was his own.

Actually, Callen spent the night sleeping quite soundly. Because, while she hadn't gotten Sam to tell her what his problem was, she now knew it hadn't been her imagination. Something serious was bothering him, other than the situation with her father. She was certain that Sam would have no choice except to confess. She wasn't going to give him any peace until he did.

Sam slept poorly in the barn. The hay in the loft was scratchy, and the wool blanket he had laid over it smelled of horse. It was also miserably hot. Sweat dribbled its way across his skin like many-footed worms. And he missed the feel of Callen lying next to him. In the hours he spent lying awake, listening to the rustling movements of the animals below, he thought about his confrontation with Callen.

He was going to have to tell her something. Otherwise she was going to ferret out the truth. He didn't want that to happen. He crept back into the house at dawn only to find his wife already fixing breakfast. He shifted his eyes to the wallpaper and said contritely, "I'm sorry. I guess I owe you an explanation."

The fool woman dropped the spatula in the pan and walked right into his arms. She felt good and smelled sweet and her mouth was warm and wet and made his body go hard.

"I missed you," she whispered in his ear. She rubbed her cheek against his jaw and made a kittenish sound in her throat that drew his body up tight. "You need a shave, Sam," she said with a raspy chuckle. At the same time, her hands came up to caress his cheeks, and she sought his mouth with hers.

A moment later she jerked herself free. "The bacon!"

He watched her race back to the stove where the bacon had kept right on cooking.

She turned back to him with a grin. "It's perfect. Sit down and eat. Once your stomach is full, there'll be plenty of time to talk."

He took her at her word. The eggs were perfectly done, over easy with the yolks soft. The bacon was crisp, but not burned, and the toast was lavishly buttered. The coffee was hot and strong. She was a darn good cook.

She waited for him to finish his second cup of coffee before she reminded him that he had a confession to make.

"All right, Sam. It's time to talk. I want to know what's been bothering you."

He took a deep breath and let it out. He had to make this good. "I—I can't do the bookkeeping."

"What?" There was a blank look on her face. Clearly she wasn't expecting anything that simple.

"E.J. used to do it. I can't seem to get the numbers to come out right, but I can't afford to hire someone else to do it. Things are in a mess."

Her whole face lit up. "Why didn't you just say so? I can do the bookkeeping for you." She lowered her lids so he couldn't see her eyes. "I mean, if you want me to."

He hesitated, as though reluctant to agree. He hadn't realized he was going to be killing two birds with one stone. Not only had he put her off the scent about his "problem," but he was also going to be relieved of the onerous task of keeping the Double L books.

"I suppose that would be all right," he said gruffly.

She left her chair and sat herself in his lap, draping her arms around his shoulders. She looked deep into his eyes, until he was sure she would see the truth. But all he saw reflected back to him was her concern.

"Don't feel bad about the bookkeeping," she said earnestly. "Some people are inclined that way and some aren't."

He felt himself flushing. She was obviously aware that he hadn't been a good student. She had said, in as gentle and caring a way as she could, that it was all right if he couldn't handle the difficult stuff. She would do it for him.

Sam had known from the first grade that he and numbers didn't get along. Reading hadn't been any easier. It had been a struggle to keep up with his class work all through school. He had been the butt of a lot of cruel teasing, and he had grown a thick skin to fend it off. E.J. had kept him from feeling like a total idiot by reminding him that he grasped most ideas readily. Thank goodness he had been fast on his feet. That had given him self-esteem and a value to his peers.

But here it was again, that insidious feeling of inadequacy, just because he found numbers more than a mere challenge. Because he found numbers impossible to understand.

He felt like shoving her off his lap, but she forestalled him when she leaned her head on his shoulder trustingly and relaxed in his arms. She trusted him. She loved him. She didn't care that he couldn't figure numbers.

The crisis was past. They could go on as before.

He let the hurt go and held her close.

CHAPTER FIVE

WHEN CALLEN BROUGHT up Sam's figures on the computer she saw right away why he hadn't been able to make them balance. Several of the numbers were juxtaposed. Instead of 312.42 for fence posts, as was stated on the invoice, Sam had inserted 321.24 on the computer. It was a simple matter, once she realized the problem, to correct the numbers and make them balance. She then wrote out checks and signed them.

It occurred to her that Sam's problem with numbers might have a source he hadn't recognized: dyslexia. Only, she couldn't imagine how he could have a problem like that and not have had it diagnosed a long time ago. The more she thought about it, the more convinced she became that Sam's difficulties in school might have stemmed from his inability to see numbers and letters as they appeared on the page.

She confronted him the next morning at the breakfast table with her suspicions. "Sam, do you have dyslexia?"

Sam stared at her as if she had accused him of having a social disease. "What?"

"Dyslexia. You've heard of it, I'm sure. Letters get jumbled up on a page when a dyslexic tries to read them. It's more common in males than females. I just thought, since you had so much trouble in school…" Callen's voice faded as Sam's features reddened. Was he embarrassed? Did he think she thought less of him because he had difficulty reading? It wasn't his fault. People were born with the problem. "I just thought you might have been diagnosed with it sometime in the past."

"I'm not sick, Callen," Sam said in a terrible, low voice. "I'm just not as smart as other people."

"How can you say such a thing!"

"Because it's true," he said flatly. "I've accepted it. So should you." He rose abruptly from the breakfast table and stalked toward the door.

She rose and started after him. "Sam! Wait! I only thought—"

He turned on her, a storm of emotions on his face. He grabbed her by the shoulders and shook her once. "Let it be, Callen. I've lived with the way I am for thirty-six years. It's a little late to be coming up with excuses for why I can't manage simple, ordinary addition and subtraction, don't you think? Accept it. I'm not smart. I never promised I was."

He paused a moment and a muscle jerked in his jaw before he said, "Maybe you should have listened to your brother. I never got past high school, and I was lucky to make it through that. You don't have to find excuses for me, Callen." And then, bleakly, "I know what I am. And what I'm not."

A moment later he was gone, and she was standing alone in the kitchen wondering what had gone wrong. She had never seen Sam so angry. Or so frustrated. She had never realized he was so sensitive about his education or his intelligence. He was wrong, of course. There was nothing stupid about Sam Longstreet. He was sharp as a whip. After what she had seen on the computer, she was willing to bet he was merely dyslexic.

Only, if he was, why hadn't someone—one of his teachers early on, or the tutors Zach said the football team had hired to help Sam pass his academic subjects—discovered the problem? More to the point, how was she going to get Sam to agree to a test to determine whether he had a reading dysfunction or not?

The problem got pushed to the background when Sam returned home hobbling later that afternoon. His face was ashen, and his body was trembling.

"My God! What happened?" Callen exclaimed as Sam lowered himself gently to a kitchen chair.

"I got stomped by a cow. Made the mistake of getting between her and her calf while I was repairing some fence. I managed to slide to the opposite side of the barbed wire, but not before she laid into me some."

"Why didn't you go straight to the hospital!" Callen exclaimed as she dropped to one knee in front of him. She reached up to unbutton his torn and dirtied shirt and hissed in a breath of air when she saw the growing bruises on his chest. "Sam, this looks serious," she said in a wobbly voice. "Please let me take you to the hospital."

"It's too expensive," he said flatly. "Besides, I've been through this before. I've got a broken rib, maybe two. The most a doctor can do is bind me up. I can do that for myself."

Callen was terrified that Sam might have internal injuries he wasn't aware of, or that one of those broken ribs might puncture a lung. "Please," she begged.

"No, and that's final." He tried to get up, but groaned and slid back into the kitchen chair. "You're going to have to bind me up. I can't do it myself."

"I can't—"

"I've got bandages I've used in the past. They're under the sink in the bathroom. Go get them."

Callen found several rolls of Ace bandages where Sam had told her to look and brought them back to the kitchen. Sam had slid his shirt off his shoulders. The skin was scraped raw in several places, and the bruising looked terrible. She bit her lip to keep from pleading with him again. In the short time they had been married, she had learned how stubborn he could be. There was no sense wasting energy arguing. She would bind him up, put him in bed and then get a doctor to come see him, whether he liked it or not.

The color was returning to Sam's face by the time Callen finished. "Do you need help getting to bed?"

"I think I can manage."

When he tried to get to his feet, he swayed dizzily. He reached out for her, and she slid herself under his arm to support him. "Just take it easy," she coaxed.

Callen eased Sam into bed and retreated to the kitchen to phone the Whitelaw family doctor. "I know you don't usually make house calls, Dr. Stephens, but Sam refuses to go to the hospital. I'm afraid he may have some internal injuries. Thanks. I'll be expecting you then."

Sam lay in bed staring at the ceiling, disgusted at having gotten himself into this situation. He didn't like depending on Callen for anything. He had to admit she had done a good job of binding his ribs. And he would have fallen flat on his face in the kitchen if she hadn't been there to catch him. But he already felt enough in her debt for all the work she had done around the house.

He had been a changed man since his marriage, rising earlier than he had in years and working late into the night. No matter how tired he was, he had always found time to make love to Callen. He had tried to convince himself it was all part of the plan. But he realized now he had done it because he had wanted to please and impress his wife. He had wanted to earn her respect. And now here he was stuck in bed, helpless, flat on his back.

He tried rising, but his ribs hurt him too much. He didn't have any choice but to stay where he was. He had just started wondering where Callen was keeping herself when he heard her talking to someone in the kitchen. His first panicked thought was that Garth had come to visit. He gasped at the pain when he tried to rise and fell back to the bed.

"Who's there, Callen?" he called out to her. His answer came in the form of a strange man in the doorway. One look at the black bag he carried, and Sam swore under his breath. He turned an accusing glance on Callen, who stared defiantly back at him. "I told you I didn't need to see a doctor."

"I have no desire to bury a husband I've just married," she replied tartly. "You'll let the doctor look at you, Sam Longstreet, if you know what's good for you."

Sam had to admire her daring, even if he deplored her tactics. He couldn't very well walk out on her this time, and so long as the doctor was here, he might as well get checked over. "All right, Doc. Go ahead and look. All you're going to find is a few busted ribs."

Sam couldn't stand the anxious look on Callen's face. "You don't need to stay," he told her.

"Just try getting me out of here!" she challenged with a spark in her eyes.

Sam turned his face toward the wall. She had him over a barrel and she knew it. Hell, it wasn't so bad having a woman hovering over him all concerned like this. In fact, it felt kind of nice to know she cared. "Do what you want," he said. But there was more resignation in his voice than anger.

Sam lay as still as he could under the doctor's poking and prodding, but more than once he wished Callen weren't there so he could let out the groans he had gritted behind his teeth.

"Broken ribs, all right," Dr. Stephens confirmed. "I don't like the looks of that bruising. Could be some internal bleeding. I'd like you to come to the hospital where I can do some more thorough tests."

"No," Sam said. "No hospital. No tests."

"Sam," Callen pleaded.

"No."

The doctor frowned. "If that's the way you want it, I can't force you to go. But I want Callen to check for tenderness in your belly here and here—" he pointed out the spots to Callen with his fingertips "—every couple of hours for the next twenty-four, and get you to the hospital quick if any tenderness shows up. Also, watch to make sure that bruising doesn't spread any farther downward."

"Will he be all right?" Callen asked.

"So long as he takes it easy until those ribs heal."

"How long?" Callen asked.

"No work for ten days, at least," the doctor said. "Two weeks would be better. Otherwise you take the chance of aggravating your injury."

Sam scowled. He already had more work than he could handle. This wasn't going to help things. He would get up when he was damned good and ready, no matter what the doctor said.

In that respect, Sam had underestimated Callen. She threatened dire consequences if he left the bedroom and brought his meals on a tray. Sam had never had anyone fuss over him in his life. At first he felt uncomfortable having her wait on him. He had done nothing to deserve Callen's concern, and if she knew the truth, she would be throwing bowls of soup at him, not serving them.

But, oh, how he relished the tender care his wife gave him! Callen crooned to him as she soothed his sweating brow with a cool cloth. She made delicious meals and served them to him with the newspaper, which she read to him while he ate, saving him the effort.

"Why didn't you tell me you were helping Jimmy Lee Johnson earn the money for a car?" Callen asked him one afternoon.

Sam felt the heat in his throat rising toward his face. "How'd you find out about that?"

"He came here looking for work. I thought he'd heard about your ribs, but he told me you've hired him to work for you every Wednesday."

Sam was expecting Callen to complain about the expense. He had opened his mouth to justify himself when she leaned over and kissed him hard on the mouth. He was too stunned even to respond.

"You are about the nicest man I ever met, Sam Longstreet. Not many men would hire a teenage boy to do work he could easily do himself and pay him money that he doesn't have, all to help that teenage boy realize his dream. Oh, I'm so proud to be your wife!"

She was gone a moment later, back to chores in the house. But the good feeling she had inspired—the simple pleasure of feeling good about himself—lasted the rest of the day.

Sam had hired Jimmy Lee because he had seen a lot of himself in the boy. Long ago he had eked out enough doing odd jobs for neighboring ranchers to buy his first motorcycle. It was sitting in the barn now. He hadn't ridden it in years, not since he had hurt his knee his senior year in high school. He had been forced to give it up while his knee mended. Somehow, he seemed to have outgrown it after that. He wondered if it would still run. Maybe when he was on his feet again, he would check it out.

Meanwhile, Callen only barely managed to deter her mother from coming over to help nurse Sam. "He wouldn't be comfortable," she explained. "He feels bad even letting me wait on him, Mom." It went without saying that going to her parents' home, even to attend their annual Labor Day picnic, was out of the question until Sam recovered.

To Callen's amazement and delight, her brother, Falcon, and his wife, Mara, ignored her warnings against company. They had driven to Hawk's Way from Falcon's ranch in Dallas for the Whitelaws' annual Labor Day picnic, and refused to leave without seeing Callen and Sam. They brought along Charlie One Horse, the ancient, part-Comanche housekeeper who had helped raise two generations of Whitelaws.

"Charlie!" Callen cried as she grabbed him by his gray braids and pulled him close for a hug. "I'm so glad you came to visit!"

She brought them all into the bedroom where Sam was propped up and paging through a stock magazine.

"Sam, I don't know if you've ever met Charlie One Horse. He's taken care of me since I was in diapers."

Sam shook hands and said, "Glad to meet you."

Callen was so excited, she barely gave them time to greet each other before she introduced her brother and his wife. "You know Falcon," she said, "and this is Mara, his wife."

"We've met," Sam said with a smile.

"You have?"

"Years ago," Sam said. "It's nice to see you again, Falcon. I'm sorry I can't get up, Mara. We weren't family the last time we met, so I didn't get a chance to hug you then. And now I'm stuck here in bed."

"I can fix that," Mara said with a twinkle in her eye. She leaned over and gave Sam a quick kiss on the cheek. She laughed at the possessive-jealous-chagrined look on Callen's face when she had finished.

"We brought some food from the picnic, since you couldn't come," Charlie One Horse said. He began to arrange a huge spread of food on a tray that he set in front of Sam on the bed.

"We came to celebrate the day with you," Mara said, "since you couldn't come to us."

"Callen and I will go get the drinks," Falcon said as he dragged her toward the kitchen. Once they were there, he turned to her and said, "What the hell's going on, Callen? Mom and Dad said they haven't seen hide nor hair of you since you got married. I don't think they believe Sam's really hurt."

"As you can see," Callen replied in an icy voice, "he is."

"That doesn't explain why the two of you haven't been to Hawk's Way to visit since you got married."

"You must have heard some of the awful things Daddy and Zach had to say about Sam before the wedding."

"So?"

"So, in time, when things cool off, we'll go visit."

"Why can't you go now, by yourself?" Falcon demanded.

"Because I won't go where my husband isn't welcome! What if Mom and Daddy hadn't liked Mara? Or didn't want to be bothered with Susannah, because she was sick with leukemia? How would you have felt?"

Susannah was Falcon's stepdaughter, Mara's daughter from a previous marriage. Her leukemia had been in remission for four years now. Another year and she would be home free.

Falcon grimaced. "I see what you mean."

"Tell Mom and Daddy you saw me, and I'm fine. And tell them Sam really does have broken ribs."

Charlie One Horse, her brother, and his wife didn't stay long, but Callen was glad they had come.

After they were gone, however, a wave of homesickness washed over her. She missed her parents. This separation was ridiculous. She became more determined than ever to make peace between her husband and her family.

Sam continued to be an irascible patient, but Callen could see he enjoyed being taken care of even though he grumbled about it. She knew because of the way his eyes lingered on her face as she sat beside him brushing a stray hank of hair from his forehead, the way he laid his hand gently over hers as she set the dinner tray before him, the way he pulled her down to kiss her lips, sending her pulse soaring as he lazily helped himself to deep, probing kisses.

Callen only managed to keep Sam confined to bed for nine days, but during that time she learned a great deal about needing and wanting and expectation. Because, although there was comfort to be found sleeping close to his warmth, and joy in his tender kisses, both of them knew it couldn't go beyond that.

Callen had been surprised at the strength of her unrequited desire. She had never realized how much she counted on the pleasure of making love with her husband at night. She had refused to let Sam exert himself until Dr. Stephens's prescribed two weeks were up, but she caught herself dreaming about the day they could resume their lovemaking.

Callen had decided to celebrate the occasion of Sam's recovery with a housewarming party. She hadn't forgotten Zach's accusation: *Sam has no friends. You'll be all alone.* The truth was, in the months since she and Sam had gotten married, not a single neighbor had come to call. Partly, Callen assumed, it was because their nuptials had been private, and they had sent no announcements. People didn't intrude on their neighbors in the West without some indication that the visit was welcome. Callen was sure that if she had given even a hint of wanting company, she would have had it.

This was confirmed when Callen began issuing invitations for the housewarming party. She discovered Sam was admired and liked by his neighbors. They had simply respected his wish to be left alone. If Sam didn't have close friends, it wasn't because his neighbors weren't willing; it was because Sam himself had discouraged the contact.

Callen was hoping the party would be the first of many, and that she and Sam would meet other young couples with similar interests who would become their friends. She hadn't counted on Sam's strenuous objection to any kind of gathering whatsoever.

"You've done what?" he exploded. "Why the hell would you do such a thing without asking me first?"

"First of all, because I didn't think you'd mind. And secondly, because I need friends. It wouldn't hurt if you had a few, as well," she added bluntly.

Sam glowered. "I don't need anybody."

"Of course not," she said with a sardonic twist of her mouth. "However, I would like to point out that if you'd had any kind of relationship at all with your neighbors you could have called on them to help out when you got hurt."

"I don't want to owe anybody anything."

"That's clear enough," Callen snapped back. "The truth is, we all need other people, Sam. Even you."

"I won't be at any party you decide to give."

"Fine. The party's off."

Callen headed toward the parlor from the bedroom in a huff. She didn't want Sam to see how shocked and hurt she was by his refusal. She had known what she was getting into when she married Sam. Her father and brother had both warned her what kind of man he was. *A loner. A man without friends.* She really hadn't considered what that might mean. She had seen in Sam only what she wanted to see. In love like she was, she truly hadn't minded the thought of just the two of them alone on the Double L.

Callen hadn't gone two steps before Sam caught her arm and swung her back around into his embrace. She immediately struggled for freedom, shoving against his shoulders and chest.

"Keep that up, and you're going to send me back to bed for another two weeks," he said with a groan of pain.

She stood frozen, her expression stricken. "What do you want from me, Sam?"

"I want you to listen while I apologize," he said in a quiet voice. He tipped her chin up with his forefinger and said, "Sometimes I can be a little unreasonable."

Callen arched a disbelieving brow. "You? Unreasonable?"

Sam chuckled as his arms tightened slightly around Callen. He hated the idea of exposing himself to all those people. He avoided crowds because he never showed well in them. But when he saw how disappointed Callen was, he conceded that enduring a housewarming party was little enough to give her in return for all she had done for him.

"We'll give the party," he said. "Invite anyone you want."

"Even my mother and father?"

Sam thought about refusing but realized there were ways to keep Garth from attending even if Callen issued an invitation. "Sure," he said. "Invite the whole family."

Callen's eyes welled. "Thank you, Sam. I will."

He fought off the stab of guilt clawing at his insides. The only way he could keep focused on his revenge was to remember how his father had looked when he had found him. Thankfully, Callen's voice jerked him from those grim thoughts back to the present.

"Maybe Falcon and Mara could drive over from Dallas again and bring Susannah and the baby."

"It would be nice to see them again," Sam said softly.

"Thank you, Sam," Callen replied with a shy smile. "I know you don't care much for company. I appreciate your willingness to give this a try."

Fortunately she chose that moment to kiss him, or Sam might have spoiled everything by admitting how little he was looking forward to the shindig his wife was planning.

Since it had been two weeks since Sam's injury, and they were in the bedroom, both Sam and Callen let themselves enjoy kissing and holding each other, knowing that their desires could finally be fulfilled.

It was amazing, Sam thought, how much he had missed those carnal sounds Callen made in her throat. He loved how she arched toward him, how she gave that little sigh as he sank himself into her to the hilt. He had forgotten the feel of her fingernails gripping his buttocks and the way her teeth nipped at his shoulder when she came.

Callen was astonished at how easily Sam could arouse her. How he knew just where and how to touch her so that she felt cherished and appreciated. She loved the way he kept his own desire leashed until she was satisfied and gloried in the unrestrained passion that caught him unawares so he cried out her name at the moment of climax. She lay beside him, her body heaving, feeling sated and happy.

Her hand drifted lightly across Sam's chest, her fingertips playing in the dark curls. "Are you all right?" she asked in a lazy voice.

"Mmm, hmm."

"I take that to mean you're fine," she said, feeling the smile grow on her face. She reached up a hand to trace Sam's lips. He was smiling, too.

"I love you, Sam."

Callen waited, but Sam didn't say the words back. She had her hands on his lips, so she felt the smile disappear, felt the lips flatten.

"Sam?"

Sam knew the smart thing to do was say the words, even if he didn't mean them. Somehow, he couldn't do it. Callen deserved better. He wasn't going to lie to her any more than he already had. She had to know he admired her, that he was grateful for everything she had done to make his house a home, that he loved making love to her. Wasn't that enough without the words?

He kissed the fingertips she held against his lips, and when she would have withdrawn, he reached out to catch her hand and hold it there. "You're a very special woman, Callen," he murmured against her fingertips. "I've never known anyone like you."

It was the truth, but so much less than he knew

she wanted to hear. He knew it was enough when he felt her relax against him. He ignored the voice that told him he needed her arms around him at night. He was a man who had never needed anyone.

Callen tried to tell herself it didn't matter that in four months of marriage Sam had never said "I love you." He had shown he cared in a dozen different ways, not the least of which was making love to her every night. They had their whole lives in front of them. She knew in her heart that someday the words would come.

She moved forward with her plans for a lavish housewarming party, inviting all their neighbors and her entire family. Mara and Falcon promised to come again and bring the baby, whose name was Cody, and Susannah. Both Zach and her parents had also agreed to be there.

When Sam heard that Callen's parents had accepted their invitation, he made a point of seeking Garth out at the Stanton Hotel Café.

He walked up to the breakfast bar and said to Garth, "I want to talk to you. Privately."

Garth rose and the two men walked into one of the hotel meeting rooms that was empty.

"I got the invitation to your housewarming," Garth said when they were alone. "My wife and I are planning to attend."

Sam shook his head. "You're not welcome in my home." For the first time Sam saw pain flash across his father-in-law's features. He knew he ought to be gloating, but he found there was nothing to be proud of in what he was doing. He wasn't finding the satisfaction he had yearned for when he had set out upon this course. He forced himself to focus on the image of his father in death. That gruesome portrait produced the anger he needed to proceed with his vengeance.

"If you show up at my door," Sam threatened, "I'll make a scene the likes of which this county has never seen. I'll make damn sure everyone knows your part in E.J.'s death."

"You're bluffing," Garth said.

"Try me."

"I want to see my daughter."

"I want my father back."

The air sparked with electricity as the two men measured one another. At last Sam said in a guttural voice, "We don't always get what we want. Do we, Garth?"

Garth hadn't believed Sam could do it, that he could so effectively cut him off from contact with his daughter. But Callen had been a married woman for nearly four months, and he hadn't once seen or spoken to her. That seemed impossible to him, given the fact all he had to do was pick up the phone to talk to her or drive a few miles to be at her front door. But it was Callen herself who had asked both her parents to keep their distance. Garth had respected his daughter's wishes, never dreaming that so much time could go by without any contact between them.

He missed her. He wanted to see her, to speak to her, to reassure himself that she was as happy as Candy said she was from their conversations on the phone. "What if I come anyway?"

"If you insist on trying to get your daughter back, I'll give her back. In fact, I'll throw her out."

"You wouldn't do that."

"Wouldn't I?" Sam stared at Garth with eyes that looked totally merciless, with features that were as hard and unyielding as granite.

Garth knew from calls Callen had made to her mother that she was more in love with Sam now than she had been when they married. It would break his daughter's heart if Sam rejected her now. He couldn't do anything that might jeopardize his daughter's happiness. But he wondered how Callen could love this misguided and vengeful young man.

Much as Garth wanted to force a confrontation, he felt that waiting Sam out was a better alternative. Time was on his side. The chances of him running into his daughter in town or at church, or catching her on the phone, were very good. And after all, his ranch and Sam's bordered each other. There was always the possibility he would run into Callen on the range.

"You win," he said to Sam at last. "I'll find a reason to stay home from the party. I assume you have no objection if my wife attends?"

"None at all."

"If we're done, my coffee's getting cold." Garth left Sam standing alone in the empty room.

Sam wondered why he didn't feel more triumphant. He had won. He was keeping Callen and her father apart. If he wasn't mistaken, he had wounded his adversary. There had been suffering visible on Garth Whitelaw's face. He knew the expression because he had worn it himself. But he felt no satisfaction in his accomplishment.

Sam knew what had marred his victory. It was the thought of the disappointment he would see on Callen's face when she realized her father wasn't coming. It was the knowledge of how unhappy he would be making his wife while he punished her father.

For a moment, a brief, flickering instant of time, he considered giving up his revenge. He considered forgiving Garth Whitelaw for his daughter's sake. He considered letting go of the past and grabbing for a future with Callen.

Then he saw his father in his mind's eye, lying in a pool of blood. And remembered the vow he had made.

"I promised you vengeance, Dad. And it's vengeance you'll have."

CHAPTER SIX

CALLEN HAD SEVERAL projects she wanted to accomplish before the housewarming party. First and foremost, she wanted to investigate further into whether Sam had dyslexia. A friend who was an elementary schoolteacher referred her to a woman who worked with dyslexic children. The specialist asked Callen to get a sample of Sam's writing for her.

Callen asked Sam to make up a list of his favorite foods. He was reluctant to write them down for her at first, but she insisted she was just too tired to write herself. She did her best to look weary when he eyed her suspiciously. He laboriously wrote a list, which she was surprised to see included a couple of dishes she had made for him since their marriage. The spelling was atrocious, and some of the words didn't make any sense at all. Callen was careful to keep her expression neutral when she took the list from him.

She met with the specialist and handed over Sam's list. "Is it dyslexia?" she asked anxiously.

The specialist, Mrs. Moran, smiled reassuringly. "It looks like a classic case. See? Some of the words are backward. For instance, *can* is *nac*. Are you sure someone hasn't told him before that he's dyslexic?"

Callen shook her head. "I guess when he couldn't read, the teachers gave up on him. And knowing Sam, he would have hidden the problem as best he could. Is there something that can be done?"

"Oh, yes. Some very bright people have been dyslexic and performed exceptionally well. Einstein, for example. Sam can be taught to recognize words for what they are, even backward. But it takes practice. Do you think he would be willing to work with me?"

Callen smiled ruefully. "The question is whether you'd be willing to work with Sam."

"I've got Monday and Wednesday evenings open. I can come to your house, or Sam can meet me at the school. Some of the local service clubs have gotten together to sponsor a fund so my services are free to whoever needs them."

Callen felt her heart racing with excitement. Her first inclination was to race home to Sam with the good news. Then she had second thoughts. What if he got angry when he found out that she had tricked him into giving her a writing sample? What if he didn't want any help dealing with his dyslexia? With the party only a day away she didn't want to start an argument with him. It would be soon enough to talk with him after the party about Mrs. Moran's conclusions and her offer of help.

"I'll be in touch with you," she told the specialist. "And thank you very much!"

THE DAY OF the party dawned bright and sunny, and Callen was nearly bouncing with excitement like a teenager on her way to the prom. Sam had never seen her so euphoric. "It's just a party, Callen," he said with a laugh after she tried putting both feet in the same leg of her jeans.

"I know. But it's the first party we've had as husband and wife. I want it to go well."

"It will," Sam reassured her as he dragged her back across him on the bed and nuzzled her neck playfully. "You've got every detail planned, right down to how we're going to get everyone out the door after it's all over so we can come in here and make love."

Callen grinned. "At least I planned the best for last."

Sam chuckled, then pressed his lips to her throat and began to suck.

"Sam Longstreet, don't you dare give me a hickey!" Callen half shouted, half laughed. She shoved at his shoulders, but he held her tight in his arms. "I bought a new dress and it'll show," she warned.

Sam stopped what he was doing, but didn't let her go. "I want every man there to know you're mine," he said. "I want to put my mark on you."

"You're the only man I want," Callen said in a husky voice. "The only man I'll ever want."

Sam felt a lump of emotion in his throat. How had she become so precious to him? How could he have gotten himself into such an impossible dilemma? He couldn't give her up; he couldn't give up his vengeance. What was he going to do?

"I…" He couldn't say "I love you." It wasn't fair. Not when he was using her the way he was.

"You what?" Callen said in a teasing voice.

"I bought some fancy new clothes to wear tonight."

Callen sat up, her legs draped across his waist. "You did? Oh, Sam, that's great!"

"I didn't want you to worry that I'd turn up looking like I did at our wedding."

"I never thought—"

He covered her mouth with his hand. "You know damn well that's exactly what you thought," he said with a grin. "I couldn't miss the shaving cream you stuck by the sink, or the boot polish that turned up on the back of the toilet seat, or the fact that you've ironed every single one of my shirts for the past week. And I adore you for it."

The words had come out before he had a chance to stop them. He didn't miss the startled look in Callen's eyes, or the way his own heart missed a beat when he said the words that were so close to what he knew she wanted to hear. He lowered his hand from her mouth, his gaze never leaving hers.

"Oh, Sam," she said. "Oh, Sam."

She was too choked up to say any more, and since his throat had closed like a vise, he used his hands and mouth to confirm what he had said. He cupped her breasts and felt the marvelous softness of them before mouthing her through the thin white T-shirt she wore. Her cry of delight made his groin tighten. Since he was naked under the sheets, it didn't take long before her jeans were off and he had her beneath him. He was lost in a world of pleasure so vast he wasn't sure he could ever get enough of it.

It wasn't until much, much later that Sam realized he hadn't used any protection. He had taken that responsibility from the first, because he knew the dire consequences that would result if he got Callen pregnant. This time he had been caught up in the powerful emotions of the moment, wanting and needing to show Callen how much he cared, how much he valued her. Birth control had been the farthest thing from his mind.

Sam couldn't imagine any other woman than Callen having his children. Only now was not the time. The game hadn't yet been played out. He told himself the chances of her getting pregnant were slim to none. But he felt his gut wrench when he realized that the possibility existed.

He forced it from his mind as he and Callen finished the party preparations together. She hadn't decorated the house so much as filled it with candles and flowers. She had polished every surface and vacuumed every speck of dust. Even he was impressed with the results.

He was quite literally stunned when he saw Callen's dress for the party. He had never seen her wearing anything so sophisticated or elegant. It was a black dress that molded her figure, cut just low enough to reveal a hint of cleavage, but not enough to really show anything. The back, however, was cut to the waist, revealing an expanse of skin so enticing he couldn't keep himself from reaching out to touch her skin.

"You're so beautiful," he said in amazement.

Callen blushed with pleasure at the look of admiration and pride in Sam's eyes. "Thank you, Sam. May I return the compliment?"

"I'm beautiful?" he said with a wry twist of his mouth. He looked down at the starched white tuxedo shirt and bolo tie he wore with a black leather vest and black trousers. "It's the clothes," he said flatly. "I look like one of those rhinestone cowboys that sit around drinking tequila in a bar back east."

Callen laughed, a tinkling sound that skittered down his spine and right back up again to catch him in the throat.

"It's not the clothes," she said. "Although I must say you're looking very fine tonight. It's you," she said as she eyed him from head to toe. "You really are quite a handsome man, Sam. I can't believe I never saw it before."

He felt himself flush at the compliment. She was looking at him as if she would like to eat him whole. Sam felt his body respond quickly and fiercely to her invitation. He kept himself a foot away from her, knowing that if he touched her they wouldn't be dressed to greet the guests that were due any minute. But he couldn't take his eyes off her, and he knew from her face that she was feeling the same need he was to wrap himself up in her and never let go.

They both jumped when they heard a knock at the door.

"Party time," Sam said, his voice harsh with desire.

Callen cleared her throat. "Shall we greet our guests together?"

Sam slipped an arm around her waist and drew her close. "Let's go."

The rest of the party was a nightmare for Sam.

He recognized their first guests as Tom Swan, who had been the center of the high school football team, and his wife, Julie. The two had been inseparable since sixth grade. Tom shook Sam's hand and greeted him with a friendly smile that Sam made himself return.

But Sam wasn't seeing Tom's smile or hearing his greeting. He was remembering the day in high school when he had overheard Tom talking to several members of the team in the locker room, while they thought he was in the shower.

"That Sam," Tom had said. "He sure can run! It's just too damn bad he can't read!"

He heard the boys he had thought were his friends laughing with hilarity at what a dumb jock he was. Oh, he had been a riot, all right. He could still feel the awful aching pain of that betrayal.

Looking into Tom's clear blue eyes, Sam knew his former teammate's opinion of him hadn't changed. Except now he couldn't run, either.

Tom was just the first of several of his high school football cronies that Callen had dredged up. It seemed people stuck around this part of Texas when they were born here.

And there was Janice Reese. She was the girl he had fallen head over heels in love with in sixth grade. He had followed her around for several weeks before she turned and confronted him.

"Why are you following me around, Sam?"

"I was just wondering, Janice, if you'd go to the Halloween dance with me."

She had wrinkled her nose at him in a way he thought particularly endearing. "What makes you think I'd go out with a dummy like you?"

He had been so shocked at the bluntness of her statement that he hadn't been able to come up with a good reason why she should want to spend time with him. He had backed away and kept to himself after that.

He wondered if Janice remembered that fateful encounter. He had never forgotten it. He had known he had trouble with schoolwork, but had never associated that deficiency with anything lacking in himself. Until Janice had called him a dummy. It was amazing how that single sentence changed his perception of himself. He began to question himself, his intelligence.

He remembered asking E.J. if there was something wrong with him. But his father had reassured him that aside from having trouble reading and with figures, he was smart enough.

"Who was it figured out a way to get that windmill working again?" E.J. had said. "Who was it figured out the spring mechanism for the stall doors in the barn? Who was it figured out that mixing feeds would increase the yield of weight on the cattle? I could name a dozen other bright ideas you've come up with. You've got brains, boy. Never doubt it."

Only he had. It had come as a relief in seventh grade when he realized he could run like the wind. It had given him a way to excel at something. It had given him self-esteem. Until he had heard what the other boys really thought about him. It wasn't enough that he could run, when he couldn't read.

He had kept strictly to himself after that. He heard what his teammates said then. He was too stuck up to spend time with them now that all those universities had come courting, wanting Sam Longstreet to sign on the dotted line to play football. He had let them think the worst of him because there was no way he could tell them the truth.

And here they were, all of them in one place, smiling and shaking his hand and acting as if everything was perfectly normal. He felt sick to his stomach just being in the same room with them. They pretended like they didn't remember how it was. But he had never forgiven or forgotten their cruelty.

There was some respite from the horror of confronting his past. Surprisingly, it came in the form of Callen's two brothers, Zach and Falcon. Zach grudgingly shook his hand.

"I can see Callen's happy," he said.

"And that makes everything all right?" Sam asked.

"Just make sure she stays that way," Zach said.

Sam could see the respect in Zach's eyes, and the challenge. He couldn't help liking the other man.

Falcon greeted Sam with his arm around Mara, who was holding a blanketed baby. Susannah, her shiny black hair hanging to her shoulders, held trustingly to his other hand.

Sam remembered Susannah from their meeting years before. At the time, Susannah had been wearing a small red hat to conceal the fact that chemotherapy had made all her hair fall out. He could see the years had been good to her.

"You've got a good-looking family there," Sam said.

"Thanks," Falcon replied. "I don't have a free hand, or I'd shake yours."

"I can shake his hand, Daddy," Susannah said, suiting deed to word.

Sam bent down and shook the little girl's hand. "You probably don't remember me, but we met in Dallas about four years ago."

She frowned. "Yes, I do. You're the nice man with green eyes. I met you the day Daddy bought my pony."

Sam smiled. "I don't think I've ever been described so agreeably."

"You've done wonders with this place," Falcon said, looking around at the improvements, which he had missed seeing in his previous brief visit.

"All the credit goes to Callen. She's the one who worked the magic."

"Where is she?" Falcon asked. "I want to say hello."

"I think she's in the kitchen with your mother."

"Is Dad with them?"

Sam worked to keep his features even. "Your father couldn't come. Some kind of emergency at the last minute, I think."

"That's too bad. I think we'll try to find Callen, if you'll excuse us."

Sam looked around his parlor at the happy, smiling people and felt alone. He wanted to be with Callen, but he knew her family was with her now. He couldn't very well go in there and drag her away from them. He searched for someone, anyone he could comfortably converse with. His gaze stopped on Janice Reese.

As though he had summoned her, she walked toward him.

"I've been hoping I'd get a chance to talk with you this evening," Janice said.

"What have you been doing with yourself?" Sam asked. "I'm afraid I haven't kept up."

"I'm the librarian in town."

Sam smiled. It was more of a smirk. No wonder he hadn't seen her in nearly fifteen years. He wouldn't be caught dead in a library. It was full of books he couldn't read.

"I wondered where you disappeared to after high school," she said.

"Oh? Why is that?"

"I've had a crush on you for years. Ever since the sixth grade in fact."

Sam stared at her, stunned. "You called me a dummy!" he blurted. His face flamed.

She laughed sheepishly. "Isn't that awful? I can't believe I was so mean to you! I liked you a lot. I just… I was a stupid twelve-year-old." She smiled and said, "I'm sorry now I didn't track you down."

"Are you flirting with me, Janice?" Sam asked incredulously.

"Would it work if I did?"

"Nope. I'm happily married." What an easy lie that was to tell. He *was* happy. But for how long?

"That's what I thought. I could see the moment I caught sight of you and Callen together that you're in love with each other. I'm happy for you, Sam."

She lifted herself on tiptoes to kiss him on the cheek. To keep her from falling when she lost her balance, Sam slid an arm around her.

At that moment Zach turned around and saw

him. He watched Zach's eyes narrow and knew he had misconstrued the situation. Callen's brother was at his side before he could even steady Janice on her feet.

"What the hell do you think you're doing?" he raged at Sam.

"Mind your own business, Zach. This doesn't concern you."

"When my sister's husband has his arm around another woman who's kissing him in plain sight of all their friends, I'd say that's my business," Zach retorted.

"Nothing happened here," Janice began to explain.

"Keep out of this, Janice," Sam said in a curt voice. "Leave us alone, please." He gave her a little shove toward the other side of the room. Once she was gone, he turned his attention back to Zach. He could see there were already a lot of eyes on the two of them. The thought of explaining himself to Zach irked him, but he didn't want to make a scene and spoil Callen's party, so he said, "That was completely innocent."

"I'll bet."

"Janice was giving me a friendly kiss, and she lost her balance. That's all there was to it."

"You bastard. How long have you been seeing her?"

"What?"

"Everyone knows you had a thing for Janice

Reese when you were kids. You mooned over her for most of junior high school."

Sam stared at Zach. He hadn't imagined he had been that obvious. He swallowed over the bile at the back of his throat and said, "I haven't seen Janice for fifteen years until tonight. And I didn't invite her, Callen did."

"You expect me to believe that?"

"It's the truth!" Sam shot back. "But then, you Whitelaws aren't too big on honesty yourselves, so maybe you don't recognize it when you see it."

"What's that supposed to mean?"

"Ask your father," Sam snarled.

Sam had forgotten discretion in the heat of the moment. He was suddenly struck by the silence around him and turned to find everyone staring at him and Zach. What he saw in their eyes made him furious. How dare they judge him! How dare they condemn him! Then he caught sight of Callen's stricken face in the kitchen doorway.

She looked embarrassed and ashamed. Of him.

And why shouldn't she be? They all knew what he was. Dressing up and putting on airs didn't change the fact he was dumb as an ox.

He shoved a hand wearily through his hair and turned his back on all of them. "Go home," he said quietly. "The party's over."

He heard shuffling and muttering behind him, heard Callen's voice thanking them all for coming. Heard her reassure Zach and Falcon and her mother that she would be fine. That she was in no danger.

Oh, but she was! She was deeply embroiled in his plan to ruin her father. He hadn't cared whether she got destroyed in the process. And now it was too late. She was going to be hurt. And there wasn't a damn thing he could do about it.

You could give up your vengeance. You could forgive Garth Whitelaw and go on with your life.

"Sam?"

He turned around and saw Callen standing not a foot away from him, her eyes filled with concern. Everyone else had gone.

He shoved his hand through his hair again. "I'm sorry, Callen."

"What happened, Sam? I thought everything was going so well. Why did you start a fight with Zach? Why did you ask everybody to leave?"

"Zach started the fight," he retorted. "And I asked them to leave because I didn't want them here."

"Why not?" When he didn't answer, she reached out a hand and laid it on his chest. "Please tell me, Sam. I want to understand."

He brushed her hand away because he wanted so badly to hold her in his arms when he knew he didn't deserve the love she offered him.

"Don't you see?" he said in an agonized voice. "They all knew."

A frown furrowed her brow. "Knew what?"

"About me."

She shook her head. "You're going to have to be more specific than that. Knew what about you?"

"That I can't read a third-grade primer. That I could barely get through high school. That I couldn't get into college if I tried. That I'm not smart." An agitated hand went forking through his hair again. "Hell. That I'm dumb as ditch water."

"You listen to me, Sam Longstreet! You *are* dumb if you think I'm buying that hogwash for one single minute. You're plenty smart. Your problem is you're stubborn as a mule."

"Oh, Callen." He drew her into his arms, unable to keep his hands off her another second, and hugged her tight. "Saying I'm smart doesn't make it so."

She freed her hands and cupped his face, forcing him to look at her. "There's nothing wrong with you that can't be fixed, Sam. The truth is, you have a reading disability."

"Callen—"

"Shut up and listen to me!" she said. "You have dyslexia, Sam." He started to let her go, so she slipped her hands around his neck and hung on tight. "I checked with a specialist. I gave her that list you made for me. You aren't dumb, Sam, you just see numbers and letters all jumbled up on the page. Einstein had dyslexia, Sam. It has nothing to do with intelligence."

His face flushed a ruddy color. "Callen…" He was afraid to believe what she was saying. Afraid to hope.

"You're a darling idiot, but you're *not* dumb," Callen repeated, looking earnestly into Sam's green eyes. "Mrs. Moran—she's the specialist— says she can teach you how to overcome your reading problem. I told her you'd want to try. Will you, Sam?"

"Callen..." His voice was hoarse and his nose stung. He felt like crying. "It's too late—"

"It is not too late! Mrs. Moran says all it takes is time and effort."

"I don't have the time," Sam said flatly.

"Make the time."

"I'm too old—"

Callen put her hand against his lips to shut him up. "You can learn to read, Sam. You can learn to add and subtract. It isn't going to be easy. And it might even be embarrassing at your age. But if you're willing to make the effort, you can resolve a problem that's obviously been bothering you for a lot of years. I'll do whatever I can to help, but really, this is something you're going to have to do yourself."

Sam could hardly force the words over the thick lump of feeling in his throat. "What if I fail?"

Callen's arms tightened around him, and her lips pressed against his in comfort, in reassurance. "You won't fail, Sam. I firmly believe you can do anything you set your heart and mind to do."

Sam had to turn his head away so she wouldn't see the tears in his eyes. His voice was gruff with feeling when he spoke. "All right, Callen. If you want me to, I will."

She began pressing light, loving kisses all over his face.

"If we're done talking, I think it's time for bed," Sam said. "We can clean up this mess in the morning." He lifted Callen in his arms and headed for the bedroom.

He made love to her almost desperately. He wasn't sure what was driving him. Fear. And elation. What if he could learn to read, after all?

He had listened to Callen's offer of help from Mrs. Moran as though it were no big deal. But deep down, in some secret hidden place where he had stuffed all the shame he had felt as a boy growing up, unable to do simple things like read or add a column of figures, a hard knot began to loosen.

CHAPTER SEVEN

ONCE SAM STARTED working with Mrs. Moran, his progress was astonishing. Even Callen was amazed at how quickly he mastered his reading disability. Not that it was easy. And it was embarrassing at times. Callen saw his frustration on occasion, when the words on a page simply made no sense to him. But with an objective in sight, Sam devoted himself wholeheartedly to learning.

Having tackled one challenge, Sam was ready for another. His hope of making the Double L into one of the finest cutting horse ranches in Texas was about to begin.

The first cutting horses arrived two weeks after the housewarming party. Sam and Callen worked together training a sleek quarter horse mare for a rich client in El Paso who wanted to give it to his daughter as a birthday present.

When they began to work with the mare, Callen saw a facet of Sam she hadn't known existed. He had an understanding of animals, a rapport with them, that was transcendent. She had great skill maneuvering a cutting horse; Sam became one with the animal.

"Why haven't you been training cutting horses all along?" Callen demanded when Sam stepped down from the saddle after working the mare. "You're absolutely brilliant!"

One corner of Sam's mouth cocked up in a self-deprecating smile. "You think so?"

"Absolutely! I've never seen anybody ride like that, and I've seen a lot of competitions in my day."

Sam shrugged. "I've always had an affinity to horses." He paused and added, "Animals don't care whether you know how to read."

"Oh, Sam." Callen stepped into his arms and hugged him tight.

"It doesn't hurt so much anymore," Sam admitted quietly. "I mean, now that I know what was wrong. I suppose it's going to take a while getting used to the idea of picking up a newspaper just like other folks and paging through it. And I don't imagine I'll ever take up reading for pleasure." He grinned charmingly. "But I won't ever feel like I'm less smart than another man, ever again. I have you to thank for that, Callen."

"Someone else would have pointed out the problem if I hadn't come along."

"No one else ever did."

How long, Sam wondered, would he have remained blind to the truth if Callen hadn't come into his life? In a matter of months she had turned his life upside down. If he held on to his goal of revenge, he might eventually ruin hers.

"Sam, I met a young woman when I was in the

hardware store having some wood cut for shelves. She seemed really nice. Her name is Natalie Folsom. Her husband, Ted, is the new agricultural extension agent. I'd like to invite them to dinner."

"Are you asking me for permission, or telling me what you've done?" Sam asked.

Callen grinned. "You know me too well. Actually, I invited them for Saturday night. I'm willing to call and cancel if you don't think it's a good idea."

Sam sighed. He would probably never be a gregarious person, but it was foolish to let his past keep him from enjoying the present or the future. And Ted and Natalie Folsom weren't from around here. They knew nothing about him. "I think it might be fun to have dinner with another couple."

The Sam Longstreet who greeted the Folsoms at the door was the man Callen had fallen in love with. Only he was clean-shaven, had his chestnut hair trimmed above his collar, and wore polished boots and a pressed Western shirt and jeans. Callen hadn't let Sam's appearance keep her from falling in love with him, but she had to admit she felt proud of the man standing beside her.

Sam felt like a different man. It wasn't just his spiffed-up clothing and appearance. The difference came from the inside. He felt more self-confident, more sure of himself. Frankly, there wasn't anything different about him except that he knew now he was dyslexic. He had a learning disability, not an inability to learn. And he was making up fast for lost time.

Natalie Folsom was a curly haired redhead, with hazel eyes that crinkled when she smiled, and a smile that took up most of her face. She was petite and looked about seventeen, even though she admitted to twenty-four. Her husband, Ted, was only a few inches taller, but he had a muscular build. He wore glasses and had a receding hairline, but his face was open and friendly. He admitted to being a wrestler back in college ten years before, which made him a year younger than Sam.

They had nothing in common, Sam thought as the evening wore on, and yet he liked Ted. He was a good listener, and he made interesting comments when he spoke. Natalie was funny, and Sam loved seeing Callen laugh at her jokes.

Then Sam mentioned he had a motorcycle.

Ted's eyes lit up. "You have a motorcycle? What kind?"

Sam grinned. "Harley-Davidson, what else?"

"A Hog? Really? Me, too," Ted said. "Can I see it?"

"It's in the barn, covered with a tarp. I haven't even looked at it for years."

"Then don't you think it's about time you did?" Ted asked.

The four of them traipsed out to the barn, and Sam pulled a dusty canvas tarp off his Harley-Davidson touring motorcycle.

Ted whistled. "What a beauty! You've had a lot

of custom work done. I'll bet all this chrome sure shines up nice."

Sam reached out and slid a hand along the leather seat. "I'd forgotten how much I liked this machine." He had spent hours working on it, tuning it, shining it. He had been lost in a world of his own.

"Sam, I didn't even know you owned a motorcycle," Callen said. "When can I get a ride?"

"You want to ride it?" Sam asked in surprise.

"I'd *love* to ride it," Callen said with a sparkle in her eyes.

"How much work would it take to get it ready?" Ted asked.

Sam shrugged. "It shouldn't take much. I put it away clean."

"Then how about if we all take a ride next Saturday, let the wind blow in our hair and the bugs catch in our teeth."

Sam grinned at the picture Ted had conjured. "Sure, why not?"

"We can take along a picnic," Natalie said.

"And I know just the spot where we can go," Callen offered. "If this very late Indian summer cooperates. Who'd have thought it would still be warm this late in November?"

That night, as they lay in bed together after making sweet, sweet love, Callen laid her head on Sam's chest and slipped an arm across his waist and snuggled close. "Did you like Natalie and Ted?"

"Yeah. They're nice." Sam was feeling good. He couldn't remember a time when he had been this contented. He wondered what it was going to be like, having a friend like Ted. It had been easy talking to the other man, easy to share stories about their Harley-Davidsons. And he owed it all to Callen. She was the one who had met Natalie and invited the other couple to supper.

"You don't mind getting together with them again?" Callen asked.

"Hell, no. I'm looking forward to it. I can't believe we're going to a picnic on motorcycles," Sam said, grinning in the dark.

"Me, neither," Callen said with a giggle. "It almost makes me feel like a kid again."

"I'll bet you were hell on wheels," Sam said.

"Wait'll you see me on Saturday," she promised.

"I can't wait," Sam said as he turned and kissed her.

He wanted her again. Incredible as it seemed, he was hard and ready. They were both already naked, so it was easy enough to lever himself over her, spread her legs with his knees and thrust into her.

"Sam." She moaned his name as she arched beneath him. "Oh, Sam."

He kissed her with joy, with thanksgiving, with the love he felt but could not speak aloud. He wasn't supposed to care. She was merely a means to his vengeful ends. But he showed her with his mouth and hands what he truly felt in his heart.

Sam spent every spare moment of the next week working on his Harley in the barn. Callen always knew where she could find him. Once they made love facing each other on the leather seat. Once, when she wore a skirt, he stripped off her underwear, then unbuckled his belt, unzipped his pants and took her standing up against the wall of the barn. Once he took her to the loft and laid her down on a blanket in the hay. They made love often, with joy in their hearts. Life seemed perfect.

Then Callen's mother called to invite them to Hawk's Way for dinner.

"Next week is the beginning of the Christmas season, and it dawned on your father and me that we haven't seen much of you lately." The truth was, Callen and her father hadn't exchanged a word in nearly six months. "We'd both love to see you. Can you come?"

"I'll have to talk it over with Sam. But I'm sure we'll be able to come," Callen said.

"That's wonderful! We'll look forward to it. Call us when you know for sure."

Callen felt her stomach do a little twist when she hung up the phone. She had been so very happy before her mother reminded her that Sam and her father didn't get along. Well, she had tackled every other problem in her marriage with determination and conquered them all. What was one more little glitch? How difficult could it be to turn her husband and her father into friends?

"No," SAM SAID. "I'm not going to set foot in your father's house. Not now, not ever."

"Why not?" Callen demanded, her fists perched on her hips. "This has gone on long enough. I want to know what you have against my father."

Sam's lips pressed flat. He had known this moment was coming, that it would arrive sooner or later. He just hadn't expected it so soon. He met her brown eyes evenly and said, "Your father is responsible for E.J.'s death."

She got so deathly pale he thought for a moment she was going to faint. He reached out for her, but she flinched away from him.

"That's impossible. Your father committed suicide."

"Do you know why my father took his life?"

Callen frowned. "Not exactly."

"E.J. invested his life savings and every bit of capital we had for running the ranch in several get-rich-quick schemes. They turned out to be swindles. He lost everything. We were going to lose the Double L. He couldn't live with knowing he'd lost the only thing he had to pass on to me. So he killed himself."

"I still don't see where my father fits into that picture."

"Your father advised E.J. to make those investments."

Callen shook her head no, slowly at first and then more vehemently.

"Shake your head all you like. E.J. never made

a financial move in his life that didn't have Garth Whitelaw's stamp of approval."

"My father wouldn't have advised E.J. into anything that wasn't legitimate. Not on purpose."

"Oh, he did it, all right. And I even know why."

"All right. Why?"

"He wanted Double L land to replace what he gave away to Zach on his twenty-first birthday."

"That's ridiculous!"

"Is it? Think about it. How many times have you heard your father wish he had back the land he gave to Zach?"

Callen sucked in a breath. She had heard her father say exactly that over the years. He had given Zach thousands of acres of Hawk's Way land, in fact, about the same amount of acreage that comprised the Double L. And of course he missed the land, because it meant he couldn't run as many cattle, didn't have as much land to grow feed, didn't have the same lines drawn on the vast map of Hawk's Way that hung over the mantel in the parlor.

Her eyes widened in fright and horror. She didn't want to believe Sam's accusation. Refused to believe it. And was horrified to realize how much Sam must hate her father if he believed what he was saying.

"How could you marry me, thinking that about my father?" she asked in a quavery voice.

"I didn't intend to share you with him," Sam said. "I thought we'd never have to see him again."

"But he's my father!" Callen protested. "I love him. I could never stop seeing him!"

"Not even for me?"

Callen paced the room like a restless animal in a cage. "I love you, Sam. But I can't stop loving my father because I love you."

"And if you had to choose between us?"

Callen turned horrified eyes on Sam. "You wouldn't ask that of me. Surely you wouldn't!"

Here it was. The moment of truth. If he had done his work well, Callen would choose him over her father. Garth Whitelaw would realize exactly what price he had paid for coveting Double L land. He had lost his chance to have the land. Now he would lose his daughter, as well.

"I am asking, Callen. I'm asking you not to go to dinner at Hawk's Way. I'm asking you not to see your father again."

Callen stood still, but her whole body trembled. "I'm going, Sam. What you're asking of me is unreasonable. I won't be forced to choose between my husband and my father. I love you both."

"You can't have us both," Sam said flatly.

"What do you mean?" Callen asked, wide-eyed with distress.

"If you go to dinner at Hawk's Way, don't come back here. You won't be welcome."

Callen laughed, a harsh, unnatural sound. "I can't believe what I'm hearing! And it's so funny. My father threatened nearly the same thing—that I would lose my job at Hawk's Way when I said I was going to marry you. Sam—" She reached out a hand to him, but he stepped back beyond her reach.

"I meant what I said, Callen. The choice is yours."

Callen slept on her own side of the bed that night, hugging her arms to her body, unable to believe the impossible choice she had been given. She loved Sam more now than she had ever imagined possible. But she would die a little inside if she never saw her father again. She supposed she could concede to Sam now, and hope that he would change his mind later. But what if he didn't?

The next morning Sam noticed the air was almost as frigid as Callen's behavior toward him. "Good morning," he said as he sat down in the kitchen with a cup of coffee. One sip of the stuff had him screwing up his mouth at the bitter taste.

"I suppose if it gets any colder we'll have to call off the picnic on Saturday," he said.

"I'm not in the mood for a picnic anymore." Callen slammed his breakfast down in front of him.

The yolks on the eggs were broken and cooked hard, and the bacon was burned. Sam's lip curled. The woman sure knew how to make a subtle point.

She plopped down in the chair across from him and settled her fisted hands on the table in front of her. "Sam, we have to talk about this. You've got to change your mind."

"No." The eggs stuck in his throat. He washed them down with a sip of bitter coffee.

"Have you talked to my father? Did he give you any explanation of what might have happened?"

"I don't need to talk to your father. I know what I know."

"You're a damn fool, Sam," Callen accused, rising to her feet, "if you assume facts without knowing them."

Sam flushed. "I know my father, Callen. He wouldn't have done anything so foolhardy as investing on his own. He knew his limitations."

"So my father's to blame? Have you ever considered that your father may have made those decisions all by himself? That my father may be entirely innocent?"

Sam had refused to consider that possibility for several reasons. First, he knew how much his father had always relied on Garth Whitelaw to advise him on his investments. Second, if his father had made those decisions on his own, then it meant he was entirely responsible for losing his fortune, and that he had taken the coward's way out by committing suicide and leaving Sam to face the consequences alone.

Sam didn't want to believe that about his father. He needed to believe E.J.'s misfortune could be laid at Garth's door, along with the responsibility for E.J.'s untimely death.

"Do you want me to call Ted and cancel the picnic?" Sam asked.

Callen thought about it a moment. She had made up her mind to attend the dinner with her parents at Hawk's Way. If Sam held to his threats, she wouldn't be seeing him again after that. The picnic with Ted and Natalie might be the last one they ever had together. She wanted that memory to take with her.

"Tell them to dress warm," she said.

Sam couldn't believe that Callen was sticking to her guns. The dinner with her parents was the following Sunday. If he couldn't convince her to stay, he was going to have to let her go.

He was terrified of losing her.

He visited E.J.'s grave three times in the next week. He sat there with his back resting against the headstone and spoke aloud to his father, venting his frustration and asking for advice. He picked one of the fall flowers Callen had planted there and twirled it in his fingers. Then he began plucking the petals.

"She loves me…she loves me not…she loves me…she loves me not…she loves me. I really think she does, E.J. And I love her. I'm not exactly sure how it happened, but I think I've loved her for a long time. I don't know how I'll live without her. It's killing me to do this. But I don't know any other way to pay Garth back for what he did to you. And I promised you I'd give you that satisfaction, at least. It'll hurt him for sure if he knows Callen is suffering because of him. And I think she will, if I force her to stay away from the Double L.

"But, oh, God, Dad. I don't want to do it! It's tearing me apart inside. Tell me what to do! Tell me how to make everything come out right!"

There were no answers from the grave.

THE DAY OF the picnic dawned sunny and brisk. Sam produced a black leather jacket for himself and one for Callen. On the back in red lettering were the words Born To Be Wild.

"Where did you get this?"

He held it for her while she slipped into it. "I bought it for you. I thought we might start riding together."

She kept her chin down and her lashes lowered so he couldn't see her face as she zipped it up. Sam had bought this jacket when he thought they had a future together. If he didn't change his mind, this might be the only time she ever wore it.

Callen had ridden horseback all her life, so she knew the thrill of having a lot of horsepower between her legs. But when Sam revved up the Harley and she sat down behind him with her arms circling his waist, she knew what it was like to fly without ever leaving the ground. She felt the wind in her hair and smiled, knowing the chance she was taking that she would end up with bugs in her teeth. It was glorious.

It took a lot of trust to sit behind Sam and let him direct their course. She felt the power of the machine and the man who controlled it. She would have followed Sam anywhere, she realized. She knew he wasn't perfect. Far from it. But then, who was? Where it counted, when it counted, she knew Sam would always be there for her, loving her.

"Having fun?" Sam shouted over his shoulder. The wind caught the sound and sent it in all directions.

With a helmet on, Callen heard nothing. "What?"

"Having fun?" he repeated.

"Yes. I don't ever want to stop," she hollered back.

"What?" he shouted.

"Never mind," she said in a normal voice. "I know the trip is almost over. I just want to enjoy what there is left of it."

They ended up at the entrance to a deep canyon where there must once have been water since several cypress and cottonwoods had grown there. The weather was brisk, but there was no wind, and the bright sun made it seem warmer than it was.

Callen spread a blanket and the two women put out a picnic fit for kings. "Come on, fellows," Callen called. "Time to eat."

Callen and Sam never referred to his ultimatum once all day. They chatted with their new friends and discovered that all of them like to do the Texas two-step. They made a promise to go dancing together as soon as they could find a time when they were all free.

Sam and Ted talked about the weather and the price of cattle and whether interest rates were going to stay down or go back up again. Callen and Natalie talked about the weather and the price of food and whether health care reform would ever become a reality.

After lunch, when the sun was at its warmest, Ted and Natalie decided to take a walk down into the canyon.

"I'd rather rest, I think," Callen said.

Sam looked sharply at her. His Callen *resting?* It was unheard of. "Are you all right?"

She smiled lazily. "I'm just fine. A little tired. I didn't get much sleep last night."

Sam knew at least one worry that might have kept her awake. "You two go on," he said to the other couple. "We'll wait for you here."

Sam set himself down on the blanket with his back against a cottonwood and patted his thigh. "You can use me for a pillow."

Callen scooted over so she could rest her head in Sam's lap. "Thanks, Sam."

They didn't talk. Both of them knew it would have meant arguing. By tacit consent, they were determined to enjoy these last moments together before all hell broke loose.

To Sam's surprise, Callen fell asleep only minutes later. He brushed her bangs away from her face, then smoothed his thumb across her cheek for the sheer pleasure of touching her skin. He wanted to hold her close and never let her go. He wanted to treasure her. He wanted to get his children on her. He knew he had created the tense situation between them, and that he had the power to end it.

Sam leaned his head back against the tree and stared up through the branches into the cloudless blue sky. How important was vengeance, anyway? An eye for an eye, a tooth for a tooth, the Bible said. He needed to see Garth pay for E.J.'s death. Needed to know his father's death had been avenged, so he could finally lay E.J. to rest. So he could go on with his life.

But what kind of life did he have to look for-

ward to if he lost Callen in the pursuit of his al-
mighty vengeance?

He convinced himself, sitting there under a leaf-
less cottonwood, that in the end she would choose
him over her father. After all, she loved him. And
she wouldn't want to hear her father say "I told you
so." She wouldn't leave him. She couldn't.

Sam hadn't realized he had fallen asleep until
he heard the quiet murmur of voices. Maybe he
hadn't slept so well himself last night. He slowly
opened his eyes.

Callen was sitting nearby talking to Natalie.
Ted was over by the cycles, polishing chrome. He
realized Callen was talking about him, about their
marriage. He quickly closed his eyes, curious as
to what she would say.

"I can't believe you actually went through
with the wedding," Natalie exclaimed. "If Ted
had shown up looking like that, I'd have bolted
for sure."

"Sam isn't the sort of man you should judge by
appearances," Callen replied. "It's what's on the
inside that really matters. He's kind. And hardworking. He makes me feel special. And he's so
very smart."

Sam struggled not to wince at that. It was taking time for him to accept himself the way Callen
insisted upon perceiving him. He remembered a
boy struggling to make sense of confusion on a
page. She saw a man with dyslexia who had accepted the challenge to read.

"And I know Sam will make a good father," Callen said.

"Are you by any chance expecting?" Natalie asked.

Callen didn't answer, and Sam held his breath. She must have gestured one way or the other with her head, but by the time he opened his eyes a slit, she had resumed speaking.

"There's only one problem with Sam," she said.

"What's that?" Natalie asked.

Sam clenched his teeth. Well, this was it. She was going to tell Natalie about their argument, about his ultimatum.

"He drives way too fast on that motorcycle!"

Sam exploded with laughter.

"Sam! How long have you been awake?" Callen demanded.

"Long enough," he said with a grin. He rose to his feet. "Come on. I think it's time we headed back. I'm going to need lots of time to get home before dark, if I don't want to drive too fast."

He held out a hand and Callen took it. He dragged her to her feet and into his arms and gave her a lusty kiss.

Callen struggled only a moment before she kissed him back. When they finally separated, she scolded him. "What will Ted and Natalie think?"

"That I like kissing you. And you like kissing me back."

Callen's cheeks were tinged with rose by the

time Sam finished kissing her a second time. "It's getting dark, Sam. We'd better be heading back."

Sam saw the sun was on its way down. This idyll, indeed, the halcyon days of their marriage, were nearly over. Whether Callen left him, or whether she stayed, things would never be quite the same between them again.

CALLEN SPENT THE entire week leading up to the first Sunday in Advent arguing with Sam, trying to convince him that he was being unreasonable. But he was adamant. On the Saturday before she was to have dinner with her parents, she brought out the big guns. She let the tears drip in cascades from her eyes, even though she knew she never looked her best when she was crying. Desperate situations required desperate measures.

The tears almost did him in. Sam was torn in two at the sight of Callen's tear-streaked face. He wanted to say the hell with it and let her go. Only he turned at that instant and spied a small stain on the hardwood floor where E.J.'s blood had soaked into the aged wood. He had covered the spot with a rug, but the rug had slid away to reveal the dark secret beneath it. His heart hardened. He had sworn vengeance against Garth Whitelaw. By God, he would have it!

At last the fateful day arrived. In the stark morning light, from the rumpled sheets he had shared with his wife the night before, Sam watched Callen dressing for dinner with her parents at Hawk's Way. "So you're going, after all."

"Yes."

She looked awful, Sam thought. Her eyes were red-rimmed from all the crying she had done, and there were shadows under her eyes that told him she hadn't slept. Hell, neither had he. He wasn't about to miss a moment of what might very well have been the last night his wife spent in his bed.

"I don't want you to go, Callen."

"Don't you see I have to, Sam? They're my parents. If E.J. were still alive, would you avoid him simply because I didn't like him?"

Put that way, his request did seem unreasonable. But the whole crux of the problem was that her father was the reason his father was dead. And if he wasn't able to keep Callen away from Garth, then he would have to put the other part of his plan into effect. He would have to do his best to make Callen miserable, and force Garth to live with the knowledge that he was the source of his daughter's unhappiness. He had to cut Callen out of his life. He had to divorce her.

Sam could see she was ready to go. "If you leave this house, don't come back," he said in a voice that sounded like a rusty gate.

"You don't mean that," Callen replied in a calm voice.

Her eyes were full of love for him. He felt like a band was tightening around his chest, cutting off his air. He stopped breathing entirely when he heard what she had to say next.

"Because if I go out that door, never to return, so does your son or daughter." Callen closed the bedroom door with a quiet click behind her.

The silence was deafening.

An instant later Sam was out of bed and had his jeans on. He zipped them halfway up and skipped the snap. They barely clung to his hips as he headed after her. "What did you say?"

Sam caught Callen in the kitchen and dragged her back around to face him. There were tears in her eyes again. He hauled her into his arms and held her there. She was going to leave him. He could feel it from the way she remained stiff in his arms, unyielding.

He hadn't figured on a child. He had used protection every time. Except that once. Just once. And there had been dire consequences for his lapse.

Sam had a decision to make. Which was more important? Vengeance? Or a lifetime with Callen and the child she carried inside her?

It was far easier to put the burden on her. He let her go and stepped back. "Don't go, Callen. Please, don't go."

"I have to, Sam." The words were wrenched from her as she turned and ran.

Sam let her go.

CHAPTER EIGHT

GARTH AND CANDY welcomed their daughter with open arms. They exchanged a look of concern over her head as they led her into the parlor to have a glass of wine before dinner.

"None for me," Callen said. "Water will be fine."

Candy poured a glass of sparkling water and added ice before she handed it to her daughter. "Sam isn't coming?"

Callen shook her head. She turned to look out the window and blinked back a tear before it could spill.

"I can't believe so much time has passed since you got married," Candy said. "We kept expecting to see the two of you here at Hawk's Way any day. Now it's nearly Christmas."

"Yes," Callen said in a voice that was commendably calm. She had already bought one of Sam's Christmas presents. She had signed him up for an audio book club, so he could listen on tape to all the books he had never read. "There was a lot to do on the Double L. Sam and I have been very busy."

Callen was a married woman and soon to be a

mother herself. If she had learned anything in the months she had been married to Sam, it was that there was no obstacle too great to be overcome. Look at everything Sam had survived. Surely there was some way to resolve this dilemma so they could all have Christmas together.

"Is Sam treating you well, Callen?" her mother probed.

"Obviously her husband isn't treating her right," her father muttered. "Otherwise she wouldn't look like death warmed over."

"I'll thank you not to say anything disrespectful about my husband," Callen said. "What goes on between Sam and me is our business."

"I'm sorry he wasn't able to come," Callen's mother said.

"I'm just as glad he didn't," her father countered.

Callen rose and confronted her father. "I mean it, Daddy. If you make one more remark like that about Sam, I'll leave."

"Please, Garth," Candy said. "Let's just have some dinner and let Callen tell us what she's been doing since she and Sam got married."

Callen saw the warning look her mother shot at her father and was grateful for the help in steering her father away from the subject of Sam Longstreet. But it was too much to hope it wouldn't be raised again at the dinner table.

"So what have you and Sam been doing that's kept you so busy you can't—"

"Garth."

Her mother's warning cut her father off and gave Callen an opening to answer his question. She told them everything. How Sam had needed her fortune to save the Double L from foreclosure. How she had remodeled the house as best she could using items she had scrounged, or bought at a discount, or repaired with a little elbow grease and the sweat of her brow. How proud she was of the result. How she and Sam had painted the house together and how good it looked when they were done. How Sam had come up with the idea of training cutting horses and how successful they had been with a mare intended for a girl in El Paso. How she had discovered Sam was dyslexic, and how he was finally, at long last, learning to read.

Of the revelation about Sam, her mother said, "That's unbelievable. I wonder why no one ever figured it out before."

Because no one cared enough to find out the truth. Because Sam never let anyone get close enough to see how he was suffering because of it. Callen couldn't say that to her parents. They wouldn't understand. And really, it didn't matter now. She was there to love Sam, to care whether he was happy. That is, if he let her come home to him after she had finished this dinner with her parents.

She didn't tell them about the baby. She didn't want it to be used as a pawn in the battle she could see was coming. Nor did she ask her father about whether he was the one who had advised E. J.

Longstreet into so many bad investments. She knew her father well enough to believe he hadn't done anything dishonest. If he had suggested some investments that turned out to be swindles, he had not done it knowingly. Besides, there was no way to change the past. What was done was done. It was Sam who had to forgive and forget.

Callen sought for a safe subject of conversation and found it. "What have you two been doing with yourselves at Hawk's Way, now that all three of your young ones have finally flown the nest?"

Her parents exchanged a tender look. Her mother flushed. Her father grinned.

"To be honest," her mother admitted, "we've had a sort of second honeymoon."

"That doesn't mean we don't want to see our children as often as they can come visit," her father said.

"I'm glad for both of you." Callen ate the last bit of apple pie that Charlie One Horse had made because he knew it was her favorite dessert and shoved her plate away. "I'm afraid I've got to go now."

"Can't you stay and visit longer?" her father said.

"I need to get home. There are lots of chores to be done. And I want to be sure I have time to cook supper for Sam."

Her parents walked her to the door, clearly reluctant to let her go.

"When will we see you again?" her mother asked.

"Soon."

"Don't make it so long next time," her father said gruffly as he pulled her into his arms at the door and gave her a hug. "I love you, Callen," he whispered in her ear.

Callen bit her lip to keep from bursting into tears. She couldn't remember the last time her father had told her he loved her. Callen hugged him hard. She peered up at him when he let her go. The skin was stretched taut over his cheekbones. He was getting older. There was more gray in his hair, and the creases beside his mouth were deeper. She glanced at her mother and saw there were lines around her eyes that she had never noticed before. Where had the time gone?

They were already grandparents to Falcon's stepdaughter and newborn son. Now they were going to have another grandchild. And she was going to have to find a way to convince Sam that their child needed its grandparents.

"Goodbye, Daddy. Goodbye, Mom," she said, giving them each another quick hug and a kiss. "Don't worry about me, please. I love Sam. And I'll find a way to make everything all right."

She was gone before they could ask her what she meant.

Callen drove back to the Double L as fast as her car could get her there. She parked in back and headed for the kitchen door. She turned the knob and shoved, but the door didn't budge.

It was locked.

She banged on the door. "Sam! The door's locked. Come on, let me in."

There was no answer. She couldn't imagine

why the door was locked in the first place. They
never locked the doors. It wasn't necessary. She
raced around the house to the front door, thinking
it might be open. It was locked, as well.

She pounded on it and shouted, "Sam! I know
you're in there! This is ridiculous! Let me in!"

A quick check revealed his motorcycle was
gone. So, he wasn't inside listening to her pound
on the door, after all.

There was a key under the mat in front, and
Callen stooped to see if it was there. It was. She
picked it up and stood in the fading light of dusk
and stared at it. All she had to do was put the key
in the lock and open the door.

Why had Sam locked the doors, but left the key,
she wondered, unless he intended for her to let herself in? But if he wanted her inside, why hadn't
he simply left the doors open? Why had he made
sure to be gone when she got home?

Callen felt a rising fury. If Sam was backing off
from his ultimatum, if this was his idea of an apology, it fell far short of what was necessary. And if
he was testing to see whether she dared to come
inside after he had made it clear she wasn't welcome, he was going to be sorely disappointed. If
Sam wanted to play games, she would show him
how it was done. He would soon discover that a
Whitelaw learned in diapers how to win.

Callen's lips twisted in chagrin. Of course, there
was the small matter of where she was going to
stay until Sam came after her with an apology on

his lips. Returning to Hawk's Way was out of the question. She got into her car and headed down the drive away from the Double L without any clear destination in mind. Not that she could see anything anyway, for the tears blurring her vision.

When she realized several minutes later that she was on the road to Hawk's Way she pulled over to the side of the road and stopped. She refused to go home to her father. She didn't belong there anymore. She turned the car around and headed in the other direction.

She had only been to Zach's ranch a few times, but nothing had ever looked as sweet to her as his whitewashed Spanish-style adobe house. She parked the car in back and headed for the kitchen. She opened the unlocked door without knocking and stepped inside. Zach was sitting at the island bar in the center of the kitchen, finishing up a supper that looked like it had gone from the freezer to the microwave. He looked up when she appeared in the doorway, startled. He rose and took a step toward her.

Callen collapsed, weeping, into her brother's comforting arms.

He didn't ask her any questions. He didn't say "I told you so." He merely put her into bed in his guest room, drew the drapes to make it dark, closed the door and left her alone.

SAM SAT WITH his back against E.J.'s headstone. Tears had dried on his cheeks. It was nearly full dark. He knew Callen must have come home by now and found the doors locked. He wondered whether she had bothered to look for the key and whether she had used it. He was afraid to go home and find out.

He had argued with himself for hours about whether he ought to simply go back to the house and unlock the doors and welcome home the best thing that had ever happened to him. In spite of all his threats, he knew he would welcome her with open arms if she came back to him. She had to know how he felt. But he had never told her that he loved her. He had never told her how precious she was to him.

Sam tried to remember what his life had been like before Callen came into it nearly nine months ago. Bleak. Lonely.

Lately it had been filled with laughter. Soon there would be a baby crying, bringing new life to the Double L. Unless Callen saw those locked doors and left. What if she didn't remember about the key under the front door mat? What if she didn't think to look for it?

He didn't know how he would live without her.

Sam jumped up and ran for his motorcycle. He lay low along the tank as the wind whistled around his ears. He felt the fear rise as he approached the house and saw it was still dark. He raced for the back door, yanked on it and realized it was locked. He pounded on it twice in frustration before he sprinted around to the front.

He saw the shine of the key in the last rays of daylight. It was sitting on top of the mat in plain sight. She had found it. But she hadn't used it.

Sam grabbed the key and jammed it into the lock. He turned the key and forced the door open, shouting as he hurried through the dark house.

"Callen? Where are you? Callen? Are you here? Callen?"

He turned on lights as he went until he had illuminated every square foot of the house. She wasn't there.

He walked back into the parlor and sat in the chair she had scrounged for him and put his feet up on the comfortable ottoman. There was no warm fire to greet him. There was no warm woman to hold in his arms. He leaned back wearily in the chair. He had never been so tired.

Where could she have gone?

To Hawk's Way, you fool. And you have no one to blame but yourself. You had a chance. You could have made a choice.

I did make a choice.

You made the wrong one.

I owed E.J.—*Do you think E.J. would have wanted to see this happen? Do you think E.J. would want his grandchild to grow up without its father?*

She'll come back.

Better if you go after her.

She'll come back.

You're a fool, Sam Longstreet.

Sam tried to find some satisfaction in what he had done. His revenge was complete. But as he looked around his empty house, bereft of love and laughter, and thought of sleeping in his bed, empty and cold, and imagined a future spent alone...vengeance suddenly didn't seem so important anymore.

It seemed a betrayal of the feelings he had for his father to choose Callen over vengeance. But vengeance was a bitter bedfellow.

Sam was torn in two. He couldn't think right now. He closed his eyes and let blessed sleep claim him.

CALLEN POUNDED ON the door. "Sam! Let me in! Sam!"

The front door opened abruptly and Callen nearly fell inside. Sam caught her firmly by the shoulders and kept her at arm's length. "You left this house, Callen. You're not welcome here anymore."

She laughed shakily. "Sam, this is my home, too. You're my husband. I want to come in."

"No, Callen."

Callen was stunned. He had meant what he had said. He didn't want her anymore. And all because she refused to love one man more than another. Callen had too much pride to beg. "All right, Sam. Have it your way."

She turned and walked toward her car. She got in and gunned the engine, spitting rocks and dust as she headed down the drive.

Only she had no place to go.

"Callen! Callen!"

It was Sam. He was calling her back. He wanted her—

CALLEN BOLTED UPRIGHT when she felt a hand on her shoulder. Where was she?

"You were having a bad dream," Zach said.

Oh, my God, it had all been a dream! Callen bit back a sob. The nightmare had seemed so real!

She looked around her, trying to orient herself. This wasn't her bed. There was no comforting warmth lying beside her. It all came back to her again with her eyes wide open. The awful confrontation with Sam. His ultimatum. Returning home to find herself locked out. Leaving the key where Sam was sure to find it and know she had chosen to leave him. Coming to Zach's house and collapsing in his arms.

"Oh, God."

"Are you all right, Callen? You cried out in your sleep."

It was still dark. She couldn't see Zach, but she could feel his arms close around her shoulders. She leaned her head against his chest and sighed. "I've made a mess of everything, Zach."

"You had some help."

"Yes. Sam isn't without blame. What am I going to do now?"

"Get a good night's sleep and go home tomorrow."

"It isn't that simple. Sam threw me out."

"He what?"

"He's got this crazy idea that Daddy is responsible for E.J.'s death."

"That's hogwash."

"He says Daddy pointed E.J. toward those investments on purpose, because he wanted him to lose the Double L."

"Why?"

"So Daddy could buy the Double L when it went into foreclosure and replace the land he gave to you."

Zach remained silent, and Callen's heart fell.

"I knew he wanted to buy some more land," Zach mused quietly. "But I thought he had Abel Johnson convinced to sell."

"You're not suggesting Daddy might have done what Sam's accused him of, are you?"

"No. Dad and E.J. were too close for that. I think if Dad had wanted E.J. to sell to him he would have come right out and asked."

"What if E.J. said no?"

"Then I think Dad would have looked elsewhere."

Callen sighed. "I thought the same thing. But Sam refuses to believe me. And he refuses to listen to anything Daddy has to say."

"Then I guess we'll just have to catch him and hog-tie him and make him listen."

Callen laughed at the image Zach had conjured. "Oh, I'd like to see you try."

"You think I couldn't do it?"

"I think you'd have your hands full trying."

"Seriously, Callen, what are you going to do now?"

"Can I stay here?"

"You're welcome for as long as you want to stay."

"I'll have to find a place of my own soon," she said.

"You'll be no bother here."

"Yes, but I have a feeling you may draw the line at hosting a squalling infant."

She heard Zach take in a breath.

"You're pregnant?"

"Nearly three months."

"Sam Longstreet is a fool."

"Right now, I'd have to agree with you." Callen felt like crying.

Zach must have sensed it somehow because his arms tightened around her and he ruffled her hair. "Don't worry, Callen. Everything will turn out fine. You'll see. First off, I'm going to see Dad and explain the situation. I may not be able to make Sam listen, but surely Dad can find a way to make him hear the truth."

"Oh, Zach, I hope you're right."

"You'd go back to him if he asked?"

"In a heartbeat. I love him, Zach. More than my own life. More than anything."

"Then why aren't you at the Double L right now?"

"Because Sam has to realize he loves me the

same way. Until he does, until he realizes that nothing is more important than our love for each other, it's better that I stay away."

Zach eased her back down. "Get some sleep, Callen. We have a long day ahead of us tomorrow."

Zach didn't go back to his own bed. He dressed and left the house, arriving at the imposing front door of Hawk's Way a half hour later. He let himself in and made his way upstairs to his parents' bedroom. The door was closed and he knocked.

He heard the rustling of bedcovers inside and then his father's voice. "Who's there?"

"Zach."

His father and mother both appeared at the door a moment later. "What's wrong?" they said together.

"It's Callen."

"Is she all right? Has something happened to her?" his mother asked.

"She's fine, Mom. She's at my place, sound asleep in the guest room."

"If that bastard has done anything—"

"Hold on, Dad," Zach said. "You'd better be sure Callen doesn't hear you bad-mouthing Sam like that. She's likely to scratch your eyes out."

"What the hell is going on, Zach?" Garth demanded.

Zach turned to his mother. "I need to talk to Dad. Could you leave us alone for a little while?"

"There's nothing you have to say to me that your mother can't hear," Garth said.

"All right. I'll wait for you both downstairs."

It didn't take long for Zach to relate everything Callen had told him. Except the fact that she was pregnant. He figured she would rather tell them that herself. "So you see, Dad, you're going to have to make Sam listen to the truth."

"You don't think Sam's version of what happened is the truth?" Garth questioned.

"No, Dad. And neither does Callen. But I'm curious. Just what did happen?"

Garth sighed. "I believe I'll save that explanation for Sam. But I don't think he's going to want to hear it."

"When are you going to see Sam?" Candy asked.

"Is tomorrow morning soon enough?"

"I guess it'll have to be," Zach said. He rose with a stretch, and yawned. "I guess I'd better get back home and get what sleep I can. I'd advise you to do the same."

Once Zach was gone, Garth and Candy walked arm-in-arm back up the spiral staircase. They went through the motions of removing robes and returning to bed. Garth turned out the bedside lamp and pulled his wife into his arms.

But sleep wouldn't come.

"It wasn't your fault, Garth," Candy whispered in the dark. "There was nothing you could have done."

"I'm not so sure," Garth said. "He was my friend. I should have been able to prevent what happened. I should have done more. I should have done *something*."

"You did what you could. You did more than most. Don't blame yourself."

"Sam blames me."

"Sam needs someone to blame."

"What if he won't listen?"

"He'll listen. And he'll recognize the truth when he hears it."

"I hope you're right."

"Try to sleep, Garth. You'll need your strength tomorrow." Candy pressed her cheek against Garth's chest and let her hand twine in the hair at his nape. "You're a good husband, Garth, and a good father and a good friend. Don't ever doubt it."

"Thanks, Candy. I needed to hear that." Garth pulled his wife close. She was the treasure of his life. The light that burned bright in his soul. He hoped his children found the same wonder in their spouses that he had found in his.

Garth lay for a long time staring into the dark. He felt Candy's breathing deepen and steady into the rhythm of sleep. At long last, he closed his eyes and drifted into sleep.

CHAPTER NINE

NO DOUBT ABOUT IT, Sam Longstreet was a changed man. And it was all the result of his marriage to Callen Whitelaw. Sam stood on his front porch, which no longer sagged, and looked around him. Not only had the rotting boards been replaced on the barn, but it had been painted a rust red. There were six sleek quarter horses in the corral, waiting to be worked. Two of those cutting horses belonged to the Double L. The rest were being trained for clients he had advertised for in quarter-horse journals. He had written the ads himself and read them when they appeared in the magazine.

He brushed a hand across his clean-shaven jaw and wiped the polished toes of his boots against the back of his jeans. There wasn't a piece of clothing in his drawers with a rip or tear, not a button missing on one of his shirts. He owed that to Callen, too.

In the distance he saw a windmill twirling like mad, but no screech of unoiled metal carried to him on the wind. He could see his cattle near the stock tank, munching contentedly on hay he had planted and reaped himself. He would be taking them to market soon, and because he was a lucky man, the price of beef was up.

The Double L had never been so profitable as it was now. He had made his mortgage payments the past few months with money earned by the sweat of his brow—and Callen's. He mustn't forget his wife when he was counting his blessings. Because she was the greatest one of all.

Sam knew what his wife had given to him. His ranch. His self-respect. Her love.

What had he offered her in return? Dishonesty. Duplicity. Deception.

He had never once told her his true feelings. Although, perhaps that wasn't surprising, since he had lied to himself almost from the first. He must have loved her even then. He couldn't remember a time when he hadn't. Only he had never told her. He had never said the words aloud. Not when she married him. Not when she made love to him. Not when she gave him back his ranch or offered him a chance to read and write when he thought such feats impossible. Not even when she made him believe there was nothing he couldn't do if he set his mind to it.

Had he made her happy, as he had promised he would on the day he proposed to her? He thought perhaps she was. Or had been, before he insisted on having his revenge against her father. If he had it all to do over again, he would do things differently. Oh, yes, he would. He would recognize the prize he had found in his wife and cherish her and protect her from anything that threatened her happiness.

He couldn't live the past again. But there was always the future. Sam headed back inside the house for breakfast. There were no days off on a ranch. Despite everything, he had work that had to be done.

He wasn't hungry enough to cook himself a breakfast, settling for two cups of coffee while he stared out the curtained window in front of the sink. It was almost painful to be in this room without her. He wanted her here. Needed her here. Wished she were here.

Callen had lavished her attention on everything from the shiny hardwood floor to the new coat of paint on the cabinets to the flowery wallpaper. She had made the room hers, made it light and lovely. It wasn't a bachelor kitchen anymore.

Sam remembered a story Callen had told him about what it was like to grow up with two older brothers. They had gotten into so much mischief the neighbors had dubbed them the Three Whitelaw Brats. She was always tagging along behind them.

"But they didn't want me there," she said wistfully. "I was in their way. They had to be more careful when I was around—although I got hurt often enough even as it was.

"I grew up thinking I could do anything they could do. Mostly, I could. It wasn't until much later that I realized I didn't want to do all the things they were doing, that there were other things that interested me more. Only, if I did those things, I wouldn't have my brothers' company. I would have to do them alone.

"It's hard to believe that with everything I had at Hawk's Way, I could have been lonely. But I was. I was too much of a tomboy to get along with the other girls when I was younger, and by the time I realized I wanted to be just like them, it was too late. I couldn't seem to go along with the crowd. I was too much my own person.

"I spent a lot of time alone. That was what drew me to you at first, you know. I saw that same look of loneliness in your eyes. And I knew we could be friends."

"Why did you marry me, Callen?" he had asked.

"I wanted someone to love. I wanted to be loved by someone. And I wanted a home and a family of my own."

She had expected so little from their marriage. And so very, very much.

Sam's neck hairs stiffened when he heard a knock at the front door. That alone announced it wasn't a friendly visit. He made his way through the house to the front door. When he opened it, he found Garth Whitelaw standing there.

"I want to talk," Garth said. "And I won't take no for an answer."

Sam hesitated before stepping back. "Come on in and say your piece."

Garth took a quick look around and saw that

more improvements had been made since the last time he had been inside. The house had a warmth and coziness that proclaimed it a home. Unfortunately, his daughter was no longer living here. It was a situation he hoped to remedy.

Garth turned to Sam and found the other man's face unreadable. Which meant he didn't detect the loathing that had been there the last time the two of them had conversed. But there was no liking evident, either.

"I knew about those investments E.J. made," he began.

Sam's hands balled into fists, which he pounded against his thighs. "Damnation! I knew it! I knew you were to blame!"

"I didn't say I was to blame," Garth corrected in a terse voice. "I said I knew E.J. invested in those deals. He came to me and asked me what I thought. I advised him against it."

"The hell you did! If you'd told him not to invest, E.J. wouldn't have invested."

Garth shook his head. "That's where you're wrong. E.J. was sick, Sam. He had prostate cancer. He knew he was dying, and he wanted to leave you more than what he had. He was hoping to make a killing, since all those deals offered a substantial return. Only E.J. got burned. I think he was afraid to face you and tell you the truth." A muscle in his cheek jerked. "Just like I was."

Sam's face had bleached white. "You're lying." E.J. sick? E.J. dying of cancer? It was all so im-

probable. So unbelievable. Only, Garth's words
had the ring of truth.

"I wouldn't have cared if he lost everything,"
Sam said in a hoarse voice. "I wouldn't have
blamed him. He didn't have to kill himself!"

"He was afraid of the cancer, Sam. I think that
was as much the cause of what he did as losing his
fortune." Garth sighed deeply. "I know it wasn't
my fault, and yet I still felt responsible when I
heard E.J. had killed himself. I felt I deserved
whatever scorn you heaped on my shoulders. I
should have interfered. I should have argued more
against those investments E.J. made. I should have
made him tell you about the cancer. Maybe then..."

Sam put out a hand to stop Garth's speech. "You
knew E.J. as well or better than anyone. Do you
really think you could have stopped him once he
got an idea fixed in his head?"

"No. You're right. He was one stubborn cuss."
Garth paused and added, "And you take after him.
I came here today to tell you the truth. And to tell
you you're a fool if you let Callen slip through your
fingers. I haven't figured out why, but my daughter loves you enough to take your side against her
own father. She threatened to leave my house if I
said a word against you."

"She did?" That was news to Sam.

"I suggest you get yourself on over to Zach's
place and get your wife and bring her home."

"I already have."

"What?"

At that moment a sleepy-eyed, tousle-headed woman came walking into the room. She walked right into Sam's open arms.

"Hi, Daddy."

"What are you doing here, Callen? Zach came over in the middle of the night to tell us you'd left Sam and were sound asleep in his guest bedroom."

"I had. I was." She shoved her bangs out of her eyes and yawned.

"Then, what the hell are you doing here?"

"Oh. Sam came and got me." She smiled a Cheshire grin and looked lovingly up at Sam. "He near pounded the door down. I guess that must have been when Zach was gone to Hawk's Way, because when I answered the door, Sam threw me over his shoulder and carried me away. It was very romantic."

Garth gawked. He couldn't help it. "You two are crazy."

"Crazy in love," Callen said as she stared into the warm welcome in Sam's green eyes. "It seems Sam can't live without me. And of course he wanted to be around while our child was growing up." She laid a hand on her belly, and Sam put his hand over hers.

Garth grinned as understanding dawned. "I'm going be a grandfather again? That's wonderful news, Callen." He leaned over quickly and kissed her cheek. He held out his hand to Sam. "Congratulations, Sam."

Sam took Garth's hand. "I'll take good care of

her, sir. You don't have to worry about that. And about the other…"

"I should have explained everything sooner."

"I should have been more willing to listen."

It was as much of an apology or explanation as either man would ever offer. They shook hands once more before Garth stepped back.

"I guess I'll be going now. Does your mother know about the baby?"

Callen shook her head.

Garth's grin broadened. "I can't wait to tell her. You can expect her to call, I'm sure."

"Tell her to make it later," Sam said as his arms closed once more around his wife.

"I'll do that."

A moment later Garth was gone.

Sam scooped his wife into his arms and headed back toward the bedroom.

"Sam!" Callen exclaimed. "What are you doing?"

"I'm taking you back to bed, where I can make love to you to my heart's content."

"That sounds like a lovely idea."

Sam knew he had made the right choice, the only choice in retrieving his wife from her brother's house. He had sought vengeance against Garth Whitelaw to salve his own hurt. It wasn't what E.J. would have wanted. When it came down to a choice between having his wife and hurting her father, Sam had known what he had to do.

Callen had made her capture and capitulation seem romantic when she related it to her father.

But it had been far more difficult to convince her to come home than Sam liked to remember. In fact, he felt lucky to have convinced her at all.

"Why do you want me back, Sam?" she had demanded.

"Because I need you."

"That isn't enough. I won't be used as a pawn to hurt my father."

He had swallowed hard and said, "I love you, Callen."

"Oh, Sam." She let one sob escape before she put a fist to her mouth to hold back the rest. "If you only knew how long I've waited to hear you say those words. But it'll tear me apart to love you, if it means letting you destroy my father."

"I don't want to destroy your father. Not anymore."

He had seen the hope in her eyes. "Really, Sam? Have you forgiven him?"

"I believe he's responsible for what happened to my father," he countered. "But I'm willing to forego my vengeance for your sake."

"That's not enough, Sam."

"What do you want from me?" he had asked bleakly. "I've chosen you instead of revenge. I've chosen love instead of hate. What more can I do?"

"Stop punishing yourself for what wasn't your fault. Forgive yourself for not knowing how upset and depressed E.J. was. Stop blaming yourself for your father's death."

"It wasn't my fault!"

"I know that," Callen had soothed. "And deep down, so do you. E.J. chose to die. He was the one who was responsible. Not my father. And not you."

"Callen... I..." She had been sitting in a chair in the kitchen. He had fallen on his knees in front of her as she opened her arms to him. He had clutched her tightly and felt her arms fold around him.

He had grieved then, the bitter tears cleansing away his anger and his guilt and, along with them, the need for revenge. He was whole once more.

He had picked Callen up in his arms, and she had clung to him, sitting close to him all the way home in his pickup. They hadn't made love last night, but had fallen asleep in each other's arms.

Then Garth had come this morning and explained about E.J.'s cancer. Sam would always regret the way his father had died. But he would be able to look back now without the terrible hate and anger that had colored the past months.

As he laid Callen on the bed and slipped in beside her, he pulled her close. "I love you, Callen. More than my life. More than anything."

"And I love you, Sam. I was just thinking..."

"What?" Sam asked as he nuzzled his wife's throat.

"I know you and Daddy would really like each other if you spent some more time together. So why don't we—"

Sam shut his wife up in the time-honored way, by covering his mouth with hers. He had the feeling he was going to spend the next few years going toe-to-toe with his bride. Which wasn't such a bad fate, when he thought about it.

"Sam—"

He kissed her again.

"Sam…"

And again.

"Oh, Sam."

"I love you, Callen."

Sam grinned as he kissed his wife. At least he had gotten in the last word this time.

EPILOGUE

"SAM, COME QUICK!"

As a new father, Sam jumped two feet whenever he heard Callen call these days. Her frantic cry from the kitchen had him sprinting there to join her. "What's wrong? Are Karen and Kayla all right?"

His question was answered before he finished voicing it. His twin one-year-old daughters were sitting happily in their high chairs with cereal dribbled across their mouths, the trays of their high chairs and the floor.

"Come here and read this, Sam," Callen said, thrusting the local newspaper across the kitchen table toward him.

Sam took the paper without experiencing the knot that would once upon a time have formed in his stomach at the mere thought of confronting the written word.

"Look at that," Callen said, her finger thumping against the paper. "I can't believe any brother of mine could do anything so incredibly foolish."

Sam read the item Callen had pointed out to him.

Wife Wanted
Texas rancher seeks honest, responsible, compliant woman for wife. Must be capable of bearing children. Contact Zachary Whitelaw, Hawk's Pride, or phone 555-6748.

"Well, I'll be damned," Sam said with a chortle of glee. "That's one way to find a wife I'd never have considered."

"Do you see what that ad says?" Callen ranted. "Compliant! He might as well have said he wants a wife who'll kowtow to everything he says. The nerve!"

"Settle down, sweetheart. Your brother's a big boy. He knows what he's doing."

Callen snorted. "That'll be the day. The only comfort I have is that the whole idea is so ridiculous, so preposterous, that no sane woman will respond."

Sam threw the paper on the table. "I guess we'll just have to wait and see. Right now, I have more important things to think about." He drew his wife up into his arms. "You two close your eyes," he said to the little girls.

Sam lowered his mouth and gave his wife a lingering kiss, doing his best to ignore the giggles from the high-chair peanut gallery.

* * * * *

WE HOPE YOU ENJOYED
THIS BOOK FROM
HARLEQUIN
ROMANTIC
SUSPENSE

Danger. Passion. Drama.

These heart-racing page-turners will keep you guessing to the very end. Experience the thrill of unexpected plot twists and irresistible chemistry.

4 NEW BOOKS AVAILABLE EVERY MONTH!

SPECIAL EXCERPT FROM

HARLEQUIN

ROMANTIC SUSPENSE

*After a suspicious death on her team, environmentalist
Emma Copley knows someone needs to investigate.
When the authorities won't, she decides to do it herself,
despite Beau Kingston's warnings. He may have a
financial incentive to stop her investigation, but he
certainly doesn't want her hurt. Can they trust each
other long enough to find the real culprit?*

Read on for a sneak preview of
Deadly Texas Summer,
the latest thrilling romance from Colleen Thompson.

She looked up at him, her expression stricken. "You don't
believe me either, do you? You don't think I can prove
that Russell was on to something real."

"I'm reserving judgment," he said, keeping his words
as steady as he could, "until I see more evidence. And
you might want to consider holding back on any more
accusations until you've recovered from this shock—and
you have that proof in hand."

"Oh, I'll find the proof. I have a good idea where, too.
All I have to do is get back to the turbines as soon as
possible and find the—"

"No way," he said sharply. "You're not going out
there. You saw the email, right? About Green Horizons'
safety review?"

She gave him a disgusted look. "Of course they want to
keep everyone away. If they're somehow involved in all

this, they'll drag out their review forever. And leave any evidence cleaned and sanitized for their own protection."

"Or they're trying to keep from being on the hook for any further accidents. Either way, I said no, Emma. I don't want you or your students taking any unnecessary chances."

"I'd never involve them. Never. After Russell, there's no way I would chance that." She shook her head, tears filling her eyes. "I was—I was the one to call Russell's parents. I insisted on it. It nearly killed me, breaking that news to them."

"Then you'll understand how I feel," Beau said, "when I tell you I'm not making that call to your folks, your boss or anyone else when you go getting yourself hurt again. Or worse."

She made a scoffing sound. "You've helped me out a couple times, sure. That doesn't make me your responsibility."

"That's where you're wrong, Dr. Copley. I take everyone who lives on, works on or sets foot on my spread as my responsibility," he said, sincerity ringing in his every word, "which is why, from this point forward, I'm barring you from Kingston property."

Don't miss
Deadly Texas Summer
by Colleen Thompson

Available March 2020 wherever
Harlequin Romantic Suspense
books and ebooks are sold.

Harlequin.com

HRSEXP0220

HARLEQUIN

Heartfelt or suspenseful, inspiring or passionate, Harlequin has your happily-ever-after.

With new books published
every month, you are sure to find the
satisfying escape you know you deserve.

HNEWS2020